I0846956

ASH AND FEATHER

FLAME AND SPARROW
BOOK TWO

S.M. GAITHER

FLAME AND SPARROW
BOOK TWO

A COURT OF THE MARR NOVEL

ASH & FEATHER

S. M. GAITHER

ACCLADIA - THE MARRLANDS UNIVERSE
VALLA
THE UPPER HEAVENS
GALATHDIEL
GATEWAY TO THE
UPPER HEAVENS
NERITHYL
THE MIDDLE HEAVENS
THE SUN
COURT
TERRITORIES
THE STONE
COURT
TERRITORIES
THE SHADE
COURT
TERRITORIES
THE
AFTERLANDS
MORTAL RESTING
PLACES
THE
AFTERLANDS
MORTAL RESTING
PLACES
THE
EDGELANDS
THE
EDGELANDS
THE TOWER OF ASCENSION
ELIGAS - THE SPACE BETWEEN WORLDS
AVALINTH
A MONSTER WHO HAD GIFTED ME THE SUN

ACCLADIA - THE MARRLANDS UNIVERSE
NERITHYL
ELIGAS - THE SPACE BETWEEN WORLDS
AVALINTH
THE MORTAL REALM
MORTAL HELLS
MERKTH
BETHORAS
NYLTH
WE WERE LIVING LEGENDS TO SOME.

THE DIVINE COURTS

AUTHOR'S NOTE

Please be aware that this is an adult/new adult fantasy book that contains explicit sexual content, violence, and adult language. It also contains depictions of death, emotional abuse/manipulation, and trauma that may be upsetting for some readers. Read and enjoy at your own risk!

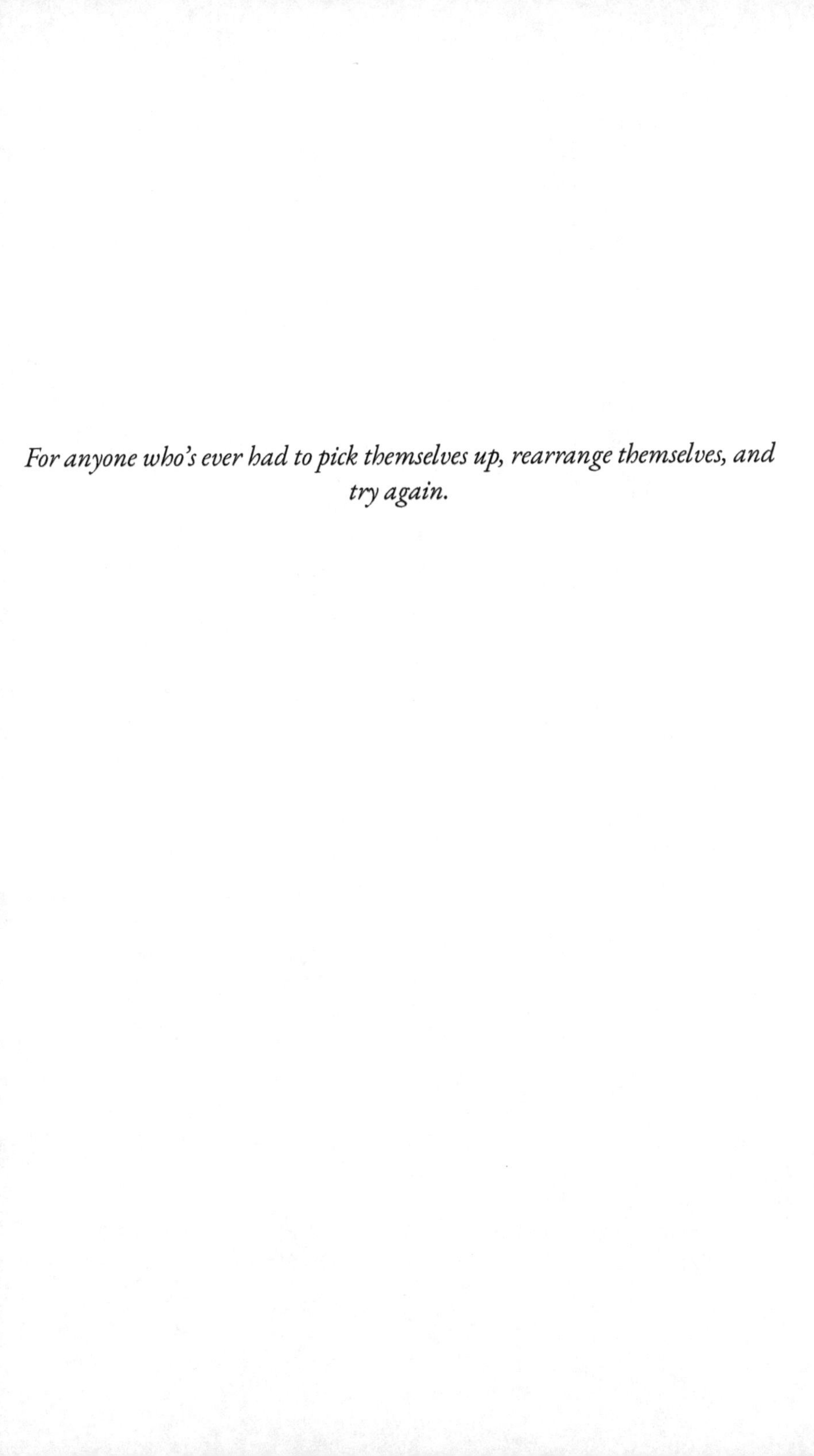
For anyone who's ever had to pick themselves up, rearrange themselves, and try again.

CHAPTER 1

Hello, Wildfire.

Dravyn's voice echoed through my mind as I stared into his storm-grey eyes.

Wildfire.

I inhaled deeply, swallowing the word down, lodging it more completely into my being. It felt like more than a nickname after all that had happened. It felt like a calling. An answer to a question I'd been too afraid to ask until this moment.

I was burning, tingling inside and out, my mind restless, filled with both too many answers and too many questions. The Tower of Ascension we stood in, which had once seemed so large and imposing, suddenly felt far too small to contain all I had become—all I was on the cusp of becoming.

I led the way to the door, Dravyn following closely behind.

The two of us stepped side-by-side into the hazy, magic-filled air of the Middle-Heavens. This air had changed, too. I'd once found it oppressively heavy...but now it only made me feel stronger, more alive as I breathed it in, like a warm breeze lifting the sails of a ship.

In the polished marble surrounding the tower's base, I caught another glimpse of my reflection—a clearer glimpse—and I gasped. The burn scars on my face and neck remained, outlines branded in place by an accidental fire I'd set years ago. But now they were... *different*. No longer scars. Not signs of the trouble I'd caused, but signs of magic I'd earned—for, with every step I took, they were transforming into the same sort of brilliantly glowing marks I'd seen on Dravyn's skin when he accessed the deeper wells of his magic.

Not proof of my mistakes, but proof of my power.

I *was* power.

I was a flame, bright and blazing a new path forward.

And I was *fast*. In the blink of an eye, I climbed the sloping hill leading away from the tower, coming to a stop at the top ridge and glaring into the distance. Far away from where I stood, a group of elves was fleeing—what remained of the faction led by Andrel, who had launched an assault on this divine realm and attempted to destabilize it for reasons I was still trying to make sense of.

Fury screamed between my ears as I thought of what they'd done. A warm, needling sensation swept over my arm. I glanced down and saw more marks like the ones on my face spreading over more of my skin. Bits of glowing, molten magic snaked along my forearms and dripped like blood from my fingertips.

When I flexed my hands, attempting to contain and control the power, the liquefied fire blazed bolder for an instant before turning to smoke. Plumes of that smoke whipped around my body, weaving amongst the sparks and embers and turning me into a moving, breathing firestorm.

Within the walls of the spinning, building storm—or perhaps just in the vortex of my own raging mind—I saw everything that had happened in the past hours: The broken barriers. The bloody battles. The bomb planted at the base of the tower behind me, and my desperate attempts to carry it away from this realm. Attempts that had succeeded. But then Andrel...

The fire surrounding me billowed and roared as I pictured his face.

My once closest friend and ally was gone—back in the mortal realm —but the ones fleeing into the distance were his followers...

Would they have stabbed me in the heart without flinching, just as he had done? Were they all willing to destroy as much as Andrel was, no matter the cost?

If I kill them now, they won't have the chance to follow him any farther.

I took a step forward, heat flaring all around me, smoke and fire engulfing me so completely I could no longer see my targets.

I didn't care that I was blind. I was still moving. I didn't need to *see* to kill, I could—

A hand reached through the storm and closed around my arm, its grip gentle yet strong, holding me back.

Dravyn.

Even through the chaos surrounding my thoughts, I recognized his touch.

"They're dangerous to us," I said, not looking at him. "And what they did was wrong."

"Yes."

"They tried to ruin this realm, the order of the world—all of it. They won't simply give up after this defeat."

I tried to pull free, but he held more tightly.

"We can't let them just *leave*," I growled. "I could stop them."

"You could."

"I could set fire to every one of them. Their ashes could fertilize the very ground they sought to destroy. They deserve it. They deserve *worse.*"

He didn't reply.

Somehow, his silence caught my attention more than any words he might have said. I stopped fighting his hold and turned my glare his direction.

His fingers dug into my skin. "I would let you go if I thought that was what you really wanted." His voice grew softer, thick as the smoke between us, as he added, "But I think you would regret it."

No, I wouldn't, I thought—and very nearly shouted it—as I ripped my arm from his hold and paced the hilltop.

My fires wrapped around me like a protective cloak, the flames rising and falling, burning brighter every time a rush of fresh fury made me clench my fists...only to recede a little with each deep breath I managed. It gave an illusion of control—which lasted until I looked once more to the last place I'd seen the retreating elves.

Their shapes were fading from sight.

They're getting away.

The fires surrounding me swelled in protest, making me feel as though I could have lit the entire world ablaze with a mere snap of my fingers.

Dravyn seemed undeterred by the threat of me, however; he closed the distance separating us, reached through the rippling fire and took hold of me once more.

He spoke my name as his fingers brushed over my arm, and I bristled at the sound as though it was an insult, a raggedy garment he'd flung at me and insisted I wear. It was tattered. Torn. I was embarrassed to slip it on, because *Karys* was the one who had given those retreating elves weapons to use against this realm.

Karys who had trusted the wrong people for far too long.

She had been a fool, weak and useless compared to the being I was on the verge of becoming—the powerful being who had raced out of the tower with fire smoldering in her veins.

I wanted nothing to do with *Karys* at the moment.

But Dravyn insisted on continuing to call out to her. He repeated the name like a mantra, a part of some ancient, revered hymn that no amount of fire or destruction or regret could erase.

Every ounce of my new, waking power continued to rebel at the sound of it. I pulled away again and started toward the retreating group in earnest, now as eager to get away from Dravyn and my old name as I was to catch and incinerate my targets.

Dravyn's voice followed me, circling around me, trying to drag me out of the dark waves and back to shore.

Miran-achth, he said, quietly, *My breath. My Wildfire. Look at me.*

I would have sworn he was speaking directly into my mind; the words were far too clear and loud given the distance between us.

I slowed, tilting my face toward him even as I continued to inch away.

"You don't want to kill them," he said, out loud now. "Not like this."

I dug my nails into my palms, focusing on the pain of it. Smoke swirled around me once more. In the thick waves of grey I no longer saw any visions of the recent blood and destruction. Instead, there came another, slightly older memory of this realm: One of glass rectangles all lined up in neat rows—too many to easily count—all shining in the scattered torchlight.

Gravestones, I recalled.

One for every person Dravyn had killed right after he'd ascended.

It was so clear it seemed as if the God of Fire had—once again—planted it directly into my mind. Whether he'd done so on purpose or not, I couldn't say, but I wondered...

Was such a thing possible, now that he'd transferred so much of his power into me?

How connected were we?

I shook my head, trying to clear it of the melancholy memories of glass and gravestones. I stumbled a few more feet away from him but went no farther than that.

He didn't try to close the distance between us this time. He watched me as I fought to steady myself, concern knitting his brows together.

Slowly, I felt my control resurfacing, the rage within me subsiding, the fires around me cooling. It took far more effort to put out the fires than it had to call them.

As the last wisps of fire shifted to smoke and drifted away, I looked, one final time, to the last place I'd seen the retreating elves.

There was nothing there but dusty ground and hills rolling toward a dark and foreboding horizon.

I exhaled a shuddering breath. A flood of emotions warred within me. Before I could untangle any of them, a sudden rush of power and the sound of wings—both leathery, booming flaps and softer, more delicately precise whispers of movement—stole my attention.

I turned and saw the Goddess of Control and the God of Winter landing side-by-side on the slope behind us.

Valas rolled his shoulders and folded his feathered, ice-glazed wings against his back.

Mairu did the same with her dragonesque appendages before turning and immediately finding me. Her eyes were as reptilian as the wings she'd tucked away—a bright, unsettling shade of yellow with black diamonds in their centers—but they became increasingly more human-like as she moved closer to inspect me.

One of her slender hands pressed uncertainly against my scarred face while the other gripped my shoulder. "Are you all right?"

My mouth felt unbearably dry, as if filled with the ashes of my extinguished fury, but somehow, I still managed a response. "Yes. For the moment."

She looked as though she wanted to press me further, but more middle-gods and goddesses were suddenly arriving, sparing me from that conversation.

One by one they appeared—the same divine beings who had walked into battle with us just hours ago.

The God of Storms came first, his dark eyes still shining with anger over the whole ordeal, his body tense as a coiled spring, prepared to launch back into battle at the slightest provocation.

Then the Healing God, Armaros, appeared in a burst of white and shimmering gold magic. He waited with one arm stretched out behind him toward Edea, the Goddess of Sky, who arrived an instant later. The Healing God's expression was grim with concern as he watched the goddess move with slow, shaky steps.

Despite Edea's unsteady appearance, my anxious heart unclenched somewhat at the sight of her. The last time I'd seen this goddess, she'd been sprawled out on the ground in the shadows of the tower. Surely dying, I'd thought. So it was a relief to see her standing on her own two feet again—to know that whatever wicked weapons Andrel and the others had devised were apparently not strong enough to kill a goddess.

Not yet, anyway.

But as the goddess's gaze swept over me, catching on my scars—which I could only assume were still glowing, however more faintly now—the tight feeling in my chest quickly returned.

She looked at me as though *I* was the one who had returned from the dead. As though I was a ghost who didn't belong in this realm, regardless of the divine magic now burning within me.

A stranger in this strange land all over again.

Stepping away from the crowd, I did my best to settle my new, burning magic further. It hurt to press it down; a tight and tingling pain along all my edges, like trying to shove a foot into a boot two sizes too small.

No one followed me as I moved away—though I could sense the curious, secretive glances they kept shooting my way, along with the building tension as the aftermath of our battle settled, leaving space for questions to rise.

What happened?

Why did it happen?

How do we keep it from getting worse?

The entire world is unsettled, our magic and power threatening to shift...

The larger problems looming over us were plentiful, but at the moment, I couldn't think of much beyond my own pain and discomfort.

The harder I tried to push my magic down, the more excruciating keeping it in became. It felt like there were heated blisters popping up all over my skin, another one bubbling up with every repressed flare— though a quick inspection revealed that, at least on the outside, I looked perfectly intact.

Dravyn continued to watch me out of the corner of his eye, a worried frown on his face. With every wince I made, or too-sharp inhale I took, he addressed the crowd around him with increased urgency.

That crowd grumbled louder and louder as the minutes passed, until Dravyn lost his patience, or his concern with me reached new heights—or some combination of the two—and he silenced the gods around him with a fiery display of furious magic.

"The battle is over, at present," he said, sharply, into the freshly stunned silence. "Obviously, we have much to discuss and deal with in the coming days, but for now I think we need to return to our respective territories and regroup; none of us are thinking clearly as we stand now."

A few grumblings followed—the Marr never missed an opportunity to argue, I'd learned—but a few minutes later, the last of the divine beings finally transported themselves away from the tower, leaving Dravyn and me alone once more.

I stopped fighting the wildness of my new magic and let it rush more freely through me. It sucked the breath from my lungs and made my legs feel like they were melting, dropping me to my knees despite my best efforts to steady myself.

"We should go back to the palace," Dravyn said, reaching out his hand as he approached, "so you can rest in a place away from the tumultuous energies surrounding this tower."

I couldn't make myself reach back. My fists pressed hard against the cold ground on either side of me as I hung my head, fighting the urge to vomit—or worse, to give in to the intense urge to search the horizon once more for our retreating enemies. I was a strange combination of sick and angry. Exhausted, yet humming with power and a dark desire for vengeance.

Dravyn stood at my side while I attempted to collect myself once again. With little more than the snap of a finger or the occasional twist of a hand, he wordlessly extinguished every furious flame that escaped my body, his gaze calmly scanning our surroundings for threats as he did so.

"I wanted to make them all pay," I said after a long silence. A confession. The quiet bloodlust in my tone frightened me; my voice didn't seem like my own.

Dravyn didn't so much as flinch at the sound of it. He only said, "I know."

"And not just them," I muttered, pressing a hand to my chest, fingertips mapping their way over the newest thick, gnarled scar stretching over my skin. The upper-gods had stopped my bleeding, healed my broken bones, and my stained tunic remained mostly in one piece...but through the bloodied fabric, I could still feel the damage that had been done.

I closed my eyes against the memory dropping into my head—the sight of Andrel's knife glinting wickedly in the sun just before it slashed toward me.

Swallowing hard, I said, "He stabbed me. Andrel, I mean. We were beside some mortal river I didn't recognize, after the chaos of traveling through Eligas, and I…" I winced as I pressed my fingers against my heart. Not because the wound there still hurt, but because the weight of what had happened settled fully against me with a violent suddenness, like a heavy iron ball I hadn't been fully prepared to catch.

Dravyn knelt before me and took my hand, drawing it away from my body and lacing his fingers through mine. "You don't need to speak of it anymore right now. I already know enough."

I gave him a curious look.

"I'm the one who carried you away from that mortal shoreline," he explained, pulling me back to my feet. "I saw what he did."

I fought my way to my feet and stepped away from him, absently touching the wrist that had, until a short time ago, held a bracelet he'd given me. That bracelet's magic had allowed me to leave this realm and take Andrel's weapon with me. It was no longer there, but it had done its job—carrying me away from the battlefield, and apparently, leading Dravyn to my side…

"If there had been time, I would have gone after him, too," Dravyn said, his tone mirroring the violence that had been in mine moments ago. "But between the weakness traversing realms had caused you, and the amount of blood you were losing, I had no choice but to focus only on saving you."

A cold sweat washed over me. "I thought I was going to die."

A haunted softness overtook his voice as he said, "So did I." I felt his gaze lifting to me as he added, "Which is why I carried you directly back to the Tower of Ascension—to its magic—and why I desperately called out for the Moraki to meet me there."

"And they actually…did." The thought made me dizzy.

He took a deep, steadying breath. "It's not how I envisioned your ascension taking place—if you decided you wanted it to take place at all. But the alternative…"

Glancing over my shoulder, I saw the guilt building in his expression and clouding his eyes, so I quickly tried to reassure him. "I don't regret anything I did. And what you did…I'm glad you did it. I'm grateful. If I'd been in my right mind, I would have made the choice myself."

He nodded, though his gaze didn't meet mine.

"I'm just a bit…dizzy. Confused." I held up my hands, trying and failing to make my skin glow at will with the magic I'd seen in my reflection earlier.

"What am I?" I wondered aloud. "I heard the upper-god of the Shade say the amount of magic you gave to me was unprecedented. How much, though?"

Dravyn continued to avoid my gaze. "I gave what I needed to."

Unsatisfied with this answer, I stepped directly in front of him and said, "You once told me that the Miratar spirits who ascend into the court of a particular Marr become like an extension of that Marr's very being. So what does that mean where you and I are concerned?"

"You aren't a mere spirit. You've been given the rank of a middle-goddess by the Moraki who reign above us."

Goddess.

My dizziness grew worse, but I steadied myself through it and asked, "We can't both be the Marr of Fire, though, can we?"

"It takes weeks—sometimes months—after ascension for the powers of any given Marr to fully establish themselves. Nothing is set in stone, as of yet. Fire will be the magic that comes most easily because of what I offered to you in order to aid in your ascension. But there's more to you than what I gave you. The Moraki granted you power in addition to mine, and it's impossible to say how much, or what you might shape that into."

I considered all this information for several minutes. "And what becomes of the magic you've poured into me?" I asked. "How does that affect you?"

He frowned. "We have a lot of things to figure out, I think."

I couldn't argue with that. And the list of things extended well beyond my powers.

One thing in particular struck me as we stood there. I said nothing of it at first, yet Dravyn still fixed me with a curious, expectant gaze; the anxiety suddenly rolling in my stomach must have been obvious on my face.

But I didn't look away.

No more secrets. We'd decided on that before marching into our last battle together—that whatever there was to figure out, we would face it together.

More than magic bound us together after all we'd gone through these past months, which was why I cleared my throat and said, "There's something else that happened beside the river. Something Andrel said to me before you caught up with us."

The mere mention of Andrel's name stirred up a scorching wind, sent it searing across my skin before Dravyn reined it in and calmly asked, "What did he say to you?"

"When I was lying there, he thought I was dying, too, I think. So he said something he probably wouldn't have, otherwise. Something I couldn't make sense of at the time, but now…"

Out of habit, I reached for the sparrow-shaped charm that had once hung so often from my neck. For so many years, it had been my greatest sense of comfort and strength.

But it was no longer there; the only thing my hand fell upon was my bloodied clothing and the bruised, scarred skin underneath it.

"Karys?"

I lowered my hand, once again looking the God of Fire in the eyes. "Dravyn…I think my sister is still alive."

CHAPTER 2

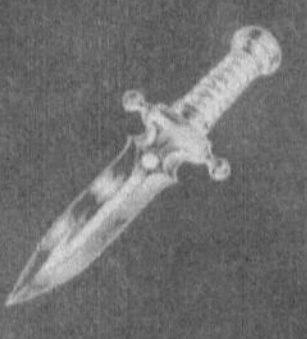

Karys

Six Weeks Later

I woke up surrounded by flames.

The world seemed to be moving in slow motion, my body growing heavier as the seconds crawled by and the fires built higher, tongues of crimson and crackling heat lashing out, blistering my skin.

I breathed in deeply. Too deeply. Smoke flooded my lungs. The choking fit that followed succeeded in waking me completely, and I rolled from the bench I'd fallen asleep on, hitting the ground hard.

My surroundings spun, but distinct, bright colors and bold shapes soon began to emerge from the jumble—canopies of silver-green leaves and twisting vines, clutches of golden flowers, statues made up of elegant edges and smooth-polished stone.

"*Elestra*," I heard myself whisper, reminding me of where I was.

What I was.

Elestra was a garden meant for middle-gods—a lavish, beautiful meeting place at the center of the Shade Court's four territories. A place that was no longer off-limits to me, its energies now inviting rather than overwhelming. Saying its name out loud grounded me somewhat, making it easier to believe this garden and the middle-heavens surrounding it were both real.

I was really here.

And I had *really* set all the magnificence surrounding me on fire...a response, I assumed, to yet more nightmares I could scarcely remember.

Frantically, I lifted my hands, trying to remember the words, the *control* I'd practiced with Dravyn over the past weeks. He could extinguish fires like this with little more than a whispered command. A wave of his hand. A tiny, deliberate breath.

Myself, I was still finding it much easier to start fires than to put them out.

I let my eyes flutter shut and focused on the feel of my fingers, zeroing in on each tip as I moved them one by one. I tried my damnedest to ignore the very real heat blanketing me, the beads of sweat soaking the nape of my neck, the acrid smoke that felt like it was leaving permanent scorch marks on my lungs....

Those things are all secondary to you, Dravyn had tried— repeatedly —to make me understand. *The fire isn't in control of you, you're in control of it.*

I clenched my eyes tighter, determined to block out the flames. More sweat built on my skin, trickling down, pooling against my lower back. High above, a branch crackled and ignited, sending a *whoosh* of heat over me before it severed from its tree and thunked against the ground, making me jump.

Just as I started to truly panic, a cool breeze caressed my cheek, followed by a distinct tinkling and cracking sound.

My eyes flew open to the sight of ice sweeping over the garden, quickly melting and sending currents of water splashing down, extinguishing the flames.

Valas.

I turned and saw the God of Winter resting casually against a distant, ivy-covered wall, arms folded in front of him, a mixture of concern and amusement gleaming in his violet eyes.

I bit my lip hard enough to taste blood. I didn't know what to say. This wasn't the first time he'd had to put out a fire for me. It likely wouldn't be the last, either. I was simultaneously glad for his help while being annoyed that I still needed it.

The Winter God's gaze swept over the charred remains of what had once been several beautiful twisting vines covered in pale blooms. He pushed away from the wall and sauntered closer. "Not making much progress with controlling your new powers, I see."

"Not while I'm asleep, at least." I shook out a cramp in my hand. "This keeps happening every time I have even a hint of a nightmare; it's as if my magic is desperate to burn away any trace of whatever I might see. Which is why I haven't slept in days...and why I accidentally fell asleep out here, I guess. I was more tired than I realized."

"So what was your plan?" He arched a brow. "To stay awake indefinitely?"

"I thought the Marr were capable of such things." I sighed. "Maybe this ability skipped over me thanks to my unusual ascension."

"None of us are truly able to stay awake forever, for what it's worth. We do still need to rest occasionally." With a yawn, he added, "And some of us just like to sleep, necessary or not. The lazier among us."

"You're one of those lazier ones, I'm guessing?" I teased.

With a sweeping gesture at his face—at his ivory skin, his sharp jawline, his indigo eyes and other undeniably divine, handsome features —he said, "Do you think I could maintain these looks without ample beauty sleep?"

Teasing him was more fun than thinking about fires and nightmares, so I gave him a sly grin and said, "If that's as good as it gets with ample beauty sleep, I pray you never develop insomnia."

"Rude," he chastised, though his grin was wider than mine; thinly-veiled insults and relentless teasing had become a major part of our shared love language. "You've been spending too much time with Mairu these past weeks," he said. "She's turning you mean."

"I've always been mean," I countered, moving to pluck a half-burned blossom from a nearby tree. "Dravyn once told me that humans who ascend tend to retain the same personalities they had as mortals; they're simply magnified by their divinity." I crushed the singed flower into a pile of white velvet petals and ash before turning back to Valas with a shrug.

He gave me another crooked, casual smile, but his eyes were suddenly alight with curiosity as he studied me. He didn't say anything, but I could guess what he was thinking—the questions going through his mind were likely the same ones going through mine.

We have a lot of things to figure out, Dravyn had said.

But the six weeks that had passed since we'd stood together in the wreckage of battle had brought more questions than answers, unfortunately. I was a strange case, after all—both because Dravyn had granted so much of his power to me, and because my mortal blood had been elven, not human.

Every other ascended Marr had once been human as far as I knew. And though the elven-kind had once *all* been semi-divine beings who walked alongside the upper-gods, we'd been cast out of such divinity generations ago. Our race had been supplanted by a new, less powerful creation—humans.

Elves and the divine beings no longer mixed; we went together so poorly, in fact, that war had been simmering between our worlds for decades now.

So why had the Moraki allowed me to have divine magic? And not only *allowed* it, but actively moved to meet Dravyn when he brought my stabbed, bleeding and broken body to the Tower of Ascension? And whatever powers they'd given me...what did they expect me to do with them? What did they expect me to become?

I was no fool; I knew the gods did not grant favors without expecting something in return.

I parted my fingers and watched ash and petals scatter down to the scorched ground, wondering, not for the first time, what I was doing in this realm, and if it—or anywhere—would ever truly feel like where I was meant to be. I was an *other* wherever I went; not a normal divine being, but also not a proper elf anymore, either.

"Do you remember what you were dreaming about?" asked Valas, a hint of concern darkening his usually carefree voice.

I narrowed my eyes on one of the fallen petals, trying to dredge up images from the tumultuous waves of my thoughts. I'd drawn a blank almost every time I'd tried this after past incidents, never able to clearly remember the nightmares that triggered my errant flames.

To my surprise, this time a few clear images *did* emerge in my mind: rocky ground, a river roaring at my back...the same river I'd nearly died next to after my battle with Andrel, I thought. And there was the familiar knife falling toward me, too, except...

Except, it wasn't Andrel wielding it.

It wasn't clear *who* it was, only that it was certainly not him—though the shadow-cloaked figure did send a pang of familiarity through me.

I tried harder to focus on the shadowy face.

I regretted it almost instantly.

Because that face...*that face*...

"Do you remember anything at all?" Valas prompted.

Shaking my head, I forcibly pulled myself from my thoughts, refusing to entertain them any further. I was tired. Anxious. Clearly my mind was only playing tricks on me.

Valas gave me a questioning look.

I rubbed at the chilled flesh of my arms, averting my eyes. "No. Just flashes of things," I said. "Nothing entirely clear."

The God of Winter was an excellent liar—and, by extension, excellent at *spotting* liars. But he didn't call me on this particular falsehood. He simply sighed good-naturedly and said, "Well, time has a way of making things clearer. Maybe if we're patient, you'll figure it out... preferably before you set fire to every thing I love in this realm."

"We can only hope," I deadpanned.

I went back to picking at the burned bits of flowers and vines and sweeping away ash, doing my best to clear away the evidence of what I'd done.

Feeling Valas's gaze upon me once more, I said, "Don't tell Dravyn about this incident, please. He'll worry."

Valas sighed his disapproval but still summoned an icy breeze to help further scatter the proof of my lack of control. As he guided a pile of scorched blooms up and over the outermost garden wall, he offered his vow: "I won't breathe a word. Of course, something tells me he'll worry about you anyway."

My cheeks flushed hot, though only for a moment; in the next beat, another blast of cold fanned across my face—another fire extinguished on my behalf. This time I couldn't help giving the God of Winter a small, grateful smile.

As we cleared away the last bits of ash and debris, a new, much warmer breeze rushed in—like some great magical beast had exhaled a sparkling breath of revival over the burned remains. The garden bloomed quickly within the shimmering warmth, bursts of color and scent exploding all around us until the space was lush and full once again, and arguably, even more beautiful than before.

No harm done, I tried telling myself. *The magic in this place is stronger than my mistakes.*

Inhaling deeply, I started for the nearest of several decorative, black iron gates. Valas followed me through it. We walked in silence into the rolling hills beyond the garden, both lost in our own thoughts for several minutes, until a niggling suspicion began to burrow into my thoughts.

"I didn't expect anyone to bother me all the way out here this morning," I began, frowning. "Did Dravyn send you looking for me, by chance?"

"No one *sends* me anywhere, just so we're clear," Valas said with a yawn. "I went to the Palace of Fire earlier because I sensed unruly company heading toward it—the God of Storms, I'm afraid. I wanted to make sure he didn't do anything foolish at the start, but I was ultimately uninterested in playing mediator between him and Dravyn. So when Dravyn mentioned he hadn't seen you all morning, I used it as an excuse to leave. You know, to find you and make certain you weren't blowing anything up. Which..." He looked back at the gardens with a long-suffering sigh.

"There were no actual explosions this time, thank you very much."

He shrugged.

I ignored the shrug and the goading smile he gave me, too busy trying to think of why the God of Storms would have descended upon the Palace of Fire without warning. We hadn't been expecting him, as far as I knew—and the Marr generally didn't arrive in others' territories unannounced unless they were prepared to start a fight.

Of course, knowing Halar, he'd likely been prepared to start a fight.

And yet, I remained hopeful he'd come for another reason. "You said Dravyn mentioned he hadn't seen me...so I take it I was a topic of conversation? Has Halar or one of his minions found something useful during their scouting?"

Valas nodded, though his eyes lacked their usual confident shine. "That was part of the reason he rushed into our territory uninvited, from what I gathered—seems one of the creatures he sent to scour the northernmost mortal kingdoms hit on something interesting."

My nerves buzzed to life, magic humming into awareness along with them. Heat filled the air. Valas gave me a wary glance, and I summoned every ounce of control I could manage so I could speak in a perfectly level voice. "What did they find?"

"Not your sister herself, based on what I heard."

My heart sank.

"But..." he continued after a brief hesitation, "maybe another sign that she is, in fact, still alive."

My breath caught as though I'd been punched in the chest.

I wondered if it would ever stop feeling like a blow to my heart, hearing that Savna was somehow still alive and well, not dead and gone like I'd believed for so long.

After I'd told Dravyn what Andrel had said about my sister, he'd been the one to lead the charge, making plans for how we might comb the mortal kingdoms in search of her.

The God of Fire was driven to find her, at least partially, for my sake, I guessed; the other Marr, however, had joined in on the search because Savna had caused them trouble in the past, and most suspected she'd had something to do with the latest attack against the divine realms as well.

They wanted to find her so they could drag information and confessions out of her, and so they could carry out whatever revenge they'd been dreaming of since she'd gotten the better of them years ago.

Which was why I was desperate to reach her first.

I had to prove that she wasn't an enemy, just as *I* was not their enemy—that she'd been tricked as I had, and the situation was more complicated than any of us could have imagined.

It was yet another point of contention between me and the keepers of the heaven I now resided in.

The countless impassioned arguments I'd had with the other Marr —many of them with Halar—had done nothing to sway their thinking on the matter. So I simply had to find Savna before they did, to find some way to prove that my sister was not the monster they believed her to be...and I needed to do it before my former allies mounted another attack against the divine. A more *successful* attack.

Every day felt closer to war, to a crossroads we wouldn't be able to turn back from. And I felt as though I held the key to stopping it all, but my sister was the locked door—and she was nowhere to be found.

I pressed a hand to my stomach, trying to settle the uneasy twisting in its depths.

"I didn't stick around to listen to the God of Storms rage and blather on, as I mentioned." Valas's tone was grim, all trace of his teasing smile gone. "I'm sure Dravyn will fill you in on the details, however... though I wouldn't go to him until Halar has made his exit, if I were you."

"I am not afraid of Halar," I snarled. "I would even be willing to speak cordially with him and help coordinate his search efforts, if he'd deign to ask for such a thing."

"Wouldn't count on that." Valas picked at a thread on his tunic. Like all the clothing I'd seen him don since we met, it was finely made, the woven patterns glistening in the hazy light of the middle-heaven sky, as though spun from some combination of magic, frost, and moonlight. "The God of Storms still thinks you aren't telling us everything you know about your sister and the other rebel Velkyn."

My blood boiled, sending another wave of heat snapping through the air and drawing another wary look from Valas.

"I *wish* that was the case," I grumbled, willing my magic to settle again after a brief struggle. "I'd give anything to actually have more information than what I've already told everyone." I shook my head in exasperation. "You believe that, don't you?"

"Will you set me on fire if I say no?"

I managed a halfhearted grin. "There's always a possibility."

"Then I've never believed in you more than I do in this moment."

My grin gave way to an actual laugh as we walked farther from Elestra, continuing our teasing and chatting. At least I had him to take my mind off all the painful, confusing things. He reminded me, in some ways, of Cillian—one of my closest friends from my old home.

Cillian.

What had become of him?

The last time I'd seen him, he'd been helping me escape that old home and a raging, murderous Andrel. I likely wouldn't have gotten away without his help...but what price had he paid after I left?

I didn't even know if he was alive or dead.

Weeks ago, at my request, Mairu had descended into the mortal realm and went to search my old home. Cillian hadn't been there. *No one* had—the once bustling nest of elven rebels had been entirely abandoned.

Just one more mystery we needed to figure out.

I'd accidentally stopped walking, my gaze sliding out of focus as I stared into the distance, overwhelmed by all of these mysteries. It took a cold nudge—Valas's magic—to bring me back.

"Sorry," I said, shrugging off the chill. "I was just thinking about... well, it doesn't matter. Did you say something?"

"I asked if you'd like me to carry you back to your palace?" He stepped back to me, offering his hand. Magic crystals of white and blue were already swirling around the tips of his fingers, but I shook my head.

The Marr could travel with ease to any place with at least a modest concentration of their magical energy. In theory, I should have had the same capabilities.

But my first few attempts had been nothing short of disastrous.

It was easy enough to let Valas or one of the others whisk me along as their passenger—as I'd done in the past—but now that simply reminded me of yet another way I was failing to figure out my new existence.

"Thank you," I said, "but I'll manage on my own."

He grimaced, likely recalling the last time I'd tried to transport myself while in his presence; I'd managed to get as far as surrounding myself in flames before I panicked. Rather than letting the fires lift me and carry me away as they so elegantly did for Dravyn, I'd struggled against the feeling of losing control and being pulled off my feet. My flailing had led to a few accidental fireballs...and I *may* have set one of Valas's favorite cloaks aflame in the process.

He'd quickly extinguished it, of course, but had teased me relentlessly about it ever since.

"Don't worry," I told him, dryly, "I'm not going to attempt magic. Nothing is going to get incinerated. Or blown up."

"Thank the Creators for that."

"I'm just going to take the longer way back to give Halar more time to finish his rampaging, as you suggested."

He looked momentarily skeptical about me agreeing with his advice, but quickly shrugged it off. "Good. That means I can go back to minding my own business at my own home, perhaps get some more of that beauty sleep, which—as you so kindly pointed out—I so desperately need."

"I've been told I'm honest to a fault," I said sweetly.

"An honest pain in the ass," he said, just as sweetly.

Despite our joking tones, concern still lingered in the depths of his gaze. For a moment, I thought he might insist on escorting me back to the palace, regardless of my wishes—but then he gave me a little salute, bade me farewell, and took several long strides before leaping backwards into a flip that sent shining particles swirling through the air. I blinked and he was gone, leaving nothing more than that icy dust as proof he'd ever been here at all.

"Show-off," I muttered, turning to scan the fields around me, seeking the creature who had carried me from the Palace of Fire to the Garden of Elestra in the first place—Zell'thas, one of the selakir, a creation of Dravyn's.

I spotted him quickly, the shifting oranges and reds of his fiery mane like a pulsing beacon against the silvery green hills.

He gave a high-pitched whinny as he caught sight of me. The sound was similar to one a horse might make, yet slightly off in a way that might have been eerie if I didn't love and trust this creature so much. He resembled the horses of the mortal realm in appearance, too—closely enough that he could be mistaken for one from a distance—but as Zell drew closer, the differences became more apparent; the small antler-like appendages, the softly glowing eyes, the impossible shades of gold he shifted between as he moved. He was clearly a divine creature born of far more magic than anything in the mortal world below us.

I didn't have to whistle to bring him to my side; he was already trotting toward me as though he'd sensed my need to move, to be carried away from my latest mistake. It wasn't the first time he'd seemed to anticipate me over these past weeks. He had been born partly from Dravyn's power, after all, so whatever increased connection my gifted magic had given me with Dravyn, I suspected I shared it with his creations, too.

As I rubbed Zell's favorite spot on his neck before swinging onto his back, I wondered again about just how deep the connection between Dravyn and I went. Not for long, however; all my questions faded mercifully into the background when Zell launched into a gallop.

This was one of the few times I was able to forget about all of the trouble surrounding me, here lately—while balanced on the selakir's back, soaring across the fields, smoke and embers swirling and blurring the world around us.

Zell was a marvelous creature, fast as the wind with grace beyond measure. Little fires bloomed and died wherever his hooves fell, and I marveled for a moment at how easily they came and went and how smoothly we soared along, wishing I could manage anything half as effortless when it came to moving through this realm.

I hardly ever needed to guide Zell; I only had to ask him to take me to Dravyn, and he always managed to do the rest. So I tilted my head back, pulled my hair free of its braid, and focused on the feel of the wind caressing me. Breathing in deep lungfuls of floral and spice-tinged air, I studied Nerithyl's strange sky as we bounded along.

There were no clouds within this sky, nor any proper sun or moon or stars. There was only a magical sort of...*haze* that shifted colors according to whatever divine energies dominated it at any given moment. Sometimes it took on the colors of the mortal realm's skies, other times it was nowhere close to them. The light shining within it depended on the gods below it; most of them could conjure up various illuminating objects if they desired it, even though they didn't need light to see in the dark. Dravyn was particularly skilled at shaping fire into miniature suns, and he'd done it often while I was getting acclimated to this realm, trying to mimic the heavenly bodies of the world I'd left behind.

Today, the sky was the color of rich cream, and the illuminated magical orbs wrapped within its haze—*forgelights*, Dravyn called them—were fading. It had been days since he'd hung them; he'd been too distracted by other things to keep up with them, I guessed.

I caught a flash of something much brighter than those fading lights, and my eyes narrowed.

"I'm not surprised," I told Zell with a sigh.

The selakir twitched his ears and picked up his speed, gleefully unaware of, or at least unbothered by, the comings and goings of gods.

I squinted harder, and I became sure of it, then: Despite what Valas had said, he hadn't gone straight back to his own territory. It looked as though he'd tried to camouflage himself, wrapping his form in magic that took on the same off-white sheen as the sky. But his wings gave him away—every occasional flap of the ice-glazed feathers created a brief, tell-tale shimmer.

Keeping an eye on me, though he would never admit to it. I was almost certain Dravyn had sent him, now. The state of things—and whatever Halar had come to discuss—must have been more serious than Valas had let on.

I leaned forward, urging Zell faster, a foreboding feeling settling in my gut as the Palace of Fire took shape far in the distance.

CHAPTER 3

Karys

I DIDN'T HAVE TO GO VERY DEEP INTO THE PALACE BEFORE I heard Halar's voice booming through the otherwise quiet halls.

I followed the thundering sound to the first staircase I came across, then up to a landing of white stone that shimmered in the glow from a tall window. Here, flanked on either side by statues of winged beasts, was a white door that led into a small library.

The door was cracked, so I let myself in, steeling my heart and mind against whatever venom Halar would undoubtedly fling my way.

As I stepped into the room, my gaze was immediately drawn, not to the occupants inside, but to the walls around them. There were floor-to-ceiling shelves on the walls behind and on either side of me, each one crammed full of books of all shapes and sizes, most of which were well-loved with worn bindings and little bookmarks and slips of paper notes sticking up between their pages.

Books were a rare sight in this realm, as many of the Marr had more efficient, compact methods of recalling and storing the information and stories of our world—magic methods. The Goddess of Stars and her servants, for example; they could conjure up records of realms and their inhabitants in the surfaces of certain reflective objects. The Ocean God, too, could use drops of water and similar spells to his advantage.

But some of the Marr still preferred the feel of actual books, and Dravyn was one of them. He'd once told me of the painstaking lengths he'd gone to in order to create this room, which was apparently a near-perfect replica of a space he'd loved in the mortal-realm palace he'd grown up in.

He didn't usually receive visitors in this cherished place—which seemed like further evidence that Halar must have blown in like some wild, unexpected storm.

One of the shelves to my left had evidence of his wildness: several jagged marks had been burned into the wood, as though the god had flung a handful of sparks into it. The damage was fresh—I could still sense the humming current of magic underneath. There were several books on the floor, as well, and papers scattered about.

My nerves clenched tighter. I forced myself to look past the shelves, and then past Halar himself, willing my eyes not to linger on the faint threats of electricity sparking in the air around the god.

I needed to keep my fear—and my own temper and magic—in check.

Beyond Halar, Dravyn was draped in the chair closest to the fireplace, massaging his temples. The chair was large, almost comically so in the snug room, but he still spilled out of it. Even in this easy pose he radiated poise and power, the edges of him seeming to glow with more than just the fire's light. I'd always found him imposing, but he appeared different to my ascended vision; looking at him was like opening tired eyes to the sight of a brilliant sunrise—my breath caught at the sight every time.

Halar, too, looked different. The sparking magic surrounding him was bolder. The human-like body he had shaped himself into seemed to ripple and bulge with his power, like a more terrible, more true form might burst out of his dark skin at any moment.

It had been easier to approach *both* of them when I was a clueless mortal with weaker eyes, blind to their true nature...there was something to be said for blissful ignorance.

I shuffled my weight from one foot to the other and took another deep, bracing breath before stepping forward.

The God of Storms spun to face me. "Speak of the demon herself."

"Mind your tongue if you'd like to keep it," Dravyn warned.

Halar ignored him and smiled at me, all sharp teeth and malice. "Were your ears burning, elf? Did you rush back to hear what I've said about you? You needn't have; I'm happy to repeat it for your benefit."

I lifted my chin, refusing to cower. "By all means," I replied, the cool smoothness of the words betraying none of the fire or fear I felt inside. "If you've something to say about me, I'd love to hear it."

The slight challenge in my tone was all the provocation the ill-tempered god needed; in the span of a breath he was inches from my face, his lightning leaping the small space between us and striking a tingling path along my skin.

I held my ground even as the buzzing power rattled my teeth and made me itch all over.

"Go on, then," I snapped.

"Answer a question for me first." He pressed even closer.

I took a single step back, caught myself, and lifted my gaze to challenge his once more. "Ask it."

"How does one live among the Velkyn for as long as you did without realizing the extent of their ambitions, their weapons, their *treachery*?" he asked, still smiling his sharp smile. "Did your eyes not work before coming here?"

The question stung. I'd asked myself the same thing countless times over the past weeks, trying to come to terms with all the mistakes I'd made. All the things I'd missed. I'd yet to make peace with any of it—perhaps I never would—but I wouldn't give him the satisfaction of knowing that.

I swallowed hard. "My eyes work fine. But the mind sees what it wants to, sometimes." Plucking courage from somewhere in the depths of my aching chest, I added, "Your eyes are much the same while looking at me, I'm afraid. They remain blind and stupid, refusing to see me for what I truly am, despite all the evidence I've given."

"Evidence..." His smile twisted. His hand lifted—

Sudden movement behind him.

And then *heat*. The room was engulfed in it, such an explosive rush that I nearly dropped to my knees, fighting the urge to shield my face, though it wasn't burning my skin.

Dravyn's fire had never burned me, even when I was fully mortal.

I couldn't see much past the large and looming, terrible figure that was Halar, but it was clear the God of Fire had risen to his feet. The flames in the fireplace leapt higher as well, popping and crackling, casting long shadows over the room.

"This meeting is over," came Dravyn's voice, darker than any of those shadows. The room seemed to be growing even smaller, all of the light and oxygen pulling toward Dravyn.

When he spoke again, the single word was like a door slamming in a deathly quiet night.

"*Leave.*"

More heat washed through the room. I felt my own magic rising in response, saw the patterns of fiery light like visible veins in my skin, bright amongst the shadows that had settled over me. I tried not to think about how little control I'd managed over those fires thus far. Books would catch much quicker than anything in the garden had...

Halar glanced back and forth between me and Dravyn. He seemed to be weighing the odds for a moment before he swept irritably to the door, pausing in front of it and turning one last glare in Dravyn's direction. "Heed what I said to you. All of it." He jerked his head my direction. "Don't let this one blind you to the truth."

And with that he was gone, slamming the door on his way out.

The room cooled. The fireplace settled; the flames shrinking in both height and intensity until they were casting a much softer, warmer glow over the room.

Dravyn stared at the door as if expecting Halar to burst back through it.

Neither of us spoke for a long moment.

As my pulse finally calmed—and with it, my magic—my gaze went again to the marks scorched into the shelf. "You two weren't playing nice at all, were you?"

Dravyn muttered something indistinguishable before prowling back toward his chair. He seemed to consider flopping back down upon it, but instead went to the nearby desk, bracing his arms against it and studying a large piece of parchment stretched across the shining mahogany top.

I moved closer, curious; whatever he was looking at was carving deep furrows into his brow and rapidly dulling his eyes from their usual shining silver-blue to a murky, frigid grey.

It turned out to be a map.

Before I could ask why he had it out, or what exactly concerned him about it, Dravyn spoke: "Valas found you, I'm guessing?"

I frowned. "So you did send him after me."

He didn't try to deny it. "The other courts are teeming with unease today, with a need to...*act*. Halar's obtained some information that's managed to get everyone riled up, all of them arguing about what to do next. It's not just the God of Storms who's restless and dangerous at the moment."

"Dangerous? Even in our own territory?"

He took a deep breath, rolling his shoulders as though redistributing the weight of the world sitting upon them. "These are strange times."

I considered the worry in his tone and found I couldn't come up with a convincing argument to dispel it. "And I'm a strange new piece in this puzzling place," I acquiesced, absently watching an ember as it escaped the fireplace and fell in a slow, twisting dance, landing and dying against the stone hearth.

"The strangest in quite some time." A corner of Dravyn's mouth quirked as I looked back at him.

My frown only deepened. "Still, you don't need to worry about me so much," I said. "There are more concerning things."

He gave a thoughtful *hmm*, almost a sound of agreement—even though he was suddenly looking at me as though I was the only thing he'd *ever* been concerned about.

Tilting my face away to hide my blush, I mumbled, "I can take care of myself."

"I'm well aware." He stepped closer. "But perhaps I like taking care of you." He reached for my hand, pulling me toward him. "Humor me, Wildfire."

His thumb absently stroked my palm. His other hand cupped my face as he leaned down and pressed his forehead against mine, sighing and relaxing against me.

We stayed pressed to one another for a long moment, huddling against the outside forces threatening us.

I might have stayed like that all afternoon, letting him lean more fully into me and trying to shift some of his worry to my own shoulders —but I was also determined to keep the conversation on track. To find out more about what he'd been discussing with the God of Storms.

"It's all just venting and throwing their weight around where I'm concerned," I insisted, taking a step back. "They'll tire of hating me, eventually. Halar is my greatest detractor, and even he seemed more subdued toward me than usual today." My eyes darted toward the door. "He left with so little argument..."

Dravyn looked to the door as well, his gaze unfocused, his mouth drawn in a tight, unconvinced line. "He was distracted."

"As are you."

He blinked, met my eyes, and gave me a small, tired smile that made my stomach flip. "Maybe."

"So what is it that's distracted the two of you? What did Halar find?" I moved away from him and circled around the desk, leaning over it as he had done, trailing my fingers along the same paths his had traveled. "This is a map of the northern territories, isn't it? The Kingdoms of Galizur and Terrath, and the no-man's land between them. The *Hollowlands*, I've heard that middle space called by human-kind, I think —though the elves have another name for it."

He nodded in confirmation, and I studied it closer.

Several of the places upon it were labeled strangely to me, the letters odd, the spellings slightly different from what I knew, while the notes along the margins were written in a language I didn't recognize at all. But the landmarks were unmistakable—the Duskryn mountain range, the upper and lower Berlnath rivers, the great Bloodroot Canyon.

I felt a strange pang in my stomach as I looked over it all, remembering the mortal realm I used to call home. "Valas told me he overheard Halar saying they'd found something of interest near the northern kingdoms, but he, too, was scant on the details with me."

Even as I spoke of those human kingdoms, my eyes kept fixing onto the black space between them. The Hollowlands. Or *Belethyn*—that's what the elves called it. A land forsaken by mortal kings and forgotten by the gods…but not truly empty, despite the dark hole representing it on the map.

There were elven dwellings dotted throughout the blackness…or at least, there had been when I was a child; I remembered my sister and father telling plenty of tales of the great warriors, deadly assassins, and respected leaders who had been shaped by the inhospitable features of that area. My sister used to say she was going to make a pilgrimage to it one day, perhaps journey deep into the darkness and carve out a greater reputation for herself within the abyss.

"Our own court has confirmed nothing," Dravyn went on, "but there are a lot of…*interesting* stirrings in the area. Rumors of a growing darkness in these so-called Hollowlands, a movement that seems to be concentrating in a village near the edge of that desolate place."

"A movement of elven-kind, you mean?" I pressed my palm to the yawning abyss on the map. "We called this area Belethyn. This map doesn't show them, but there are more elven dwellings here than human ones."

"You're right," he agreed, looking oddly uneasy about having this knowledge, as though he had firsthand experience he didn't want to dwell on. "Anyway, the rumors have it that those dwellings have increased in size and number lately. The Velkyn are reaching outward, threatening the human establishments along the edges, while planning and preparing for who knows what else from the strongholds they've made within those shadowy lands—strongholds we suspect they've been reinforcing in recent years."

I started to reply, but couldn't right away; a lump had lodged in my throat. My heart felt as though it was being pulled apart, the two different sides of it both vying for control. Because here was yet another reminder: Dravyn and I might have ascended into something different, something more equal to one another, but the places and beings we'd risen from…they were still enemies.

After swallowing hard, I said, "Do you think they're also trying to provoke the Marr through these threats and such?"

The Marr, who were tasked with watching over human-kind. The elves considered both of these groups their enemies. *Us against them all*, Andrel and all the other rebel leaders used to say, vacillating between which one they hated more on any given day.

"Likely so." Dravyn's tone was solemn. "Or, at the very least, trying to distract us, potentially leaving us vulnerable and stretched thin if they're planning another assault on our divine realm. And perhaps they consider victory close at hand, too, a return to the power they once had—power they intend to wield from human thrones after they've won whatever battles necessary to assert their dominance... I can think of several reasons for their sudden activity, really."

He turned away from the map and busied himself with studying the contents of a nearby shelf. I got the impression he was biting his tongue, not wanting to dwell on the bloody relations between our origin races any more than I did.

As though we could ignore it.

Even though he'd stopped speaking of it, the history of us hung over the space like a foul cloud, making it hard to breathe. I cast my eyes about for a window to open before remembering there wasn't one.

Clearing my throat as best I could in the thickness, I pressed on. "You said the movement seems to be concentrating in a village near the edge. Where, exactly? Does this village have a name?" My fingertips went back to trailing the weathered parchment, seeking but finding no dot or label to indicate any villages right along the Hollowlands' edge.

Dravyn glanced back but didn't reply. There was a distant, troubled look in his gaze—a sort of glazed-over sheen that gleamed brighter as the firelight caught it.

An uneasy shiver crept down my spine.

A sharp rap at the door interrupted us. Rieta stepped inside without waiting for an invitation, carrying a tray of food. Dravyn started to protest, but I was glad for the sight of her, even if I wasn't hungry; she'd broken through the dark cloud that had been settling over the room.

With the arrival of food came a predictable scavenger as well, and another welcome interruption: Moth. Another of Dravyn's creations—this one much smaller and considerably more dramatic.

As Rieta placed the tray on a small table in the corner, the fiery little griffin attempted to help himself to one of the flaky bread treats upon it.

He was thwarted in his efforts by Dravyn, who was familiar enough with Moth's antics that he managed to catch the griffin by the thick ruff around his neck before so much as a claw scraped the fine metal tray.

Dravyn plopped him onto the ground, giving him a stern look. He then poured himself a cup of whatever steaming concoction was in the small kettle in the tray's center—it smelled like oranges and cloves—and carried it toward the fireplace, ignoring Moth as he slid dejectedly under the table, a pitiful warbling sound rising in his throat.

I thanked Rieta as she left, then settled into the chair beside the corner table and absently nibbled on a bit of toast, thinking.

While Dravyn stared into the fire, I took a piece of fruit from the tray and slipped it to Moth, nearly losing the tip of my finger when the griffin's sharp beak quickly closed over it.

I jerked my hand away, smacking it hard against the bottom of the table as I did. At the sound, Dravyn looked back, eyes dancing from me to the flaming tip of Moth's tail, which was sticking out from under the tablecloth and thumping happily as he ate.

Dravyn's disapproving frown twitched only slightly when I gave him a rueful smile.

"The Hollowlands," I prompted, rubbing my stinging hand. "We were talking about the Hollowlands, and the trouble spilling over the edges of them."

"Right." He placed his cup on the shelf beside him, folded his arms across his broad chest and tilted his head toward the ceiling in thought. "According to the information Halar brought with him this morning, the unrest is centering around a certain figure that might be meaningful to you—one they're calling the *Godwalker*."

I stared at him, both desperate and terrified for him to elaborate.

"One who earned this nickname because she allegedly walked among the heavens and then returned to the mortal realm in one piece..." He lowered his gaze back to me as he added, "I'm sure you can draw the same conclusion I did about this figure."

My breaths grew short, ragged. A dozen different, warring emotions flooded me, and my lower lip trembled from the effort of trying to keep steady within the waves of them.

Moth abandoned his scraps under the table and climbed into my lap instead, nuzzling my hand until I started to absently pet him.

After several moments, I managed to find my voice, even though it came out thin and shaking. "Belethyn...we have to go there, don't we? We need to collect evidence for ourselves. Not just about my...about this *Godwalker*...but also...what if this is the place Cillian and Andrel have relocated to as well?"

Dravyn's face became an unreadable wall.

Frustration bubbled up inside me, expanding until it lorded over all the other emotions I was fighting with. My skin flushed, my muscles drew taut, and the flames in the hearth danced dangerously bolder and bigger. Moth lifted his head from my lap and gave a wary purr.

Without a word, Dravyn looked to the fireplace and exhaled, settling the building flames with all the effort of extinguishing a single candle. But despite the ease of the motion, he looked visibly more weary when he turned back to me.

The space between us seemed to expand as it darkened, as he fixed me with an expression that was still guarded, but clearly concerned.

"You can't expect me to just stay here and wait for more reports to trickle in from the likes of Halar, or from others who don't have the same connection to the elves that I do," I argued. "If there's a chance my sister is out there, or if—"

"I don't think it's safe for you to step outside of this realm until you've managed better control over your new powers. No one acclimates to these things in a matter of weeks. You're doing better than most, but it would be unwise to push it at this point."

I started to hurl several arguments at him only to catch them at the tip of my tongue and drag them back.

He had a point, loathe as I was to admit it.

I tried to keep my composure. Tried to make my expression as placid as his, even though all I was suddenly thinking about were my nightmares and the infernos that had followed them...

The gardens had grown back easily enough, thanks to the magic in the soil there. I'd set a few fires within the palace itself, too, but Dravyn or his servants always managed to put them out, and within no time at all these places were always restored. No lasting harm done.

But a mortal garden—or house...or worse, an entire town—wouldn't fare as well, and we both knew it.

And with that thought came another frustration, another question: What else did we *both* know?

Quietly, I asked, "Could you sense what happened earlier? Were you able to see what I...what I did in the garden?"

It took him a long moment to reply. "I'm not doing it on purpose, but it's becoming increasingly difficult to separate my power from yours. And when you call on the fire I shared with you, sometimes I see flashes of whatever that fire is surrounding. And sometimes I hear your voice..." He hesitated. "You don't see me in the same way, I take it?"

"No. Not as of yet, anyway." I went back to stroking Moth. The downy fluff of his fur and the silk of his feathers were soothing to focus on. "Although as I was approaching the palace earlier, I could feel your frustration and anger toward Halar, I thought."

Dravyn opened his mouth to reply, only to close it and fall into a thoughtful silence instead.

I averted my eyes, still unsure of how I felt about this latest development between us. There were few secrets I wanted to keep from him at this point, but I was still not used to feeling so...*known*. By anyone, really—much less a god I used to hate so intensely.

Somehow, our deeper-than-ever connection made the loss of my former life and identity feel all the more jarring, and thus, the need to see my sister—and to reconcile all the lost and mixed-up pieces of me—felt all the more desperate.

"It's not uncommon for divine beings who share the same threads of magic to be able to hear one another's thoughts and communicate mentally, even over long distances," Dravyn reminded me, taking command over a flame in the fireplace as he spoke, twisting it this way and that. "But it's usually more subtle and more controllable." He tilted his gaze toward me. "Perhaps once you have a better handle on—"

I shook my head, cutting him off. "Never mind it," I said. "It's just as well. You saw the truth, and you have a point—there's a chance that I would do the same thing in the mortal realm, where the consequences could be much more dire."

I got to my feet, placing Moth in the chair instead of my lap. I could no longer keep still. My frustration felt like a living thing crawling over me. I needed to shake it off.

Dravyn watched me for a moment before he came closer, taking hold of my arm to stop my restless wandering and fidgeting. "If I hadn't believed you could wield the fire I offered," he said, "then I would not have given it to you. You just need time."

"*Time.*" The word slipped from my lips in a whisper, dripping with bitterness. "What time do we have, with everything that's happening?"

He didn't reply. I felt foolish and weak in the shadow of everything we faced, like a child staring down a wolf with nothing but a stick for a weapon.

I considered storming from the room as Halar had done, but Dravyn grabbed my other arm and fixed me in front of him. He brushed a hand across my cheek, wiping away a tear I didn't even realize had fallen. I felt even more foolish. Crying was not going to bring me any closer to my sister. It would not give me the strength to keep my feet in the shifting, relentless waves of our battles, nor would it help me wield the fire burning wild inside my body.

I broke free of Dravyn's hold, scrubbed away the beginnings of more tears with the heel of my hand, then went back to the desk and the map upon it. I needed to trace a clear path of some kind along the parchment. A visible route to...*something*. Anything.

"What is the name of the village where they're concentrating their efforts?" I asked again.

As before, there was a hollow, haunting sort of pause before he replied. But this time, no one interrupted us, so he eventually managed to answer me: "Ederis."

"Ederis...why does that sound familiar?"

His entire body went rigid—a reaction that passed so quickly I might not have noticed had it not been accompanied by an equally abrupt shift in his power. I felt the fluctuation in his magic like the snap of a sail in a sudden wind, jolting me more sharply into awareness.

And after only another moment of thought, I remembered where I'd heard the word before.

"Ederis...that's the elven city you destroyed when you first ascended, isn't it?" The assassins who killed his younger siblings were said to have hailed from there, which was the reason he'd targeted it—yet more painful knots in the tangled web that was our histories.

All of the air seemed to be fleeing the room as he thinly, quietly, said, "Yes."

I braced both hands against the table, pressing against it for balance.

"Apparently, despite the destruction I caused, the roots of that city run deep and they held fast." He spoke without emotion, as if reading directly from a script so he wouldn't lose his nerve. "And now, the revitalized version of it is proving an even more dangerous hotbed of rebellion and power than what was previously there."

I stared, unseeing, at the map beneath my fingers. My mind was full of horrific images of gods and elves clashing while countless humans were caught in the crossfire—and one elf kept coming to the forefront of it all. The same one my nightmare in the garden had been about.

Godwalker...

Was my sister really at the center of this newest, burgeoning uprising? What was she planning to do next? If she was in Ederis, did that mean...

"This city and the rebellion gathering and festering there..." The words cracked as they crawled from my dry throat. "It's close to your old kingdom."

Dravyn nodded, staring blankly at the map under my hands as he said, "The past, it seems, is not finished with either of us."

CHAPTER 4

Dravyn

I PACED THE ROOF OF THE TALLEST WESTERN TOWER, staring out over miles of grey ground and cracks filled with molten fire, focusing on nothing in particular while I tried to decide what the hell I was meant to do next.

The sky was growing darker. It matched my mood, and so I couldn't bring myself to summon another orb to brighten it; too many other things were weighing too heavily on my mind, anyhow. And my magic —namely, the strange way it had been ebbing and flowing since Karys's ascension—was certainly not the least of these things.

I stretched my hand out and summoned a small flame. Whispered to it, twisted my wrist, watched the tendrils of red and orange move in accordance...

Effortless enough.

But then again, it was a weak spell. And Karys was not far away from me at the moment. That was the one element that seemed to be consistent with my wayward-as-of-late magic: It was stronger whenever I was close to her, for better or worse.

So I hadn't gone far—just to find some clearer air. Meanwhile, she had insisted on staying inside and looking closer at the maps I'd had out, gleaning whatever extra information and ideas she could from them and the books stuffing the shelves.

I could feel her easily from where I stood, like a second heartbeat pulsing and fluttering through my body. The beating of her magic had been restless for the first hour after I'd left her, but it seemed to have leveled off now...so one of us was clearing their mind, at least.

With a sigh, I closed my hand into a fist, extinguishing the fire in my palm. It was time to admit defeat; this clearer space had done nothing for me. My thoughts still drifted in hazy, aimless patterns, unable to decide on a solid shape, much like the smoke now slipping through my clenched fingers.

Swatting that smoke away, I went back inside. I wandered the halls for a bit until I felt a pull—as I so often did lately—that led me back toward Karys; I returned to the small library and found her still in the middle of it.

The bookshelves, I immediately noticed, had been rearranged in the short time I'd been away. She had color-coordinated them, then lined them up according to the height and width of their spines.

Despite my weary mood and battling thoughts, I felt a small smile curving my lips.

It wasn't the first time she'd done something like this. I could picture the scene even though I hadn't witnessed it; she'd likely started off trying to clean up the mess Halar had made, only to get carried away. Those books were easier to organize than most of the messes we were facing, and finding ways to impose logical order on things brought her comfort, I knew. So I didn't begrudge what she'd done—even though it meant I likely wouldn't be able to find the next book I went looking for without a struggle.

Reimagining the space had apparently worn her out; she'd pulled a stool up to the table where the map of the northern kingdoms was still laid out—one of the only things untouched during her redecorating— and she was resting with her head upon it, her breathing slow and steady.

Asleep, it looked like.

It had been such a long time since I'd seen her surrender to sleep like this that the sight of her stillness concerned me for an instant.

"Seems like it worked," came Rieta's voice.

"What worked?" I asked, looking over my shoulder as she followed me into the room.

"Earlier today, she asked me for something to keep the nightmares at bay. So I gave her a balam dust concoction."

A lead weight settled in my gut at the word *nightmares*. They weren't a new occurrence—the first weeks after she'd gained her divine powers had been full of such horrors—but I didn't realize she'd still been having them. I'd been a bit...preoccupied lately.

And, knowing her, she'd done everything she could to keep me from seeing her struggle.

Rieta went to the desk, gathering up a few scraps of parchment that had fallen to the floor at Karys's feet. Notes she'd been taking; I recognized her small, painstakingly neat handwriting even at a distant glance.

"Likely the first sound sleep she's had in weeks," Rieta said, quieter.

The weight in my stomach sank deeper.

"I got the concoction from the Healing God. Told him I needed it for myself, so don't worry—he and the rest of the Stone Court don't know that anything's plaguing her. She wouldn't want them to know what she was going through, I suspect."

"No. She wouldn't." I moved closer to the desk, taking care to step lightly and not wake her. My gaze fell to her right hand, the only part of her that remained tense under the balam's influence; a pen was clenched in it, its sharp tip pointing upward as though she'd fallen asleep prepared to brandish it against any nightmares that might slip through the Healing God's potion.

More to myself than Rieta, I said, "I wish I knew how to make these nightmares stop permanently."

"Stop?" she repeated with a sniff. "My dear, the kinds of things she's been through will never just *stop*. Some hurts echo on indefinitely, in nightmare form or otherwise. Quieter after a time, maybe, but still there, just waiting for some new thing to bounce off and amplify themselves by. I told her the same thing." She sighed wistfully, her warm brown eyes crinkling at the edges as she focused them on Karys. "But she's strong—she'll push through whatever hurt there is to push through, don't you worry."

These last words brought little comfort, but I nodded all the same; I'd learned long ago not to argue with this woman who had practically raised me.

"Speaking of hurts that echo…" Rieta began, stacking Karys's notes into a neat pile and adding them to the organized shelves as she spoke, "I accidentally overheard some of your conversations in here earlier."

"*Accidentally* overheard?" I huffed out a laugh, knowing better. "Or eavesdropped on them?"

"Either way," she said with a shrug. "I would have known something was bothering you even if I hadn't heard a thing."

Again, there was no point in arguing.

"You're thinking of leaving, aren't you?" Rieta asked, casually, still busying herself with the piles of notes. "You're worried about your brother."

"It's my job to be concerned for human-kind," I said evenly. "Especially their leaders."

"I'm rather sure this concern has little to do with your godly obligations." She pinned me with the same sort of look she used to give when scolding me for not caring enough about my school lessons. "Nothing wrong with wanting to see your brother."

"I'd hardly consider us true siblings at this point." Karys stirred, burrowing her face more completely into her folded arms, and I lowered my voice as I added, "I am not the little brother I once was, trailing like some lost little puppy on the heels of the future king."

"No, you're not. But you'll forgive an old woman and her poor eyesight, won't you? Sometimes I blink, and I still catch a glimpse of that little princeling in the corner of my vision." Rieta's tone had taken on the pensive, wistful quality it sometimes did when she was recalling our past life in the mortal realm.

I was not fond of that tone.

I exhaled a slow, concentrated breath, as though I could expel all the memories of my old life if I just focused hard enough.

Unsurprisingly, this didn't work.

There was no forgetting where I'd come from—and no denying that I needed to go back there, sooner rather than later.

Glancing at Rieta, I said, "I suppose you were also eavesdropping when I told Karys it would be too dangerous for her to visit the mortal realm alongside me."

"I heard no part of that conversation." She coughed. "But I suspected you'd feel that way."

"I'm not being unreasonable."

"No."

I wasn't sure which one of us I was trying to convince more. "If she were to lose control of her magic..." Violent images of smoke and ash and flame exploded in my mind—a still-too-clear memory of Ederis burning. I shoved it down as best I could. "She would never forgive herself, and I won't risk her suffering or having to carry such a weight if I can help it."

Rieta's hand rested upon Karys's notes, fingertips drumming thoughtfully against the parchment. "Forgiving one's self is a difficult thing to do, isn't it?"

I felt her gaze slide toward me, but I ignored it as Karys stirred again, clearly unable to get truly comfortable against the hard desk.

I still had not made up my mind about leaving for the mortal realm, but I was done talking about it. For now, I focused on picking Karys up, gently cradling her against my chest and carrying her toward a more comfortable bed.

She felt feverishly warm, and a thin sheen of sweat coated her skin— a side effect of unsettled magic? Or of nightmares that were trying to push through?

"The balam potion should keep her at peace through the night, at least," Rieta called to my retreating back.

The unspoken meaning was clear enough: *Go do what you need to do and be back before she wakes up.*

I pulled her more securely against me and trudged onward without another word to Rieta.

Karys seemed to get even warmer as I walked, as if the fire contained in her skin was rising up and trying to reach mine. Her eyes blinked open as we reached the stairs that led to my private chambers. She appeared disoriented for a moment, body squirming, hands fumbling for purchase among the folds of my shirt, until her gaze finally found mine. "Where are we going?"

"I'm carrying you to bed."

Her hold on my shirt tightened. A grip of panic—likely at the thought of sleep and the nightmares waiting for her there.

"I'm not tired," she protested, words slurring, eyelids fluttering and fighting against closing. "I'm wide awake."

"Yes," I said with a touch of amusement. "Clearly wide awake."

She nodded and half-yawned, half-mumbled a response that was fully lost as she buried her face against my chest.

After a few more steps, her fingers relaxed, and she made no more protests. Even as I opened the heavy bedroom door, sending a rush of warmer, smoky, wood-scented air flowing over us, she still did not stir.

Concern gnawed at my insides as I wondered at the amount of the Healing God's potion currently flowing through her veins. But I trusted Rieta—she'd nursed me back to health often enough—and I knew she wouldn't have given Karys anything she didn't feel was completely safe.

Karys had her own room, her own bed, but I much preferred her in mine. There were several reasons why, but tonight it was mainly because of the tower it was located in; the wards surrounding said tower were older and ran deeper than anywhere else in my territory.

I wanted to believe she would be safe here, even if I disappeared for awhile.

You once thought your family was safe in their guarded tower, too, came a faint voice in the back of my mind—the too-familiar voice of a monster that seemed to always be lingering at the edges of my thoughts here lately, waiting for an opportunity to creep in.

I gave my head a shake, tossing the monster as I'd done before. Then, as carefully as I could, trying not to wake her again, I settled Karys onto the bed and drew the covers up over her.

I remained at her side for several minutes afterward, watching to make certain the Healing God's potion was truly doing its job.

I wanted to stay longer. To crawl into bed beside her and pull her close, let the feverish heat of her skin transfer to me, along with her nightmares, her pain, her fear—all of it. I would have carried it all for her if only there was some spell to make such a thing possible.

But our magic was capable of nothing like that.

There were other problems to see to this night, too, whether I liked it or not. And if she truly *was* resting peacefully for the next few hours...

Holding in a sigh, I rose soundlessly and started toward the door.

Ramoth slipped through that door at the same moment, tail swishing and talons scratching softly along the wood floor.

"There you are," I mumbled. "Finished stealing and hoarding your fill of baked goods, have you?"

He wiggled his shoulders and puffed out his chest—clearly proud of all he'd collected this evening—before trotting his way over to the bed and pausing next to it. His tail ceased its swishing as he took in the sight of Karys lying motionless on the bed. An uncertain purr rumbled in his throat as he cocked his head back toward me.

I nodded to the empty space near Karys's feet, granting him permission—though the little shit likely would have ended up in the bed even if I hadn't.

"Gently," I warned. "Don't disturb her."

He gave his tail a haughty flick, but he obeyed, softening his steps before taking a flying leap and landing gently on the mattress. He burrowed under the covers, looking positively smug about how warm and comfortable he was.

"I really did create a monster with you, didn't I?" I muttered.

He yawned, closed his eyes, and snuggled closer to Karys.

Again suppressing my desire to crawl into the bed myself, I turned away and forced myself to leave. I descended the steps outside in a daze, crossing much of the palace with the same lack of focus. My movements felt detached, as if controlled by some unseen puppeteer, but I was still very aware of all the individual thoughts racing through my head. All the possible paths I could travel. All the ways those paths could prove wrong and deadly.

By the time I made it to the entry hall, I'd finally, reluctantly, settled on my next move.

Almost as if summoned by my decision, I heard footsteps in the hall behind me, soon followed by a familiar voice: "You're planning on going to Galizur tonight, aren't you?"

I didn't break my stride as the sound of Mairu's voice reached me. I wasn't surprised by her arrival, or that she knew what was going on; Valas had overheard enough earlier, and the God of Winter had never managed to keep anything to himself for longer than a day—if that. Her palace had likely been his very next stop after escorting Karys back to me.

Mai stepped directly into my path, fixing me with an expectant glare.

"I've thought about it, yes." I wasn't in the mood to discuss this any further. I just wanted to act. To do what needed to be done. "And I've already made up my mind regarding it. So your visit is in vain, I'm afraid."

She set her jaw. "Don't you think you're being reckless?"

"I've been there countless times since my ascension."

"Never with the mortal realm in such a state as it's in now. It's a mess, and frankly, so are you. Your magic is—"

"Enough." I didn't want to talk about what my magic was. Or wasn't. It was just another complication in a long list of them. I would deal with it in stride, along with everything else. "I'll be careful," I insisted. "And I won't let him see me. I never do."

Though I'd gone back to my old home countless times over the past years, I hadn't actually spoken to my brother, Fallon—now the King of Galizur—since shortly after I'd ascended. Given the chaos and bloodshed that surrounded my ascension, I doubted he would *want* to have any sort of conversation with me. And I didn't want to speak with him, either.

It was simply easier this way.

Mai was relentless, as per usual. "Let me go instead."

"You don't know the royal city or its palace like I do. I can move much more quickly."

"Until your magic fails to bring you back to this realm *quickly*. Or at all. What will you do then?"

I shrugged. "I'll walk back. Do you know I used to be very fond of walking when I was a human? I could journey for miles in the forests around my city, solely on foot."

"Be serious," she hissed.

I mirrored the clench of her jaw, started to speak several times, but ultimately decided to keep my mouth shut. I pushed by her and exited the palace, setting my course for the magical waterways that would carry me to the mortal realm.

Mai followed. "Does Karys know what you're doing?"

I slowed, shooting her a cross look. She'd wielded Karys's name like a weapon—the only sharp edge that could have given me pause just then.

"I didn't have a chance to tell her," I said. "She's resting at the moment."

"You're sneaking away while she's asleep. Coward."

"And you're painfully accurate and aware, as always."

"I'm only trying to help."

"If you really want to help, then stay here and keep an eye on things until I get back."

She clenched her fists against an obvious surge of irritation, her controlling magic seizing the trees around us and making their branches go unnaturally taut. But then she glanced in the direction of the tower that held my bedroom.

The tree branches swayed as she breathed out and released them, several leaves snapping loose and drifting to the ground as she did.

I could see the thoughts churning in her mind, her concern for Karys slowly outweighing her disagreement with me and my plans.

"Fine," she grumbled.

"Thank you."

She chewed on her bottom lip, contemplating for another moment, before removing one of her many rings and offering it to me.

It was golden in color, the band made to look like the curled body of a serpentine dragon—her favored form to shift into when she wasn't masquerading as a human. The dragon's head was slender, its eyes made up of two shining, scarlet-colored stones.

"Take this, at least," she said, placing the ring into my palm. "It won't make up for the...troubles you're having with your own powers, but it will help hide you, at least for a time. Not indefinitely, mind you. And if its power wears off and your reckless ass is still in the middle of someplace you shouldn't be, I am not coming to save you. Just so we're clear."

"You'd come for me."

She rolled her eyes.

I smiled.

She bared her teeth at me, only to relent with a snort. "Eventually. Maybe. After you had time to suffer and think about what a godsdamn idiot you'd been."

"That's fair."

"Hurry up and go," she said.

I went. Over hills of cracked and smoking ground, through a small forest of white trees, and finally into a small clearing where a silvery pool awaited.

This pool was called Galim. Five rivers twisted away from it, and dozens more branched out from those five farther downstream. The waters of the rivers were thick, rolling like molten silver, and each one corresponded to a certain area of the mortal realm below this one. They would bear you smoothly through the spaces in between the realms, typically spitting you out on the other side within moments.

These waterways were mainly utilized by lesser divine creatures or spirits. Only occasionally did gods such as myself use them—and only when traveling to places we weren't personally connected to. If not for my magic's currently unpredictable behavior, I would not have needed any river to carry me into my old kingdom.

I might not have needed it now, either, but I didn't want to risk it; traversing the realms by way of the waterways was less taxing than using one's own power.

I needed to conserve all the power I could for the night that lay ahead of me.

So I knelt, placing my palm flat against the water, and I ignored the warning building in my gut as I pictured the place I had once called home.

CHAPTER 5

Dravyn

I SURFACED IN THE MORTAL REALM JUST AS THE SUN WAS slipping behind the hilltops, splashing swirls of pinks and orange over the sky as it sank.

The river that had carried me here roared restlessly at my back. All the paths and waterways that snaked through Eligas—the name we gave to the space between the mortal and divine realms—felt restless as of late, ever since Karys had gone to battle in that in-between space.

During that battle, she'd managed to sweep a powerful elvish weapon away from the middle-heavens and into Eligas, preventing said weapon from doing catastrophic damage to the Tower of Ascension.

But the weapon had still ignited.

We didn't know how far the destruction had spread; Eligas was a strange place, difficult to map, its many shifting layers nearly impossible to truly inspect for damage.

All I could say for certain was that it felt different traveling through it now.

Everything felt different about this trip compared to the dozens of times I had made it in the past. And the restless, warped energy rising from the river, combined with my own strangely off-kilter powers meant I was already more tired than I should have been, even before I'd taken a single step onto mortal grass.

I soldiered on, all the same, my gaze fixed on a halo of light in the distance—the glow above the royal city of Altis.

I could only just make out my family's palace on the far side of the city, and only because the setting sun's light was reflecting off a wall of its windows with a dazzling shine that was difficult to miss.

I knew what room that was—the one with all those windows—even from here. It was an expansion of the study that lay behind it, a sunroom my mother had requested as an anniversary gift. My father had immediately dismissed the idea of a room with so many windows, and in such a precarious spot...only to summon the kingdom's greatest architect to the palace the very next day to make it happen.

A funny feeling spread through my chest as I thought about my parents—like an itch below the surface of my skin, just out of reach.

They had died several years ago. Mother first, from a terrible sickness that shriveled up her lungs, and father soon chasing after her as he'd been doing since the day they'd met. I'd heard about it secondhand from the Goddess of Stars—the one who kept record of all mortal lives and deaths—and I'd watched my brother's coronation from the shadows a week later.

He'd looked so alone.

Our siblings gone in the span of one violent night, and then our parents taken almost as quickly...yet, somehow, Fallon had stood tall and managed not to flinch as they placed the heavy crown on his head.

It was the only time I'd come close to regretting my decision not to show my face or speak to him.

I hadn't left him entirely alone, however; there were magical wards of my making around the palace here just as there were around my palace in the middle-heavens. I'd put them in place on his coronation day, and I returned regularly to make certain they were still intact.

I kept my eyes on the gleaming wall of windows as I walked—a room I'd taken especially great care to surround in hidden spells.

Some of my earliest memories were of sitting in it with my mother and my siblings, playing childish games, pretending to be dragons sunning ourselves in the warm beams of sunlight. I remembered few details, now; whenever I tried to focus on them, I was usually met with nothing more than a hazy, hot feeling, and occasionally visions of sunset colors bursting behind my eyes.

Reaching the edge of the city, I paused. I could have surfaced into this realm somewhere closer to the palace, but I'd wanted distance while I tested the current limits of my magic—and also to test out the ring Mairu had given me. As I twisted it a few times around my finger, the ruby-eyed dragon in its center emitted a soft hum that vibrated up my arm, tickling my skin.

I exhaled, surrendering to the spell.

As easy as that, my body began to shift its appearance whenever I moved, taking on the colors and textures of whatever I stood in front of. It was a weaker spell than what she could have performed in person; she was capable of more than mere camouflage, able to transform entire bodies into *other* bodies if she wanted to. But I could rely on stealth for my plans tonight, so this borderline invisibility would serve my purpose well enough.

"I suppose I owe you for this," I thought aloud, watching the ruby-eyed dragon shine in the setting sunlight.

It seemed to wink at me in response.

I summoned a few flames to my hands next, testing both their strength and my hold on them. Once I felt in control of the various magics at my disposal, I set off at a quick pace into the city.

I kept to the outskirts, stealing up and down smaller side streets I still vaguely remembered.

The air was filled with dozens of scents, each more tantalizing than the last. One could never predict the smells they might encounter when strolling through the streets here; Altis was a crossroads city, frequented by travelers journeying along the three major roads that ran through it. The exceptional amount of foot traffic drew merchants from far and wide. Tonight, the place smelled strongly of spices—mainly cinnamon and cardamom—mixed with the pine forests hemming the city in.

The sounds were more predictable. Shopkeepers pushing their goods in the common tongue or in occasional, heavily accented Galithian. Buyers bartering. Coins clinking as they exchanged hands.

As the sun dipped lower, the hum of noise featured more idle chatter and gossip about the day's events, with the competing chimes of the three temples serving as background music.

A few people shivered with awareness as I passed them, some looking twice at what maybe appeared to be a strange ripple in the air.

But no one truly *saw* me.

Sometimes they stared at the space where I stood for an unsettlingly long time, but ultimately just said a quick prayer under their breath, often while making the sign of the Sky Goddess—the deity best known and worshipped for her protective magic—before they turned and hurried in the opposite direction.

It was a strange feeling, this invisibility. I used to sneak out of the palace as a young adult, wide-eyed and following my older brother as he made his rounds at various questionable locales, drinking and gambling and swapping contraband goods with his friends. I hadn't wanted to be seen then, either, but it was a different kind of stealth. It had been exhilarating—a game.

My current invisibility felt more like being a ghost walking through a graveyard full of all the people and places I'd once loved.

I was very clearly *here*, but without being able to share that existence with anyone, did it matter?

As I drew nearer to the walls around the palace grounds, searching for the easiest place to quietly scale them, a sudden commotion caught my attention.

A small, harried unit of soldiers was converging on the main gates at a frantic speed, their leader shouting orders as they came. Two bodies were draped over two horses at the center of the company. It was difficult to see them from where I stood, but I was certain the bodies were barely moving, if at all.

I drew closer, first out of curiosity, and then because I saw the opportunity the clamor created for me: The guards at the main entry point had flung the gates wide open to allow the injured men to be carried inside.

Nobody noticed when I calmly made my way in behind them.

I'm not sure they would have noticed me even if I *hadn't* been using Mai's magic, given the levels of panic and disorder among them.

"Take them to the garrison and see to their wounds as best you can until the healer arrives," said a voice that sent a shiver of familiarity through me.

The voice's owner lowered his hood as the gates groaned shut behind us, and I was unsurprised to see a face I recognized glowing in the fading sunlight.

Black strings of hair framed a hollow face with silver-green eyes that were nearly always casting about in search of trouble. He moved with a slight limp, the result of a riding accident that had left his right leg mangled, its bones shattered too completely to properly set.

Captain Sordrin.

He'd served my father since before I was born. A decorated and well-respected soldier, advisor, speaker...and often the one who had caught my brother and me during our clandestine adventures into the city.

He growled out a few more orders to the rest of his soldiers before turning and striding toward the main doors of the palace.

I followed closely behind. If anybody was going to have useful information for me to gather tonight, it would likely be him and the circle he surrounded himself with.

My hunch about this was further confirmed only a moment later, as another familiar face—Lord Ryltar—met him on the front steps. Ryltar's eyes were wide as he watched the group in the distance carrying away the wounded, his rotund body shaking with anxiety as he wheezed for breath. "What the hell happened? You were on a routine patrol, yet I've heard—"

Captain Sordrin held up a hand, his gaze sliding toward the handful of people close enough to listen. "Not here. Gather whatever council we have available and meet me in the north-view room. And ready a messenger to send to His Majesty; he'll want this report as soon as possible."

A messenger?

So my brother wasn't here, it seemed.

Just as well.

It would be easier to focus on what I needed to find out if I didn't have to worry about seeing him—or him seeing me. I didn't *want* to see him. Regardless of what Rieta believed, I could in fact separate my divine obligations and plans from whatever lingering, complicated feelings I had toward what remained of my mortal family.

I paused with my foot on the top step, just for a moment. Though I had returned to this palace—and the city around it—numerous times over the past years, I rarely went inside the building itself.

But Sordrin and Ryltar had already slipped through the door and started down the hall.

Just as the footman pushed that heavy, steel door closed, I made myself step forward, darting inside, the drag of metal on marble covering the sound of my footsteps.

For a moment, I paused in the center of the atrium, staring at my family's coat of arms. It had been etched in gold against the floor—a shield wrapped in brambles with an eagle on one edge, wings unfurled, talons stretching toward a sword on the opposite edge.

Familiar sounds and scents assaulted me as I stood there. It was officially sundown—the hour when prayer and occasional fasting and offerings began among the more devout palace inhabitants—which meant smoky trails of incense, pungent whiffs of floral offerings, and the hum of prayer and soft chants as people made their way to the various shrines spread throughout the palace and its grounds.

It didn't escape my notice how amusing these humans were, preparing prayers and offerings to gods without realizing one was currently walking among them.

I didn't recall there being so many devout palace inhabitants in the past. How much did they all know about what was happening to the north? Maybe they were praying more earnestly because they were afraid of more men returning to the palace, lifeless, on the backs of their horses.

In my experience, few things inspired prayer more than fear.

I knew where the north-view room Sordrin had referred to was located, so I didn't worry about losing track of him. Instead, I took my time as I walked through the halls of my old home, studying it closer— but not too close.

In truth, I struggled to strike a balance; I'd come to gather information, which necessitated a closer look and an eavesdropping ear toward everything...but to look or listen *too* closely was to invite a trip down memory lane that I had no interest in taking.

As I reached my destination, several members of the summoned council reached it simultaneously. I hesitated, waiting for the right moment to make my next move.

I ended up slipping in alongside Lady Meira, an elderly woman who'd served as an advisor to my family for so long she was even closer to a ghost than I currently was; needless to say, her deteriorating eyes saw nothing out of the ordinary as I slid past her.

Once inside, I moved silently to the wall farthest from the table most of them were gathering around, pressing back against it and narrowing my gaze on Captain Sordrin.

As expected, he spoke first.

"One dead, two severely wounded."

A chorus of disgust and outrage rippled through the room.

Sordrin held up his hand, silencing them as he had Lord Ryltar earlier. "We never made it to Ederis proper, as we'd planned—only to what appears to be a new base they're trying to establish just north of the upper Berlnath river. A base very close to Ghaun. We spoke with some of Ghaun's inhabitants, and they confirmed that our old enemies have been terrorizing them. Nothing too harrowing, as of yet—only petty thievery and threats. But the citizens of Ghaun are afraid."

Ghaun was a small village with a dwindling population; it had once been a booming town, but most of the younger, more able bodies had migrated further south over the past decades—into Altis. So its population was elderly, its resources scarce, its ability to defend itself nearly non-existent.

The room turned Sordrin's words over in silence for several moments, until a man with ash-colored hair and unsettlingly bright green eyes sat up straighter in his seat, cleared his throat, and said, "So they're spreading beyond even the places we originally feared. Out of the Hollowlands and into the kingdom at large. Creeping their way closer to our own fair city. And attacking Ghaun along the way? By the gods... what business could they have in that peaceful place, if not abject destruction? They are the lowest of the low."

I braced my hand more firmly against the wall behind me. The grey-haired man's words mirrored what Halar had told me: The rebel Velkyn were in fact spreading, positioning themselves in threatening ways, likely preparing for larger attacks.

Now the main question I had was what the human kingdom planned to *do* about this encroachment.

How close were they to a true war?

How much time did we have to get control over these things?

Unfortunately, the council before me seemed incapable of agreeing on any plans. They went round and round for what felt like hours, proposing ideas that were all immediately criticized and picked apart, bickering with one another and hurling insults until it was all I could do to keep myself still and silent. If my brother had been here, he would have silenced them all and taken control of the conversation, steered it in at least a somewhat productive direction—something Captain Sordrin was trying but repeatedly failing to do.

But Fallon is not here, I reminded myself. *So stop thinking about him.*

I watched the chaotic scene unfolding around me with perfect silence and stillness, until finally, it seemed to be decided: they would station defensive units around Ghaun. That much was easy.

Then, if their king approved, they would mount an offensive attack to try and drive the elves back into the shadowy bowels of the Hollowlands. Those elves could not be allowed to believe that they had the freedom to go wherever they wanted to, to make whatever messes they cared to.

"They think we're afraid to answer their threats with fire of our own," said a woman I didn't recognize. "They will find that they are sorely mistaken about that."

A low murmur of agreement filled the room.

The words left me feeling as if I was witnessing a dangerous shift, like the beginnings of an avalanche breaking free while I stood, powerless and unnoticed, at the bottom of the mountain.

After a bit more discussion, the councilmen and women filed out of the room, still conversing among themselves with rapid tongues and serious tones.

Captain Sordrin was soon the only one left. He stood silently, nursing a pewter mug full of something a servant had brought him, as he stared out the room's only window.

I looked to the window, too. It seemed pitch black outside; how long had I been hiding in this room? I chanced a few steps closer for a better view, but froze as the captain glanced my direction, his ever-alert eyes darting about as they usually did.

I kept perfectly motionless, holding my breath.

And yet, as his gaze seemed to meet mine, for a brief, foolish moment, I found myself wanting him to see me. To find me as he used to. Even if it meant trouble. Even if it meant answering to my older brother—or worse, to my father. I might have welcomed an excuse to be dragged before the feet of either of them.

But Father was dead.

Fallon was not here, and even if he had been, he was complicated and potentially dangerous.

So I kept still, clutching the Serpent Goddess's ring and willing myself to remain unseen.

A moment later, Sordrin slammed the cup on the table and left the room, his injured leg dragging even more so than usual, as if close to buckling under the weight of all that had been discussed.

CHAPTER 6

Dravyn

I waited until Captain Sordrin had been gone for nearly a full minute before I exhaled the breath I'd been holding. Another minute before I chanced movement, and one more before I dared to step back into the hallway.

The palace was quieter than it had been upon my arrival. It meant less questioning gazes and bodies to avoid, but unfortunately more silent space for my thoughts to run wild in.

These thoughts kept circling back to my brother, wondering if there was more I should do where he was concerned.

I knew—better than any of the council I'd just witnessed—what the elves were truly capable of and what they might be planning. Did I have an obligation to wait until my brother returned so I could tell him these things? A duty as his family? As a god his people worshipped?

Or maybe Rieta was right, after all, and I was simply looking for an excuse to see him.

No; I wouldn't see him this trip, I decided. I'd risked enough already. I'd collected good information—information that I needed to take back to the divine realm. That would be enough for tonight.

And yet.

And yet...

When I looked up, I found myself standing at the head of a familiar hallway. This one was silent, completely devoid of any people or signs of life. The air hung stale and heavy, as though it had been undisturbed for a very long time.

My chest caved in, slowly but surely, as I realized where I was. I should have been paying more attention to where I was going. Because this hall...of course I found it familiar.

My room had once been behind the second door on the left.

And all my siblings...their rooms had been here, too.

My older brother might not have been in the palace—physically— but it didn't matter. These halls still held him. They still held *all* of us. I didn't dare open any doors to see if their rooms remained intact, but I swore I could hear the laughter of my younger siblings echoing out from them.

I could smell Elora's paints, her latest work of art still drying on one of her many easels.

Closing my eyes tightly caused shining blobs of black and blue to spill into my vision—like the splatters of ink that always covered Sylas's hands and clothing, remnants from his hours of studying and note-taking.

My heart pounded as if we were playing a game, as though they were all looking for me.

Why was I hiding from them?

Then the smell of blood eclipsed it all.

So much blood.

Then screaming. Pounding footsteps. A weight against my chest— the weight of my little sister, too heavy for my younger arms to bear. Too heavy, too heavy, *too heavy...*so I was too slow.

Too late to save her.

The memories rose like waves, each one crashing with more violence than the last. Cursing under my breath, I staggered back, kicking free of the shifting water and sand I imagined around my ankles, refusing to let it pull me into deeper, darker depths.

As calmly and quietly as I could, I turned and hurried away from the hallway.

Only to round the corner and find myself facing a dead end, looking up at a half-covered portrait.

The black mourning shroud that had been hung over it had begun to droop on one side, revealing part of a painting of the once-complete royal family.

There was my father—whom everyone always said I favored—with his serious glare and a crown of twisted, diamond-studded gold resting on his dark blond waves.

There was my mother, somehow striking a perfect balance between power and warmth as she clutched one of our family heirlooms: a golden sword with outstretched eagle wings forming the guard.

My elder brother stood beside her with a proud smile and his hand on my shoulder; even now I remembered the way he'd dug his nails into me as we'd sat for the painting, trying to goad me into crying out. He'd been unsuccessful. I had a high tolerance for pain—then and now—and the painted version of my younger self wore a determined, grim expression.

My younger brother and sister were below me, still covered by the mourning shroud. It was a small mercy, not having to see their faces; I might have stared at them forever if given the chance. The temptation to uncover them was enough to make my fingers cramp and itch with the need to move, but I kept my hands at my sides, unflinching.

It's time to leave. Over and over I told myself this—*leave, leave, leave.*

But the truth was that I had never truly left this place.

I didn't know how to.

Countless years had passed, but I still remembered all the horrors that had happened here with a kind of cruel, brilliant clarity.

I closed my eyes, trying to make it easier to turn my back on the painting of my family.

An instant later, I felt a series of sharp pains on my ring finger, as though the dragon there had coiled more tightly around my skin before biting into it.

Looking down at the dragon's sparkling ruby eyes roused me back into something like awareness. I didn't know how long I had until Mai's spell wore off—but I knew I couldn't be standing in this cursed hallway when it happened.

I made my way back to the lofted area overlooking the entry hall. I wanted to sprint down the spiraling staircases and out the front door faster than I'd ever sprinted in my existence. Maybe I could finally shake this palace and its memories off my trail if I just ran away from it all fast enough.

But I walked, because running would have been too loud, and the palace seemed to be filling up with more and more people all of a sudden; I couldn't risk bumping into someone.

The extra bodies were dangerous, but the walls were worse—they felt like they were shifting away from me, dragging at my hair and clothing as they went, like a beast trying to inhale me, swallow me whole, never let me leave the belly of despair ever again.

Somehow, I put one foot after the other and marched on.

Somehow, I slipped out the same door I'd come in, through a city turning sleepy and quiet, and then beyond that, into a forest of thick pine filled with the beating of owl wings and the competing songs of chirping insects.

And *somehow*, finally, I stood before the restless river that would bear me back to the divine realm.

Head pounding and heart hammering, I knelt and pressed my palm against the surface, just as I'd done in the divine realm on the other side.

The water should have turned thicker, closer to the consistency of molten metal, as it was in that other realm. But the river didn't shift, not in the slightest, as though it didn't recognize my authority at all.

I suspected—hoped—it had less to do with my wayward magic and more to do with a lack of concentration. I was too far removed from my divine existence in that moment; I couldn't travel to the middle-heavens while so many images of my mortal life remained dominant. I couldn't belong to both worlds.

I tried harder to push the images of my family and my old home away.

I *had* to push them away.

But no matter how I tried, I couldn't form even the faintest image of the divine realm in my mind—and so the river would not take me back to that realm.

My fingers dug into the cold mud on either side of me.

Magic stirred in my bones, tempting me to use it instead of the river.

The pools of water around me dried with the heat I gave off, rising as steam into the night air. Little fires began blooming in the grass and mud. They crackled and hissed against the damp ground, the sounds seeming to whisper words that were at once taunting and encouraging.

You don't have to surrender to the mud. You're a god. You don't need a river to carry you anywhere. Your magic can take you away from this place.

I realized then how little I'd come to trust that magic of mine…so little that I wouldn't even risk a simple transporting spell. Mai had been right; I was a mess.

The fires were becoming brighter, more numerous. I didn't feel out of control of them—they were still harmlessly small—but they were popping up breathtakingly quickly. This was fast becoming a nightmare.

Nightmare.

The word stirred something inside of me. My hands lifted of their own accord, shaking away mud and putting out several fires with the same motion. And as quickly as that, I could picture the divine realm again—or a small part of it, anyway: my bed, with Karys resting in the center of it.

What if the potion Rieta had given her hadn't worked? What if another terror had awakened her by this point and she was wondering where I'd gone?

My fingers reached out, hovered over the cold water. Instead of trying to picture the heavens themselves, I only tried to picture Karys's face. It was surprisingly easy to do, even with the fires still building around me and the blood-stained memories still clawing at my back.

I could—I *would*—make my way back to her, even if I had to crawl to her through fire and mud and memory, and whatever else tried to come between us.

With an effort that sent a painful spasm up my arm and drew a deep groan from my chest, I forced all the fires around me to extinguish.

Darkness engulfed me. Fire started to rise within me, but I resisted the urge to let it overtake me again.

Instead, I leaned forward and dipped my hand closer to the river's surface, still not quite touching it. I kept perfectly still as the water moved toward me. It rose almost tentatively to my fingertips, like a lover slowly moving in for a kiss, until finally, it swept over my hand, up my arm, and pulled me fully down into its embrace.

It was not a smooth journey. The waters seemed to have grown darker and even more restless in the short time I'd spent in my old king-dom. I was tossed and battered about, striking rocks, getting caught in violent currents, washing onto what seemed to be shorelines, only to be yanked back—almost as if Eligas could not decide what to do with me.

Once I finally reached a familiar shoreline, I stayed sprawled out by the water's edge for several minutes, unable to bring myself to move. I was sore. Exhausted. And afraid to open my eyes completely, convinced that even after all that painful tumbling around, I was still in the mortal realm. The water hadn't felt right. The air here didn't feel right. *Nothing* felt right, except...

When I focused, I could feel a second, fluttering force of magic alongside the heartbeat of my own.

Karys.

Closer. She was closer, and certainly in the same realm as me. So I was back in the heavens I'd been aiming for. But I still had at least a mile to go to reach her. Picturing her face once more, I shoved myself upright and carried on.

I made it back to the palace, all the way through the front door, and nearly to my tower before I had to kneel and catch my breath.

It was in this frustrating, embarrassing position that Mai happened across me. She scrutinized me from head to toe—likely making sure I wasn't in any immediate danger—before scrunching up her nose and sniffing as though I'd dragged something dead in alongside me.

"You look like shit," she remarked.

"Thank you," I said, wincing as I took a deep breath. "That's helpful."

Her hands went to her hips. "Well? What did you find out?"

The images from the night's travels raced through my mind. I shook them away. "Later," I told her. "I need to go wash the pieces of that realm from my skin."

Mai's gaze turned softer and brighter—a mixture of concern and curiosity—but she only bit her lip and gave an understanding nod.

"Karys," I began, "is she…"

"She's fine. Still asleep, last I checked."

I gave her my thanks and staggered to my feet, waving her away as she tried to offer a hand for balance. I managed to stand and walk well enough on my own, and without another word, I climbed the stairs toward my bedroom.

CHAPTER 7

Karys

I WOKE IN THE MIDDLE OF THE NIGHT, NOT BECAUSE OF nightmares or flames building around me, but because of a sudden pressure in my chest—like someone had taken hold of my heart and was trying to wrench it out.

I sat up in a daze. The potion Rieta had given me made my head feel as though it had been stuffed with dandelion fluff. It took several moments to form a coherent thought. Several more to blink my eyes back into focus and remember where I was.

Dravyn's room.

His bed.

He'd carried me to it, hadn't he?

Beside me was Moth; he'd slipped under the covers and now rested on his back. His beak was hanging open, little snores occasionally slipping out of it.

It was colder than it usually was in this room; the fireplace was full of nothing but glowing coals.

How odd.

I'd never seen that fire go out.

I rubbed my eyes, blinking a few more times to make certain I was seeing clearly...and what I saw made the uncomfortable pressure in my chest even worse.

At the foot of the bed sat Dravyn, his eyes closed, his head bowed low, his hands clasped together in front of him. His hair was damp. He smelled of mint and soap and oil, and his arms looked to have been scraped roughly enough that welts had formed on his skin, as though he'd gotten carried away while trying to scrub himself clean.

"Dravyn?"

He didn't reply. Didn't lift his head or stir at all, even as I sat up straighter and leaned toward him.

"Are you okay?"

Still no reply. I threw the covers aside—waking Moth and earning a disgruntled growl as I did—and I crawled toward Dravyn.

He jumped slightly as my hand fell upon his arm. Up close, I confirmed what I'd suspected: several of the welts looked prominent enough that they'd likely bled before closing into the raised wounds I saw now. Nothing terribly deep, certainly not concerning for a god; they would be healed in the next few minutes, most likely.

But what had caused him to do such a thing?

He still didn't look at me, so I cupped my hand against his jaw and turned his face toward mine. He didn't resist. As our gazes met, I had to fight the urge to jump myself. His eyes frightened me. They were glassy, wide, seeing right past me. And his skin...it wasn't *cold*, but it was not full of the warmth I was used to from him.

I drew my hand down, pulling it into a fist against my chest as I tried and failed to suppress a shudder.

He finally came back to life at this—maybe because he could see the fear he was causing me—and he mirrored my earlier movement, lifting his hand and pressing it to my cheek. His fingers trembled against my skin, but touching me seemed to give him strength. He managed a deep breath.

As he exhaled, the room warmed the tiniest bit.

"I didn't mean to wake you," he said, lowering his hand and trailing his fingers up and down my arm. "I just needed to be near you again. I hope you don't mind."

"Mind?" I whispered, mouth almost too dry to speak. "Of course I don't mind."

His fingers came to rest in the spaces between mine. He squeezed my hand tightly, holding it as though I was an anchor keeping him from drifting away again.

I squeezed back just as tightly.

He felt...*strange*. Like part of his magic had been drained. I don't think I'd fully realized how in sync I was with that magic until this moment, when the waning of it made it feel like a hollow cavern was opening in my own chest.

"What happened?" I demanded. "Where did you go?" I had a sinking suspicion I already knew the answer to that last question.

He hesitated only a moment before he told me the details—how he'd gone back to his old kingdom just as I'd feared. How he'd witnessed death and chaos starting to build, confirming the awful warnings Halar had given us. How he feared war was unavoidable, and that, when it came, what remained of our respective mortal families would be standing on opposite sides of the battlefield.

As he spoke, Moth crawled out from under the covers and curled up in my lap. Within moments, he was snoring again.

"It feels intentional, the elves targeting my old city all of a sudden," Dravyn said, absently scratching the griffin between its tufted ears. "As if they are trying to draw you and me into the fold, likely in hopes that we'll also pull other divine beings down with us. Chaos and complications—whatever it takes to undo the hierarchy of power as it is now."

I should have been focused on the bigger picture as he was, perhaps.

But at the moment, all I could think about was the danger he'd put himself in. And the pain. The haunted look in his eyes, the way his fingers had trembled against my skin only moments ago...

"Did you see your brother when you were in Altis?"

His gaze snapped to mine as though I'd uttered some heinous, unforgivable curse.

"No," he said, with obviously practiced indifference. "I didn't see him."

The words—and his obvious attempt to hide behind them—only made me more curious about what he *had* seen.

I swallowed down the frustration starting to build in my throat and quietly said, "You shouldn't have gone alone."

"It was faster that way. Easier."

"Not easier for *you*."

"I've faced far more difficult things."

"That's not the point."

He stood, dropping my hand and making his way over to the fire. He rekindled the flame with a bit more effort than it usually took him; he actually had to kneel before it and shift the wood into a more deliberate position to help it catch properly.

"The past isn't finished with either of us, as you said." I got to my feet as well, gently placing Moth in a pile of blankets behind me. The griffin snored on, oblivious to the conversation around him. "But you don't have to face that past on your own."

He grabbed the metal poker and started stoking the fire. I'd rarely seen him use that poker, or any of the other tools on the hearth, for that matter; it wasn't as though the flames burned him when he used his hands.

Maybe he just wanted an excuse to stab something.

"Next time you do something like this, we go together." My words were firm. Unyielding. I felt bolder, stronger than I had in weeks. Maybe it was the balam potion—the fact that I'd finally managed to truly rest because of it.

Dravyn shook his head. "I barely made it back to this realm in one piece. If you had been there..."

"Then maybe we could have made it back easier."

He didn't reply.

"You're stronger when I'm closer to you," I said. "Admit it. Do you think I haven't noticed the way our magic reacts and builds when we're near to each other? Sometimes it's enough to take my breath away. Maybe it's not as overwhelming for *you*, but you must feel some sort of shift, too."

He relented with a sigh. "Yes. But that's a very simple—too simple —explanation of what's happening between us. There are too many unknowns. You need to get a firm grip on your own power in a safer, less volatile environment."

"*Are* there any safe, less volatile environments for me, at the moment? If so, I'd absolutely love to hear about them."

A muscle in his jaw ticked.

I'd made a point he couldn't refute.

Nevertheless, he didn't give in. "You're right—I *do* feel a shift in my magic when you're close. Sometimes it feels like I'm drawing more in, my power feeding from yours because you haven't yet learned how to hold your own. Don't you see how this could be dangerous? Destabilizing? I won't risk finding ourselves in a desperate situation where I end up taking from you and—"

"You aren't taking anything, you idiot. I'm freely offering it. No matter what happens, we're supposed to face things together, right? And there's more to my power than the fire you gave me. Remember? You said that right after I ascended."

He didn't take those words back, but his gaze remained troubled.

"Either way," I continued, "we can't avoid these complications forever. We have to figure out how to make sense of these new versions of ourselves."

For a long moment, he regarded me with the same practiced, stony expression he'd used when I'd mentioned his brother.

Then, without answering me, he straightened back to his full height and turned all his attention to the fire he'd built.

"I already made up my mind earlier," I pressed, stepping toward him. My words were sharp-edged, honed by the frustration building inside me. "I'm going to work harder to control my divine powers so you *can't* inadvertently take them, and so nothing else can go wrong in that regard. I'll focus on my ability to transport first. I'll prove to you that I can use magic to get myself out of danger, same as you. Will that make you feel better?"

He slowly drew his gaze back to mine, turning to meet me as I approached.

He still didn't speak.

I swallowed down more sharp words, trying to ignore the painful way they carved and settled into my stomach.

The fire burned brighter the closer I came to him. Brighter as I exhaled as much of my frustration as I could, and brighter still as I wrapped my arms around him and rested my head against his chest, watching the flames dance to the rhythm of his breathing.

His body was stiff at first, each muscle clenched impossibly tight. But the longer I held him, the more he relaxed against me.

Finally, his hands moved, abandoning the rigid grip he had on my hips. He circled his arms around my waist instead. Pulled me against him. Buried his face in my hair, breathing in my scent, his hands moving over my body and tracing the curves and lines of me as though he was trying to convince himself that I was solid. That I was real and safe and *here*.

I stretched up and pressed my lips to his, so he could taste the realness of the moment as well as feel it.

He kissed me back, fiercely, fingers threading through my hair, clenching hard enough to draw a small gasp from my mouth.

His hold relaxed at the sound, but not by much. He was holding on just as he'd held my hand earlier—as though he was worried he might float away without me to anchor him down.

Even when he ended the kiss, he stayed close, his fingers still tangled in my hair.

I wondered again at what he'd seen and experienced while I'd slept. I didn't ask this time, but he soon offered up more on his own, his voice barely audible even though his lips were close enough to brush my ear when he spoke.

"I had a vision earlier," he said, "while I was trying to wash up. In it I...I was carrying you through the halls of my former palace. You were bleeding. I'd moved too slow. I..." His hold on me tightened even more as he trailed off.

My heart skipped several beats as I realized what had caused him to dig so deeply into his skin: He'd been trying to get my blood off his arms. My invisible blood.

"It wasn't real," I whispered, leaning back so I could see his face. I brushed strands of damp hair from his eyes, willing my fingers not to shake. His expression was frightening again—distant and almost... *panicked*.

I'd never seen him like this.

I did my best not to let my fear show, closing my eyes and pressing my lips to his again, trying to say with my kiss what I couldn't manage with words.

He kissed me back, but with less force than before. Less awareness.

"It wasn't real," I whispered again.

He nodded absently.

But no matter how many times I repeated the words, the guilt still remained in his eyes, haunting and dark, even in the bright glow of firelight.

CHAPTER 8

Karys

Later that day, Mairu and Valas both met me in the open fields just south of the Palace of Fire.

Dravyn had gone to speak with Halar and the rest of the Sun Court after promising to help me practice my magic whenever he returned. He'd seemed more like himself before he'd left, but I was still worried about him, in need of a distraction—and impatient, too—so I'd asked the others to help me practice in the meantime.

"You sure you're ready for this?" Mai asked.

I nodded, turning my attention away from thoughts of Dravyn and focusing fully on her. She looked beautiful, as always, her hair plaited in rows and woven through with strands of shimmering gold. She wore a fitted top paired with a skirt that flowed beautifully around her, shifting between all the colors of a sunrise-splashed sea with such perfect precision that I wondered if she'd spelled it with her magic.

She smiled as I nodded—but it was a propped-up sort of smile, one that was trying too hard to pretend everything was fine.

Valas arrived a few minutes later, looking as though he'd just been roused from a nap. His shirt was untucked, his hair disheveled, his saunter the definition of effortless.

Mai gave him a disapproving look.

He only smiled and yawned in response, ring-laden fingers sparkling as he brought his hand up to cover his mouth.

Mai rolled her eyes, but she was biting her lip as she looked away, and I could guess at what she was thinking easily enough: It was unfair for anyone to look that good when they'd just woken up.

"All caught up on your beauty sleep?" I asked, arching a brow.

His expression brightened. "Almost."

In the distance, Zell trotted and pranced around, occasionally leaping straight up, kicking his feet and sending ribbons of flame into the air.

Moth soared in and out of these ribbons, trailing his own fire behind him—ribbons of a bolder red than Zell's. The combination of the two of them was mesmerizing.

I watched their show for a moment, smiling at their antics, trying to concentrate on anything but the task before me in hopes of soothing my nerves.

Mai was much more focused than I was. She wasted no time declaring the lesson officially in progress, signifying its start with a sharp clap. "The first thing I believe you should work on is *relaxing*."

Just the word made my stomach lurch and my hands shake in a decidedly *un*relaxed manner.

"This ability to traverse instantly from one place to another is one that almost all divine beings share," Mai went on, "and in every case I've known, it's a magic that works in essentially the same way: You can't out-stubborn it or force it into submission, no matter how powerful you become."

"Can't I try?" I asked with a rueful smile. "I'm much better at being stubborn than I am at relaxing."

Mai gave me a stern frown, shaking her head.

"This should go well," Valas said, settling down on a lush patch of the silver-green grass. He sat cross-legged and propped a hand under his chin, grinning like a child eager to watch a funny play.

I shot him a dirty look. "Did you tag along just to antagonize me?"

"Of course he did," Mai said.

"Don't worry," said the Winter God, still grinning, "I made sure to wear clothing I didn't care about this time, so we're good in the event that you accidentally set me on fire."

"What about if she *purposefully* sets you on fire?" Mai inquired sweetly.

He scoffed. "That won't happen, because Karys and I are best friends."

I snorted. "No forcing it," I said to Mai, reminding her of where she'd been interrupted. "What else is there to know?"

She thought for a moment before continuing, using her hands to mime the concept as she explained it. "Imagine a current that weaves between all the places of the world. It carries you on its own; you don't control it any more than you control a rushing river. It's a bit like the paths that twist and turn through Eligas: You simply surrender to its power, but tell it where to let you out of the waters by picturing or feeling a particular place. A place that, as you know, is much easier to travel to if you've left a marker there, so to speak—a concentration of your particular brand of magic."

I nodded, feeling a touch more confident. I *did* know how it worked —and had for some time. Putting it into practice was simply the next step.

I could do this.

"We'll stay close to the palace," Mai said, "since it's drenched in Fire magic residue, obviously. It will draw you toward it, so even if your spell goes way off course, you shouldn't end up too far from here."

My gaze swept over that palace, studying its twisting spires and white stone, admiring the colorful glass windows that had all been personally crafted by Dravyn.

Out of the corner of my eye, I saw fire building in the distance— Moth and Zell, still playing. Their burning display drew me in just as before, and now it gave me an idea.

"Could I try to move myself toward their fires?" I asked, nodding in that direction. I felt a connection to them and their magic—more so than to the palace itself.

"Good thinking," Mai agreed.

The praise gave me another surge of confidence that lasted for approximately five seconds—until I turned and fully focused on the hill the two playful creatures were tumbling around on.

They seemed much higher up and farther away all of a sudden.

"Relax," Mai reminded me.

"I'm here to extinguish whatever you inevitably set aflame," Valas added, ever so helpfully.

I closed my eyes, trying to empty my mind of everything except the image of the fire show Moth and Zell had been putting on. I tried to imagine being a part of that show, sitting astride Zell's back, flames dancing all around me—and *from* me. We drew from the same divine source of fire, so now I just needed to let it pull me in.

Same fire, same fire, same fire...

I clenched my eyes even tighter for several beats, then opened them, blinking slowly.

Nothing had happened.

I tried again with the same results.

"Well, at least nothing's on fire yet," Valas said cheerfully.

"That's not helpful commentary," I heard Mai hiss.

They both sounded very far away, even though I hadn't managed to move an inch.

I ignored them and tried again.

And again.

And again.

Whatever it took, whatever I had to endure, I would not stop until I got this right.

Hours later, my head was pounding and sweat dripped down my face, stinging my eyes. My bones ached as though some invisible force had been trying to rip them from my body—which I suppose wasn't far from the truth; though I hadn't managed to transport myself anywhere, it *did* feel like every attempt rattled something inside me a little looser, and it was only a matter of time before all those broken pieces ended up flying out in all directions, out of my control like everything else seemed to be.

Mai had assured me this was a normal feeling and that it would pass.

Valas had volunteered to help me collect my bones and organs whenever they inevitably scattered, which earned him another scolding from the Serpent Goddess.

I'd lost track of the exact time, but it felt like we'd been at this for almost an entire day now.

And I still could not get the spell anywhere close to right.

I'd managed to wrap myself in flames repeatedly—a good start to a method many divine beings used. I'd seen Dravyn do the same thing before he disappeared, essentially letting his magic bleed out of him in order to make it easier to surrender to the older, deeper magic that allowed one to be carried away on that *current* Mai had spoken of.

A few times, I'd even felt the tips of my fingers and toes starting to disappear while I was surrounded by the flames. But every time, I'd panicked at the thought of being there one moment, gone the next.

Just *gone*.

I couldn't do it.

It made no logical sense. I couldn't map the space between where I stood and where I was transporting myself to, and so my brain simply refused to believe it was possible to make such a journey on my own.

My latest attempt had resulted in a transfer of what seemed to be only my magical essence—I had remained perfectly solid at my starting point, but a ghostly figure that vaguely resembled me had appeared on the targeted hilltop.

Mai had nearly panicked at this. Apparently, it wasn't unheard of for a divine being to splinter themselves this way and then not be able to put the physical body and the magical soul back together again.

I needed to take a break, she'd decided, before I did permanent damage to myself or my magic.

So, I was taking a break.

I'd sank down to the ground several minutes ago, oblivious to the mud I landed in—mud from melted Ice magic that had extinguished my chaotic fires, as Valas had promised to do. I sat stiffly, my fingers drawing random objects in that cold, dark mud—a flame, a feather, a sword plunging through a crown—until I could no longer stand the silence or the dismal mood settling over us.

"On a scale of one to ten," I said with as much humor as I could muster, "how hopeless would you say I am?"

Mai knelt beside me and put a comforting hand on my shoulder.

"I'd say you're around a six or seven," Valas said.

"Be quiet," the Serpent Goddess snapped.

"What?" He yawned. "I didn't say *ten*, now did I?"

I rose to my feet and stretched, trying to work the soreness from my bones and loosen up my muscles in hopes of trying again. I couldn't end the day without at least a *bit* more progress.

I looked once more to the hilltop I'd been trying to reach. Moth and Zell were still there, now curled up together. Moth slept using Zell's golden flank as a pillow. The selakir was sniffing at the air, searching the space where my ghostly apparition had been minutes ago, his ears twitching beside his stubby antlers.

He must have felt me staring because his head swiveled toward me, intelligent black eyes meeting mine and holding them.

We stared at one another until he gave a sudden snort and a swish of his tail. Then he was rising elegantly to his feet and trotting down to me, leaving Moth without a pillow; the griffin voiced his displeasure with a loud wail that lasted until Valas aimed an icy spell in his direction.

As the grass turned to frozen, glittering blades beneath him, Moth rose with a huff and shot upwards, disappearing into the sky.

Zell circled me, tossing his slender head about and stamping his hooves. He seemed eager to run—and to take me with him.

I drew him close and stroked the bridge of his nose, considering the offer for only a few seconds before I made up my mind.

"I'll be back," I told the others, swinging onto Zell's back. "I need to clear my head."

Mai nodded, frowning thoughtfully.

Valas gave me a salute and then laid back in the grass, crossing his arms behind his head, looking happy for the opportunity to take a nap. It would likely be a short one; Moth was hovering high above him, and I suspected the griffin was preparing some sort of revenge for the Winter God's icy attack.

Part of me wanted to stay around to watch that, but instead, I urged Zell into a gallop without any particular destination in mind.

He didn't need much encouragement to reach his full speed. Nor did he care that I'd given him no direction. He would likely have run without ceasing to the very ends of the heavens if I'd let him, and he would have enjoyed every stride.

When we finally slowed several minutes later, trotting to a stop next to a small pond I didn't recognize, my hands were shaking from a strange combination of exhilaration and anxiety. My hair had shaken loose from the elaborate braids Rieta had woven it into. My heart was racing. My thoughts were pounding...but also clearing.

I looked back in the direction I believed the palace to be in, and images of what I needed to do—and what was at stake—flashed through my mind.

I couldn't keep running away.

I had to figure this out.

"There doesn't seem to be much magic in the air here, compared to where we were practicing before. Maybe that will actually be more helpful to me?" I reasoned aloud. "The greater contrast between where I'm standing and the palace might make it easier to focus on the magic at said palace."

Zell snorted and swung his head to fix his inky eyes on me. I couldn't say if it was an encouraging look or not, but I wanted to think it was.

I slid from his back and readied myself for one more try. My theory made sense, I'd decided; I was confident I'd be able to pick out that great concentration of magic around Dravyn's palace. Then I only had to surrender to its pull.

Surrender. Surrender. Surrender.

I repeated the word as I stared at my reflection in the glass-like surface of the pond.

I watched the familiar-by-now flames flicker to life and start to wind around me.

I watched my mirrored self take a deep breath, then another, silently urging her to stay calm.

Zell took a few steps back, eying me carefully. He went completely still as the fire swallowed me up to my shoulders. Not the spooked stillness of a frightened animal, but the intelligent, stoic stance of a partner trying not to break my concentration.

I looked down at my boots. Imagined them gone. Blinked.

Still there.

But then a deep breath, another blink, and it was finally happening: I was disappearing, feathered flames whisking away from me and leaving nothing but air where they'd just been burning.

It had likely only been seconds, but time seemed to move in slow motion as I watched the process spreading up my legs, my waist, my chest.

Surrender. Surrender. Surrender.

"Don't panic," I ordered myself in a whisper.

My body—what was left of it—no longer felt like my own. Then it didn't *feel* at all. I was untethered, terrifyingly light and aimless. Panic rose, but with no body left to hold it in I found it easier to let go of it. I could imagine it scattering into the wind, frail and harmless and no longer my problem.

But I cannot scatter with it, I reminded myself—one of the lessons Mairu had been repeating all morning. *I have to stay on the path I decided on.*

There may have been no map to help visualize that path, but this time I tried to imagine one—even going so far as to lift my hands before me and pretend I was trailing my fingers between points on a piece of parchment.

I was so close now. I would not fail.

I *would not.*

As soon as I declared this to myself, I felt my body being pulled forward. All around me was darkness, but warmth kissed my face. Distant, teasing warmth—like the tiniest ray of sunlight penetrating a dark forest I'd been wandering in for ages. I imagined myself embracing it. Reaching up, parting the canopy of leaves, letting more light in.

I knew where this light was coming from. This warmth. I closed my eyes and pictured moving toward it—the palace.

When that didn't make me budge, I pictured something more specific: Dravyn descending upon that palace. Wings of fire flared wide, burning so brightly they blurred away all but the faintest outlines of everything around me.

The warmth became more intense, pulling me along, farther and faster.

Faster, faster, almost there, *surely, I was almost there—*

Something caught me, jerking me violently to a stop as if the pocket of my tunic had caught on a door handle.

I was no longer light and floating, yet I still felt suspended and fragile...less like a feather and more like a rock upon thin ice. Cracking, breaking, and then I was sinking through cold, such awful cold, faster and faster, until finally I hit the ground *hard*.

I knew instantly that I'd managed to bring my physical self with me this time—because pain blossomed from a half-dozen different parts of my body. I tasted blood on my lips, and I heard myself cry out, the sound echoing in air that was much more frigid than what I'd left behind.

I opened my eyes.

Darkness surrounded me.

Why was it so dark?

I lifted an aching, trembling hand and tried to summon a small flame. It sputtered to life in my dirt splattered palm, its glow illuminating a landscape of black, rocky soil dotted with a few scraggly white trees. Clearly not the same place I'd just been. Yet my flame continued to burn—so my magical soul was intact as well.

I hadn't splintered.

My whole self was here, when a breath ago, it had been somewhere else.

I'd done it.

A giddy, nervous laugh escaped me. I couldn't believe I'd actually *done it.*

My glee was short-lived, however, as I studied my surroundings more closely.

I still expected to see the familiar palace, even if it was far in the distance. Its stained-glass shining, its towers looming, maybe Dravyn standing on one of the many balconies, calling me home...

Instead, black ground stretched in every direction. A fine, shimmering mist rolled along the land, and to my distant right, there were jagged cliffs that plummeted down farther than I could see. The air smelled of rot and dust.

"This isn't right," I said—to no one. Zell was gone. The palace was nowhere in sight, and neither were Valas and Mairu.

In fact, this didn't seem to be Dravyn's territory, at all.

A chill breeze rose at my back, raising the flesh along my arms. I spun around and saw strange shadows tumbling toward me, rolling as if they were riding that wind...and all at once I realized where I was.

Because I'd been here before.

This was the Death God's territory, and judging by the glowing eyes that had just appeared in the shadows, I was not as alone as I'd thought.

CHAPTER 9

Karys

I'D MADE A MISTAKE.

As I backed away from the shadows full of glowing orbs, an explanation occurred to me.

The cliffs to my right...I'd found myself on them months ago, soon after my mortal self had first started to explore these heavens in earnest. The Death God, Zachar, had cornered me there. His magic had been horrible; I could still imagine the cold claws of his dark power raking against my skin, draining me of all sense of life and hope.

Dravyn had appeared at the last moment, wielded his fire against Zachar and chased him away. It had seemed like an incredible amount of power at the time, but now I understood just how much it had truly been—enough that it had left behind a mark on this spot, a residual pool of magic.

And that pooled magic—and perhaps my memories and feelings of being astonished by his power—had pulled me back to this place.

I stopped backing up as I felt another burst of cold at my back, more intense and concentrated along my spine this time, as though someone had slipped a block of ice down my tunic.

Shadows were closing in on every side. Some of the glowing eyes were coming closer, the beastly creatures they belonged to emerging from the dark, trailing black ribbons behind them as they did.

Then came the Death God himself, a tall figure wrapped in a grey cloak with a pack of shadow cats snarling and spitting at his heels.

He looked more human than I remembered him looking before. His hood was lowered, revealing normal ears where there had once been horned appendages. He wasn't as pale as I recalled, either, his complexion still fair, but far from the ghastly shade of bone it had once been.

Nevertheless, he was still terrifying. His body was still too long, too jagged and uneven, too...*something*, and it moved with a strange grace just shy of seeming human.

I fought the urge to keep backing up. Instead, I stood taller, meeting his eyes, which were the color of twilight, their glowing pupils like the only stars that had appeared in the sky thus far.

"So here you are again." His voice was a serpent slithering in and out of my head. The words were accompanied by a dark cloud, like breath fogging in the cold—except the breath, like so many things in this territory, was made of shadows. "Once again an uninvited guest in my dominion."

"Uninvited, yes. But also an inadvertent one," I said flatly.

"You mean you weren't dying to come see me? Even though we haven't seen one another since your ascension? I pushed for your divine blessing, you know. If I hadn't helped you, you wouldn't be standing here now, invited or not. I thought perhaps you had come to thank me."

"*Thank* you?" I should have held my tongue. No good had ever come from provoking this god. But his slithering tone and smug expression had both slipped under my skin. "You didn't help me. And why would I be happy to see you? You betrayed me. You told Dravyn my thoughts, my secrets, my plans—plans that I'd already abandoned, by the way—and you nearly ruined me."

He laughed.

I clenched my teeth. "I don't find any of it funny."

"No? Still essentially a short-sighted mortal, then, even with all you've been given. How disappointing."

"And you are still a traitorous time-waster who talks in riddles and circles. *How disappointing.*"

His smile crept slowly across his face, beautiful but deadly, like an early frost in spring choking out any chance of life. "I am no traitor, girl," he snarled. "For me to have betrayed you, I would have had to swear allegiance to you, first. I did no such thing."

"True enough," I snarled back. "My mistake for assuming you were decent, like the rest of the Shade Court turned out to be."

"My *decent* fellow court members forgot themselves in the chaos you brought into this realm. I alone remembered that we are meant to answer to a higher power—in the matter of you as in the matters of all things. And it was me who first suggested to my higher power that you might find a place here in His court. I helped devise the trial Malaphar ultimately offered you, and I set that final trial into motion."

I started to object, but a memory dropped suddenly into my head, snapping my mouth shut as it landed.

Everything that had happened in the Tower of Ascension was a blur...but when I focused, I remembered the powerful, quiet voice of the Shade God speaking over my battered body.

You were dying on the shore of the mortal lake known as Irithyl. I had my servant—you know him as Zachar, I believe—stall your soul's passing long enough to transport it here...

The Death God had clearly been following orders from a higher power then, as he claimed. So was he telling the truth about other things? Had he been helping to arrange my destiny according to his upper-god's wishes the whole time?

Could I trust him?

I didn't know. But I was too tired, and too frustrated from my day of failing at magic, to think about how I might have gotten my opinion about him wrong, too.

His smile brightened as he watched me, as though he could hear my warring thoughts and was delighting in my confusion.

"If you are telling the truth," I said, smoothing some of the edge from my voice, "then I suppose you have my thanks. But unless you are going to help me with my current trouble, I'd appreciate it if you'd leave me alone. I didn't mean to come here, anyway, as I told you."

Our gazes remained tensely locked until I worked up the nerve to turn my back on him. I wasn't sure this was a wise move, but I knew I wouldn't be able to even *attempt* to transfer myself back to my own territory so long as I was near Zachar and the heavy, depressing air that hovered around him.

So I trudged through the dark on foot, putting space between us, vainly trying to rub the chills from my arms as I went.

Though my breath steamed in the air, I wasn't as cold as I'd once been in this dominion—my internal Fire magic was useful even if I couldn't control it very well; I simply ran hotter these days. And though the Death magic was draining me, I still felt strong enough to walk all the way back to Mai and Valas, if necessary.

And luckily, Zachar didn't seem to be following.

I started to chance a glance over my shoulder—just to make sure— when he called out to me.

"You might find it beneficial to let some parts of yourself properly die off."

Against my better judgment, I slowed to a stop. "I'm perfectly content with keeping all my parts intact, thank you." I'd spoken under my breath; I didn't know if he'd even heard me.

He didn't answer for a long moment.

The air grew warmer, almost balmy, and I thought maybe I'd finally vexed or insulted him enough that he'd given up on me and left.

But then he was very suddenly *there*, a shadow slowly taking on the form of a man right in front me.

He wasted no time continuing his speech; as soon as his mouth took shape—before it even had the company of those cold twilight eyes of his —he said, "Have you ever noticed the way people get shy around the subject of death? And around me? They forget that *rebirth* also lies under my rule. And that there can be no rebirth without death."

That last part struck me as strange—wrong. "I thought Valas was the Marr associated with rebirth?"

"The threads of magic within the Marr often intertwine, particularly within their given court. We all carry different shades of a magic that pertains to such—and you could wield your own power of renewal too, if you decide to. But death must come first." His eyes finished forming and blinked several times. "I wonder...could you wield that, too?"

I couldn't think of a response to this.

He didn't seem to really want one.

"You're lost at the moment," he went on, the rest of his features emerging from the shadows and arranging themselves.

I still didn't speak, partly because I was mesmerized by the way he effortlessly put himself back together, and partly by the finished product taking shape; he was so close, and—like most of the divine—a horribly beautiful creature, even when in pieces.

His words were even more hypnotizing, though.

Lost?

I was not lost. At least, not at the moment. I knew exactly where I was and exactly where I wanted to get to—back to the Palace of Fire.

I started to tell him so, but found the words caught in my throat for some reason.

"Physically, you cannot control your new magic," Zachar told me, as though I needed a reminder, "because mentally you are still trapped in a past where you felt powerless. Some part of you still *likes* being in that past, I suspect." He looked around, his attention lingering the longest on the exact spot on the cliffs where he'd once trapped and threatened me. "So here you are, as before."

I, too, found myself staring at those cliffs. I couldn't recall many times when I'd felt more lost—or powerless—than the moment when I'd been trapped on the edge of those rocks. That much was true.

But I hadn't *wanted* to return to this moment, or to this place.

That was nonsense.

Almost everything he was saying was ominous nonsense, as per usual.

"Perhaps the reason you cannot move forward is because you cannot heal from what's happened to you," Zachar mused, "and that is because you are trying to return to a person who does not exist anymore. To an old self that is trying desperately to die—a powerless self that you love and thus keep breathing life into."

I glared at him, all my frustrations with the day bubbling to the surface. "I don't want to be powerless. And I don't love that older version of me. At all. I *hate* her, and I'm happy she's gone—not that it's any business of yours, whether you're the God of Rebirth or anything else."

"You don't *seem* happy," he remarked.

"You have me all figured out, do you?"

"Not you, specifically. But I have watched mortal beings coming and going for long enough now—one starts to notice patterns after a while." He lifted a hand in front of him, curling a clawed finger. The motion summoned a small shadow to his palm, and he watched it twist into different shapes as he said, "None of them like change, even when it's *good* change."

"I am not a mortal any longer," I reminded him fiercely.

He breathed in that slow, unsettling way he often did, as if he was inhaling the air and tasting all the unspoken words and emotions within it.

My skin heated with discomfort, tiny flames flickering to life in the space around me.

He eyed those fires with a hungry sort of interest. "You seem frightened, little goddess."

I shook my head, even though it was true—his words had struck a note of terror deep in some buried part of myself I didn't want to examine. I would not give him the satisfaction of knowing that, however.

"I am not afraid of change," I said. "And I am not afraid of *you*. But I *am* leaving. Go find someone else to haunt."

This time when I walked away, he didn't stop me. I soon felt his stare at my back, though, and his shadows trailing me, nipping like restless dogs at my heels.

I walked faster.

As it turned out, I hadn't managed to travel as far as I'd thought. Disappointing, but also relieving—because within only a few minutes of walking, I spotted the pond I'd left Zell next to.

I gave a sharp whistle, and soon the selakir was racing to my side once more.

I rode back to the palace with my body pressed flat against Zell's back, my cheek resting on his muscular neck and my hands fisted into his fiery, silky mane, oblivious to the flames that would have burned anyone other than Dravyn and me.

Zell went slower than usual, keeping his gait as smooth as possible so as not to jar me from my troubled thoughts.

I kept replaying my conversation with the Death God over and over, even though I didn't want to. Even though I came to the same conclusion every time.

He was wrong.

I was not afraid of change or power or anything else.

I couldn't be. I had no time to think of the past me, or grieve the loss of her, or wonder what might have become of her if she'd survived taking a knife to her heart. I was not a mortal. Not an elf.

I was—as Zachar had called me—a goddess.

He had said it mockingly, but it still resonated. It was simultaneously like a beautiful song stuck in my head and a splinter under my skin that would not stop aching.

It was the first time someone other than Dravyn had called me a goddess.

Goddess.

Did becoming one require me to burn away all that I'd been before? To starve her of oxygen? Every part of her? Or...how did one decide what was meant to stay, and what was meant to go?

I focused on the rhythmic clipping and clopping of Zell's hooves rather than the questions battering my brain, letting the sound lull me into a restless sort of daze.

On and on we galloped, until Zell suddenly slowed, his head lifting toward the sky.

I knew why he'd slowed. I'd felt it, too: Something powerful crossing overhead, heading in the same direction we were.

"Dravyn is back, isn't he?" Power surged through me as I said the words, my magic rising and stretching as if just awakened from a deep sleep. Magic that felt both certain and wild, capable and unpredictable.

I wanted more than anything to be near him now, wrapped up in his arms. To feel the magic passing between us like a shared breath, a heartbeat I didn't even have to think about.

As I stared at the sky, an idea struck me.

I wanted to be near him. *More than anything*. Isn't that what Mairu said I needed? A clear vision, a clear feeling about where I wanted to go.

Little else felt clear to me at the moment aside from Dravyn.

He was not a place, but he felt like home, and where could I trust my magic to carry me to, if not home?

"I'm going to try one more time," I warned Zell.

A shudder rippled through the selakir; maybe a touch of concern on my behalf. But he kneeled without protest and let me slide easily from his back, giving me an encouraging nudge with his nose as I found my balance.

I started the same way I had so many times today: deep breaths, letting flames rise around me and swallow me up, beginning with my fingers.

"No panicking," I reminded myself.

Bit by bit and breath by breath, I turned once more to flames, and then to smoke, and then to *nothing*.

Again I was untethered, terrifyingly light and aimless for what felt like several minutes.

Darkness prevailed once more; I still could not see the path between where I was and where I wanted to go. It still made no sense, all this floating in between nonsense. No way of properly mapping it all out, no way of leaving a trail to find my way back to my starting point...

But maybe, just this once, I didn't need a map.

It felt like stepping off a cliff while wearing a blindfold, but I did it.

I let go.

CHAPTER 10

Karys

THE DESCENT BACK INTO MY PHYSICAL BODY WAS LESS jarring this time—and less painful—because Dravyn was there to catch me.

Or to break my fall, at least.

I hurtled into the palace surrounded by tumbling flames, passing seamlessly through walls and magical wards before finding myself hovering above the stairwell leading up to Dravyn's bedchamber, of all places. From the looks of it, I'd caught him mid-ascent.

The cramped passage allowed little room to maneuver, but the instant the flames began to clear—and he spotted my face within them —he reacted, snatching me from the air as I plummeted to the floor.

We still tumbled down a few steps, thanks to my momentum, crashing hard onto the nearest landing. Dravyn caught himself against the wall beside a tall window, bracing me in front of him, hands tightly gripping my sides.

Bits of fire drifted around me. As Dravyn held me more tightly, more securely, the flames lengthened and drew closer, like a second embrace melting into my body as though to build it up and fortify it.

Dravyn kept me steady, looking me over as if he still wasn't convinced I'd really just appeared out of thin air.

Honestly, I wasn't entirely convinced myself.

I wrapped a hand around one of his arms. Squeezed. *Definitely solid.* I lifted my other hand to his face, brushing his cheek, letting my fingers linger against his skin. *Definitely warm.*

He was real—and more importantly just then, *I* was real.

I was *here.*

Slightly dizzy, yes, but the entire experience wasn't as disorienting as I'd expected it would be. My mind was already clearing, my nerves settling, ready to do it all over again.

I felt I could have gone anywhere in the realms in that moment—especially if I knew I could find my way back to Dravyn like this. That he would break my fall and catch me no matter the flames and chaos I carried back with me.

"Hi," I said to him, brightly.

He cocked his head, regarding me with a wry smile. "Will you ever stop surprising me?"

"I don't plan to," I replied, smiling back.

He looked up at the ceiling, like he still thought there must have been some hole in it that he'd missed, some skylight I'd actually tumbled through.

"Do you realize what I've just done?" I asked, nearly bouncing from the excitement humming through my veins.

Several emotions seemed to be competing for dominance within him as he lowered his gaze back to me. Concern flashed briefly over his features, but he settled them into something closer to admiration as he said, "The lessons with Mai went well, I take it."

"Actually, they were disastrous for most of the day."

"They were?"

"Yes. But I felt you returning to this palace moments ago, and I was able to focus on you at that point. My magic seemed to do the rest. It was almost...*easy.*"

He didn't appear terribly surprised by this. "I felt you, as well. I knew you were drawing closer—though your entrance was still unexpected, I'll admit."

"I'll try to aim for a door next time."

He laughed a bit at this, the look in his eyes deepening to something more than admiration. Something I couldn't readily name, but which made my entire body flush with fresh heat.

I felt you, as well.

It was rapidly becoming more than a mere feeling. The longer we stood there, wrapped in our shared flames, the more it was becoming like a compulsion—a need to be even closer to him than I already was, like a wave pulling back to the sea it was a part of.

He arched a brow. "Are you all right?"

"The magic...it still feels like it's drawing me toward you." My words were little more than breath between us. "Even though you're right here."

He considered this for a moment, his hand lifting and caressing my cheek. "Magic can...*intensify* whatever emotions you might be experiencing in a given moment. It's probably that at work, more so than the lingering traversing spell."

"*Intensify?*"

"Anger, fear, sorrow. Or in this case..." He let the sentence hang in the air, his gaze dipping briefly to my lips as he dragged his thumb across them.

Unmistakable hunger flashed in his eyes, and a shiver curled my toes as I silently finished his sentence for him.

Or in this case...desire.

I was elated at my newfound ability. Drunk with accomplishment. And the way he was looking at me, the way all the fiery parts of him twisted and tumbled with mine...it was intoxicating me to the point of foolishness.

Without much thought beyond that happy, drunken foolishness, I threw my arms around his neck and pulled his mouth down to mine.

As our lips met in a crash of heat and need, I understood—in a single, electrifying instant—what it *truly* meant to have the same power flowing through our veins.

To be connected in such a way was nearly overwhelming.

My heart ballooned to the point of bursting. My arms trembled against his neck. My knees buckled.

His hands were on my sides again just as quickly, steadying me once more, his touch drawing even more heat between us as his fingers dug in —not my heat, nor his.

Ours.

He backed me toward the wall, pressing me into cold stone that proved an arousing contrast against the fire engulfing us. His hold fell to my hips, taking a more commanding grip and hoisting me up, pulling my lips more fully into his.

I lifted one leg and wrapped it around his waist, then the other.

His hands slid to my thighs to better balance me between him and the wall.

Maybe it was the heat searing all reason from my mind, but I don't think he'd ever kissed me quite like this. It was wild and feverish, terrifying yet exhilarating. I wanted more of it. I didn't care if the fire building between us burned us and everything else to ashes. I didn't care about the hard stone digging into my backside.

My fingers curled like claws around his shoulders. I remembered at the last instant that I *did* have retractable claws—a feature I'd had as a mortal and retained through ascension—and I caught myself just as they started to unleash and draw blood.

He only laughed at the sharpness that had briefly pricked his skin, a deep, rich sound that vibrated through me and made me want to dig even more deeply into him, so deep that there would be no telling where I ended and he began.

"Easy," he whispered, nipping at my earlobe as he spoke. "I can't tell if you want to maim me or make love to me."

"I'm not sure I know, either. The heat of this new magic is *intensifying* things, as you said."

Another gruff laugh. Another vibration that sent shivers racing through me, shaking off more of what little restraint I had left.

"Should I be afraid?" he asked, lips dropping to the hollow of my throat, warm breath spilling along that sensitive spot and somehow making me burn even hotter.

I pretended to consider the question for a moment. "I think the pain will be worth it."

"I've no doubt." His fingers pushed through my hair and gripped my skull, gently angling my face upward so he could more easily press his lips to the most sensitive parts of my neck.

My fingers moved in turn, trailing along the strong curve of his jaw before sliding along one of his broad shoulders, slipping beneath the rumpled collar of his shirt and finding searing hot skin.

Despite our teasing words, we slowed for a moment, savoring the feel and taste of one another.

He readjusted his grip on my thighs, dropping me lower, pinning me against the wall with his body more than the strength of his arms.

With no space between us, I could feel the hardened length of him pressing into me, each throb of desire making the fires around us flare a little more brightly.

"Next time I need to find my way back to you," I said, in between catches of breath, "maybe I'll just picture you and me like this. That should create a strong enough pull."

He chuckled against my throat before lifting his gaze to mine. The grey in his eyes seemed darker than usual, heavy with both magic and desire. "I'm glad to be of use to you."

"And you can picture the same thing, and whatever connection we have will surely help draw me in."

"That could be dangerous," he said, planting kisses along my shoulder and up the side of my neck, "considering how often I find myself imagining you like this."

"I'm sure we'll manage, as needed."

"So, you're saying I can have you this way whenever I like," he whispered into my ear. "I just need to picture you up against the wall like this. To imagine myself touching you, tasting you, taking you...and you'll come crashing into my arms."

He leaned back, allowing me to catch my breath.

"Whenever you like?" I coyly lifted a brow. "Let's not get carried away."

He gave me a crooked grin. "I'm afraid I already have."

"Well, perhaps summon me to a more spacious and private location next time," I suggested, glancing around. "Especially if you intend to *have* me once I arrive."

"I think this stairwell will do just fine, personally."

"It's rather narrow," I said, stretching the tips of my fingers outward for emphasis.

"I love a challenge."

"You do, don't you?"

"Part of the reason I fell in love with you," he murmured, lips once more against my skin. "And also? You underestimate my ability and willingness to fuck you in just about any and all locations."

My breath didn't merely catch this time—it left me completely for a moment, leaving me briefly dizzy and glad for the firmness of his body against mine, holding me up.

"And the door below us is locked, for what it's worth," he added. "Only you and I hold the key to this tower. It's private enough." His tongue flicked against my pulse before he drew back to meet my eyes, a wicked smile now in place of the crooked one. "Though the sound does tend to echo in here. So you'll want to be mindful of that."

"Maybe I want it to echo," I whispered back, thrilling at the way the words made his eyes darken even further with desire. "Maybe we could be loud enough for the other courts to hear us—make them *really* hate me."

It was reckless, foolish talk, but magic was still circling around us and within us, still making me feel stupidly elated—and bold.

Bold enough that I wasted no more time fighting against what I wanted.

I dropped my hands below his waist, sinking my fingers into his thighs, yanking him harder against me while adjusting my weight so his arousal slid more completely between my legs.

His head tilted back as a groan left his lips. He pulled away from me slightly, allowing my legs to drop. Once my feet were firmly balanced on the floor, my hands moved deftly over his clothing, undoing buttons and clasps and buckles.

He pulled his shirt over his head and tossed it aside, then reached back to do the same with mine, making quick work of it and everything underneath. He was no longer forcibly pinning me against the wall, but I was still completely enveloped in him, held there by his power, his heat, by the sheer size of his body.

I ran my fingers along the hard ridges of his stomach, down to the waistline of his pants, pulling them off far enough to allow his cock to spring free. The fire between us again made me bolder than usual; I took him in my grasp without hesitating, stroking until his head fell back once more and curses replaced the appreciative groans.

One of his hands cupped one of my breasts, his thumb teasing its center into a stiff peak. The other hand curved against the small of my back and dragged me away from the wall. He started to lead me up the stairs, in between kissing and caressing and fondling, but after climbing the first few steps, he stopped.

For a moment, he seemed to be considering picking me up, throwing me over his shoulder, and carrying me up to his bedroom. But as his gaze swept up and down the stairs around us, a better idea appeared to strike him.

A better *challenge*, maybe.

He went to the steps just below the landing we stood on, taking his coat and shirt and spreading them along the stone, creating a softer floor to kneel on. Then he returned to my side and pulled me back into another series of breathless, fervent kisses, while guiding me toward this spot he'd created.

Once there, his hand raked through my hair, grabbing a fistful of it and tilting my head back, aligning my ear with his mouth so he could whisper, "On your hands and knees for me, Goddess."

I pressed back against him, making the hand fisted in my hair clench tighter as he buried his face into my neck and barely suppressed a raspy growl.

"On hands and knees doesn't seem like a position befitting of a goddess," I teased.

It took him a moment to collect himself enough to say, "Give me a few minutes to worship you while you're in that position, and I think you'll change your mind."

The words sent more pleasant lightheadedness washing over me, leaving me breathless and dazed, so I didn't resist when he moved to put me into the position himself.

His one hand remained tangled in my hair. The other traveled along my body, smoothing down over my stomach and towards the apex of my thighs.

Then it went lower.

It was automatic, the way my body bent, the way it moved to accommodate him as his fingers drew achingly near to my center. And as soon as my knees had bent, it was hard to resist dropping the rest of the way down. Soon I was kneeling, most of my body braced on the landing except my knees, which were on the step below.

Dravyn stood on the steps just beneath me, watching me as I followed his command, and he didn't move after this—not right away. He didn't speak. Didn't touch me. He scarcely seemed to be breathing.

It felt deliciously vulnerable, exhilarating, *maddening* waiting for whatever he planned to do next.

Then came his hands, slowly working their way around the top of my leggings, sliding them and my undergarments down inch by inch until my backside was fully exposed for him.

He left the unraveled clothing bunched around my ankles, a sort of restraint that added to the feeling of vulnerability and surrender, that raised chills over every inch of my exposed skin.

Another few tantalizing moments of nothing but the sound of his harsh breaths, followed by the sound of the rest of his clothing slowly being pulled off and dropping to the stone steps.

Then his hands were on me once more, caressing, tapping, stretching. Positioning me better against the steps as he knelt behind me. He traced his fingers over my curves, gliding the tips lightly over the dampness between my thighs a few times before plunging two of them inside of me. While they beckoned the first shivers of orgasm forward from inside, his thumb worked against the sensitive bud outside.

He drew his hand away far too soon, but his mouth followed before I could protest, kissing a similar path. His tongue was more brutal than his fingers had been as it swept over me and inside me, tasting me relentlessly, like a man half-starved, reducing me to a quivering mess.

My body shook against the steps, already prepared to curl into my release and let it rock through my body. The magic seemed to be *intensifying* this, too—what usually started as a slight tingling already felt close to a full blown release, and somehow it was continuing to build. I was going to shatter quickly. Violently. Fear gripped me for an instant, though it was still mingled with arousal—I felt too hot, too out of control.

"Not yet." Dravyn's voice hummed with the command and control I lacked in that moment. If I'd been with anybody else, the panic might have continued to grip me more and more tightly, but his voice was all I needed to bring me back to the state of pure bliss I'd been in.

"Not yet," he repeated. He cupped a hand between my legs and pulled me back into my original position. "Not yet, Wildfire. Not until you've taken all of me."

Some cross between a whimper and a moan of pleasure left me as he said this, as he shifted his stance and took hold of my legs, urging them farther apart before easing his length between them. He moved back and forth against me for a minute, sliding the tip of his cock over my center and adding to the wetness he'd already created there until finally, *finally* he pushed inside me.

He grabbed my sides and pulled me back to him, thrusting slowly, filling me more fully with every lift and sway of his hips.

I quickly understood why he'd decided against the bedroom—the stairs created precisely the height difference needed to allow him to drive more deeply into me than ever before. He pulled me down while he pushed up, and it was almost too much, the way this position filled and stretched and wrecked me so utterly and completely.

"*Fuck,*" I cried out as he began to drive harder into me—though I didn't realize I'd said the word out loud until I heard him laugh.

"That one echoed," he murmured approvingly.

I moaned something incoherent in response.

The sound urged him back to his thrusting. He placed one hand between my shoulder blades, pressing me more firmly down. Holding my upper body in place against the stone landing gave him the leverage he needed to push deeper and faster.

The stairwell was soon filled with the echoing cries of our combined gasps, our curses, and the swishing, rushing sound of sweat-slicked skin meeting skin.

As my upper body melted against the landing—too spent to move thanks to the waves of pleasure rocking through me—Dravyn's hands slid from my back and hooked around my hips. He gripped them tightly, lifting me up to more fully meet each of his increasingly ravenous movements.

The next cry that left my lips eclipsed all the sounds we'd made thus far.

He answered it by raking his fingers into my hair once more, gathering the strands together into a fistful which he tugged, forcing my back to arch, drawing him more completely into me.

His other hand slipped between my legs, caressing as he pushed in. It was the last touch I could take before unraveling—I came with a breathy cry and was lost in a field of fiery stars bursting before my eyes, in an inferno of passionate flames swirling around us.

Some of those flames were real, responsible for an increasing number of scorch marks on the stone around us. Some of them were likely imagined. I couldn't tell the difference. I didn't care to. All of the burning felt good in that moment, and I just wanted it to keep building, swallowing me up, incinerating every thought from my mind.

Dravyn continued to move. To pound into me with ever-increasing speed and power. His hands moved from my hair and roamed along my body, grasping at my flushed skin, keeping me close as I trembled and tingled with the rush of my release.

As I coasted along the ripples of that release, he pulled me upright, my back flush against his stomach. His arms crossed tightly around my breasts, holding me in place as he balanced himself and then drove upward, deep into my tightly-clenched core. Another peal of orgasm rang through me with the motion, his own following with an answering roar, his hold turning crushingly tight as he emptied himself into me.

After several breathless moments, he finally loosened his hold. I managed a few shallow breaths. He moved toward the support of the wall, dragging me with him. As he settled against it, I turned around so I was facing him, his knees hemming me in.

I stared at him for a moment, overcome by the way the wisps of fire around us caught on every beautiful edge of his face. My breaths remained ragged and shallow. I planted a clumsy kiss on his lips, still halfway caught up in a shaky, delirious euphoria.

He took the sides of my face in his hands and held me still before drawing me in for a slower, steadier kiss. As it ended, I closed my eyes and leaned forward, falling against his chest as his arms gathered me in.

I was still coming down from my high when I felt him lifting me, carrying me up the steps toward his room. Everywhere his fingers touched was still sensitive, setting off little explosions that all ran together, cocooning me in blissful heat.

Once we reached his room, I cleaned myself up while he went back and gathered our discarded clothing from the stairs. I didn't bother putting more clothing on; the heat still radiating from my skin would have made even the lightest garments uncomfortable.

Dravyn wore only loose-fitting linen pants when he crawled into bed alongside me a few minutes later. His skin still burned as hot as mine did. I briefly wondered what this bed was made of, to keep it all from combusting in moments like this. Could it continue to withstand both of our fires?

I closed my eyes, drifting in the warmth, trying to keep the images of the last hour locked inside my head.

Dravyn didn't disturb me for several minutes, though his body never moved more than a few inches.

As I settled down and my mind cleared, I pressed my palm to his. He wove his fingers into the spaces between mine and loosely held my hand as he quietly asked, "What are you thinking, miran-achth?"

Miran-achth. My breath. The one that was missing.

I scooted closer to him, burrowing my face into his shoulder, holding his hand more tightly as I considered the question.

"That it's been too long since we did that," I finally said, truthfully.

In the weeks since my ascension, the chances we'd had to spend together—just the two of us—had been too far and few between.

Everything was more complicated now, including intimate moments like the one we'd just shared.

He was quiet for so long, contemplating, that I nearly dozed off. "I was worried it would be too intense for you until you had gotten used to your magic," he eventually said. "I wasn't sure how our powers would... *play* together."

I thought of the fear that had briefly gripped me and made me feel out of control—and not necessarily in a good way. "There were overwhelming moments," I admitted, still curled against his shoulder. "But I'm not afraid of them. Not when I'm sharing them with you."

He gave my hand a little squeeze, but this was the only reply he offered before he sat up and pulled away from me.

I lifted my head, blinking my eyes open to find him studying his arms, tracing them with the tips of his fingers. His touch was light, absent-minded, but it brought back memories of last night, when he'd been trying to scrub my invisible blood from his skin.

I sat up as well, drawing my knees to my chest and wrapping a blanket around myself. I wasn't cold. I couldn't remember the last time I'd felt cold. But a different kind of chill was winding through my body —one I couldn't shake.

My insides twisted at the haunted look in Dravyn's gaze, but I said nothing. Maybe because I didn't know what *to* say. Or maybe because I was a coward who didn't want to talk about the overwhelming parts of our relationship. I'm not sure which it was.

My eyes drifted to the window instead. "I didn't check in with Mairu and Valas," I said, the realization—and all the world outside of the two of us—suddenly catching up to me. "They'll be worried."

"They'll have felt your energy coming back here, along with mine. They should be able to tell we're together, so they shouldn't worry too much." A corner of his mouth edged up, as if he was fighting a smile despite the troubled look still glazing his eyes. "They might ask questions about what you and I have been doing to keep you from checking in with them, though."

I couldn't help blushing, already imagining the inappropriate commentary I would have to endure from Valas.

Dravyn shook a little further from his haunted stupor, his smile breaking through as he pressed a hand against my flushed cheek. "Rest while you can. We'll see to them tomorrow, along with everything else."

Something about the way he said *everything else* made my stomach clench. "Speaking of which...did you accomplish what you set out to do today?"

He looked away from me, his hand lowering, and stared at the ceiling as he answered. "I've spoken with all who would grant me an audience. They'll be gathering here first thing tomorrow to decide what to do about the mortal realm. If—and how—we will intervene."

I had expected as much. I knew such a council had to happen. Still, the thought of the Marr holding court in this palace was not a soothing image to fall asleep to; it was always chaos when a group of them gathered, and I never felt more out of place in this realm than I did when all those perfect, powerful beings were surrounding me.

Dravyn was watching me closely, his brow furrowed. Could he hear my jumbled thoughts? Could he feel the anxiety humming through my veins?

"Rest," he suggested again. "Tomorrow will be here soon enough."

He didn't seem prepared to take his own advice. His gaze had shifted to the door; he looked ready to bolt the instant I fell asleep. But to where? Back to his old kingdom again?

The thought struck sickening fear into my heart.

"What about you?" I asked.

He hesitated.

"Stay with me?" My words came out quickly, but quietly, my voice breaking a bit toward the end. It wasn't on purpose, but the broken sound seemed to catch his attention, pulling his eyes away from the door and back to me.

"If it will help you to sleep," he said, "I won't go anywhere."

I nodded, and he slid his arm around me, letting his hand come to rest lightly against my lower back. I curled closer to him, laying my head on his chest. His heartbeat was soft, fluttering, like a tired bird ready to collapse into its nest.

And collapse he did; now that he'd turned back to me and stopped fighting the urge to leave, he seemed to give into whatever weariness he felt. His eyes closed. His breathing slowed. Even the fiery flush of his skin cooled slightly.

It was rare to see him relax like this. Maybe he was doing it partly for my benefit—to help me feel less like an outsider; most divine beings didn't think of sleep nearly as much as I still seemed to. Maybe he wasn't even truly asleep.

I didn't try to rouse him, but I continued to study him, thinking.

The moment felt, like it so often did with him, as if I'd drifted into a dream where I couldn't quite tell what was real and what was make-believe.

And though I tried to stop my thoughts from racing, they soon traveled once more to last night, to waking up to the sight of him coming undone. I wondered again about what he'd seen and heard in his old kingdom, and what would happen next time he went there...

No, when *we* went there.

How did this end between us?

How else *could* it end, except unhappily?

His old kingdom hated the world I'd come from. So did most of the gods I now lived among. This council tomorrow, and everything that would follow it, regardless of what was decided...

Where was I supposed to stand among all this?

A tear slid down my cheek. I hastily wiped it away before it could drip onto Dravyn's bare chest. But more followed, along with a sudden rush of despair so violent it nearly made me choke.

As quietly as I could, I slipped from Dravyn's grasp and rolled away from him.

Breathe, I reminded myself. *You have to keep breathing.*

But how could I?

I didn't belong in this new world, no matter how hard I practiced or how much magic I learned. I felt like an imposter in my own skin, and I feared I always would. Even if Dravyn called me *Goddess*. Even if he treated me like one.

I stretched a hand toward the fireplace. Twisted my fingers and managed some semblance of control over a bright ember, drawing it up into a tendril of flame and making it dance to a silent tune in my mind.

Goddess, I tried telling myself. *This is what I am now.*

But all I could think about were the ties I still had to the world below. To my sister. To the rebels I had once considered my family...my *everything*. Even the tune I sang in my head—the one I made the dancing flame keep time with—was an old song my sister used to sing me to sleep with.

The Death God had insisted I needed to kill those things off.

Maybe that was true.

But what difference would it make?

Dying did not undo a life that had been lived.

In my case, all the pieces of that life were still waiting for me in the messy realm below. I would have to face them sooner or later. And my sister...

As I lay there, scarcely breathing, my cheek sticky with dried tears, her face became all I could think about.

Soon enough, I'd made up my mind.

Whatever the council decided tomorrow, I was going to find Savna, and I was going to find a way to put all the broken pieces of us back together.

CHAPTER II

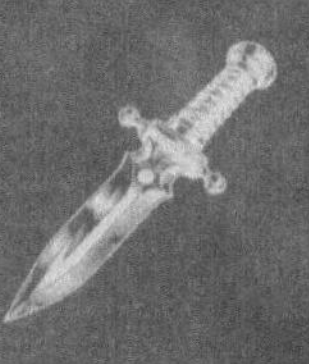

Dravyn

I woke up in my bed with no clear memory of falling asleep.

I'd been more tired than I cared to admit, it seemed.

Karys was curled against me, her head resting on my chest. I brushed aside the hair in her face. Just grazing her skin with my fingertips flooded me with fresh desire, warming the space around us and making the dim flames in the fireplace jump.

I halfheartedly tried to force the energy down, but it made no difference; her magic was already responding, simmering to life and intertwining with mine, adding to the heat and light blooming around us. Faint marks appeared on her arms—swirls of black and red that pulsed bright one moment, pale the next.

My marks.

My claim, growled some deep, primal part of me that I didn't particularly like. It sounded like the same monstrous voice that I'd battled as a younger god. A violent voice I thought I'd gotten rid of—but now it was back. It had been coming back more and more frequently ever since I'd let myself fall for the one sleeping beside me now. And it was insistent, trying to convince me that violence and bloodshed were the only solutions when it came to keeping her safe.

A sliver of the brighter firelight caught on the edge of her jaw and throat, illuminating the old burn scars covering those spots. My gaze lingered for a moment on them, then dropped to her chest, still as bare as mine.

Even though she was pulled against me in such a way that most of her was covered, I could still see the top of the newer scar that ran alongside her heart.

I had to turn away again at this point, to put more space between us —not because I was fighting a desire to claim her, but rather to murder someone on her behalf.

The room was heating to the point that even I was starting to sweat.

Moth, who rested on the perch I'd built for him by the window, lifted his head and gave me an uncertain look. His ears drooped, his tail was tucked, his ruby eyes were wide. Afraid.

I breathed out a long sigh.

I was going to have to get a hold on all these violent cravings. There were too many battles ahead of us—enough to have me running in circles until the end of my days if I didn't stop chasing every vicious urge I had.

I reclined stiffly against the pillows, still close to Karys but not quite touching her; it was easier to think clearly when we weren't touching.

I stared at the ceiling for the better part of the next hour, lost in thought, until I felt a telltale shiver in the air that warned me of approaching power.

Moth hopped from his perch to the windowsill and peered outside, letting out a low, anxious purr.

"Company," I muttered to him.

Expected company, but the feel of magic foreign to my territory still triggered a response, sending more heat rushing from the core of my being to the surface of my skin.

As before, I tried to settle the borderline violent energy, but Karys again must have felt it—or maybe sensed the approaching company herself—because she stirred, reaching for my arm.

"What is it?" she asked softly. She pulled closer to me without opening her eyes, pressing her face into my arm as though she didn't want to see whatever *it* was.

"The meeting I mentioned last night...the others are arriving."

"Already?"

"We've been asleep for quite some time, I think."

She mumbled in protest but slowly rolled away from me and sat up. She looked disoriented for a brief moment, hair sticking out at odd angles, sheets clutched against her breasts. But then she was on her feet just as quickly, a determined look overtaking her face.

She went to one of the wardrobes in the corner and hesitated only a moment before yanking it open, mumbling to herself as she pawed through the garments inside. Though it was smaller than the wardrobe in her own room, there was still no shortage of things for her to choose from.

Rieta had been excited for the chance to fill all of these closets; she'd been fond of sewing when we lived in Altis. She'd created many of the garments by hand, rejecting all offers of magical help, and Karys had willingly assisted her by drawing up patterns and the like.

Karys draped one of those garments over her arm before disappearing into the adjoining washroom.

She reemerged a few minutes later, fully made over. Her hair was woven into a crown of braids, her eyes bright and fierce in the firelight. The dress she'd chosen was quite simple, falling in tiers that draped longer in the back than the front, its color reminiscent of the shadowy green of a deep forest. It had none of the enchanted embellishments that often featured on the clothing donned by our kind—yet somehow the mortal-styled clothing made her look *more* like a goddess, not less.

I didn't realize I was staring until she drew to a stop, frowning.

"What's wrong?" she demanded, looking herself up and down. Her hands smoothed invisible creases from the dress, the agitated movements betraying the true nerves she felt about what awaited us outside this room.

"Nothing is wrong," I told her. She didn't look completely reassured, so I added, "Except that seeing you in that dress makes me want to skip this meeting and pull you back into bed."

She smiled a bit at this—that soft, barely-there smile that always drew me to her side without fail. I briefly forgot about the battles waiting for us as I went to her and kissed her forehead, and she curled against my chest with a sigh.

After she stepped away, I left to make myself more presentable as she had done, returning to the bedroom after several minutes to find her standing by the window, her eyes narrowed in concentration.

"Is everything all right?"

She startled at my voice. "Yes. I just thought I saw some sort of shadowy...something." She pressed closer to the window. "A creature of some kind, maybe. One I've caught glimpses of a few times over these past weeks, but never long enough to actually make out what it is."

I started toward the window as well, but froze as a possible explanation occurred to me.

This *creature*...I wanted to be wrong about what it was, so I hesitated to give my opinion on the matter—and she waved a dismissive hand before I could speak, anyway.

"Never mind," she said quickly. "It's probably just a trick of my tired mind. And either way, it's not as important as the council awaiting us, is it?"

She turned to face me, Moth dangling from her arms. The griffin was nibbling the edges of her clothing and swatting at loose tendrils of her hair, but she was paying him little mind; her eyes were on the door that led downstairs.

I walked over to pry Moth from her arms just as he got his beak around the tip of one of her braids, starting to unravel it in earnest. I dropped him unceremoniously to the floor—ignoring the hiss he gave before catching himself in mid-air, remembering his wings, and streaking toward the open window.

Looking back to Karys, I frowned. "You seem worried about that council."

She didn't disagree, but her expression hardened as though determined not to show any more of that worry. "Whatever this council decides to do about the impending war in the mortal realm," she said, "I want to be a part of it."

I nodded, though her tone made me uneasy. She sounded as though she'd spent the night plotting.

Knowing her, she likely had.

"And if we agree that my sister is at the center of whatever scheme the elves are preparing," she pressed, "then I want to be the one to find her. To confront her."

"...If it comes to that."

"I don't see how it won't."

Truthfully, I didn't, either.

I just didn't want to think about it.

I took her hand, absently tracing her skin with my thumb. "Today we should focus on the bigger picture, I believe. At least for this meeting."

"I *am* focused on it. My sister just happens to be a part of that bigger picture."

"I don't disagree. But I think it would be wise not to draw attention to your complicated relationship with her. The other Marr will see it as weakness and a potential temptation for betrayal—as evidence that you're clinging to your old loyalties and life."

She pulled her hand from mine. I could sense the frustration simmering inside her—it made her magic burn hotter, made it reach for mine. I fought the temptation to reach back. It wouldn't do us any favors, combining and unleashing our fire before we'd even made it out of the bedroom.

"We can discuss the matter of your sister more fully amongst ourselves later," I offered, attempting to keep the peace. "It will be safer...and probably more productive than any conversation we might have with the others about her."

She looked unsatisfied by this answer. We were interrupted, however, before I could come up with anything more to say; both of us sensed more deities appearing somewhere in the palace below us.

It felt as if everyone was now here.

"Come on," I said, "we shouldn't keep them waiting." I offered her my arm.

She took it without a word, avoiding my gaze as we left the room.

I DIDN'T HAVE much experience with wartime councils and the like from when I was a human prince—I'd been young, and not as interested in conquest and bloodshed as my father and older brother would have liked me to be—but I'd come to the conclusion that the gods played at war in much the same way that so many mortal leaders did.

They sat in their comfortable chairs, eating and drinking, pushing plans around as though it were a game with clear-cut winners and losers, with wooden pawns instead of living, breathing beings.

The game had been underway for an hour already.

At least.

We had taken up residence in the largest of the courtyards scattered around my palace grounds. A fence of fruit trees hedged us in, their scent sickly-sweet. A great black table stretched between us—one I'd personally made, mostly by hand, from a slab cleaved from a large vein of onyx on the edge of my territory.

In the chairs surrounding the table sat six deities from outside of my own court. The Healing and Ocean Marr represented the Stone Court. The Sun Court was here in full, the goddesses of Sky, Star, and Moon all present, along with the Storm God.

Karys and Valas sat to my left, Mairu to my right. Zachar had initially refused to join us, but had shown up several minutes into the meeting without speaking a word to anyone. He now stood a short distance away, leaning against the largest of the trees, his dark shadows gathered around him like a second cloak.

Following the aforementioned hour of bickering and gamesmanship, a tense silence now stretched over our group. I suspected most of those present would have been fine with leaving things in this unsettled silence—they'd shown up and had a discussion, and that was doing enough work for one day, as far as they were concerned.

Before anyone could start any dramatic exits, however, Armaros, the God of Healing, broke the stalemate.

"We've heard all there is to hear about the matter," he said, in his predictably pontifical tone. "We could dissect and discuss the evidence for a millennium, but it won't change any of it. Let us make a decision about our next move; I'm growing weary of this conversation, and more weary, still, of doing *nothing* while the situation continues to escalate."

"We are meant to watch over human-kind from afar—not to hold their hands through every moment of their existence," Kelas, the God of the Ocean, countered. "I say we let them work it out among themselves."

"The only thing they will work out is a massacre," the Sky Goddess replied, bluntly. "The weapons the Velkyn threaten them with are not natural. They wield an alarming amount of power against our divine energy, if you've forgotten—so even the humans we've blessed with magic will struggle against them, I fear."

"Yes; those weapons they're creating are vile, even by my standards," agreed the God of Storms, sparks flashing in the air around him, accompanying the words.

Karys shifted in her seat. A barely perceptible movement, but I was too aware of her not to notice it. I pretended to sip from the wine-filled chalice I'd yet to actually drink from, letting my gaze slide toward her. Waiting for her to raise an argument in favor of her former allies.

She didn't say a word.

And that concerned me more. It meant she was calculating, continuing whatever plotting she'd started last night.

I had a sudden, desperate urge to bring an end to this meeting.

"The evidence we have isn't sufficient," Mairu said, with a meaningful glance at Armaros. "However much we dissect and discuss it, it doesn't matter if we're working from incomplete information."

The Goddess of Stars looked her direction, her silver eyes flashing with their usual contempt; the two of them rarely got along.

But, to my surprise, Cepheid slowly nodded in agreement with Mairu, adding, "We can't be sure of their numbers. We've collected rumors—nothing more—about what's happening in those so-called Hollowlands and the cities within. There's a haze over these places that makes even my magical sight murky. Unless one of us is willing to venture into the depths for ourselves and see what's happening there, we'll be making any decision blindly."

The words settled darkly over our gathering, like a sudden cloud overtaking the sun. One heavy with an oncoming storm.

Then Karys rose to her feet, her chair scraping over the stone with a sound like a distant crack of thunder.

"I am going to Ederis," she said. Loudly. Clearly. "So I...I will be able to see for myself what is happening underneath that haze."

A horrible silence followed this proclamation. The others all looked to her, and then several of them looked to me as well, assuming I must have been aware that she had planned this trip into the heart of such a dangerous place.

Which was almost certainly what she was hoping they would think —that we'd been scheming this together all along, just waiting for the opportunity to announce it.

I am going to Ederis.

Not *I would go* or *I could go.*

She had already made up her mind, likely before this meeting ever started.

And she knew I couldn't—*wouldn't*—deny her right in front of them. It would be dangerous to let the divine beings around us think that she and I were not on the same team. Either I supported her or I left her vulnerable to their attacks and criticism.

She'd forced my hand.

I was annoyed, but not surprised, even though sometimes I forgot who she'd been before I found her: A dangerous, manipulative rebel who had done whatever she needed to in order to carry out her missions.

She continued speaking before I could calm myself enough to add anything to the conversation—not that I knew what I would say.

"We've already decided it," she told the room with a pointed glance at me. "No one could blend better within an elven stronghold than me." Her eyes stayed on me. Hopeful. Expectant. A bit apologetic, maybe.

I rolled away the weight that had settled on my shoulders and mirrored her decisive tone, trying not to let my irritation show.

"It's true," I said. "She knows their languages, their customs, their mannerisms. There will likely be plenty of faces there that she'll recognize, too. She will be able to navigate their ranks better than any of us could."

"What about the fact that *she* will be recognized?" Halar wanted to know. "And after what she did during the last battle we fought against the Velkyn, it isn't as though her old friends are going to welcome her in with open arms."

Karys met the Storm God's heated gaze without flinching, though she didn't answer his question.

"My magic can disguise her and make her look like any common elf," Mairu chimed in, as though she'd been a part of the plan all along. Maybe she had been.

I fought the urge to rake my hand across my face in exasperation.

"Her divine power will give her away," argued the Goddess of Sky. "She isn't in control of the new magic inside of her; one wrong move, and she will cause more chaos than this plan of hers could possibly be worth."

Zachar moved toward the table, shadows preceding his steps, sending cold rippling outward. "There are ways to at least partially suppress that, too."

I glared at him, shrugging off a shiver. The crawling down my spine was less from my own discomfort at those damn shadows of his and more from the plan he was suggesting.

His draining magic could temper hers—but at what cost? She would be walking into enemy territory with either potentially out-of-control magic or a subdued version of that magic...

I wasn't sure which would be worse.

I chanced another glance in Karys's direction; the faint glimmer of fear in her eyes suggested the Death God's offer was unexpected to her as well.

She recovered from any trepidation she felt quickly, however, blinking it away and nodding along with Zachar's words as though this, too, had all been a part of her plan. She calmly sat back down. Her performance was convincing. Composed.

It was hard not to be impressed despite my irritation.

The conversation around the table fast returned to bickering, which lasted several minutes before the Goddess of Stars cleared her throat and spoke—an unusually assertive gesture for her, which might have been why she actually managed to quiet everyone enough to be heard.

"The God of the Shade had his reasons for allowing her to ascend, mysterious as they may remain to all of us." She gave Karys a long, hard look. Then her gaze lifted toward the sky, her fingers moving as though she was walking them through a tapestry of stars no one else could see, trying to find some telling constellation or revelation we'd all missed. "Perhaps this is part of a grander plan. She is an interesting pawn, isn't she? One with connections to multiple worlds."

I bristled at the word *pawn*, though I knew it was accurate. Whatever powers we had, they paled in comparison to the ones above us, and those upper-gods rarely missed an opportunity to remind us of that.

Another few minutes of arguing commenced, but this time it trailed off on its own. A feeling of reluctant resolve overtook our gathering, and no one—not even the God of Storms—offered any more protests against Karys's plan.

"So it's settled, then," said the Healing God, his expression solemn. "We'll allow our fledgling goddess to gather more information from the heart of the Hollowlands before deciding if and how we intervene in the conflicts plaguing Avalinth." The god's golden eyes fixed on Karys. "Remember the divine blood that now flows in your veins," he said. "And do not disappoint us."

Karys sat up straighter. "I won't."

I got to my feet, my gaze shifting toward the marble arch that led out of the garden—a wordless dismissal. No one objected to it. Most disappeared instantly, filling the space with a faint medley of magical energies on their way out.

Soon, only our own court remained in the garden.

Karys stayed in her seat, her hands clenched on the table before her, her head bowed in thought.

I stared at her, unsure where to start. Unsure I *trusted* myself to start.

After a moment, she lifted her head and glared back at me but said nothing.

Valas rose from his seat, stretching. "I'm sensing a bit of tension in the air."

He moved toward me, but I ignored him, keeping my stare leveled on Karys. Quietly, as calmly as I could manage, I asked, "What were you *thinking*?"

"I told you what I was thinking before the meeting started."

I caught a flash of something black and shining at her hands—claws.

She tucked them out of sight, clenching her fists tighter against the table. "I told you I was going to take the opportunity to find my sister if I was presented with it," she said. "And the council needed someone to make a decisive move. It made sense."

"What happened to *we'll discuss it later*?"

"I'm saving us some time on that discussion," she said, matter-of-factly, as she stood and stepped away from the table. "The easy part is decided: I'm going. Now we can focus our efforts on how to get me in, how I might be able to best help our cause, and how I will then manage to get back to you and this realm in one piece."

She lifted her chin, daring me to argue. Bits of fire swirled in the air; I wasn't sure which of us had summoned them. Maybe both of us.

"If I have to do this myself, then I will," she said, turning and starting toward the palace.

I grabbed her arm and jerked her to a stop more roughly than I'd meant to—roughly enough that she let out a small gasp before yanking free and spinning furiously around to face me.

Valas started toward us as if to intervene, but Mairu stepped into his path. Zachar stood as he had for most of the morning—keeping his distance without saying a word, his eyes slightly aglow as they tracked our movements.

The three of them lingered at the edges of our conversation, but Karys didn't seem to be paying them any mind; her gaze had not left mine.

"Go on, then," she challenged, "yell at me if you'd like." She gestured to the scraps of flame floating around us. "Set this whole courtyard on fire. Do whatever you need to get it out of your system. But you should know that it doesn't matter what you do...I've made up my mind. I *have* to go, Dravyn."

"Karys—"

"Please. Understand."

I wanted to take hold of her and shake her until all thoughts of dangerous missions in the mortal realm fell out of her head.

I wanted to wrap her in flames and whisk her away from this garden and all the fallout of the meeting that had taken place here.

In the end, I forced myself to back away from her. I paced restlessly for a moment before returning to the table, gripping my chair for balance.

"I know you would lock me in the towers of your palace indefinitely if you could get away with it." I could feel her stare digging into me as she spoke.

I gripped the back of the chair harder. "That isn't true."

"You can't protect me from everything." Her voice softened a bit toward the end, as if she knew her words would drive deeply and she was trying not to draw blood.

I shook my head, not wanting to dwell on this weakness she'd struck.

Valas and Mairu crept closer, both looking anxious for a resolution. Zachar kept still, leaning against a vine-wrapped wall, but his attention was zeroed in on us, the weight of his stare uncomfortably heavy.

I sighed. I couldn't think of any more arguments—none that would sway Karys, anyway

"We'll go together this time," I said to her, "as you said the other night."

"That sounds like a disaster in the making," Valas interjected.

"He's right," Mairu said. "My magic has limits. I don't know if I can keep a spell around both of you for as long as we'd need to, especially if you're going deep into that elvish territory. We don't know what kind of anti-divine wards they're using there. The simpler—and quicker—we can keep this first mission, the better."

Worse and worse.

I was gripping the chair hard enough at this point that I'm surprised I didn't crack it.

"Fine," I growled. "But even if I don't go all the way into that territory with her, I'm going as close as I can to the perimeter. It will be easier for her magic to transport herself to me, and to someplace in the same realm, than it would be for her to try and make it all the way back to the middle-heavens."

"I'll go as well," Valas offered. "We can both stay close by. Run interference and extraction, if necessary."

Karys considered this plan for a long moment, her gaze occasionally flickering toward me, as if waiting for me to change my mind and go back to arguing.

I *wanted* to keep arguing—but how could I fight her on this?

She was right. Of course she was right. I could not keep her here knowing that the wars outside of these grounds belonged to her as much as any of us. I didn't want to cage her; I only wanted to keep her safe.

She still looked suspicious. Her arms were folded tightly across her chest, hands tucked within—still hiding her claws. She started to speak several times, only to fall silent. Looked around at the little embers still floating in the garden, as though she wasn't sure how they'd gotten there or whether or not it was safe to let them go.

Yes; she'd clearly expected more of a fight.

She'd been fighting her whole life, after all, and we'd been enemies for far longer than we'd been allies.

And then there were the ones she had *believed* to be her allies. Her sister—among others. Worthless pieces of shit who had betrayed her in so many different ways...

No wonder she didn't trust anyone but herself to carry out her plans.

It stung to realize how far we still had to go. To wonder if we could ever get to a place where we might stop playing these games and truly trust one another. But now was not the time to dwell on that particular challenge we faced.

She finally agreed to my part of the plan with a stiff nod, and there was no going back after this point.

"So," I said, detaching my tone as best I could from the uneasy feelings tumbling in my gut, "we need to figure out how we're going to get her safely inside our target area, and *keep* her safe."

Zachar moved from his place by the wall and joined Mairu in discussing the particulars of this.

By the time their discussion finished, both had left marks on Karys's skin—powerful, if temporary, shades of their respective magics. Shades that would last longer than the impromptu trinket Mairu had given me during my last visit to the mortal realm.

These borrowed powers would be enough to change Karys's appearance and to keep her own divine magic in check, at least for a little while. She was part of our court, her magic derived from the same ultimate power as both Zachar and Mairu's—so the spells would hold almost as if they were her own.

She would be fine.

I had to make myself believe that, somehow.

The others continued to talk, going over the finer points of the plan. I tried to listen and contribute, but their words quickly became nothing more than empty noise. It didn't matter what they said, or what else we decided to do to keep Karys safe; it didn't change the fact that I had a bad feeling about this.

All of this.

And if something happened to her, I was not sure the world could survive the fires I would unleash upon it.

CHAPTER 12

Karys

THE HOLLOWLANDS TURNED OUT TO BE NOTHING LIKE I'D imagined they would be.

I'd pictured shadows upon shadows in my mind, each one concealing a danger more deadly than the last. I'd braced myself for air that reeked of rot and poison. For traps the lightest misstep would trigger. For whatever horrifying formations had earned the area the name *Hollowlands*; to stumble upon great gaping pits filled with endless darkness, or to look to my left and right and see the bones of hollowed-out beasts caging me in.

Instead, the landscape I found myself navigating through was almost...*pleasant*.

The air was balmy and smelled faintly of honey. It was dark—save for a bit of setting sunlight still weaving through the sea of branches overhead—but it was a cozy sort of darkness, like the kind that came after a well-spent day when all you had left to do was get a good night's sleep.

Deep and gold and glowing with promise. It made me think of younger years—simpler years—when my sister and I ran wild through the woods surrounding our family's farm. Those woods had been filled with old pockets of magic. Even as a mortal elf, I'd been able to sense it —and harness it, in some cases, into healing spells.

But I felt no real magic in this place. And even if I found my sister, this was not somewhere she and I had discovered together, like so many of the magical paths and make-believe castles in our old woods.

No; it was a part of her life that she had concealed from me. One of *many* things she'd apparently concealed.

And I needed to remember that.

In an effort to remind myself of the mission I was on, I found a small pool of water and crouched down to study the face peering up at me—not my face, but that of an older, wiser looking elven woman with dark red hair curling around a pale, lightly-freckled face. My eyes were an arresting shade of violet that I had a hard time looking away from.

Mairu's spell was very convincing; no one would recognize me.

The strange thing was that I still *felt* like myself. Even as I stared at the unfamiliar face in the water, I felt more like myself than I had in weeks.

Maybe because I was back in the mortal realm, drawing nearer to the elves.

Or maybe it was just part of the spell—a charm on the mind to make one calm enough to walk in whatever skin they found themselves in. If this was the reason, I silently hoped that part would linger even when the rest of the disguise faded away.

I returned to the road I'd been following. Though *road* was becoming a misnomer the deeper I went; it was turning more and more into an overgrown, barely-there path.

There were others moving along this path, however—elves passing me occasionally, going in both directions. They seemed to have set destinations in mind, and were untroubled by the increasingly wild landscape. So I pretended I wasn't troubled, either.

I belong here, I kept telling myself. *I know where I'm going.*

I trudged forward. I couldn't hesitate. I wouldn't show fear. It felt like I had the entire divine world watching me, pressing against my back, waiting for me to fail or succeed.

I blinked and slowly scanned my surroundings more closely. I was supposed to be acting as the eyes and ears for the Marr. Whether literally or not, it still wasn't clear; the Star Goddess had said something about how this territory limited her divine vision...but Dravyn had occasionally been able to see what my eyes were seeing, thanks to our connection.

Could he see through my vision now?

I wouldn't truly know what he was seeing until I returned to him, I supposed—although every now and then I would have sworn I could hear his voice in my mind, telling me to be careful. Just occasional, quiet words—only a memory, perhaps.

Or was it?

After a few more minutes of walking, the road began to widen and clear once more.

Soon after this, I came upon a junction of sorts, with five different roads leading in different directions. A nearby sign indicated that each road led to the same city—Ederis—but to different entrances.

I didn't know which entrance would be most conducive to my mission, so I stood to the side of the sign for a moment, pretending to be adjusting the fastenings on my cloak while I observed the passersby.

Most seemed to be taking the center road. And the more common and well-trafficked the entrance, I decided, the easier it would be to slip in unnoticed.

Once I'd made up my mind about this, I waited for a large group I could follow and integrate with; it didn't take long before a promising crowd appeared, talking and laughing, paying little attention to me or anything else outside their boisterous conversation.

I exchanged a few pleasantries and then followed them closely for a half-mile, without incident, until a glimmer of something in the air ahead brought me abruptly to a stop.

It was barely noticeable—like a finely spun spiderweb catching a bit of the sun—but I could feel the web's energy radiating outward. It was strange. Uncomfortable. A faint wind swirling toward me, catching at my hair and clothing and pulling, almost as if it was trying to suction the life from my body.

I'd encountered a similar energy before, while traveling into a different elvish city, so I knew what this barrier was: A ward against divine magic.

This one felt stronger than any other I'd come across, however.

My heart raced even though we'd expected this sort of anti-magic. I absently wrapped a hand around my right forearm; the mark Mairu's magic had left was hidden there, gently pulsing beneath the long, flowing sleeve of my shirt.

Was her spell deep enough to withstand what I was walking into? That ward...would it simply prevent anyone from doing magic once they passed its threshold, or would it also *undo* any spells that were already in progress?

Only one way to find out.

Bracing myself, I hurried forward. As I walked through the barrier, the uncomfortable pulling sensation grew briefly more intense before fading to a mere tickling against my skin.

Once I was on the other side, I ducked off the path, hiding behind a group of trees as I looked myself over, watching for any changes in my appearance.

I waited as long as I dared—until the group I'd been following was nearly beyond my range of hearing.

Nothing changed.

Mairu's spell still looked to be perfectly intact.

There was no telling how many more wards I'd have to walk through, however, or how their collective energy might chip away at my disguise over time. But I'd known the risks going into this, so I didn't let them stop me.

I quickly carried on—though I did take greater care to memorize the route I was following, now, leaving occasional claw marks on the trees I was passing; if I was going to return myself to the divine realm using magic, as planned, I likely wouldn't be able to do it unless I was first able to get back to clearer air. I couldn't afford to get lost.

The road stretched on and on beyond the first anti-magic ward, winding much deeper than I expected, and still there was no city in sight.

Every step I took made the way back seem a little more daunting.

I caught up to the group I'd been trailing, and soon after, I *finally* spotted a sign of civilization rising from the wilds: the tops of buildings and colorful tents peeking above a stone wall with a black iron gate in its center.

A roar of noise rose up to meet me as I closed in on the wall, accompanied by a plethora of scents—the competing aromas of food, of flowers, and of a cold, metallic odor I couldn't place.

The pillars on either side of the entrance gate were inscribed with words written in an ancient form of elvish that I had to work to decipher. On the left was the city's name, along with a list of elves I assumed were instrumental to its founding. On the right was a phrase that meant something akin to *To enter here is to wipe the dust of the world behind.* Or maybe it was *Wipe away the dust of the world first or do not enter?*

Either way, it gave the unnerving impression that whatever waited beyond this gate was set apart, the ones inside of it not concerned with the current order of the world outside.

A guard stood to the right of the gate, studying his sword with a bored look on his face. He was barely glancing at anyone walking past him, which made me feel as though I'd chosen the correct, least-conspicuous entrance.

I made it through with little resistance and was instantly met with a flurry of activity on the other side.

I don't know what I'd expected, but what I found was a town that might have been mistaken for any other ordinary town—one with the expected clusters of shops and houses surrounded by crowds going about their business.

It all seemed so normal that it was almost unsettling, like a set propped up on a stage; I could easily imagine a strong wind knocking it all down.

If there were more anti-magic wards hanging in the air here, I didn't notice them from where I stood. My skin still tickled and itched occasionally, but it was easy enough to ignore. There were too many other things drawing my attention.

As the minutes passed, however, more things started to strike me as odd. The gate guard had seemed indifferent toward me, but the rest of the city's residents were more discerning, even if they were discreet about it. Eyes followed me as I passed. Vendors stopped calling out their prices when I walked by. Groups went out of their way to put space between themselves and me.

They knew an outsider when they saw one, it seemed.

Once I moved farther from the entrance, many of the buildings I passed were boarded up. The coverings were neatly placed, aligned so at first glance they seemed to be only a part of the existing architecture. But in addition to these boards, heavy locks hung from most of the doors, of both shops and houses alike, and beside them there were often cryptic inscriptions that read like requirements for entry.

Moving freely in this place was clearly not going to be as easy as I'd initially thought.

After walking on for some distance—through another gate that required more precise timing and a diversion to slip through—the scenery began to change.

Gone were the colorful stalls full of sundries, the sweet and sultry scents of food, the chatty gossipers. They were replaced by neatly organized, drab tents; the scent of metal and rust; groups of solemn-faced elven soldiers everywhere I looked.

The street was also less crowded. I could see to the end of it, and at its terminus stood what looked like barracks that could have easily held hundreds.

I moved toward it with determined steps, despite the sick feeling growing in my stomach.

There was no mistaking this city for what it was at this point: Precisely the rebellious stronghold we'd feared.

A stronghold preparing for war.

I wandered through this budding war zone for what felt like hours. My head was spinning. My chest ached as though it had been cut open by Andrel's knife all over again. And all the while, horrible images tormented me—scenes of the last battle I'd fought against my own kind, when they'd broken their way into the divine realm.

I'd been so sick to my stomach during that battle I could hardly stand. I wasn't sure I could do it again, regardless of whatever loyalty I now held to the gods.

Looking around me now, I wondered if I'd have a choice.

Many of the elves walking around in the area wore insignia I recognized—the symbols of familiar elven houses, though often altered in some way. There were even a few carrying a symbol of the ancient bloodline I belonged to: The feather-wrapped sword and the jeweled goblet of the once-powerful House of Mistwilde.

The legacy of that house was so tarnished, and buried so deep, I'd rarely given much thought to it while growing up. Some still clung to the power it had once represented; I was not one of them. Even when I'd still considered myself a part of the rebellion, I'd been more focused on my family's future, rather than its history.

But I still silently cursed myself for not thinking of bringing something of my own that featured my house's symbol—it would have helped me blend in. I didn't have any of the actual items from my old home, but I could have fashioned a replica from memory easily enough.

Not everyone wore symbols, at least. They all seemed to have a purpose, however; there was no idle standing around. Like cogs in a machine, they darted this way and that without ceasing. I was going to stand out if I didn't figure out a role for myself.

I walked on with purpose, covertly scanning and studying things more closely.

All the information I could glean proved frustratingly superficial. The doors were all locked. The conversations were all hushed, difficult to eavesdrop on, even with my excellent hearing. I was drawing too many curious stares—though less than when I'd initially entered the city; the ones in this area seemed more interested in their own duties.

I was preparing to hide somewhere to regroup and come up with a new plan when I heard a voice that brought everything else to a jarring halt.

Dread twisted my stomach. My muscles seized, making it painful to move, but I forced myself to walk toward the sound, and then to peer toward the side street where it was coming from.

And there he was—a tall, familiar figure with dark hair giving instructions to a small group of soldiers, his voice as arrogant and smooth as ever.

Andrel.

CHAPTER 13

Karys

I FOUGHT THE URGE TO REACH FOR THE SCAR NEAR MY heart.

My stomach twisted more violently.

Move, I silently commanded myself. *You have to keep moving.*

I'd known there was a good chance I would find him here if this truly was the heart of the elven rebellion. It shouldn't have been such a shock to my system.

But it was, it so painfully *was*, and the storm of emotions that roared through me nearly knocked me off my feet. I tasted bile in the back of my throat but swallowed it down. I tried—and failed—to follow this with a deep breath. Dizziness threatened.

Suddenly, warmth blossomed in my chest, right below the scar, spilling through my veins and somehow making it easier to breathe. To move.

I couldn't say if it was Dravyn—his magic reaching across the space between us and wrapping protectively around me when I needed it most. But I *wanted* it to be him. I needed it to be him.

I needed to know I wasn't alone in this place, if only for a moment.

I steadied myself in that warmth for the span of a few breaths before reminding myself that, even if Dravyn could catch glimpses of my thoughts and feelings, he wasn't coming in here to rescue me.

That wasn't the plan.

It was up to me to make something of this mission. To prove myself to the divine courts.

And Andrel presented an opportunity, loathe as I was to get closer to him.

I leaned casually against the closest building, out of sight, but still near enough to catch snippets of the conversation he was having.

That conversation was already drawing to a close, however. As it trailed off, I chanced a quick look around the corner. The men he'd been ordering around were giving quick salutes before leaving in the opposite direction. Andrel walked toward me, coming uncomfortably close to where I stood, before turning down the main street and heading toward the barracks.

I watched him out of the corner of my eye as he made his way into that set of buildings. He was one of several coming and going without any fuss—it was a low-security, residential establishment, as I'd suspected. And it was the only place that didn't appear entirely locked down.

There was nothing to do except follow him.

Inside was a maze of doors and hallways. I lost sight of Andrel almost instantly. But I knew his scent better than most, even if every part of me wanted to forget it. I could follow it with little effort, too, given that my godly senses were even stronger than my elvish ones had been.

My tracking skills only got me so far, however; I eventually came to a locked door—one he was clearly on the other side of.

Luckily, no one saw me pulling on it in vain, nor heard the curse I let out before I turned around and ducked into the nearest open room to calculate my next step.

There were no lights nor windows in this room, and I was so distracted by racing thoughts of Andrel that, at first, I didn't realize I wasn't alone.

A young elven woman sat by an unlit fireplace in the corner. She held a small glass orb in her hands—a bomb of some sort. Five more lay beside her in a neat row. I could smell sulphur and charcoal, and I saw that little flecks of a crushed red...*something* coated the floor around her.

Corpseroot powder, I thought; I'd seen Cillian make explosives with similar ingredients.

The woman glanced my way but said nothing. She seemed to be hoping I'd realize I was in the wrong place and leave.

Maybe I should have. But something about those bombs—and the pang of familiarity they caused—made me stay put.

"You're a new face," the woman eventually said without looking up.

"Sorry to interrupt you."

She waved a hand as if she was unbothered by my hovering, though her expression suggested otherwise.

Despite her obvious annoyance, I still didn't budge. I'd seen Andrel. Did that mean Cillian was here as well? What had happened between the two of them since my messy exit from the former home we'd all shared?

"Is there something I can help you with?" the woman mumbled.

"No," I said quickly. "Just the bombs you're working on there...they caught my eye. The root powder that's used to make them is quite rare, isn't it?"

"Yes."

"I've only seen it in a region far south of here."

"It's called corpseroot," she said, still mostly ignoring me, her fingers working deftly on twisting the bomb's fuse together.

"Yes. I know. I...I know someone who is a master at making these bombs—an old friend of mine. From that same southern region, actually."

She kept working without comment.

I looked back toward the hallway, making certain the two of us were still alone before I said, "His name is Cillian."

Her fingers stilled against the bomb. "I know who you're talking about. Used to live in the old Morethian Manor for a time, I believe."

My stomach heaved. "That's right."

Her gaze lifted to my face, though the rest of her remained perfectly still. She studied me for a long, uncomfortable beat before she went back to fiddling with the weapon and said, "It's been weeks since I saw him around here."

He was here.

The revelation made my pulse quicken, but I stopped myself from commenting on it and revealing my ignorance.

"I haven't seen him lately, either," I said, calmly. "I've been wondering where he was."

She gave me a puzzled look. "You're a friend of his. Surely you know he couldn't pass up an opportunity like the one in Stillwind."

Stillwind?

I was desperate to know more, but before I could think of a way to pry information out of her without seeming suspiciously clueless, she swept her unfinished bombs and ingredients into a bag, slung it over her shoulder, and got to her feet. "Sorry to run," she said, "but I've got people expecting me elsewhere."

With a casual wave, she was gone.

I stood alone in the room for a few minutes, staring at the shining remnants of corpseroot powder on the floor. Memories of Cillian flooded the space, threatening to drown me. Memories I didn't have time for.

I had a confirmation that he was alive now, at least.

No matter what else happened, that alone made this risky venture worth it to me.

I doubted most of the gods and goddesses waiting for me would agree with this sentiment, however. Clenching my fists at the thought, I hurried back to the hallway—

And nearly collided with Andrel as he emerged from the locked room.

"Watch yourself," he growled, snatching my arm and pushing me aside.

"*You* watch it," I growled back.

I knew it was a mistake the instant the words left my lips. I also didn't care. All of the loss and confusion and anger I'd carried into this city was winding up so tightly inside of me that I was going to violently, irrevocably snap if I didn't release *something*.

Andrel's fingers remained tightly wrapped around my arm. He watched me without speaking for a long moment.

Too long.

Why was he studying me so closely?

Was my disguise wearing thin?

I'd made sure to change the sound of my voice—but had I not done enough?

"Who are you?" he asked. "I don't think we've had the pleasure of meeting before." His expression softened, a corner of his lips quirking and a touch of curiosity lighting in his bright hazel eyes. To someone who didn't know him like I did, he would have seemed friendly. Charming.

"Elora Estel."

"Estel?" He considered the false name. "From the Calan region, I'm guessing?"

I nodded.

"I wasn't aware our message had gotten through to any of your clan. The lord of your people has been rather...*stubborn* in all our dealings thus far."

I forced myself to adopt a tone I knew would flatter his ego. "Some of us are able to see as clearly as you can, despite what our leaders want us to believe."

He smiled. "Happy to hear it."

He finally released my arm, though he remained entirely too close. Every second of that closeness was making my nausea worsen. My mind kept attempting to shut down, to somehow protect me from the visceral memories of everything he'd done to me.

Just as the urge to back away from him became nearly unbearable, a rope of heat snaked through my body. It felt the same as earlier, and I was almost certain of it, now: Dravyn could sense my fear, my panic, my disgust...and his magic was responding to it, subtly but surely.

I stood taller, willing my expression into something blank, unreadable, just as a soldier rounded the corner and headed straight toward Andrel.

"We have a situation in the square that Captain Raegel thought you'd want to be present for," the soldier said. "Spies from Galizur. Four of them."

Andrel no longer seemed interested in who I was or why I was here, for better or worse.

"They're apprehended?"

The soldier nodded. "And we've sent for...*her* to deal with them, as she requested. The required ones are gathering to hold trial."

"Good," Andrel said. "Let it be quick, so that we might send a message to the ones hoping for their safe return."

He sneered the last two words with such cruelty that it took all the restraint I had not to whip the knife from my hip and plunge it straight into his stomach.

After a few more brief words, the messenger left.

Andrel lingered, tilting his head toward me and studying me once more. "You'll join us at this exciting event, I hope? And then feel free to write to your lord back home with all the details later; perhaps we can enlighten him, yet."

"Of course," I replied, still fighting the urge to reach for my knife.

Maybe I imagined it, but it seemed as though his lips parted in a slight, mocking smile—almost as though he could sense my violent desires and was daring me to act on them.

I kept still.

Somehow, I kept still.

He said nothing else before turning and walking away.

I watched him leave, heading in the same direction as the messenger. He was nearly out of sight before I managed to make my feet move.

I stepped outside, shielding my gaze against a sun that had grown brighter during my absence. As I moved through the city, following Andrel at a safe distance, I kept an eye out for potential escape routes I could take.

I would see what I needed to see of this trial, and then I would be gone before Andrel could look my way again—that would be enough for now.

It would have to be.

It was much quieter in the streets than before, even once I passed back into the more residential area of the city. Although, if I strained, I could hear the roar of a crowd building far in the distance—most of the city was gathering toward the square the soldier had mentioned, I assumed.

Somewhat reluctantly, I kept moving toward that sound. I was looking more and more closely at potential getaway routes as I drew nearer—which is what led to me staring down a narrow, winding path lined with blue flowers.

On the other end of it, I could just make out the edge of what looked to be a monument made of white stone.

The stone was so massive, and shining so beautifully in the sun, that curiosity got the better of me.

I followed the path and found myself facing a wide open, natural space that seemed completely at odds with the city behind me. I forgot about the stone monument for a moment as I kneeled, pressing a hand into impossibly lush grass. Hills of that grass rolled in all directions, dotted with more blue flowers that shivered in the slight breeze.

Trees bursting with blossoms were spaced evenly along the edge of the space, blocking out much of the noise from the city. The quiet made the place feel oddly solemn, maybe even sacred, and I wondered again what the monument at the front of it stood for.

Only as I started to make my way back to the street did I pause long enough to study that stone more closely, and what I saw sent chills racing through my entire body.

It was covered in names.

Hundreds of names.

I didn't count them all. I didn't have to. Dravyn had already told me the exact number months ago. And the reason for the lush, fertile grass and the strange, solemn air of this place suddenly became clear.

It was a mass grave.

I backed away slowly, not stopping until I was surrounded by grey streets and buildings once more. The city reeled around me. I resumed my original path with shaky legs, only this time I kept my eyes straight ahead and didn't stop until I reached the crowd at the square.

It was even more massive than I'd expected.

I disappeared among the shifting, jostling bodies for several minutes, grateful for the noise that drowned out my thoughts along with my pained, uneven breaths.

Once I'd somewhat collected myself, I moved to a clearer space and stretched taller, surveying the area, still determined to finish what I'd set out to do.

There were four humans standing upon a small platform I hadn't noticed during my earlier walk through this part of the city. An elven soldier stood between them with a roll of paper in his hands, reading the charges against them. The noise around me made it hard to hear what he was saying, but whispers carried through the crowd quickly enough, repeating his words with increasing fervor.

Spying, trespassing, thievery—all the things I was also guilty of, but which I'd gotten away with merely because I looked like I could belong here.

My gaze dropped to my boots. I didn't need to watch any of these executions. It was enough to know they were happening.

I didn't need to look.

Why, why, *why* did I look?

I didn't know why, but as several members of the crowd inhaled sharply, I lifted my head. I looked toward the platform just in time to catch a sword gleaming in the daylight.

Just in time to see the executioner's face before she turned her back to me.

Everything seemed to crash to a stop.

Because the one holding the blade was my sister.

And before I could even whisper her name, she swung.

CHAPTER 14

Karys

I DIDN'T SEE THE HEAD HIT THE GROUND—I WAS TOO BUSY staring at my sister's smiling face—but I heard the sickening thud as a brief hush swept over the crowd.

Savna winced at the sound, but her smile never faltered.

The longer I stared at her, the more disconnected I became from myself and my surroundings.

I was not here.

That was not my sister.

It could not be my sister.

She was speaking. Lips moving, hands gesturing. Her words didn't register. The crowd responded with enthusiastic cheers to whatever she was saying. I felt my body moving toward the noise like a moth drawn to fire, knowing it would hurt but unable to resist the urge to get closer.

The crowd was too thick to push through, so I located a fenced-off yard nearby and climbed onto the wooden railing. I found my balance, one boot pressed against a thick, splintering post, just in time to get a clear view of my sister lifting her sword for another strike.

The blade gleamed brilliantly in the sunlight, its edge splattered with surprisingly little blood. Her first strike must have been clean and quick, aided by her inhuman strength. All elves possessed it; my sister had always been one to train to the point of obsession, trying to make herself even stronger.

She twisted the blade with the flourish of a performer, continuing to smile at the crowd. That smile looked just as I remembered it. Warm, confident, unyielding. The same expression, the same face I'd pictured for years while trying to fall asleep. Thinking of her used to chase away the nightmarish things pressing in.

Now, she *was* the nightmare.

But that was not her, and I was not myself, and I was not here, not here, *not here...*

The blade sliced forward only to leap back before touching skin. A practice swing. Another swing, faster this time—

"Savna! No! DON'T!"

I hadn't meant to shout it, or even say it out loud.

She heard me, I think—enough that she flinched—but I don't know if she saw me or truly recognized me.

I never found out.

In the next instant, a hand was on my leg, startling me and causing my balance to sway. I pitched backwards, someone grabbing me and yanking me further off balance.

I was dragged from the fence and far away from the restless and noisy crowd. Slammed against the side of a tall grey building. My breath left me in a violent *whoosh*. My vision twisted and flickered.

"How dare you speak her true name," came a growling voice. "Who the hell do you think you are?"

I blinked, trying to fight through the dizziness. A furious elven man came into focus, his face mere inches from mine. He wore a jacket with a symbol sewn into its collar—an upside-down triangle with a sun around its lowest point. More regalia adorned his sleeves. His skin was lined with scars, his breath sour, his eyes a deep brown flecked with red that made me think of dried blood.

I fumbled for a response to his question. It hadn't occurred to me that *Godwalker* was more than just a nickname for my sister—that maybe it was an entirely new identity she'd taken on to help hide her until she was ready for...

For *what*?

What the hell was she *doing*?

When I couldn't manage a reply quickly enough, Blood Eyes shifted one of his hands from my arm to my neck, pushing me harder against the wall, choking tightly enough to make our surroundings spin.

A second solider emerged from the churning scenery, a dagger drawn and ready in his hand.

I fought the urge to cough and sputter, trying to remain calm and take small, consistent breaths. But these breaths weren't enough; my vision started to dim. My body slumped. I forced my eyes to stay open, even as my surroundings spun; the sickening churning was better than surrendering to the darkness.

"Gentlemen," came a familiar voice.

Andrel.

The spinning slowed for an instant, then got worse as he drew nearer and continued to speak.

"What is going on here?"

The grip on my throat loosened the tiniest bit as Blood Eyes glanced over his shoulder.

I managed a somewhat normal breath. Black dots still danced in my vision, threatening to take over, but I focused on the color in between them.

"Clearly she is a guest in our city, unaware of our customs." Andrel's gaze darted to the hand on my throat. "And that is no way to treat a guest."

The second soldier lowered his dagger, but Blood Eyes kept a secure hold on me until Andrel spoke again, a hint of warning in his otherwise casual tone.

"Stand down," he ordered.

Reluctantly, my captor released me. Both soldiers took a step back as Andrel moved in, though they remained uncomfortably close—one on either side—giving me no real space to make a run for it.

Andrel regarded me with a cocked head and a cold smile. "I should have known I'd bump into you again. You had a troublesome air about you."

I had no reason to believe he knew my true identity, but I didn't like the way he was looking me up and down as though trying to place it.

I kept silent, motionless, fighting the urge to claw his eyes out as they took me in. I hadn't forgotten what was at stake, and I'd already messed up enough for one mission.

"Who are you—*really*—and how is it that you know the Godwalker's true name?" he asked. "She's gone to great lengths to keep that identity a secret from all except the highest-ranking soldiers and leaders among us."

So the ones who'd grabbed me were not merely common, overzealous guards; they were potentially both as powerful and dangerous as Andrel.

Just perfect.

"Well?" Andrel prompted.

"I...I knew her when she was younger." It was perilously close to the truth, but what else could I say?

I kept my gaze on his as though I had nothing to hide.

He stared back, silent for several moments past the point of uncomfortable, but all he said in the end was, "Interesting."

I held in a relieved sigh.

He had a short sword hanging from his hip—one that hadn't been there earlier. His fingers absently tapped the jeweled handle, but he didn't draw the weapon. He didn't have to; I was already breaking out in a cold sweat at the mere sight of it, images from our last meeting playing rapidly through my mind. The rocks against my back. The river roaring nearby. The glint of the blade as it stabbed toward my heart...

Pain spasmed through my chest.

I willed myself to continue taking small, consistent breaths.

I could still slip away from this city without causing a real scene. I just had to survive Andrel's questioning, his cold scrutiny. I'd managed that for years when we lived together; why should now be any different? If anything, I was stronger now. I was not the same person he'd nearly killed weeks ago. Not the same one he'd used and abused for so long. I could handle this.

"You know, every elf I've ever met from the Calan region had very specific markings under their left ear." He tapped his own slender ear for emphasis before dragging his finger downward. "Three dots that ran down here." He reached and gently pushed the hair from my neck, revealing the unmarked skin underneath. "I couldn't help but notice that you *don't*. I started to ask you about it earlier, before we were so unfortunately interrupted."

"You clearly haven't met many from my region," I said, with as much haughtiness and confidence as I could muster. "Or else you would know that most of my kind abandoned that tradition a generation ago."

"Is that so?"

"It was an old homage to the old gods who have abandoned us," I said, "and we have little allegiance to those Creators now. So why should we continue to honor them?"

This seemed to please him. I knew it would. It didn't matter if it was true or not; he just wanted to hear more voices speaking ill of the gods.

His hand fell away from my ear, only to brush against the side of my face. It lingered there as if he was feeling for something else—for scars, I feared.

No.

My disguise was still intact. He couldn't possibly have realized there were marks hiding beneath Mairu's magic.

Marks he could likely map better than anybody. I cringed at the thought. Our history was a stain I couldn't seem to get out, no matter how hard I scrubbed.

He finally drew his hand back. Yet something about the way he continued to study me made my insides feel like they were turning to liquid. I subtly shifted my stance, bracing a hand against the wall behind me.

"It's clear we have a lot to learn from one another." His gaze shifted between the restless crowd at his back and the two soldiers who were helping to corner me. "Escort her to my office," he told them.

Panic bloomed in chest, crowding against my lungs and making it hard to breathe. I couldn't risk meeting anywhere private with him again—or being stuck in this city long enough for my disguise to wear off.

"Make sure she's comfortable," Andrel said. "I'll be in to finish our meeting once everything settles down out here."

"You aren't taking me anywhere," I snapped.

"We'll see," Blood Eyes replied, cracking his knuckles as he stepped forward.

Reflex snapped my hand forward, wrapping it around his forearm as he reached for me. He tried and failed to break out of my grip. The spell Zachar had laid over me had suppressed my magic, but it had done little to dull my divine strength.

I pushed my enemy away with relative ease, shoving hard enough that he stumbled back against Andrel.

Andrel threw him forward in a rage and Blood Eyes did his best to right himself, lunging for me.

I easily sidestepped his uncoordinated attempt to grab hold of my arm again. I twisted fully out of his reach and turned to run—

Only to be cut off by the second, sword-wielding soldier.

Sword Soldier lifted his weapon toward my throat once more, trying to threaten me back against the wall. Back into submission.

I parried the blade with my bare fist—a desperate move to knock it away from more vulnerable parts of me. It sliced through my skin, leaving a gash across my knuckles and spraying the ground with my blood.

My balance swayed, my vision momentarily blurred from the pain.

He tried to pin me with his fist, this time, snatching for the collar of my shirt. I clumsily ducked his reach and darted forward, sweeping a low kick toward his ankles as I went. He leapt, avoiding the brunt of the blow, but I still managed to catch part of his foot and knock him off balance.

While he staggered and caught himself against the building behind him, I ran, refusing to look back.

The commotion I'd caused had pulled some of the crowd away from my sister and toward me; I could feel their stares. But I couldn't think about them now—and I couldn't risk meeting my sister's eyes by looking back. She would only slow me down.

I had to get out of this place while I still could.

Footsteps pursued me.

Andrel's voice rose even louder than the building roar of the crowd: *"STOP HER!"*

The path in front of me was suddenly blocked, dozens of bodies converging onto it—soldiers who'd sprung into action from seemingly nowhere at all.

I spotted a narrow side street that remained unblocked and veered toward it. It turned out to be littered with trash and debris, each object I had to knock aside slowing my pace a little more.

Andrel didn't follow me.

But as I careened around a corner, I found him already waiting for me on the other side.

I stumbled away from him, only to hear more soldiers closing in from behind.

I had nowhere to go.

Blood continued to pour from the gash on my hand. My pain became panic that rolled into fear before igniting into fury. I closed my eyes to try and ground myself, and I instantly had a vision of fire—of great wings of flame unfurling and wrapping around me. I felt myself sinking into their embrace, my own power fluttering as they did, rising up until...

Gasps sounded all around me.

I opened my eyes and immediately realized my mistake: There were little fires everywhere. Bits of trash had ignited, as had leaves and patches of grass. Embers swirled and sparked through the air.

It was a weak display, dampened by the Death magic spell, but it was obviously magic, and equally obvious that I had summoned it. Smoke trailed from my skin. Heat flooded the space around my body, intense enough to make the air ripple.

I couldn't move right away, frozen with horror at myself for losing control.

Andrel snapped out of his shock faster than I did; I couldn't maneuver quickly enough to avoid his hand.

He snatched my arm in a bone-crushing grip and roughly shoved my sleeve up. He was searching my skin for a divine mark, maybe—a sign of magical ability usually only found on humans.

I held my breath until I saw for myself that both the marks Mairu and Zachar had branded onto my skin were no longer visible. Even as another wave of heat surged through me—a combination of both my own rage and Dravyn's, I thought—nothing appeared.

They'd been there at the beginning of this; were the spells wearing thin?

Andrel continued to scrutinize my skin. I must have made frustratingly little sense to him, but even if he didn't realize who or what I truly was, he clearly suspected I was at least connected to the divine more than any elf should have been.

His grip didn't let up, fingers digging in so tightly I wondered if he was attempting to break the bones in my wrist for a second time.

"Let go of me," I hissed.

"Not until you explain who the hell you really are."

I kneed him in the stomach instead.

My strength and speed seemed to catch him off guard. I didn't land as hard of a blow as I wanted to, but it was enough to knock him back and loosen his grip on me. I wrenched my arm the rest of the way free, biting back a cry as the violent twisting motion sent pain stabbing up my arm.

He shook off my attack and dove for me again.

I swung my throbbing arm forward, slamming my palm upwards into his nose. It was cathartic, the feel of that nose crumpling under my furious strength, and the blood that gushed out and rained over me.

But as much as I wanted to stay and break every bone in his face—to make him truly pay for the things he'd done—I knew when the odds were against me. And those odds were getting worse by the second, with more and more soldiers drawing closer and threatening to intervene.

I saw an opening behind him, and while he was busy wiping the blood from his face, I moved.

I sprinted past him, racing toward the gate I'd entered the city through. I changed direction before I reached that gate, though, heading instead for a small road I'd noted on my way in. It led to what looked to be an older, smaller entry point with a much less impressive wall stretching out around it. I made my way to a partially-collapsed part of this wall and vaulted over it. My injured hand burned in protest, but I fought through the pain, landing lightly on the other side and scrambling for the cover of the thickest bushes I could find.

A crowd was gathering at the main gate; I was still dangerously close to it, able to hear what I could only assume was a hunting party preparing to come after me.

Was Andrel among that party?

Was my sister?

I sank deeper into the foliage. Hand shaking, I picked up a stick and sketched precise little lines into the dirt, recreating the mental map I'd made of the route between Ederis and the first anti-magic ward.

Somehow, I had to get to the other side of that ward.

CHAPTER 15

Dravyn

"This place reeks," Valas grumbled, "of elves and something even more rotten."

"Do me a favor," I replied, hacking an overgrown vine from our path, "and complain more, why don't you?"

"I'm only trying to make conversation."

"Silence is golden, my mother used to say."

"In here it's just eerie," Valas countered. "Why do all of these plants give off such a hostile, dark energy? It's strange. Cursed, it feels like."

It's because this place isn't meant for gods, I thought. But I made my way to a clearer path and continued walking without comment.

We'd spent hours hovering on the outskirts of this wild forest after parting ways with Karys. Tense, excruciating hours with nothing to do but wait and hope she returned to us in one piece before the day was over—until, finally, Valas and I had both reached our limit and decided to move.

We'd ventured well-beyond our previously agreed-upon boundary, and we now found ourselves deep in the Hollowlands. How deep the lands ultimately stretched, I couldn't even guess at.

It was a foreign feeling, that uncertainty; ever since my ascension, there were few places I did not feel comfortable walking in, and fewer still where I didn't feel like I had some measure of control and dominance. The upper-god I served was the one who had imposed order and knowledge over the world, after all.

But this place...

I wasn't convinced the upper-gods had truly been involved in its creation in any way.

We soon came to a threshold of sorts; the path widened up ahead before branching in several directions, but before that crossroads was a nearly-invisible wall of magic. It glistened in the twilight, giving off a sinister, pulling energy, like the sea rolling away from the shore and trying to take my balance with it.

"A barrier," Valas commented, summoning a tumbling ball of ice and shaping it into a small knife. He threw the knife casually toward said barrier. It collided with a violent spark of white light before it disintegrated completely, leaving little more than a faint shimmer behind. "And suddenly, this place feels even *less* inviting."

I started to head off in search of a different path, but stopped as I caught sight of a small gash in the trunk of a nearby tree—a claw mark.

"...She passed this way."

"You can sense her?" Valas asked. "That weird connection between you two again?"

"No need for that," I said, pointing. "She's marked the trees."

"Ah. Clever."

We pushed through the barrier, through an immense pressure that gave me the brief, mad desire to shed my human form in an attempt to deal with the discomfort of it.

"What the fuck is this ward even made of?" Valas growled.

"I don't know, but let's just keep moving. Maybe the pull will subside once we put some distance between ourselves and it."

"It feels like it's trying to latch onto my magic and rip it out. How did Karys stand this?"

I didn't answer, because I didn't know—and I didn't want to think about her suffering the way we were currently suffering. Maybe her elvish ties protected her somehow, or maybe the spells Mairu and

Zachar had laid upon her were better at countering this hellish attack...

Hopefully.

We reoriented ourselves as best we could and picked up our pace, committed to our plan, even though it was feeling more and more like a bad idea.

I thought of being pulled out to sea again—except this time I was wading willingly into it, deeper and deeper, ignoring how close the waves were to crashing over my head. I ignored the sick feeling in my stomach, too—along with the uneasy chatter of birds overhead, the foliage that seemed to be alive and closing in around us, the briars that caught at my hair and clothing.

Pain sliced through my hand, sudden and sharp.

I peered down, expecting to see the evidence of brambles catching, digging in and scraping their way over my knuckles...

Nothing was there.

My fingers were unmarred, yet the pain lingered, unmistakably real. A surge of emotion soon followed it—fear. Panic. I'd been catching flickers of similar things for the past hour; glimpses of what I assumed were the feelings Karys was experiencing, though the barriers between us made it difficult to see what was causing them.

Did this pain in my hand belong to her as well?

Had something happened to her?

I pushed my own fear down and focused on action. The pain felt clearer than anything yet—which hopefully meant we were getting closer to one another.

I paused, bracing myself against the closest tree as I tried to reach for her, to feel the familiar beat of her among the hostile energies and thick, suffocating air of this hellish landscape.

An urge to move soon overcame me, pulling me back the way we'd come. As if we'd missed her somehow. Months ago, I would have thought it was foolish to even think of obeying this instinct.

Now, I followed the inexplicable pull with little hesitation.

Valas trailed closely at my heels. We ran for no less than a mile, until I felt another, equally strong and equally unexplainable urge to change direction. Following this pull had us veering from the clear path, battling our way through thicker forest as the scent of blood and burning things grew more and more prominent.

Finally, we cut our way through a cluster of vines and made our way into a small clearing where Karys was kneeling, surrounded by a circle of burned vegetation.

The spell that had changed her appearance had faded away. Ribbons of fire surrounded her. Her head was bowed, eyes fluttering open and shut, as though she was meditating, concentrating on not letting her fiery walls fall.

I stepped through the fire and knelt in front of her. She didn't seem startled or surprised by my sudden appearance; she'd likely felt me approaching.

"What happened?" I demanded. "Are you hurt?" I answered my own question as soon as I asked it, reaching for her hand only to draw back when I noticed it was covered in blood. There was dried blood on her other hand, as well, but it didn't smell like hers.

She stood without answering me. Her movements were mechanical —slow but determined. She looked ready to collapse against me as I moved closer, but fought the urge with a shake of her head, then started to walk away only to pause and look over her shoulder.

Her gaze narrowed on a distant spot of forest. Her lips parted as if she'd spotted something horrifying, but when I looked, all I saw were thin, rickety tree trunks clacking and swaying in the breeze.

"You look like you've seen a ghost," Valas said. "What the hell went on back there?"

It seemed to take a moment for the question to register. She looked to him, briefly, and in a low, brittle voice she said, "My nightmares were right. My sister, the blood, the destruction, all of it. I..." She trailed off, fists clenching, her expression caught somewhere between utter grief and painful fury.

I moved to her side once more, taking a closer look at her hand, gently feeling my way along the wound underneath all of the blood. Most of that blood was fresh—still flowing freely enough to rapidly coat my fingers. The airs of this place seemed to be affecting her divine ability to heal.

"Your sister did this to you?"

She shook her head vehemently. She started to explain what had truly happened, but Valas cut her off.

"Perhaps now is not the time for this conversation," he said, gaze jumping to the same spot Karys had been staring at a moment ago. "Sounds like we have company."

I looked to that spot again just as an elven soldier broke through the trees, immediately followed by two more.

One of them tossed a shining ball toward our feet. As it hit the ground, it shattered, filling the air with a bitter-scented powder.

Breathing in the bitterness made my throat instantly, unbearably dry. The trees spun around us. My eyes watered. I wiped away tears, and through my blurred vision I saw eight more soldiers emerging.

"We aren't far from the barrier we passed through," Valas said under his breath. "We'll be able to make a clean getaway easily enough on the other side of it. Running would be wiser."

"It would," I agreed.

But I was staring at the blood on my hands as I said it, and thinking of the blood that had covered Karys when I'd carried her away from that mortal river and into the Tower of Ascension...

I unsheathed my sword.

Valas sighed but followed my lead. "Let's make this quick," he muttered, waving away a lingering cloud of the bitter powder. "Every breath I take is making me feel more sluggish and stupid."

I didn't have time to reply—the enemy was already advancing.

The same one who'd thrown the bitter-scented bomb lunged toward me first, a curved blade drawn and prepared to swing.

I shoved Karys behind me and met him with my own blade in a single-handed parry that sent him flying backwards.

He looked momentarily startled—as though he'd expected his bomb to have rendered me entirely useless.

He'd miscalculated.

Badly.

I gripped my sword more tightly in my bloodstained hand, moving without mercy to finish him off before he could regain his balance. My blade plunged so deeply into his chest that it was difficult to draw it back out again.

A second soldier rushed me from behind. I dislodged my weapon at the last moment, and in the same smooth, uninterrupted motion I twisted around and swung, slicing into his neck.

A single gasp turned into a choke, then into silence. Blood spurted, showering me before I could avoid it. The soldier dropped as though made of stone, his body sounding a heavy *twhump* as it hit the ground.

I spun around, looking for my next target.

My pulse quickened as I saw how many more had joined the original eleven.

Valas backed toward me, surveying the increasing number as well. Karys had moved to the edge of the battle—far enough outside the concentration of bomb powder that she'd been able to summon more fire to shield herself with. It was a weak spell, but it seemed to be keeping our enemies away from her for the moment.

Valas's words rang through my head.

Running would be wiser.

"That powdery shit is making magic even more difficult to draw upon," he said.

"It doesn't matter," I replied, rage tightening my voice as I wiped the blood from my hands. "They can die by the sword just as easily as by fire or ice."

It was more satisfying than magic, too—the feel of my blade sinking in, the crunch of bone as I slammed its hilt into skulls, the spurts of blood as I struck precisely the right places.

Line after line of soldiers advanced upon us. We cut them down, over and over again. They didn't seem to care how fast they were falling; more simply appeared to take the fallen's place. The air grew thick with the scent of blood and sweat and other bodily fluids, and somewhere in the back of my mind, I knew this would do nothing to diffuse the wars that were building, threatening the stability of our realms.

The ones littering the ground would serve as proof that the gods were merciless beasts. Maybe they had even been sent as intentional sacrifices to further enrage and rally others to their cause.

Several minutes and too many bodies later, the dryness in my throat and the dizziness from the powder was starting to truly get to me. I felt the first tinge of exhaustion creeping in. A moment later, I stumbled, righting myself just in time to see a soldier racing toward me with his sword at the ready.

I staggered back and tried to rebalance my own weapon in time to block.

I was too slow.

A flash of steel flew in from my left, impaling the soldier in the stomach and driving him back just before his blade met my chest.

Karys.

I hadn't even sensed her moving. She'd taken a sword from one of the fallen elves, and now she clutched it in her hands as though it was her last tether to reality.

Stepping into the tainted air had made most of her fiery shield disintegrate, save for a few stray embers that reflected hauntingly in her eyes. The green of those eyes seemed darker, almost black, clearly mirroring the fire swirling in and around her.

Did she even realize there was fresh blood covering her skin? The one she just killed...was it someone she'd known before today?

Protecting her suddenly seemed more important than avenging her.

"Come on," I said, wiping the blood from my sword as quickly as I could before sheathing it. "Let's get to clearer air so we can leave this realm."

She snapped out of the trance that had overtaken her and nodded, still holding tightly to her stolen sword as she hurried off in the direction of the barrier we needed to cross through.

We were close, as Valas had assessed. But as we started to brace ourselves for passing through that barrier, a familiar voice reached us, imploring us to *wait.*

"Let's keep going," Valas urged.

I looked to Karys. She'd slowed down, though her eyes were still on our escape route. Her face barely hinted at the war raging inside of her, but I could feel it as clearly as I'd felt her pain slicing through my hand.

I glanced back.

Some of the soldiers we hadn't killed had caught up to us. There were new reinforcements, as well, and each one of them carried what looked to be bombs similar to the first one thrown at us.

All of these things were concerning, but I didn't give a shit about any of them.

Because my vision had tunneled toward the one standing in the center of them all—Andrel.

I turned to face him more fully, all thoughts of running away momentarily forgotten.

He wasn't looking at me; he only seemed to be aware of Karys. He was studying her, his stare far too intimate for my liking.

My fingers twitched as I thought of how satisfying it would feel to carve his eyes out with the knife I had strapped to my ankle.

"So it's as I suspected," he called, stepping forward while motioning for his soldiers to remain at ease. "You *really* thought you could trick us with some ridiculous magical disguise?"

I started forward too, but Karys stopped me, placing a hand on my chest. She took a deep breath, concentrating. Heat bled into the space around us. I met it with my own, pouring as much into her as I could manage after breathing in so much toxic, anti-divine powder.

Her fingers clenched into my shirt as she balanced herself. Looking down, the depth of the wounds on her fingers became more obvious than ever.

"Did he do that to you?" I demanded.

Again, she shook her head.

Nevertheless, I was calculating how many more I would have to kill to get to him when Karys suddenly stepped away from me, turned around, and strode directly toward our enemies herself.

She stopped several feet away from Andrel. Valas and I both moved closer, hands gripped tensely on our weapons, eyes scanning the restless soldiers all around us.

"How low we've sunk," Andrel continued, still only focusing on Karys, "that you feel the need to employ tricks, to creep around in my presence rather than meeting me face-to-face. There was a time when we didn't hide anything from one another. Do you even remember that? Or have these beasts taken that from you as well, along with your sense of self-respect?"

Karys stiffened, but kept her head up and her voice level as she replied. "I'm not hiding, now, am I?"

"No. Though it's arguably worse, what you're doing. The company you're keeping."

"I've kept far worse company than this," said Karys.

He considered the statement for a moment before chuckling darkly. "Are congratulations in order, then?" he sneered. "I suppose I'm meant to cheer for you, now that you've become a filthy servant of the divine? Will you also be changing your name? How should I address you going forward? A servant of the—"

"She is no servant of mine," I interrupted. "She is my equal. And you may address her as *Goddess* or not at all."

Andrel finally turned his head toward me.

The entire circle of soldiers seemed to be looking at me as well, all of a sudden.

I fed off their glares, forgetting myself for a moment, letting chains of fire whip outward from my body. The ground beneath me heated to the point that little fissures began to spread out from under my feet.

All of it was subdued by the poisons they'd filled the air with, but there was still enough flame and fury in the display to make Andrel flinch—though he quickly recovered and hid the movement with a smile and said, "Well, I'll be sure to start building a temple to her, in that case."

Molten fire filled one of the cracks in the ground, pouring toward him. It moved more sluggishly than it would have under normal circumstances—the only reason he was able to dance back and out of the way before it swallowed him up in a violent, deadly rush.

I reached for my sword instead, but a hand clamped down on my shoulder, preventing me from drawing it. A cold breeze stirred, snaking around me before weaving into the streams of fire I'd unleashed, cooling them back into relatively solid ground.

"We were heading for clearer air," Valas reminded me in a low voice.

I shrugged free of his grip.

He was relentless, stepping more fully into my line of vision and jerking his head in Karys's direction. He didn't say another word, but his meaning was clear enough.

We should get her out of here.

Somehow, I managed to pull my hand away from my sword.

He took the lead, grabbing Karys's hand and dragging her toward the barrier.

I moved more slowly, watching our enemies crowding in, daring any of them to try and stop us from leaving. Once Karys and Valas had crossed back over the barrier—and I felt their magic building as they prepared to transport themselves—I finally relaxed enough to turn toward the exit point myself. I fixed one final glare in Andrel's direction before walking away.

"We aren't finished," I promised him.

He gave a slight bow. "Until next time, then."

CHAPTER 16

Karys

Two days after my mission into Ederis, I stood in the smaller of the Fire Palace's two kitchens, obsessively counting out the ingredients to an old family recipe I'd made at least a hundred times before.

I'd memorized the steps to it years ago, yet now I found myself second-guessing every measurement, checking off ingredients only to throw them back into their containers so I could take them out in a different way, line them up in alternative rows, count them by twos instead—whatever it took until they finally felt *right*.

It was the first time I'd been out of my room since returning to this realm. I'd been determined to make it out today. To not let myself be overwhelmed by the sights and sounds throughout the palace, the things that reminded me of what I'd become. Where I lived now. What I couldn't go back to.

Don't look back, don't look back...

I just had to find something to distract myself with and I would be fine.

The distraction of cooking had been Rieta's idea—she'd reminded my shocked and addled self that I had loved it, once upon a time, and she'd rearranged the kitchen in a way she thought would suit me best before kicking all of the usual servants out of it.

Mairu had offered her help as well, and had ventured briefly to the mortal realm to gather up authentic ingredients that I was used to working with, even though they didn't compare to the quality of the ones that originated in the divine realm.

They had both encouraged me to dig into these old recipes, to lose myself in the thrill of creating as I'd once been able to. They weren't trying to erase my past; it was *me* who couldn't seem to hold both Karys the goddess and Karys the elven rebel in her mind at once. It felt like trying to walk with two separate people controlling my legs.

I took a deep breath.

I was out of my room and moving, at least, even if I occasionally stumbled. Even if I didn't feel like I could create anything real or worthwhile at the moment.

I was fine.

Everything was fine.

I surveyed the kitchen, pointing and calling out the things I would need for the next steps of the recipe. It was an old trick my sister had taught me—when my unconscious mind tried to overtake things and deaden my emotions, forcing it to focus on tangible things brought me back to the present. We used to turn it into a game, sometimes, trying to see who could point and call out the next tool or ingredient first. I could still hear her laughing when I stumbled over the words in my haste to get them out.

"Have everything you need?" came a voice from the doorway.

I wiped a tear from my eye before turning to find Rieta standing there with a box resting on her hip. "Yes, thank you."

She studied me, her fingers tapping rhythmically against the box. "You look disappointed. I s'pose you were hoping I was the God of Fire?"

"No, it's not that."

She clucked her tongue in a disbelieving sort of way, but ultimately didn't argue as she stepped inside and placed the box on one of the marbled countertops, mumbling to herself as she pawed through its contents. It looked to be more ingredients Mairu had sent.

"He'll be back soon, I suspect," Rieta said, more to herself than me.

I had barely spoken to Dravyn since our return, except to numbly recite the things I'd heard and witnessed. Not because I didn't want to talk to him more, but because I didn't know what else to say.

The space between us felt like a deep, dark ocean, the lands we'd come from too far apart from one another. And I was too tired to try and swim.

He'd spent much of these past days away from the palace and out of reach in all ways, anyhow. He was off setting fire to things on the edges of his territory, creating volcanic upheavals, *and who knows what else*, Rieta had explained. He seemed determined to reshape the very slopes and edges of his domain with violent, relentless energy.

I would have known this was what he was doing even if she hadn't told me; I felt him and his restless magic clearly enough.

"He's furious about what happened, isn't he?" I asked, studying my knuckles. After two days, my divine blood had done its job, leaving behind little evidence of the cuts I'd sustained. "Furious with me for talking him into my plan...I should have known there would be things in that city I wasn't ready to face."

"He's not furious with *you*, love," she replied, gathering up an armful of the dishes I'd dirtied and carrying them over to the wash basin. "He simply needs to be alone."

I didn't believe her, but I didn't have the energy to argue, so I simply went back to my cooking. I had finally committed to the order I'd placed the ingredients in, and even though my hands itched to keep rearranging them, I resisted the urge.

I was determined to finish at least *one* recipe before the day was over.

Rieta busied herself with the dishes, polishing and drying nearly every cup and spoon before she spoke again.

"He's always done this, ever since he was younger. Sometimes he'd disappear into the woods for days on end. He knows his temper, and he knows when he needs to walk away from things. Usually. The few times he hasn't succeeded in doing that, well..." Her hands shook slightly as she tried to place a glass cup on the drying rack; it slipped, falling back into the wash basin, and the sound of glass striking metal reverberated throughout the room. "It's better to let the fires have a chance to settle."

My gaze caught on the bright red coals beneath the oven. "Or else innocents die in those fires," I mumbled. "Like the elves of Ederis did."

"Yes. And he's never forgiven himself for that. I'd hoped he might make some kind of peace, with you now at his side, but with everything that's happened lately..." She trailed off, sighing and shaking her head.

The past, it seems, is not finished with either of us.

Those haunting words Dravyn had spoken had already proven more true than I think either of us were prepared for.

"He's not as far away as he may seem, for what it's worth," Rieta added after a moment of thought. "He's been back periodically to check in on things here. To check on you."

Warmth crept into my cheeks. "I still have a hard time seeing him as someone who could level an entire city without flinching," I told her.

Even after personally witnessing how easily he could kill, it still felt at odds with the rational, protective god I knew. The one who was distancing himself now until he felt more fully in control of his anger and magic. The one who had protected me time and time again.

"No one is fully good or bad," Rieta pointed out with a shrug.

I considered this as I measured and sifted flour into a bowl. "I expected to struggle more with the monstrous side of myself when I ascended," I admitted. "Sometimes it doesn't feel like I truly ascended at all. Or like I only made it halfway."

"It's been different for you, I believe, because of how close you are to Dravyn, and how tightly your magic is woven together."

I hadn't forgotten the bloodthirsty drive I'd experienced when I first walked out of the Tower of Ascension, but she was right—the God of Fire had been there from the moment I'd woken up, talking me back from the ledge.

The same god who had recently returned to this realm covered in the blood of my enemies.

And they *were* my enemies, weren't they?

To say that no one was fully good or bad felt like a gross oversimplification.

I massaged my temples, trying to soothe away a building headache.

"But even Dravyn was fully monstrous in the beginning, based on what he's told me."

She frowned. "I suppose it can be argued that he was—at least for a time. Like most new gods. And yet, even then..." She hesitated, as if on the edge of revealing a secret she wasn't sure she trusted me with.

I gave her an imploring look, and her gaze slowly softened until she finally relented and continued to speak.

"Do you know how I came to live in this realm...a mortal being blessed with enough magic to be able to survive here?"

I shook my head, fully intrigued, the spices I'd just started to measure momentarily forgotten. "No. But I've always wondered."

"His brother—the one who is now the king of Galizur—wanted me put to death for failing to do anything to stop the assassins who killed their younger siblings. I was in the room when their sister was stabbed. I hid, Prince Fallon thought. Truth is I simply froze, and was lucky enough to go unnoticed.

"Still, I could have done more, I know, and Fallon wanted someone to blame for what had happened. But Dravyn stopped the execution order. And once he became a god, shortly thereafter, he returned to the royal city and took me away. Brought me here. A single life saved among all the chaos and bloodshed of that night probably doesn't seem like much, but...well, it wasn't meaningless to *me*, obviously."

I went back to the spices, double and triple checking their measurements before dumping them into the bowl one by one. Quietly, I said, "I don't think it was meaningless, either."

I wasn't entirely sure *what* I thought. But chasing all the possibilities around in my head eventually led me to a single horrible one: If he could be good despite the monstrous things he'd done, then my sister could be a monster despite the good she'd done.

I wanted to shrivel up with the pain of this realization one moment. In the next, I wanted to rage against the very idea of it, to set fire to something, *anything* to get it out of my head and stop the burning ache it caused in my heart.

But I refused to do any of these things in front of Rieta; I understood Dravyn's need to be alone more than ever, suddenly.

She seemed to pick up on this. "I'll come back in a bit to check in on you." She eyed the stack of dishes she'd finished washing. "Do me a favor and try not to be so damn messy going forward, hm?"

I swallowed hard. My throat felt like it was full of broken glass. "I'll try."

She watched me for a bit longer, concern clouding her eyes, before she finally left.

I spent the next several hours alone, thinking of nothing except the steps to whatever I was cooking. I finished the first recipe—dozens of cinnamon-dusted cookies that had once been my father's favorite treat —and then I jumped straight into another before my mind had any time to wander.

I wrote down each of these recipes in painstaking detail before I attempted them. Even though I likely could have made them from memory alone, the act of writing out each step brought me a greater sense of peace.

As long as I had lists and directions I could check off, I could keep moving. As long as I methodically followed them, I would make it through the day.

I passed the hours with one successful baked creation after another, falling into a daze that was, if not entirely peaceful, at least bearable. With each finished product, I slipped away a little more, until I was no longer present and hurting—I was the past me, back in my childhood home, and things were as they had always been.

I finally broke from my trance at what must have been close to the middle of the night, and only then because my magic stirred in a way I couldn't ignore. It brought me to a stop in the middle of the kitchen, nearly causing me to drop the bowl of dough I'd been mixing.

Dravyn walked into the room a short time later.

A searingly hot wind preceded him. He still carried the wild scent of where he'd been, of sweat and scorched earth and smoke. His skin was unsettled, the divine symbols on it glowing faintly. His eyes were brighter than usual, too, a fiery gleam weaving through the steely blue— though their color settled somewhat when they fell upon the counters, which were full of my neatly organized rows of sweet and savory pastries, breads, muffins, and more.

His expression flashed between impressed and dubious as he said, "You made all of this?"

"I just...I needed a distraction, that's all."

"And you're still going," he commented, eyeing the bowl I clung to. "Moth will be thrilled."

I nodded.

We stood silently for a moment, staring at one another as if it had been much longer than two days since we'd had a proper conversation.

Finally, he pointed to the latest piles of neatly-stacked ingredients I'd laid out and asked, "Can I help?"

I exhaled slowly, the deliberate breath finally breaking me from my stupor. "Yes. You can. But you have to wash up first."

He smiled slightly at this, but obeyed, disappearing for a few minutes before returning with his hands and face scrubbed clean.

He presented himself to me as if for inspection, that slightly crooked smile still on his face. I played along, taking his large hands in mine and turning them over, one by one, tracing my fingers along the lines of his palm.

"That will do, I suppose," I informed him.

He still smelled of broken and burning things, but I tried not to think about those things and focused only on the task before us once more. I grabbed a paring knife and handed it over, instructing him to gather and chop the chocolate I'd planned to fold into the bowl I held.

And I was fine.

Everything was fine.

For a few, blissful minutes I managed to believe that once again.

The night moved on and we transformed into the settled, easy version of us that I quietly, desperately longed for. Talking. Laughing. Tasting the things we'd made. Plotting ways to make them better. Making a mess that I was sure Rieta wouldn't be pleased about.

But there was an ache building steadily in my gut as I went through the motions. A grief that grew heavier with each stir of a spoon, with every check of the recipe's steps—with the increasingly clear realization that I would likely never, ever do these things with my sister again, even though she was alive.

It was as if she'd died all over again.

As I watched Dravyn adding the last ingredients to the cake we were attempting to make, a memory struck me—that of the first time I'd cooked after my sister disappeared. Of how wrong I'd gotten the dish without her there to look over my shoulder while I prepared it. Even though I'd been cooking on my own for years before that, without her there, everything I did had suddenly felt so...*unbalanced*.

A tremble went through me. I braced my hands against the counter, trying unsuccessfully to hide it.

"Karys? What is it?"

I shook my head, but Dravyn's gaze was insistent.

"You're doing it wrong," I said quietly.

He gave me a confused look.

"It's all wrong," I said, angrier. The same anger I'd felt toward myself all those years ago was suddenly resurfacing, except now I couldn't bear to keep it inside of myself as I'd done back then. There was no room for it along with everything else.

"It has to be all lined up perfectly," I insisted, furiously. "It has to go in the right order. If something is missing or wrong, the foundation is *ruined*. And if the foundation isn't right, then everything else crumbles."

I didn't take my eyes off the bowl he held, barely resisting the urge to knock it from his hands.

"Everything crumbles," I repeated, trying and failing to keep my voice from doing the same.

He slowly placed the bowl on the counter and started to reach for me, but I shook my head and backed away.

I needed to keep moving.

I tried to keep speaking, too. Tried to explain myself, but I couldn't get my voice to work.

My knees suddenly felt weak. Despite my best efforts to pace the room with precise, purposeful steps, I ended up sinking against the door to the pantry, wrapping my arms around myself as I fought against the urge to slide down into a miserable heap on the floor.

I had to stay on my feet, at least.

If I collapsed now, I worried I'd never find the strength to get up again, so I bowed my head and concentrated on staying upright.

Moments later, I heard Dravyn coming closer. He reclined against the wall beside me but didn't speak. I didn't either. I didn't even lift my head—though after a minute, I did move, leaning against his shoulder as I tried to stifle the sob building in my throat. I only partially succeeded; the cry ended up silent, but the tears came anyway, quickly drenching his shirt.

His hand found mine, holding tightly to it even as more tremors of rage shot through me.

"You don't have to stay," I said quietly.

"I want to stay."

"I might start throwing things next."

"I'll catch them."

I didn't know what to say to this, so I said nothing, only let my head rest more completely against him while the tears continued to fall. I'd given up fighting those tears; I'd run out of them, eventually.

Running out took several minutes, but when it finally happened, the anger inside of me had subsided enough that I finally trusted myself to speak again.

"She used to be the one I turned to when things crumbled. Even after she di—left." I sucked in a breath. "Even after she left, she was still my foundation. I built myself around the absence of her. Isn't that stupid? To build everything around that emptiness. Of course it didn't hold up. I'm a fool for thinking it could."

"You are not a fool for doing what you needed to do to survive."

But I am a fool for not seeing the truth sooner.

He shook his head, as if he'd heard the thought even though I hadn't voiced it out loud. "You were lied to. Manipulated. Abused."

My heart clenched. He was right. I knew he was right. I don't know why I couldn't agree with him. Maybe I wanted to blame myself because it made things feel like they were still in my control, somehow.

Maybe the God of Death had been right the other day...maybe I *was* clinging too tightly to too many parts of my old life.

I curled closer to Dravyn, burying my face into his chest. He wrapped his arms tightly around me but didn't say anything else. There didn't seem to be anything else to say just then, so we simply stayed that way for a while, until I found myself and my thoughts growing restless again.

"What am I supposed to do now?" I asked, hoarsely, more to myself than him. I didn't really expect an answer.

Because what could you do, when the person who used to help you through all the hurt became the *reason* you were hurting?

Dravyn was quiet for a moment. Then his hand found mine once again, and he started to pull me away from the door as he said, "Let's finish making this cake, shall we?"

"What?"

"The cake. What's our next step?"

I lifted my gaze, half-expecting to see a teasing smile and laughter dancing in his eyes.

His face was entirely serious.

"Come on," he said, continuing to guide me back toward the abandoned ingredients. "And I'll need you to explain it to me more carefully this time; I've never been good at this sort of thing."

I stared at him. And at the counter covered in flour, the splatters of batter, the broken eggshells and dirty spatulas strewn about...it all suddenly seemed so ridiculous in the midst of all we were facing that I found myself laughing at the very notion of finishing.

But he was insistent.

So I picked up the recipe I'd written out once more, and together, step-by-step, we found a way to keep moving.

CHAPTER 17

Dravyn

It had been four days since our return from the mortal realm, and every day had brought more challenges, more impossibilities, more weights that were steadily tipping the mortal realm toward war.

I'd spent most of the morning in my office, nursing a goblet of wine while poring over records of previous conflicts in Avalinth, until the God of Winter interrupted me with a report I'd been waiting on—one filled with more bad news from that realm below us.

I reluctantly put my notes aside, drained the last of the wine, and went to pass this news on to Karys. I couldn't keep it to myself; as much as I wanted to shoulder the burden alone, I'd promised her I would keep her informed of everything I could—the good, the bad, the in-between.

I found her in the main gardens, braiding a crown of flowers that she was attempting to place on Moth's head.

Unsurprisingly, the griffin was not being particularly cooperative; he already had one string of battered blossoms hanging from his beak. More scattered the ground, seemingly crushed and ripped apart by his paws. A few were burned almost beyond recognition.

I paused at the garden gate, watching them, wishing I didn't have to interrupt the quiet scene with more talk of war and ruin.

Karys ultimately proved more stubborn than Moth, successfully adjusting the string of white and blue flowers so that it balanced perfectly on his head. She sat admiring it for a moment, assuring the griffin of his handsomeness and sternly commanding him not to ruin her work.

She kept her back to me as she called, "You know I can feel you standing there—and sense your troubled thoughts—even if you don't speak, right?" She glanced over her shoulder, not quite meeting my eyes. "You have bad news?"

I moved closer, leaning my back against the wall she sat beside, crossing my arms in front of my chest.

Moth sprang onto the top of the wall and paced it, preening before me, tilting his head this way and that to make certain I saw what he was wearing. Now that the job was done, he seemed less interested in eating the crown and more interested in showing it off.

"We've successfully scouted the place you mentioned to me," I told Karys. "The area where your old friend Cillian is supposedly hiding out."

"Stillwind, you mean?"

"Yes."

She stood, dusting the dirt from her pants, her expression unreadable.

"Stillwind is the name given to the region as a whole, but in the center of it is a military post long used as a training ground for the Galithian army," I explained. "*Mindoth's Keep*, it's called. Valas sent one of the spirits who serve him into the mortal realm yesterday, and they spent the night watching the place."

"And what did they find?"

"The grounds of Mindoth have been on high alert for weeks, dealing with intruders and the occasional covert attack...mostly cloak-and-dagger antics, for the time being—but if things continue to escalate as they currently are, a full-scale battle seems imminent."

She picked off a white blossom clinging to her sleeve, tracing its delicate petals as she said, "We need to stop that battle from happening."

"Ideally, yes."

"How?" Her voice was quiet, her gaze intently focused on the flower.

"I'm not sure. I haven't spoken to anyone other than you and Valas about the matter yet. But it's part of our duty as Marr to be aware of Avalinth's major problems and conflicts...so the other middle-gods must be informed of what we've learned, at least. After that, we'll have to decide, once again, whether to intervene. And to what extent."

"Another council?"

"Maybe. Unfortunately."

She shuddered visibly at the prospect.

I didn't blame her.

"...For now, let's just go for a walk," I suggested. "There's something I need to check on—something that I've been wanting to show you. We can talk more on the way."

She agreed. We followed the well-worn path through the garden, beyond the vine-wrapped trellises, alongside fountains lined with colorful glass tiles, and finally past the stone walls and out to a point where the packed dirt trail gave way to wildness.

The land rolled out for miles before us. I breathed in the warm, spice and smoke-scented air, feeling somehow both unsettled and at peace as I took the scenery in.

I was not the first of my order, so I had not been the hand that originally shaped this territory. But I'd reworked some places in the years since my ascension, partially with the help of magic from the Towers of Creation that were scattered throughout the middle-heavens—the same magic that had aided me in creating creatures like Moth.

The area we traveled through now was perhaps the closest thing to *mine*. The pockets of ghostly white trees were of my design, as were the swaths of fiery red and orange flowers. While much of my territory was barren stone with bright veins of molten earth weaving through it, the ground here was covered in rippling, bluish-green grass.

I'd also rerouted and widened the creek running through it all, lifted the flat ground into rolling hills, and enchanted the winds so that they often blew warm and dry, and from a southernly direction—work that, collectively, made this small part of my domain resemble the kingdom I'd grown up in.

I'd never admitted this to anyone. In some ways, it felt like a weakness, this clinging to where I'd come from. What I couldn't seem to forget. Like a child afraid to let go of his mother's hand.

"I've never been this way before," Karys remarked, running ahead and summiting a small hill to get a better look. She circled the hilltop, surveying the land around us with one hand raked into her hair to keep the wind from blowing it into her eyes. "It's beautiful here."

"Yes," I agreed, coming up beside her. It was on the tip of my tongue to tell her that I'd modeled it after my old home. I'm not sure why I didn't. Maybe because I found myself thinking less about the past and more about the future whenever she was close to me.

She tilted her head toward me, eyes lighting with curiosity as they took in my pensive expression.

Maybe I didn't *need* to tell her what I was thinking; maybe she already knew.

I cleared my throat. "Come on—we've still got a ways to go."

I pointed her in the proper direction. She nodded and raced down the hill, arms stretched out, hair flying wildly behind her. Moth soared above, his crown delicately clutched in his front claws and dangling beneath him.

The three of us eventually made our way to Galim, that pool that was connected to so many of the inter-realm waterways. But instead of following any of the rivers branching out from it, we walked due north, over more wild land devoid of any marked paths.

Though I'd often traveled to the place we were heading to, I didn't usually walk the entire way. Normally, I took Farak. Or, if the selakir was not in the mood to be bothered—which happened often—I traveled by way of wings or magic.

But I was in no hurry to deal with all the bad news on our horizon, so today I was perfectly content to walk as slowly as possible toward whatever came next. To savor the relative peace we were enjoying.

All too soon, we came to the spot where I normally touched down: the head of a twisting trail packed with fine grey sand. Following it led down into a valley, where the land grew flat and dozens of small pools awaited us.

I guided Karys to the pool in the very center, an uneven circle rimmed in cheery yellow flowers. The water, by contrast, was the color of a skull that had been left to bleach and rot in the elements. Occasionally, it bubbled with a darker substance, turning the liquid briefly to the shade of charred wood before it returned to its pale state.

"This is Elandrach," I said. "A Watching Pool. It's tied to the mortal realm, and it's one of several such pools scattered throughout the middle-heavens. Different pools correspond to different areas."

"And this one corresponds to the Kingdom of Galizur, I'm guessing?"

"Yes."

"So what can you see in them?"

"Their waters are a gauge of sorts, showing us the general state of Avalinth at a glance. The more unsettled or murky the water, the more unsettled the mortal realm is. The color changes at times, as well. In this case, those bubbles you see have been growing steadily darker for weeks."

Moth swooped down for a closer look. He carefully placed his crown on the sandy ground before trotting up to the pool and inspecting it. Karys knelt beside him, catching him and pulling him back when he leaned too close and nearly tumbled into the water. He slipped behind her, sniffing at the pool from a safer distance, while she scooped a handful of it up.

"It feels strangely thick," she said, studying it as it slowly trickled through her fingers. "Like...blood, almost."

"It's not truly water," I explained, "but a liquified concentration of special magic created by the Moraki."

She turned her hand this way and that, coating it in the thick, shiny substance.

"Some of the Marr can manipulate these pools into showing them more details about the places they represent. I'm not one of them, unfortunately."

"It's clear enough, isn't it?" she asked, softly. "A feeling of blood, and a growing darkness...it seems like an obvious omen."

I didn't disagree, though I couldn't bring myself to say this.

She paused with her fingertips hovering just above the pool and looked up at me, expectant.

"...I don't know how to put an end to this without more bloodshed," I admitted.

She stopped herself from scooping up more water, clenching her hands into fists that she pressed into the sand next to her.

"I don't think I even fully understand what they hope to gain from escalating this into a full war," I continued, wandering through the collection of pools as I spoke.

The one Karys knelt beside rippled with the darkest of warnings, but all of them had changed over the past month; I'd witnessed various shades of those bubbling warnings, and not a single surface experienced sustained calm, now.

"They must realize they can't annihilate all of the gods," I said. "No matter what weapons they manage to create, they aren't strong enough to take on the upper-gods above us. They'll overstep with their demonstrations and warmongering, and the Moraki will intervene eventually and finish them off. I'm certain of it."

Karys's breath audibly hitched, and hastily I added, "Though, obviously, I'd rather it not come to that."

She shook her head, eyes shining with an emotion I couldn't easily name as she looked up at me. "It isn't about annihilating the Marr entirely. It never has been."

I made my way back to her, my gaze curious, urging her to continue.

"It's all a ploy to get the Creators to regret their decision to cast us from their graces in the first place," she continued after a pause. "It's all some of the elves think about...all they've thought about for *decades*.

"When I was growing up, almost every gathering of my kind led to the same conversations about it. So even though I don't remember a time when we were the most powerful beings in Avalinth, I still grew up feeling like I had been personally cheated out of an inheritance I was owed. Like I was a victim of the tyrannical Moraki. And that if I made them regret their decision badly enough, I might be able to claw back some of the power we once had."

I didn't reply right away, trying to imagine a younger version of her sitting among a budding, rebellious movement, absorbing all the frustration and anger being poured over her.

The emotion simmering in her eyes was clearer now—a tired resolve mixed with quiet sadness, a feeling even deeper and more complicated than these pools that reached all the way to the mortal realm.

Moth took his crown in his beak and carried it to her, nudging it into her hands as if to offer a distraction. She took it absently, her fingers carefully tucking and smoothing some of the bent blossoms back into place.

"And what about now?" I couldn't help asking. "Do you still feel cheated?"

She was quiet for a time, looking back at her reflection in the pool, eyes narrowing as if trying to recognize the face within it.

"Not entirely. We were stripped of our stronger magic, that's true— but we weren't stripped of *everything*. And we weren't completely wiped away as we could have been. We had other chances, other ways we could have rebuilt. But once you've had so much power, I suppose it's hard to learn to live with less. Most humans now refer to us as the *Fallen*, but we actually called ourselves that first. And now we have extremists alienating us further and further..." She shook her head, placing the crown back on the head of a surprisingly accommodating Moth, then rose back to her full height while swiping sand and bits of flower crown from her palms.

"I'd always thought it was more complicated than what many of my kind insisted," she went on, "even before I met you. I didn't *want* it to be complicated, though. Blind hatred is easier, after all." Her heavy gaze fixed on me. She sighed. "Sometimes I wish I could still hate you the way I once did."

She mirrored the grim smile I gave her as I closed the space between us, taking her hand in mine.

"If only," I said.

She stared at our intertwined fingers as she continued. "I'd started to think I could be a bridge between our two worlds—that maybe that was the destiny the Moraki had intended for me when they allowed me to accept your magic, even though I was...well, you know what I was."

I found myself wrestling with the same question as before: "And what do you think now?"

She lifted her eyes to me. "After what I witnessed in Ederis...I'm not sure. I don't know how I can walk back across the divide, face my sister, and..."

I waited patiently for her to finish. When she didn't, I merely gave her fingers a little squeeze. I wouldn't force her to keep talking. Especially not when I didn't know what to say or what to think, either.

She moved away, weaving through the pools until she found a long stick next to one of them. She used it to trace lines and circles in the sand, as if mapping out our next moves.

Moth intently watched the tracing, his flame-tipped tail flicking back and forth. More than once he started to grab the stick only to be stopped by a stern look from Karys.

"We have to go to Mindoth's Keep, don't we?" she decided after a few minutes of silent debate. "To protect the humans there, de-escalate the battle somehow. That's ultimately your charge as a middle-god..." She trailed off, forehead creasing in frustration, as if she'd just remembered that she, too, was technically a god.

I could hear her thoughts relatively clearly. They grew louder with her increasingly troubled emotions, just as mine had when I'd hesitated by the garden gate earlier.

But I could have guessed what she was thinking even without our connection.

Where was her ultimate obligation supposed to lie?

I decided to stick to talk of strategy instead of trying to answer that question. It was easier.

"They'll be expecting us to come to the aid of the humans they're attacking," I said. "Which means they'll be prepared, if and when we do."

"So they're escalating things because they think they have enough power and weaponry to deal a blow to both humans *and* the gods?" she wondered.

"I'd call it hubris on their part, but...who knows what sort of weapons we'll be dealing with? I suspect—as do many of the other Marr —that part of the reason for their assault on this realm weeks ago might have been about stealing things they could take back and corrupt into fuel for their weapons. I'm sure there are things that were taken while we were busy battling at the Tower of Ascension."

"I hadn't thought of that." She went back to mapping out her thoughts in the sand, her brow creased in concern.

"So walking into Mindoth will not be without significant risk," I said. "At the very least, the humans of that training compound will potentially glimpse weakness in our ranks. They'll see these weapons that can actually do harm to the middle-gods."

"Which is likely part of the goal of the elves," Karys said. "It's the same reason my fellow rebels and I destroyed temples and did our best to slander the role of the divine—to make the Marr seem more like flawed, fallible creatures."

I nodded slowly, understanding. "To weaken the hold we gods have over humans, to encourage them not to worship us, and to keep us from becoming a united force against them."

"Exactly."

"An ambitious goal," I said, frowning. "And again, I wouldn't have thought it within the realm of possibility months ago, but now..."

She made a frustrated noise before swiping away whatever she'd been drawing in the sand. Her fist clenched more tightly around the stick as she looked over the ruined lines and symbols.

She started to attempt several more diagrams, but never managed to commit to any of them for longer than a few seconds.

Her thoughts raced. I could sense the anxiety surrounding them, could hear occasional bits and pieces of them—a jumbled mess of ideas, questions, plans. Nothing that took root. Every promising idea was met with painful realizations before circling back to a single defeated question, the same one I'd been asking myself all morning.

How do we even begin to fix this mess?

As if she heard the echo of this question in my mind, she turned to me with a decisive look and a quick suggestion. "You promised you would help me practice magic the other evening. We never got around to that, did we?"

"No, we didn't." I arched a brow. "I was ambushed in the stairwell, as I recall, and the rest of that evening is a blur."

My sensitive hearing caught the sound of her heartbeat speeding up. "A pleasant blur," I added with a grin.

Another quick flutter of her heart, and this time my pulse skipped with it as images of that stairwell encounter flashed in my mind. My stomach clenched. My cock twitched at the thought of her pressed against the wall, surrendering to my strength, her skin hot and body quivering at my touch...

She tossed the stick aside. "Well, back to business this afternoon, then," she said, clearly trying to focus through what I assumed were her own heated memories. "If we'll be heading into what sounds like a war zone, then I need to be ready."

CHAPTER 18

Dravyn

Somewhat reluctantly, I cleared my mind of all other thoughts and said, "Agreed."

Moth stayed behind, napping on the hilltop overlooking the pools, while Karys and I traveled farther north in search of a place that felt suitable for the work we intended to do.

The ground gradually became pale stone, smooth and shimmering, rather than grass. The hills straightened into a grey expanse that stretched beyond where we could see. The sky was darker here, the nearest forgelight now some distance behind us, casting everything in a shadowy, violet-edged, twilight kind of glow.

Finally, Karys paused, bracing her hand against a skinny tree, and said, "The air feels different here. Clearer."

I nodded. "What should we focus on, then?" I asked. "Do you want to practice transporting again?"

She bit her lip. Shook her head. "I don't want to practice running away."

"No? Then what?"

She considered the question for a moment, focusing on twisting her hair into a long braid and tying it off with a strip of leather she pulled from her coat pocket. Her hands fisted together as she lowered them back to her sides. The clenching motion quieted the restless fire that had begun to stir within her—a trick she had employed often during these past weeks. She was remarkably good at keeping herself from erupting, in spite of everything she'd been through. It was a talent I sometimes envied.

But now that we were out in the open with no one to witness it, with the warm breeze weaving encouragement and temptation around us, her fire didn't stay suppressed for long.

Little curls of flame appeared in the air, following the slender curve of her hand. She lifted that hand and stared at the smoke drifting up through the lines of her palm. Her breathing stilled and her eyes widened as though she was seeing her power—truly seeing it—for the first time.

Her voice was soft but certain as she lifted her eyes to mine and said, "I want to set fire to something."

A chill rushed over my skin. I knew the feeling far too well.

Gesturing to a grove of small, skinny trees in the distance, I said, "Take aim, then, Goddess."

She needed no more encouragement than this.

More flames sprung to her fingertips, wild and powerful—more powerful than she'd intended, I think.

She inhaled sharply. Refocused. Her chest heaved with the effort of taking deep, concentrated breaths. She swung her hand forward. The fire rushed out in a wave that overtook several of the trees—not just the ones she'd been aiming for, I gathered, based on the feeling of frustration that washed through her.

"Too messy," she muttered.

She tried again, summoning more fire, attempting to hone it into a spear-like shape. The form didn't hold; it got away from her as soon as she tried to throw it, the flames taking on a mind of their own, stretching wide and engulfing everything in their path once more.

She cursed.

I watched quietly, not intervening until her gaze flicked to mine with a silent plea, her lips curved down in uncertainty.

I stepped closer, then, placing one hand against her side to steady her while I brought the other one up to help guide her magic. I didn't try to control it or shape it myself; I merely countered it with my own power, forcing it back into form when it tried to rage out of control. It gave her more of an opportunity to focus on aiming. Allowed her to take a deep breath.

That was all she needed, really; her next attempt saw a precise arrow of flame strike the closest tree and set it—and only it—ablaze. It stood like a burning beacon, a herald of more power and precision to come.

She grew even more accurate once her initial fury and pent-up powers were released.

As the hour passed, she began hitting more and more targets, eventually challenging me to follow her shots with my own.

It quickly became a competition between us, trying to see who could strike the most targets, the most accurately, in the least amount of time. The small grove of trees was fast burned beyond use, so we left the smoldering corpses of them behind and raced across the land in search of more targets.

With every cluster of trees we ignited, her confidence grew and her restraint lessened. I'd rarely seen her so open, so relaxed, so...*free*.

And for what might have been the first time, the guilt I'd carried since stepping out of the Tower of Ascension with her eased somewhat.

Because in that moment, it was impossible to look at her and think she could have been anything other than a goddess, whether of Fire or otherwise.

We came to a hill overlooking a narrow creek. The trees along its banks were sparse, staggered, bent at odd angles in the mud—a challenge.

Karys summoned another javelin of flame, but paused to consider her attack.

"Getting tired?" I teased.

"Hardly," she panted.

I smiled.

"I could do this all day." She stood up a little straighter, catching her breath. "But let's say the next series of targets will decide the winner between us."

"Very well. A fair warning, though: if it's a proper competition, now, then I'll be taking it seriously."

She scoffed. "As if you weren't really trying before."

"I wasn't," I told her. "But *now* I will be. And I don't lose, I'm afraid. I don't think I even know how to."

"That's too bad." She finished catching her breath before smiling sweetly at me and adding, "I'm sure you'll get better at losing, though, the more we practice together."

I laughed at the taunt, summoning a spear of my own fire. "We'll see."

Her gaze narrowed on me at the challenge, and she kept it there as she pointed her fiery weapon toward the nearest tree.

Without warning, I swung my fire-wrapped hand forward, launching the javelin of flame toward the same tree.

She threw even faster, and her aim was deathly precise; the first target was hers.

With that, we were off, the game officially underway with a rush of smoke and searing wind.

After beating me to a dozen more targets, she glanced back while still racing forward. Her eyes blazed. Her smile was bright, her nostrils flaring as they inhaled what she believed to be the sweet scent of imminent victory. I even heard her thoughts already claiming that victory: *I win*.

But I'd spoken the truth.

I had no intention of losing.

I pushed harder, gathering speed before leaping into the air. Wings unfurled from my back, sending a shower of embers raining down. I soared high enough to see the entirety of our course trailing out below me. Fire swirled around both my hands this time.

I forged more than spears; the flames started as these simply-shaped weapons, but soon sprouted claws, lithe bodies, angled heads, and wings that rivaled my own in strength and size.

A controlling flick of my wrist, and the beasts roared brighter before combining into one that spiraled down, down, down, past Karys, weaving a path back and forth across the creek, setting fire to every tree and bush along the way.

We reached a spot where the creek spilled into a small, turquoise-colored lake—a finish line. I landed lightly on the edge of this larger body of water, turning to face Karys as she caught up.

"Better luck next time," I said, grinning.

"Cheater," she grumbled, tucking pieces of her disheveled braid back into place. "First the wings, and then summoning an extra beast to do your bidding?"

"It was not a separate beast," I informed her, still grinning despite the sour look she fixed on me. "It was an extension of myself, as are the wings."

She let out a sigh. "Fine. You win. *This time*, at least."

I flexed my right wing, concentrating magic toward a spot where the feathers were losing some of their definition. "It would probably be helpful if you remembered that, too, by the way—that your magic is an extension of you, I mean. Not a separate beast to be mastered."

I'd mentioned this to her before, but now, it seemed to trouble her for some reason.

She averted her gaze as she considered the words.

"Maybe that's my problem with all of this," she said after a moment. "I can't think of *anything* as an extension of myself for too long, because I'm not sure who that self is anymore. One moment I want to embrace the new wildly powerful, magical side of me. The next, I'm thinking about who I was before. I know it's useless, standing in the middle, yet I can't seem to get myself to step to one side or the other most of the time. So I keep losing my balance when the stakes are raised."

I frowned. "You've already managed to balance an impressive amount of magic for such a short period of time. More than any other goddess or god I can think of."

She shrugged off the compliment. "Maybe."

"And maybe you're being too hard on yourself."

She didn't respond to this. Her gaze drifted to my wings. "How long did it take you to master that particular extension of you?"

"Much longer than you've had," I said, pointedly.

She was undeterred. "Is traveling with them more difficult than transporting yourself from place to place with magic?"

"Yes and no."

She narrowed her eyes and crossed her ams, clearly not satisfied with this response.

"It requires more concentration in the beginning of the spell," I elaborated, "as well as more of your own power. But after that, I think it's easier, being in full control of where you're going."

She turned this over in silence, craning her neck to better see her back, as if mapping out the best spots and proper angles any appendages could sprout from.

"It's harder to do it when you're standing perfectly still on the ground," I told her, "and not in *need* of wings."

"So you're saying I should wait until we're in the middle of a competition...when I need to cheat in order to beat you?"

I smirked. "Well, yes, necessity can be an excellent teacher."

"In other words, you're admitting you *needed* to cheat to beat me?" She poked me in the chest. I feigned a pained expression as I caught her hand and stopped its jabbing, making her laugh and roll her eyes.

Absently intertwining my fingers with hers, I said, "I still remember the first successful flight I managed."

"And what *necessitated* it?"

"Valas shoved me off the top of my palace's tallest tower."

Her brows lifted at this, but her expression quickly turned thoughtful as she turned to stare in the direction of that palace we'd left behind—thinking of potential high places that could be utilized, I suspected.

I shook my head. "I will not be shoving you off a tower. Don't get any ideas."

Her lips quirked as she looked back at me. "Find another way to teach me, then," she said, eyes burning with this new challenge.

There would be no talking her out of at least *trying* to fly today, I was certain.

"See what you can do on the ground, first," I suggested. "Summoning the wings themselves is the first step. Then we'll see about using them."

"You said it was harder to summon them while on the ground."

"It is. But it's also safer, and if you can master it under these circumstances, then calling them forth when you actually *need* them should be even easier."

She didn't argue against this logic. She fell silent and watched me expectantly, studying my every breath and movement as I made my wings disappear, only to bring them back with a burst of smoke and heat.

She copied my movements with the methodical precision I'd come to expect from her. It wasn't enough; not even a hint of feathers appeared at her back.

"It's not the sort of spell you can memorize and go through the motions with," I explained. "You have to feel it out."

She exhaled a quiet, frustrated little noise.

"Just imagine they're already there," I offered. "Something that has been inside of you all along...tucked inside your coat at the moment, perhaps."

She looked doubtful, yet determined to keep trying. Her forehead creased in concentration as she closed her eyes. They remained closed as she shrugged free of that coat.

No wings emerged as the heavy garment fell away—but after a minute, something else did.

The outline of a massive creature began to take shape around her, its lines of fire etching into the air, the glowing strokes extending far higher and wider than either of us.

I blinked several times, and the form being drawn grew clearer—similar to the eagle I often became, but altogether different. More elegant, more smooth...not like that hulking bird that featured on my family's crest, but more like a creature I'd only ever witnessed in paintings and in storybooks as a child.

A phoenix?

The form never fully materialized. It was gone as quickly as it appeared, lasting no more than a single, awestruck breath. The glowing edges gave way to smoke and ash that fell like snow over Karys, prompting her to sneeze and open her eyes.

She didn't seem to realize she'd done anything impressive; she watched the ashes fall around her with her lips pressed into a clearly disappointed pout.

I tried not to stare.

How could I explain what I'd just seen?

Had I imagined it?

No, I didn't think so. There was more power sleeping within her than either of us realized. And I still had no desire to push her off a tower, but maybe...

"On second thought, let's try something different," I said, abruptly. "Something more challenging."

She stopped wiping the ash from her shoulders long enough to give me a bemused look.

I didn't explain, or give her time to protest or overthink what we were doing. I swept forward, gathered her into my arms, and we were soaring toward the sky before she could even let out a gasp.

CHAPTER 19

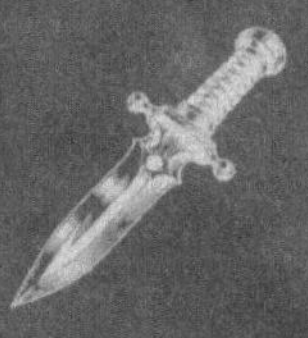

Dravyn

HER BODY TENSED AS WE ROSE HIGHER. IT WAS LIKE LIFTING a statue—not particularly heavy, but awkward and stiff and nearly impossible to guide.

I pressed my mouth closer to her ear, making sure she could hear me within the roar of wind rising around us. "Relax. I've got you."

She gave a barely perceptible nod, but remained entirely too stiff. I kept an arm around her, pulling her against me while I moved my hands over hers. Once our hands were securely locked together, I shifted so we were more side-by-side, my arms braced and holding her up as I stretched my wings more fully. In the same moment, I summoned flames far below to create a warm, uplifting draft to help support us. It built and built, becoming a thick cloud of energy that gave a sense of solidness beneath our feet. Between it and the strength of my hold, soon she was essentially walking through the air alongside me.

She relaxed a bit more with each step, allowing me to focus on my own balance and lift us higher with several strong beats of my wings.

"Don't look down," I warned.

She started to do exactly this, but caught herself and instead fixed a determined stare straight ahead. She trembled from what felt like a combination of fear and anticipation.

I waited until the shivering had stopped, until she was able to calmly glance my way for more instruction, before I said, "Now, try summoning wings as you did before. Feel the fire pooling around your shoulder blades...and just let it extend from your body the way it wants to."

Her breath caught as she tried to take a deep breath. But she managed another nod, and then a slow exhale that brought magic with it. Little bits of fire appeared at her back, fluttering without any control or direction. They were followed soon, however, by the budding foundation of solid wings.

She closed her eyes. Took another deliberate breath. The fire dancing behind her pulled in toward her back—almost as if she'd inhaled it—and melded with the start of those wings, building them up and outwards.

I concentrated on keeping my own magic separate, neither pouring into hers nor pulling away from it; I was determined to make sure she could do this on her own.

After a few more breaths, she'd managed to wrangle all the loose embers into the wings. She looked over her shoulder, eyes widening slightly as they took in the feathered flames sweeping and curling out behind her in a relatively orderly, solid shape.

"Don't overthink them," I said. "Just let them work."

She gave a nervous laugh at this, glancing my way as if to remind me she didn't know how *not* to overthink things.

Before her mind had time to race, I let go.

Her expression turned to panic, then horror.

Then instinct kicked in, followed by a flare of light and power as her wings became bolder, their outline more defined. They fanned out, catching the warm updraft I'd created, lifting her higher without much effort.

I darted higher as well, curving into the space in front of her. Her gaze caught mine. For a moment, she seemed too elated to think of her panic or fear. Too overcome by her accomplishment to think of anything other than flying.

But it was a short flight.

The initial elation wore off as soon as she took her eyes from mine. I felt her focus snapping, saw the exact moment she recognized I was no longer holding her, followed by the mistake of looking down and seeing nothing between her and the faraway ground.

In the next breath, bits of her flaming feathers started to peel away.

She plummeted for an instant before managing enough control to stop the rapid disintegration of her wings. They no longer remained solid or strong enough to carry her upward, but enough gathered together to fan out once more and slow her descent.

As she approached the final stretch of that descent, I sensed her magic truly start to flicker—then go out—and only then did I intervene, swooping down and wrapping her up in my arms once more.

We were perilously close to the ground by the time I properly caught her, making it difficult to adjust for a graceful landing, so I simply pulled her against my chest and maneuvered as best I could to cushion her fall.

Despite the bumpy landing, she was laughing as we rolled to a stop in the long grass.

I ended up on my back with her straddling my waist. My wings stretched out on either side of us, burning an impression into the ground and sending little swirls of smoke into the air.

As those wings faded away, Karys leaned forward, pressing her lips to mine. The last of her hair slipped free of its binding, falling in wavy curtains around our faces.

I took her head in my hands, pulling her deeper into the kiss.

Our hearts pounded from the fall. Our bodies shivered. The pulse of our magic was wild, heating the space around us to a point that made it ours and only ours. We were the only two who could have withstood this burning—set apart from the rest of the world and its problems, if only for a moment.

I stopped trying to keep my strands of magic separate from hers, instead taking the full heat of her in, letting all her breaths and beats tangle up with mine.

"I'm going to seriously injure you one of these days," she mused, lips still hovering close, "if you have to keep breaking my fall like this."

"You're easy enough to catch."

"One misstep and..." She shrugged, and then her forehead wrinkled with thought. "Can gods break their bones?"

"Whatever corporeal forms we take are susceptible to all kinds of injuries, yes. But you've seen how fast we heal other injuries. Bones aren't much different, and they're stronger, harder to break in the first place compared to mortals. So it's unlikely you're going to shatter me beyond repair."

"But it's possible."

"So little faith in my abilities," I laughed, sitting upright, shifting my grip to her hips and repositioning her with enough quick, easy strength to make her gasp.

She settled into my lap, hooking her arms around my neck for balance. "More like 'so little faith' in my own coordination."

"For a first flight, that could have gone much worse," I pointed out.

She lifted her gaze to the sky, to the remnants of her wings drifting over us as ash and glowing-edged feathers. Her mind was racing along with her heartbeat.

I shouldn't have intruded on those racing thoughts, but it was nearly impossible not to in moments like this—when she was so maddeningly close and so much of her was wrapped around so much of me, physically and otherwise.

She wore a knowing look as she lowered her eyes back to mine. "You hear what I'm thinking, don't you?"

"Not anything specific."

Her hands roamed over my chest, fingers smoothing my shirt before hooking around the collar of it and using it to pull my lips toward hers again. Her kiss was soft, a brush of velvet and fire. I felt the smile curving her mouth when I tried to deepen it.

"Impatient," she chided, teasingly.

"No one has ever mistaken me for the God of Patience," I countered, sliding a hand against the back of her neck, holding her in place as I leaned more fully into her.

As my tongue slipped into her mouth, her grip on me tightened. The harder I kissed, the more fiercely she held, and the bolder the fire inside of her blazed. The strength of her hands, the heat of her waking magic...I could have gotten drunk off the sensation of these things alone —and yet I found myself craving more.

When I finally drew back for breath, her hands roamed a bit longer before slipping under my shirt and settling against my back. As her fingers dug into burning hot skin, I couldn't stop myself from imagining them in other places. Around other things.

I drew back to find a faint hint of red spreading over her cheeks. Could she hear my thoughts as clearly as I could hear hers?

Likely *more* clearly, I realized—she didn't have enough control over her new powers to be as selective about what was slipping its way in.

I lightly gripped her chin and tilted her face so our eyes met. "Blushing?" I murmured, trailing my fingertips down her throat. "Now I'm *very* curious about the specific things racing through that mind of yours."

Her lips parted, a soft little noise escaping them. The muscles in my stomach flexed. My fingers moved to her face, running along her lower lip, pulling her mouth open wider; I wanted to hear her make that sound again.

She shuffled in my lap, repositioning her knees on either side of my hips and settling her weight more completely onto me.

I inhaled sharply as her lips closed around the tips of my fingers in a slow, sucking kiss—a wickedly deliberate kiss that sent a shock of desire through my core.

I slid my other hand to the small of her back, firmly holding her in place because...*fuck,* she felt good sitting on me like this.

I swallowed down both the groan and the curse rising in my throat and, as calmly as I could, I said, "No more magic practice, then? Seems like you've gotten distracted."

"It's not my fault my teacher has been trying his best to seduce me."

"I've hardly been trying," I informed her with a smile. "I think you just want to be seduced."

She scoffed playfully at this, but the sound gave way to a gasp as I took hold of her hips, digging my fingers in.

"If I was trying," I told her, "then I might have done something more like *this*."

Her mouth formed a small '*o*' as I lifted my hips slightly upward, just enough to let the softness of her collide more fully with my growing hardness.

"And I would have told you to strip off all that unnecessary clothing for me," I added, "because it was impeding our ability to practice."

"Impeding it, hm?"

"I need to be able to feel the heat of your skin," I said, slipping a hand beneath her shirt, "so that I can properly gauge your fire."

A corner of her lips inched up at this last part, eyes lighting with mischief and desire. Without taking her gaze from mine, she pulled her shirt over her head and tossed it aside, leaving only the thin, supportive undergarment underneath. That garment hung haphazardly, one of its straps dangling off her shoulder. Her breasts nearly spilled from it, stiffened peaks pressing through the silky fabric and begging to be touched.

I brought my lips to her shoulder, kissing along the path where the strap should have been while reaching to slide the other one off as well. Then I rolled the entire thing farther down, leaving her breasts fully exposed and pushed upward.

I cupped one breast, lifting it toward me as I bowed my head so I could trace the velvety tip with my tongue. As it hardened more completely, I took it in my mouth, sucking as slowly and teasingly as she'd sucked the tips of my fingers a moment ago.

She leaned back, adjusting the angle of her body so my mouth could more easily reach her. The movement shifted her hips as well, sliding her center over my stiffened cock. I felt a throb of need go through her, and my mouth grew rougher in response, sucking harder and scraping teeth over her pebbled, aroused flesh.

Her mind was racing again. And again, I tried not to intrude on her thoughts...but I still caught flashes. Visions of us intertwined. Ideas that caused her blush to deepen, and rushes of need that might have been hers, or mine, or some combination of both.

"We could use the connection our minds seem to have to our advantage, you know," I said.

"How so?"

"Use your imagination."

"Walk me through it, instructor," she teased.

I brushed my knuckles across her cheek. "If I can see what's going through your head, then I'll know exactly how you want to be touched." My fingers swept lower, down her neck, along the curve of her chest. "Tasted." The word drew her toward me. Our mouths collided once more, and her hips rolled eagerly against me as I sampled that taste with my lips, my tongue, my teeth.

Her breaths grew more shallow. More needy. I slid my hand between her legs. Even with her bottom half fully clothed, she still shivered with pleasure and anticipation, her hips working even harder to find a rhythm that would meet the need burning more and more strongly within her.

I matched her strength and speed with my own caresses, curling my fingers and penetrating her, cloth and all.

"And most importantly," I said, emphasizing the words with small but powerful twitches of my fingers, "I'll know exactly how you want to be fucked."

Her head tilted back. Her eyes closed as she breathed slowly in and out; she seemed to be concentrating on trying to draw out the pleasure of the moment for as long as possible.

"Yet another advantage of this whole divine business," she said.

I laughed, planting another kiss on her exposed throat.

She looked down at me as I drew my mouth away, her eyes smoldering, her cheeks flushed. "So if you actually *try* to see and hear my thoughts, do you think we can clearly communicate in this way?"

"Most likely."

Her smile turned mischievous once more. "So I could imagine anything I wanted to..."

I lifted a brow. "At your own risk."

"Meaning...?"

"Meaning if you start putting ideas in my head, I can't guarantee I won't act on them. I only have so much self-restraint." I repositioned my hands on her hips, holding her more firmly against me as I added, "And you're already sorely testing it, sitting in my lap like this."

A familiar look crossed her face—the slightly parted lips, the wild gleam in her eyes, the determined set of her jaw. The look of a challenge accepted.

She lifted herself slightly from my lap, shuffling backwards until she was at a better angle. She balanced there as her hands moved along my sides, sliding down, fingers fumbling with my clothing. Unbuttoning my shirt. Unbuckling my belt.

I relaxed my mind. I was not actively trying to keep her thoughts from it, but not pushing them out, either.

The images became clearer. Visions of her kneeling before me. Then me before her. And then...

My pulse quickened. "You're actively trying to torture me, aren't you?"

"What do you mean?"

As if she didn't know.

"You weren't listening when I told you to be careful of what you thought about."

"Wasn't I?"

I ran a hand along the curve of her breast, finding her hardened tip once more and giving it a flick. "Wicked thing."

She smiled. "So we're getting better at communicating through our thoughts. Which means this still counts as practice, I think."

"I feel like we're moving outside the realm of the training we'd planned on."

"Maybe. I'm always trying to improve in *all* areas, though."

"I don't believe you need training in this particular area, for what it's worth." My voice dropped lower, thick with want as I took a handful of her hair in my fist and pulled her into a quick, rough kiss. "But if this is what you want, I'm still happy to provide guidance, of course."

She kissed me back, her hands feeling their way over my pants, pulling them farther down until she'd freed my cock. Her hand wrapped around it, somewhat tentatively at first, but growing more confident as it gave an enthusiastic twitch beneath her warm touch.

I exhaled a slow, raspy breath.

Her eyes flashed up to mine. She licked her lips—a small, unconscious motion, but it undid the last of my restraint.

I gripped her hair more tightly in my fist and offered that guidance I'd promised, pulling her head downward. I needed her mouth around me.

Now.

She needed no more persuasion—or guidance, for that matter—as she ran her tongue along the length of my cock. Slowly. Tantalizingly.

Her hands joined in the stroking after a moment, closing around me once again and moving up and down in a perfect, excruciating rhythm. At the same time, her mouth teased the tip of me as she'd done with my fingers, lips brushing in the faintest of kisses before sucking and pulling away.

"Wicked thing," I repeated in a growl.

It was an enormous test of control, fighting the urge to drive myself deep into her throat.

I couldn't keep myself from *thinking* about doing this, however—an image that grew bolder with every lash from her tongue and caress from her fingers, until I was sure she'd seen it clearly, judging by the way her strokes grew more purposeful. More persistent.

She adjusted her stance, sinking lower onto her knees so she could take more of me into her mouth. My thoughts seemed to implode, swallowed up by that mouth, lost in the wake of her touch.

With slightly shaking fingers, I pushed her hair from her face, tucking it behind her slender ears. Pieces of it slipped free again within moments. Wild. Beautiful. Messy.

"Look at me," I commanded.

Her gaze fluttered up while her mouth continued to work. The sight of her like this—eyes heavy with lust, lips glistening, breasts heaving—was one of the most beautiful fucking things I'd ever seen.

I wasn't going to last as long as I wanted if we kept this up, so I pushed the loose strands of her hair back once more, cradled her face more gently, and eased her away from me.

"As much as I love the idea of dripping down your throat," I ground out, "I think we have more things we should *practice*."

She responded by resisting my touch, leaning up and taking half my length into her mouth once more, gripping the other half with soft yet certain hands.

After a moment, she pulled up slowly, eyes fixed on my face the entire time, and I nearly lost myself in the rush of hunger that radiated through me.

Wicked thing, indeed.

"Not following directions...that's the sort of thing that could get you in trouble during these lessons," I warned.

She ran her tongue over the dampness coating her lips, her eyes still on me, as if daring me to punish her.

I twisted my hand tightly into her hair again and used the grip to pull her head forward again. I slid deep into her throat. She managed to take nearly two-thirds of my length before I felt the vibrations of a building cough. I held her there for several seconds before allowing her to come up for air.

She sucked in several deep lungfuls of that air only to immediately bring her mouth back, drawing enough of me in to nearly choke once more.

A glutton for punishment, apparently.

I caught her jaw between my fingers, tapping the bulging outline of my cock against her cheek.

"I appreciate your enthusiasm for learning," I growled, pulling away from her, "but we're moving to the next lesson. Turn around."

She gave me a curious look. I grabbed her pants and ripped them down, not bothering with loosening ties or buttons or anything else. The sound of ripping fabric was eclipsed by her sharp gasp.

I barely heard either of them over the thunder of my own pulse and the throb of my magic as it burned hotter, desperate to take her in.

"Turn around. Now."

She did. I finished stripping off the rest of her clothing, then leaned back, taking hold of her legs and prying them apart as I went.

She resisted at first, self-consciousness keeping her thighs close together as she hovered over me. I ran my hands over the soft and ample flesh of her thighs, waiting for her to be ready. Truthfully, I was no God of Patience, but for her, I would take my time. I would have spent an eternity mapping out the shape of her, worshipping and memorizing the mere outlines of her body until she felt comfortable enough to let me into the softer, more sacred parts of it.

As my light, admiring touch circled its way along the back of her thigh, the tension began to slowly melt from her muscles. Her spine arched and her legs eased apart—an invitation.

"Wider," I encouraged, my hands moving to her center, the heat of my fingertips meeting the damp warmth of her arousal.

A quiver went through her. I slid my hand more deliberately against her, cupping her sex, teasing the swollen bud of it with my fingertip. Her legs opened more completely, all sense of hesitation abandoned. I took hold of her once more, positioned her with a few powerful tugs, then wrapped my arms around her waist and pulled her center down to meet my mouth.

She cursed as I planted a trail of soft kisses against her. Several more curses followed as I pressed my fingers hard against the small of her back, holding her down, allowing me to devour her without any more mercy or restraint.

She tasted like she belonged to me. Marked by my fire—like smoke and salt and that particular zest of magic. But there was something else, too, a soft spiciness that was undeniably *her*.

As my tongue pushed deep inside her, driven almost completely mad by the need for more of that spice, her hands found my hardened shaft once more.

Her mouth soon followed.

Her tongue swept across the head of my cock. I groaned without taking my mouth away from her. The vibration of sound and the warmth of my breath spilling over her folds caused her legs to clench together. Her mouth soon returned the favor, lips sucking the tip of my length before closing over it and sliding down, up, down, up.

She moaned as she worked—a particularly sweet sound while she had a mouth full of me—and my hands gripped her legs, fingers digging into her soft skin. Her hips rolled against me, growing increasingly desperate, chasing release.

I considered giving it to her. The way I could have spread her thighs wider and licked, kissed, sucked until she was writhing on top of me, all restraint forgotten. It was enough to drive me mad with desire, just thinking about it, yet it wasn't enough—I wanted more. *Needed* more. Needed to be buried deep inside, filling her with more than the fire and magic I'd already given her.

I didn't bother with commands this time. I simply grabbed her and spun her back around into the position I wanted her in.

I settled her into my lap once more, but this time my cock was free, fully erect and there to meet her. She slid onto it without hesitation. Warm. Dripping wet. Perfect. A little whimper left her as she sank lower, and I moved my hands to her hips, helping to ease her down.

"I know you can take all of it," I murmured, pressing my lips to her hair.

She wrapped her arms around my neck and rocked her body against mine, grinding her way down, slowly taking more and more of me in until her soft cries of pain shifted to pleasurable moans.

"Good girl," I mumbled against her, voice wavering as a shiver went through me.

"Goddess," she corrected, breathlessly.

"Goddess," I agreed, smiling.

I rose onto my knees, adjusting for balance and leverage. My hands slid to her thighs, holding her in place while I drove more fully into her. I moved subtly inside her at first—and occasionally not at all because it was mesmerizing just to be still and watch her face, to see her eyes widen and her lips part as I stretched her and throbbed inside of her.

Her hold around my neck tightened as her head tilted back. I took her by the hips and lifted her slightly, just enough to give myself room to push harder, faster.

She cried out with my first full, fast thrust. The sound was like the first taste of a divine, perfect fruit, leaving me desperately hungry for more. The fire inside me roared, determined to meet hers more completely.

A few more thrusts. A symphony of beautiful sounds cascaded from her mouth. Her back arched with increasingly perfect timing to meet my pounding movements, and a dangerously feral need began to rise within me.

I lowered her onto her back, keeping myself buried deep inside her.

She reached a hand toward the pinnacle of her thighs, fingers sweeping over the dampness we'd created. Her touch grazed my erection as she moved it more furiously against her sex. I matched her quick, needy caresses with faster, deeper thrusts. Her eyes soon fluttered shut, and she started to stretch out her hands, abandoning her sense of control, ready to surrender.

I caught her wrist and held her hand in place. "Keep touching yourself."

She did, her eyes flashing open and fixing on me. Her stare was deliberate. Her touch was equally so, each increasingly fervent stroke pushing her closer to orgasm.

"That's it. That's my goddess."

Her breath caught at the low rumble of my voice. She stroked even harder. Faster.

I lifted her legs, hooking her ankles over my shoulders, elevating her lower back and taking advantage of the angle to drive more deeply into her.

She kept her fingers moving over her center. Her other hand soon joined in. The position pressed her breasts together between her arms, and I was forced to amend my earlier thought—she was even more fucking beautiful now than she'd been with my cock in her mouth.

I tossed my remaining restraint aside and gripped her legs more tightly, rocking harder against her until I felt her climax building, her body shaking from the effort of trying to hold on to the last shreds of control.

I leaned over her, pushing even more completely inside, leaving no space between our bodies. No space for *control*. As I pinned her down, her hands fell to her sides, fingers clawing into the ground. Fire bloomed in her palms. The scent of smoke and scorched earth enveloped us.

I brought my lips to her neck, to the sensitive spot just below her earlobe. The slightest pressure from my tongue made her hips lift and her back arch. I met the movement with one last, powerful thrust. She came as we collided more deeply, her cry echoing through my body, my soul, sinking in and drawing my own release in answer.

We remained pressed together, sweat-slicked bodies heaving for breath, for several moments after. She continued to move beneath me, slowly twisting and turning, wringing out every last drop of pleasure. The air hummed with heat and hints of our still restless, aroused magic.

Once the world ceased its spinning, I wrapped my arms around her, pulling her upright as I settled back into a sitting position.

She cupped her hands against my face, holding herself steady as she pressed her lips to mine. Everywhere we touched still felt electric, tingling, sore in the most pleasant sense of the word.

A cocoon of warm magic settled around us as we drifted down from the heights we'd reached. I closed my eyes and leaned my forehead to hers. She continued to kiss me, her lips dragging lazy, savoring paths over mine.

"You know," she said, finally pulling her face away from mine, "these sort of endings make the training sessions a lot more bearable."

I chuckled. "Agreed. I find it's always good to end on a positive note."

She snorted at this before crawling away and reaching for her clothing.

We dressed, mostly in satisfied silence save for the teasing lecture she gave me about ripping her clothing. Luckily, with a few minor adjustments, these things remained wearable enough—at least for the trip back to the palace.

As she finished fixing her attire into place, her back was to me, her gaze fixed on some distant point on the horizon. I wondered what she was thinking, but I didn't try to pry my way into her thoughts.

Her cheeks were still flushed with the heat of our encounter when she looked back to me. Her hair fell in wild waves around her face. Her eyes seemed an even bolder green than usual. I exhaled slowly, trying to keep my balance.

She was fire and fierceness, my brightness and breath.

She was the most beautiful thing I'd ever seen.

She was also talking—I saw her lips moving, though the words didn't register in my mind right away.

She fixed me with a wry look as she stepped forward and smoothed the front of my shirt, which was still rumpled from being so hastily discarded.

"Are you even listening to me?"

I gave her a roguish smile. "Sorry. I was distracted."

"I asked if we needed to head back," she said. "Valas will have gone to Mairu by now and told her what he told you. They'll want to discuss what comes next; we shouldn't keep them waiting."

"We shouldn't," I agreed, my tone calm and even despite the sudden weight in my chest.

Neither of us felt like walking, but we both wanted to drag this trip out a little longer, I think—which ruled out transporting instantly back into the problems that awaited us at the palace.

I called the selakir instead, summoning the particular vein of magic I shared with the creatures, connecting specifically to that bond I'd developed with Farak over the years. He appeared, accompanied by a gust of wind and spiraling threads of fire, a few moments later.

Zell followed soon after, eagerly kneeling before Karys and allowing her to climb onto his back. The pair of them rocketed forward without hesitation.

Farak snorted at the sight, clearly disgruntled by the overzealous behavior, but he didn't resist when I urged him into a gallop to catch up.

We retraced the path Karys and I had taken earlier, eventually making our way back through the valley full of the Watching Pools. Karys slowed Zell to a trot as we wound our way through them.

"Is it my imagination," she asked, frowning, "or do several of the pools look different than they did a few hours ago?"

I swept my eyes over the area, eventually focusing on the pool in the center—the one that corresponded to my old kingdom. Karys was right; its waters had shifted to an even more ominous shade of dark grey, like heavy storm clouds.

"...More things we need to discuss with the others," I said, nudging Farak back into motion. "Let's keep moving."

She nodded. Though she looked hesitant, Zell was already breaking into a run once more, his form becoming little more than a fiery gold blur as he swept up the far hillside.

Farak, perhaps sensing my unease, carried on at a much slower trot, occasionally tossing his head and fixing his shining dark eyes on me as if to ask, *What is happening?*

We reached the top of the hill overlooking the pools. I glanced back one last time, my eyes immediately finding the one in the center.

And I would have sworn its waters had already turned even darker.

CHAPTER 20

Karys

THREE MORE DAYS PASSED IN RELATIVE PEACE AND QUIET. I continued to concern myself mostly with practicing magic, letting Dravyn focus on gathering and sorting through reports about the mortal realm and the things threatening it.

He'd left earlier that morning, his sights set on making his way into the training grounds he'd told me about—Mindoth's Keep. I'd considered going with him, still unable to forget the state he'd been in after his last visit to his old kingdom. He'd insisted I stay and keep working on my magic, however. And I needed all the practice I could get; I couldn't argue against that.

So Valas had gone with him instead, and I'd done my best to stay calm and focused on what I needed to do, while trusting that they could take care of things elsewhere. Dravyn wasn't alone in that kingdom of blood and bad memories... That was the most important thing. He would be back soon. He would be fine.

He would be fine.

That still didn't stop me from focusing my inner fire every few minutes, thinking of him and hoping I would feel his warmth reaching back.

In the meantime, Mairu and I had made our way to the outermost edge of the Fire Palace's grounds. There was an observatory here, a tall tower made largely of glass. It had several balconies, as well as wide, decorative ledges that were easy enough to access by climbing through the countless windows.

A variety of prime launching spots, in other words.

So far, I'd only worked up the courage to jump from the second-lowest balcony and the ledges around it. It was proving helpful, though —necessity was an excellent teacher, as Dravyn had pointed out, so I simply kept jumping and forcing myself to further develop my wings on the way down.

I still hadn't accomplished much in the way of sustained flight. I'd managed to not crash or break any part of my body, though. And after several hours of practice, my landings were becoming *almost* graceful. My confidence was soaring a bit as well, so I decided to chance a higher jump.

I pushed my worries about Dravyn and the mortal kingdom down and marched to the next highest balcony. To reach it required walking through a room that smelled of leather, old books, and ink. Diagrams lined the walls. Most featured what looked like the sky filled with different sized spheres—forgelights, I realized.

There were copious notes about different luminosities, angles, and more, all written in Dravyn's blocky, heavy handwriting; this tower must have been where he worked on perfecting those creations of his.

It was oddly comforting, seeing these displays. So much of this realm and its magic seemed effortless...it was nice to know he occasionally had to take notes and experiment with things.

I pulled the doors open and stepped onto the balcony, squinting in the bright haziness. The sky was the color of watery milk and glowing softly, courtesy of one of those burning forgelights in the distance.

Heart pounding, I walked to the edge of the balcony and hoisted myself up onto the railing, one hand pressed against a column for balance. I made sure to step onto the rail left foot first—an old habit I fell into when I was trying to avoid catastrophes. Pointless, maybe, but I couldn't keep myself from completing the ritual.

One foot, then the other. The ground seemed a million miles away. Warmth pooled against my back. I closed my eyes, imagining that warmth turning solid and shaping into feathers.

As my wings took shape, they caught more of the heat rolling off my body and started to lift, carrying me up to my tiptoes before I came to my senses and grabbed the column once more.

Mai waved from below, signaling that she was ready to intervene in case of disaster.

Stepping off the edge was always the hardest part. To have solidness beneath me one moment, only to lose it the next...I hated that sensation. So I didn't hesitate more than a few seconds. I would lose my nerve if I did.

Two deep breaths.

One big step.

Then *whoosh*—I was falling, ground rising fast below me, wings flaring out beside me, body twisting in a wild, ultimately useless effort to right itself.

As my wings extended further, more fiery feathers building upon them even as I fell, my descent slowed. I jerked nearly to a stop in mid-air. My stomach heaved. The sky spun around me.

I was no longer thinking about merely surviving the fall—which should have been freeing. But instead, I became all too aware of every single feather and flame holding me up. Of how little control I had over these things. How little I understood the magic that had created them.

I started to sink.

The harder I tried to understand it all, the faster I fell.

The wings resisted my every attempt at control. I was careening faster than ever toward the ground and failure—too fast.

Much too fast.

Just before I hit, I managed to twist so I could break the fall with my wings rather than my body. I rolled across the ground, wrapped in flames and feathers, eventually coming to rest flat on my back.

I stayed there for a long moment, every part of me aching. Heat still blazed against my back, hotter than ever, even as my wings were disintegrating, pieces of them floating away into the sky.

Mai grabbed my hand and pulled me to my feet. "I thought you were going to properly take off on me that time," she said encouragingly. "You're getting closer."

I sighed, absently twisting my hand through the smoke and embers over my shoulder—what little remained of my wings. "It's the same problem I had when trying to master the transporting spell."

"Thinking too much?"

I nodded. "As soon as the wings slow my descent, there's too much space in my mind for calculating. And by my calculations, none of this magic makes any logical sense."

"Who needs logic?" she teased.

"*I* do."

"Right." She waved a dismissive hand. "Well, we just need to find a way to make you *stop* thinking."

"Valas suggested I try it in an *altered state of mind*. It sounded ridiculous at the time, but I don't know. Maybe I'd be more successful if I was drunk—and relaxed—right now."

She gave me a crooked grin, shaking her head. "If he offers you something to alter your mind, I'd strongly suggest *not* taking it. It might help you fly, but there's no telling where to, or what kind of state you'll be in when you land."

"You speak like you have experience."

"An embarrassing collection of experiences I'd rather not talk about."

I mirrored her grin. "Noted."

"Let's take a break," she suggested. "They should be back soon."

I wasn't ready to give up without more progress, but I was eager to see Dravyn and Valas as soon as possible, so I agreed, picking up the coat I'd draped on a nearby tree and slinging it over my shoulder.

We started to set a course back toward the main palace but only made it a few steps before I sensed foreign energies coming toward us.

"A guest?" I wondered, looking back.

"Two of them."

I concentrated on trying to feel out their identities. They carried Sun Court energy, I thought.

"Keep your head up," Mai said under her breath. "Don't let them get under your skin. I'm sure they'll try to."

They emerged from the backdrop of bright sky a minute later—two of the Sun Court Marr, both shifted into beastly forms.

Cepheid, Goddess of Stars, came first. She was in the form of a great stag. I'd never seen her in this shape before, but the patterns on her body gave her identity away—inky black as a night sky with swirls of shifting lights upon it. Each point of her massive antlers shimmered, too, as though she'd speared stars onto the ends.

The Sky Goddess, Edea, resembled a lankier version of the panther-like shape Valas often took. The coloring of her form made me think of clouds that were edged in gold from hiding the sun. A telltale trail of her cerulean-colored magic followed in her wake.

The two goddesses touched gently onto the ground, their shapes shifting into more humanoid figures as they approached us—though Cepheid retained a smaller version of the stag's star-tipped antlers, and Edea's cerulean magic still trailed after her, the shape shimmering as it swished and curled like a cat's tail.

My mouth had fallen open, I realized. I quickly closed it and tried to avert my eyes. I wanted to appear indifferent, but it was hard not to be overwhelmed by their display of power. Hard not to wonder if I would ever manage to shift and move through the realms as easily they did...

This last part seemed unlikely after a day spent tumbling from the tower behind me, giving everything I had just to keep myself from crashing.

"We've come to speak with the ruler of this territory," said the Star Goddess in her soft but unsettlingly powerful voice. "Where is he?"

"Dravyn isn't here." I lifted my chin. "You can speak to me."

The two Sun Court Marr exchanged a slow, meaningful glance. They spoke to one another in the language of their own court, the words rapid and tense, their gazes occasionally drifting in my direction. They didn't bother trying to hide their disdain.

Clearly trying to rattle me, as Mai had predicted they would.

I cleared my throat. Loudly. "You can sense the magic of your fellow Marr, can you not?"

They stopped their private conference. The Goddess of Sky gave a single, slight tip of her head.

"But you couldn't tell Dravyn wasn't here? You must have felt little difference in my magic and his before you arrived, then. So why treat me differently, now?"

Edea sneered at my challenge before turning away and scanning the palace in the distance, as if she didn't fully believe Dravyn wasn't here— as if I might have been hiding him somewhere.

The Star Goddess looked me in the eyes, at least. "A fair point."

I glared back at her, refusing to back down, even as the silence between us stretched far beyond the point of comfortable.

"Very well," she finally said. "You can serve as a messenger, I suppose." Her gaze darted around the space, taking in the few embers still burning here and there. Were those yet more errant bits of my broken wings?

I wondered if Cepheid could sense my failed attempts at flight. Her magic gave her an eerie ability to see past, present, and future; what did she see when she looked at me?

"Tell your God of Fire that our court is not interested in the wars building in the mortal realm," she said. "We have decided to let fate run its course without any guidance from our hands. Not that he needs us to help with whatever meddling he and the rest of your court intend to do." She swatted at a floating bit of fire as though it were an annoying fly.

"Clearly, you have all the power you need, anyway," the Sky Goddess added, nodding toward a cluster of my scattered embers with a smirk. "And it's perfectly under your control, isn't it?"

I didn't reply.

I simply reached out a hand and curled my fingers into a fist. The motion—and the furious power simmering beneath it—brought all of the wayward embers flying back toward me, swirling them into a torch around my clenched fist.

I didn't try to shape them into wings this time. Instead, I imagined a sharp point. I stretched out my fingertips until the fire stretched with it, creating a flaming blade twice the length of my arm.

I inhaled and exhaled a deliberate breath that brought more fire flickering into the air around me.

Without taking my eyes of the Sun Court goddesses, I twisted my wrist as if rebalancing my sword. The small movements drew the newly-summoned embers in tighter, solidifying and lengthening the flaming weapon.

The Sky Goddess tossed the thick waves of her shining black hair over her shoulder and averted her gaze, pretending to be interested in something in the distance.

The Star Goddess watched my sword building, her disdain turning to curiosity as I pointed the burning tip at her chest.

"If that's all you needed to tell me," I said, "you can be on your way now."

Cepheid didn't flinch.

Edea started to move on her behalf, but the Star Goddess held up her hand and brought her to a stop.

Cepheid's eyes remained cold and fixed on me.

I willed myself not to shake, to not let the blade drop.

"An impressive weapon," said the Star Goddess. The words bordered on mocking, but her lips curved in an odd way as she looked the fiery blade up and down—as if something like begrudging respect was starting to break through.

I was probably imagining it.

She took a step back, rolling her shoulders. As she did, starry ribbons shot out from her back and twisted into the shape of bat-like wings. They were nearly transparent, save for their edges, until she gave a slow, lazy test flap. Then they came to life, the thin membranes darkening from pale blue to a rich shade of indigo dotted with glowing bits of white. It was like watching a sky turn from midday to midnight in a matter of seconds.

"Make sure you give the God of Fire my message," she said.

"I'll make it my top priority," I replied.

If she could read the sarcasm in my tone, she gave no indication of it. In a slightly lower voice, she added, "I won't intervene, but I'll be watching the movements of that mortal realm—and you—with great interest."

Before I could think of a response, she gave a slight bow of her head and then leapt into the air, soaring and twisting away with breathtaking grace and ease.

After one last smirk in my direction, the Sky Goddess followed, disappearing in a flash of turquoise light only to reappear at Cepheid's side far in the distance.

Alone with Mairu once more, I flicked my wrist, breaking up the shape of my summoned sword and sending the pieces of it flying in all directions.

"That *was* impressive," Mai said, watching the scattering sword for a moment before collecting her bag, which was hanging from the same tree I'd used as a coat rack.

I took the first deep, normal breath I'd taken in several minutes. "It was mostly fueled by spite," I admitted.

She shrugged. "So? I'd say at least two-thirds of what I do is motivated by spite." She took an apple-like fruit from the bag, polishing it on the flowing hem of her shirt before she added, "Some days it's the only reason I get out of bed."

I giggled a bit at this, releasing more of the tension that had gathered in my chest. She tossed me the fruit, took out another for herself, and we strolled side-by-side back into the palace while enjoying them.

"Dravyn once told me you and the Goddess of Stars don't get along very well," I said, in-between bites.

She snorted. "It's complicated."

"Why am I not surprised? The Marr are complicated in general, aren't they?"

"Yes. But in this case...I am the goddess most often associated with change and control," she reminded me, balancing her half-eaten fruit on the tip of her outstretched palm.

I watched as she narrowed her eyes in concentration and the fruit began to spin, its shiny skin unraveling in a tidy spiral to reveal the juicy pink flesh underneath.

"Cepheid is more concerned with fate and the glimpses of destiny she sees in her stars," Mai continued. "She's inclined to believe that mortals are bound to these things. And many of them are, of course—but there are always a few who rebel against the stars' control and make a mess. I champion those mortals who aren't afraid of these messy, daring changes; she can't stand them. So we're at odds to begin with.

"And over the years we've gotten into many arguments regarding such things." She shrugged. "I'm not surprised they won't be joining us. Cepheid doesn't meddle in the affairs of the mortal realm whenever she can help it, and she's the oldest and arguably most powerful of her court. When she refuses something, the others tend to follow her lead. Even Halar."

I tried to picture the demure Star Goddess commanding the brutish Storm God.

I couldn't.

"It's probably just as well if Halar doesn't join us if we do descend upon Avalinth," Mai said. "He'd likely only make a bigger mess of whatever we ultimately try to do, or whatever battles we end up fighting."

I agreed, though it would have been nice to have some of the Sun Court alongside us. The Sky Goddess, for example...so many mortals prayed to her and built temples to praise her for her protective magic, and for what?

Just so she could turn away from them when their world and its wars got too messy?

"Hopefully, it won't come to a battle," I thought aloud.

Our current plan was not to choose a side or fuel the animosity between them, but rather to try and find a way to de-escalate the situation.

It had been my idea. If Dravyn and Valas could track down Cillian, then I could do the rest. He helped me escape my old home, after all—he was one of the few willing to disagree with and stand up to Andrel. So whatever operation he was helping to lead in Mindoth...I could convince him to put a stop to it.

I hoped.

We reached the main doors to the palace. Moth swept down from his perch on one of the nearby turrets, greeting us with a series of flying loops before crashing into my arms with enough force to send me stumbling backward. As I caught my balance, he peeked up at me through the waves of hair he'd tangled himself in. His owl-like eyes blinked in an almost sheepish manner.

"Still a better landing than any I've managed today," I reassured him, carefully untangling his head from my tresses.

He snatched a lock of hair in his mouth and clamped down on it in reply, his tail swishing affectionately.

Mairu walked ahead of us, letting herself through the massive iron doors. Her footsteps echoed loudly across the marble floors, making the palace sound even more empty than it felt. She paused as she reached the center of the atrium, the corners of her mouth twitching as if fighting off a frown.

"Still no sign of them," I said.

Uncertainty flashed in the Serpent Goddess's usually confident gaze. "I have a few other things I need to take care of," she said, "but I could stay and wait on them with you, if you'd like me to."

"I'll be okay on my own, thank you."

Moth gave the hair in his mouth a sharp tug.

"I'm not *entirely* on my own, after all," I amended.

Mairu smiled wryly at the griffin's antics before lifting her gaze back to mine. "I'll return soon," she promised.

I waved goodbye and made my way farther inside, searching for things to occupy myself with other than worrying.

I found Rieta asleep by one of the fireplaces in the main study, a basket of cloth and other supplies at her feet, her body hunched over a garment she'd been sewing. Another shirt for me, it looked like. The deep scarlet fabric pooled in a beautifully soft manner. She'd woven slightly darker, shinier red threads in subtle patterns along the flowing sleeves, and movement—her body rising and falling along with her snores—made those threads gleam faintly in the firelight. A simple yet elegant piece, flirting between mortal and divine in appearance; she was a master at creating such garments, I'd found out.

It would have been nice to talk with her—I'd thought of approximately a thousand more questions about her and Dravyn's life in the royal city of Altis since we'd last spoken of it—but she was sleeping so deeply I didn't want to bother her.

Instead, I eased her into a more comfortable position, grabbed a throw blanket from a chest in the corner, draped it over her shoulders, and quietly continued on.

I soon regretted not asking Mai to stay.

The palace was too large, too dark, too quiet to wander in alone. It might have been my home now, but it was harder to think of it as such whenever Dravyn wasn't here.

Even my room, which had been filled to the brim with gifts and decor curated specifically by me and for me, didn't feel right. I rested on my bed for only a few moments before I felt the urge to get up and head back into the main parts of the palace—just in case I'd somehow not sensed Dravyn and Valas returning.

But no...still no sign of them.

I soon sensed another presence, however; a surge of power that rushed in and then immediately flickered to a barely noticeable hum— like something had transported close by and then tried to cloak its arrival.

I went to the nearest window, searching.

A spidery, shadowy form scurried just out of sight—the same shadowy form I'd seen outside of Dravyn's bedroom days ago, and a few times before that.

I was becoming more and more certain of it: Something was following me.

Watching me.

I was afraid to get a closer look, but I did it anyway, pressing into the large, curving window and angling myself so I could study the thick rows of hedges that stood around the yard. One of those hedges rustled with movement. Glowing eyes peered through a tangle of leaves and branches.

I stumbled back with a gasp.

The instant I caught myself and moved forward once more for a closer look, the spying creature was gone.

"Did you see that?" I asked Moth, who was busy chasing his own tail, trying to put the flaming tip out by smashing it under his paws. The griffin stumbled to a stop at the sound of my voice, settling back on his haunches and cocking his head in confusion.

Clearly, he hadn't seen or sensed anything.

Dravyn hadn't seemed overly concerned when I mentioned it the other morning, either. So maybe it was nothing? Just a trick of the light and magic in this place—part of its strangeness that I was still trying to get used to…

I went back to wandering. I eventually ended up in the same place I often did: Within the gallery of glass art Dravyn had created.

It spanned several rooms, the largest of which served as his workshop. It smelled as if the oven in that workshop had been used recently —he must have been working in here after I'd fallen asleep last night.

On what? I wondered.

I lit the torches by the doorway while Moth bounded ahead of me into the first room, his eyes wide and his body trembling with excitement as he took in the beauty gleaming all around us.

"No touching anything," I warned him. He had a tendency to try and steal the shiny glass figures; I'd already stumbled on several tiny hoards he'd stashed throughout the palace.

His wings and ears drooped at my command, but I didn't give in.

"You'll be all right without more shiny objects," I said, bending and scooping him into my arms. "You have plenty of other things to entertain yourself with." He had more than enough, really.

Despite Dravyn's insistence that Moth was a monster he could do without, he absolutely spoiled the creature with toys and trinkets.

I held Moth to my chest as I circled the room, studying each of Dravyn's creations. Most of the collection was familiar to me by now, yet the light never seemed to hit the figures in exactly the same way; I always felt like there was more to see and discover within the colorful prisms.

As I came to the table that held rows upon rows of red, rectangular sculptures, I froze in place, thinking again of the monument I'd encountered in Ederis.

Two-hundred and thirty-two, he'd told me—one red rectangle for each of the elves he'd killed when he'd leveled that city years ago.

I'd never actually counted them, but I had memorized the pattern they stood in—so I noticed it had changed since my last visit. He'd added more to the right of the collection. Markers for the ones killed in recent weeks, I assumed.

The graveyard was getting very crowded.

My muscles tensed. I squeezed Moth more tightly without realizing I was doing it, causing him to let out a little squeak before giving my arm a vicious poke with his beak.

"Sorry." I loosened my hold on him, though I hardly registered the pain from his attack; I was too busy thinking of the lush grass, the blue flowers, the towering white stone...

I hadn't spoken to Dravyn about the stone or all the names that had been etched into it. I'd tried—several times, in fact. The words always fell short.

What else was there to say about the matter?

We both knew what he'd done. There was no undoing it. We had decided to move forward, and that was that.

I pried my gaze away from the grave markers.

My attention moved instead to a pale blue willow tree on a nearby table—another sculpture that had caught my eye the very first time I'd visited this room. I'd since learned that Dravyn had made it in memory of his sister.

Carefully, I put Moth down, and I picked up the tree and studied it. I'd never found the courage to lift this fragile object before, but this time the compulsion was too much to resist.

His sister's name was carved into the bottom of the trunk, I noticed.

Elora.

As my fingers traced the thin, swirling letters, it was hard to keep my mind from jumping to thoughts of my own sister.

My chest burned as if the scars upon it had ripped open. My hands started to shake. Moth weaved in and out of my legs, occasionally nuzzling his head against them.

"Why did I come in here?" I asked, giving him a sad smile. "I'm such an idiot sometimes."

I placed the tree carefully back in its spot and started to turn away, but something else caught my eye as I did—another new figure.

It stood alone on the other side of the table: An elegant, magnificent bird with flowing wings and a trailing tail, its feathers rendered in a myriad of fiery colors. Reds and oranges, warm hints of purples and blues…how had he managed all these different colors? What had inspired such a masterpiece?

My heart pounded as I stared at it, though I had no idea why.

Before I could reach for it or study it closer, a sudden flood of warmth overtook me.

Moth abandoned me and pranced over to the door, tail swishing expectantly.

Neither of us was surprised when the God of Fire joined us a minute later.

And despite all of my confusing, messy thoughts, the sight of him standing in the doorway still pulled a sigh of relief from my lips.

I still went to his side and wrapped my arms around him, losing myself in his strength, in the smoke and cedar scent that clung to him. I still wanted to stay caught up in these things, indefinitely.

I still loved him, mess and all.

Or maybe it was *because* of the mess. Because he'd trudged through the wreckage to find his way back to me, time and time again. Because he knew how to live in the shadow of graveyards, and how to navigate around ruined and broken things, same as I did.

He kissed the top of my head before drawing back. Torchlight spilled over his face. I noticed how dull his eyes were, how tightly his jaw was clenched—how tightly *every* part of him was clenched. It was as if he was afraid he might collapse into total exhaustion if he relaxed even the tiniest bit.

"You seem tired."

"Much less so," he insisted, "now that I'm back at your side."

I warmed at the words. My hand found his, and I focused on that warmth, letting it build between us since it seemed to help ease the stiffness from his tired shoulders. I wanted nothing more than to lose myself more completely in him and our kindling heat, to pull him toward his bedroom—toward rest—and lock the doors behind us.

Instead, I told him of my practice and the goddesses who had stopped by for a visit. I delivered Cepheid's message word for word… though I left out the part where I'd nearly impaled the Star Goddess with a blade of fire. He clearly had enough on his mind; there was no need to add to it.

His gaze was distant as I finished, fixed in the direction of the bird statue I'd been studying.

"What happened in the mortal realm? You and Valas were gone much longer than I expected you would be."

He didn't reply right away, but I could sense the unease rolling off him. The torches reacted to his mood as well, their fires dancing brighter, wilder. The flare of extra light made the glass figures gleam brighter, highlighting all their edges.

It felt like we were surrounded by swords, suddenly, all their sharp tips shining, pointed directly at us.

I locked my eyes with Dravyn's, urging him to continue.

"We've found Cillian," he said after a pause. "And if you're going to speak with him as planned, we need to move quickly. I don't think we have much time left before everything in Avalinth goes to hell."

CHAPTER 21

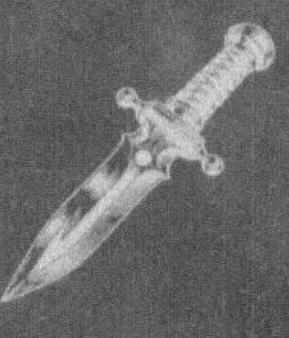

Karys

THE FOLLOWING EVENING, DRAVYN, VALAS, MAIRU, AND I traveled together to the easternmost edge of the Kingdom of Galizur.

As Mairu had predicted, the rest of the Star Goddess's court had followed her lead and chosen to ignore whatever was happening in Avalinth. The Stone Court had been of a similar mind—though the Healing God had mentioned he'd be monitoring the situation and willing to aid us if we returned with any injuries, at least.

The final member of our own court rarely visited the mortal realm, so it was no surprise when Zachar also declined to join us.

So the rest of the Shade Court came alone to where the land narrowed into a peninsula that jutted out into the tranquil turquoise waters of the Kelden Sea.

Mindoth's Keep, the premier training grounds of the Galithian Army, stood in the center of this jutting land.

The waters on either side were filled with ships. Warships—manned by trainees and seasoned soldiers, alike—made up the bulk of them, but there were also vessels carrying various goods of all kinds, most of them hailing from the continent to the north, or the islands in between that continent and Galizur. Part of the training that took place here involved protecting incoming supplies and seeing them properly distributed.

Given all this, the area was well-protected, overall—save for one unfortunate feature: There were an astonishing number of tunnels that crisscrossed beneath it.

Some were natural, a vast network of beach caves that started along the shores of the peninsula, weaved throughout it, and reached for several miles inland. Others were manmade extensions of those caves that had been dug out decades ago. They provided an extra place to hoard supplies, or even to hide people. A few were long enough, and strategic enough, to provide relatively safe, secret routes in and out of the region. Useful in many ways—but they also created a weakness that could be exploited.

Most of the caves had been closed off in recent years, Dravyn told me, because their potentially vulnerable points outweighed their possible benefits.

I knew Cillian, though. He didn't need much to work with to get his job done.

If *any* vulnerable point remained, he would find it—and he would know the exact weapon to use to bring it crashing down.

As the four of us made our way through the forest of towering pines on the outskirts of the training compound, my mind raced with memories of all the things I'd watched Cillian destroy over the years.

Soon my lungs were burning, my eyes watering, as if I was standing once more in the rubble and dust of one of his explosions.

Dravyn spoke quietly as we darted through the trees, briefing us again on the things he and Valas had discovered previously.

I wiped the moisture from my eyes and tried to hang on to his every word, letting those words pull me away from thoughts of exploding and collapsing things.

"We spotted two encampments during our last visit," he was saying, "one to the north of the Greyveil Peninsula, one to the south. There may be more scattered about. But Cillian was in the northern one, so that's where we're heading. Not far, now."

To our right, we often caught glimpses of the sea and its ships, as well as the occasional outline of walls and battlements, of high watch-towers and drably-colored, sprawling garrisons.

Dravyn knew the area fairly well, as he'd spent some time there with his father and older brother, making inspection rounds and getting first-hand reports from the officers. He'd never taken part in the actual train-ings that went on, but he could answer most of my questions about what we were seeing—even the questions I didn't ask out loud—which helped me map out our surroundings and plans, calming my nerves somewhat.

After a few minutes we veered away from the sea. The ground grew more hilly, the trees thicker. We reached the crest of a particularly steep slope and paused. Valas pointed at something far in the distance. Squint-ing, I could just make out the tiniest glimmer of light through tightly twisting tree branches.

"Lantern light?"

The four of us crept toward it.

We came to a group of guards before we reached the light, but we disposed of them quickly and silently; Mai used her magic to control the very breath in their lungs, holding it until all five of them slumped into unconsciousness.

"I sometimes forget how efficiently you can kill," Valas told her, eyes widening slightly. "It's absolutely terrifying."

He sounded like he was complimenting her, but her gaze was fierce as she snapped it toward him and whispered back, "I didn't kill them."

I wondered how many she *had* killed in the past, suddenly realizing I didn't know much about her ascension. She was a master of control, now, but had she been a monster in the beginning, too, like so many of the other Marr? A slight chill swept over my skin.

Now wasn't the time for that conversation, maybe.

"It's still quiet," Dravyn commented, motioning to the camp ahead of us.

"That's a good thing, right?" Mai asked.

I tentatively agreed, though I shouldn't have. After years of rebel missions alongside Cillian, I knew the calmness before an explosion all too well...how quickly things could go from absolute stillness to total madness.

We moved to a better vantage point where we could size up the camp in its entirety. It was small, but tightly packed and buzzing with activity. Like a hornet's nest.

"So Cillian is likely here somewhere..." I began.

"The question is *where*?" Valas wondered. "We probably shouldn't go person to person inquiring about him. That might look a touch suspicious."

"And we need to move quickly," Dravyn added. "It's only a matter of time before someone notices that their watchmen are unconscious and stuffed in the bushes."

We considered the problem for a moment before Mairu offered a solution. "If one of us creates some sort of commotion, it will likely draw their leaders' attention, if only briefly."

"Flush them out, you mean?"

"Exactly."

I nodded slowly, understanding. "...And one of those leaders will be Cillian."

Valas cleared his throat and gave a little bow. "The God of Commotion and Chaos, at your service."

"Just enough chaos to get their attention," Mairu warned. "We aren't here to escalate this war, remember."

"You speak as though you think I have no self-restraint."

She gave him a withering look.

He smiled.

She coughed. "Right. Moving on." Her gaze narrowed on the camp. "We should probably have eyes and ears in the midst of the camp itself. I can disguise myself and walk among them easily enough, which should allow me to overhear the information we need to pinpoint Cillian."

"And once we do," I said, "I can corner him and talk to him alone."

"And I'll stay close and make sure you aren't interrupted," Dravyn added.

"Perfect," said Valas, rubbing his hands together. "There's no way any of this can go wrong, right?"

I laughed nervously.

"Let's just get on with it," Dravyn said.

Mai was already changing. In the span of a few heartbeats she had lost the radiant luster of her divine body and transformed into a perfectly dull figure with pointed ears, mousy brown hair, and a pleasantly warm, round face—a stark contrast to her normal, fiercely beautiful appearance.

She looked expectantly to Valas before turning and heading into the camp.

The God of Winter set off in the opposite direction.

Dravyn and I held our position, watching and waiting.

Soon, I could no longer see Valas—but I could sense his magic rising.

He began sowing his chaos by targeting the dim lanterns spaced throughout the camp. One after the other they went out, ice crawling into the glass and choking out the flame within.

As the darkness deepened, ice overtook the branches of the trees surrounding the camp as well. Creaks and groans filled the air, followed by violent cracks and crashes as the weight of the ice snapped the weaker branches and sent them plummeting downward.

Lastly, a shimmering, cold mist swept over the area, moving in a way that was clearly unnatural. It left a fine, sparkling film upon everything it touched. In some places the mist pooled, gathering into the shape of beasts that roamed about like ghosts.

These phantom creatures were the breaking point—as soon as they appeared, the shouts began in earnest, panic spreading from one end of the camp to the other as the elves rushed about grabbing weapons and searching for the source of the frigid, invading magic.

"The ghosts are a bit much," Dravyn said under his breath.

"If they keep eyes off us, I'll forgive his showiness, just this once."

"Fair enough."

We drew our hooded cloaks tightly around ourselves and carefully weaved into the chaos.

Between the hoods, the increased darkness, and the distractions Valas had created, we were able to almost completely avoid unwanted attention.

I listened for the sound of Mairu's voice among the shouting. She was melding perfectly with the panicking crowd, calling out orders to stay calm—as if she was not only an elf who belonged in this place, but one with authority. She was also calling out a question that seemed perfectly reasonable from a person trying to maintain order: *Cillian... where is Cillian?*

After she'd gotten her answers, I felt her magic crawling over me, turning my head in her direction. She discreetly signaled for me to walk toward her.

We stepped away from the crowds, and she covertly relayed the details she'd gathered to Dravyn and me.

Following her information brought us to the very edge of the camp, to a sloping hill that led down to a clearing where a circle of tents had been erected. Dravyn paused at the top of the hill, keeping one eye on the chaotic camp behind us while I crept my way toward the clearing below.

I caught a flash of blond hair darting between the shadowy trunks. A male figure moving on light, silent feet. His gait seemed familiar.

Cillian?

I pressed myself flat against the nearest tree, holding my breath as I studied his tall figure in the falling darkness, making sure it was really him.

It was.

He spoke briefly to a soldier who had been standing guard at the largest of the tents. He waved this soldier away—pointing him toward the chaos still building in the main camp—then he disappeared inside the tent.

Nothing between us now except a short stretch of forest and a flimsy flap of canvas.

Dravyn stayed on top of the hill, keeping watch. The space between us felt vast, but warmth reached through it a moment later, settling in my bones, and I heard his voice in my mind—

I'm watching over you. Go.

Before I could lose my nerve, I went.

I ran straight for the tent, hesitating only an instant before crashing inside, nearly colliding with Cillian in the process.

He stumbled back, reflexively whipping the short sword from his side and pointing it at me.

I lifted my palms and moved into the soft glow of the lantern hanging from the tent's center.

He gasped. Shook his head. Slowly lowered his sword. "Karys? Is that really you?"

I was speechless for a moment, all of my carefully-rehearsed lines forgotten, my body trembling as I tried to suppress the storm of emotions rising inside me.

"What the hell are you doing here?" he asked.

I forced myself to remember the plans I'd made, the lists of questions I'd planned to ask. The storm inside me quieted. I lowered my hands and took a step closer to Cillian. "I've come to stop you."

"...Stop me?"

"To make you see reason. I...I know what you and the other rebels are planning to do tonight, and you *can't* go through with it. An attack on this place will trigger complete war."

He stared at me as though I was speaking an entirely different language.

Because *complete war* was the plan, of course. I knew that. I was just hoping he would deny it.

I wanted him to lie. To try and hide what he was doing, because that would mean he was at least somewhat ashamed of it. And if he had shame—and regret—somewhere in his heart, maybe I could still get him to change his mind.

He sheathed his sword, turning away from me and walking to a small folding desk that had been set up against the back of the tent.

The space seemed to expand around us, the air thinning as it did.

"I'm glad you're safe." His voice was quiet. Conflicted, I thought, which gave me a glimmer of hope.

But then he looked over his shoulder, and I saw the resolve settling among the shadows on his face. He looked older than I remembered, and somehow smaller—like a distant relative of the person I'd known.

"I'm glad you're safe," he repeated, quieter. "But that doesn't change what has to be done tonight."

"Nothing has to be done," I whispered, fiercely.

"No? So things stay the same, then. The humans continue to multiply and drive us to extinction while the gods champion their cause." He braced his hands against the table. Several of his fingers were wrapped in dirty bandages, I noticed. Another tattered strip of cloth covered his right forearm.

It was not surprising; he was always nicking or burning or otherwise maiming his skin during all his experiments with weapons. This, combined with my talent for healing, had given us plenty of opportunities to bond over the years. And perhaps I had exchanged my healing prowess for more fiery ambitions, but I still had to fight the urge to scold him for not keeping his bandages cleaner.

"Have you already forgotten what it was like to live in this realm?" he asked. "To be beaten down a little more each day? To be fallen and cursed?"

I moved to the other side of the table. There was a symbol carved into its center, dissected by the line of its hinged folding point—a circle containing the vine and thorn wrapped daggers of the once-powerful elven House of Moreth. It made me think of Andrel and his family's manor—this symbol had graced so much of the furniture back in that old home of his.

My stomach twisted. I couldn't bring myself to touch the wood, to steady myself against the table even as Cillian lifted his gaze to me and my balance swayed.

His smile was strained. He refused to let it disappear entirely—like he was trying his best to return to an easier time, when we used to spend hours talking about anything and everything—the good, the bad, the messy. "You don't remember, do you?"

"Cillian, I..."

He averted his eyes. "I heard rumors that you snuck your way into Ederis a few days ago."

I didn't deny it.

"Some of the witnesses swear they saw you summon fire."

My breath hitched.

"Is it true? Are you so close with the gods now that they've granted you divine magic?"

He didn't have any idea just how *close* I was.

None of them did, I realized.

Andrel knew more than anyone, probably, but who knew what he'd told them—how he'd picked apart and distorted the truth to suit his own agenda. I was scared to think about it.

"I'm glad at least one of our kind has the power we once did, and yet..." He stared past me, frowning. "Whatever they've given you, I'm sure there will be a steep price for it. Monsters don't give without expecting anything in return."

"Not all of the gods are monsters."

He hesitated. Had he even heard what I said? Was he truly considering the possibility?

Another flutter of hope stirred in my chest as the seconds ticked by.

But then he asked, "What about our kind, then? Are we the monsters? All of us?"

I fumbled for a response but didn't find one before he kept talking.

"The humans think so. They treat us as such no matter what, so how could we act any different?" He spoke in a quiet, almost thoughtful tone. Even now, while my own heart felt like it might pound right out of my chest, he was the pillar of calmness he'd always been to me.

"You aren't a monster," I told him. "Not the same kind as Andrel and his followers. I *know* you aren't. You helped me escape the last time we saw each other."

I had replayed that scene endlessly in my mind over the past weeks, but there was no flash of recognition in his bright green eyes as I spoke of it.

It felt very far away, suddenly, as if it had happened in another lifetime. In some ways, I guess it had.

"Cillian, *listen to me*. Please. It isn't so black and white as we—as I—once thought it was."

He again seemed briefly intrigued by the idea, only to ultimately shrug it off. The gesture felt more tired than dismissive, like he was on the verge of giving up, too exhausted to keep carrying the crushing weight of all our kind's struggles on his shoulders. Like he needed to shrug at least some of it away if he was going to keep moving.

"I don't mind being called a monster, for what it's worth," he said, his tone still hushed. "Sometimes, it takes a few seemingly monstrous actions to make things happen for the greater good. You know that. How many conversations have you and I had about this very thing?"

A lot.

More than I could count. But he seemed different from the Cillian I'd had those conversations with.

Or maybe I was the one who had changed.

My heart no longer pounded. It felt like it was shriveling up instead. I desperately wanted to let the rest of me do the same, but I kept talking.

"How many?" I asked. If I couldn't talk him out of his plans to cause further destruction, I at least needed to gather details about what those plans entailed.

His eyes turned glassy. He didn't answer me.

"Cillian, *how many weapons have you planted*? How many soldiers are you ordering into the keep tonight?"

Still nothing.

"How many lives are you planning to take?"

He finally snapped out of his stoic stance. His tone was a mixture of barely-suppressed anger and bitterness as he said, "It isn't about taking individual lives. It's about the bigger picture. The future. *Our* future. You were an important fixture of that future, once upon a time."

"I haven't abandoned you all, I speak for the gods at the moment, but I...I..."

"If you are here to speak for the gods, then you speak in favor of the ones those gods are ultimately sworn to protect. In favor of humans, in other words. And you know as well as I do that both are—and always will be—our enemies."

I opened my mouth. Closed it. My hands were burning. I bowed my head and stared at my palms, at the lines of fire starting to show upon my skin.

"Just answer one question for me," Cillian said.

The weight of his gaze made me feel like I was sinking.

"Whose side are you on?"

I clenched my hands into fists. The heat in them continued to build, but I ignored it as I lifted my eyes to my old friend and tried—unsuccessfully—to answer without letting my voice break. "It's complicated. We can talk about it later, I swear, I just need you to stop whatever it is you planned to do tonight so that tomorrow we can—"

"It's too late for that."

"It *isn't*."

"You should go. There are more of our rebels coming, and tonight is about more than just blowing random things up, it's..." He trailed off, shaking his head. "Just leave, Karys. Please. You can't win this particular battle." The glassy look in his eyes cracked, letting a glimmer of his usual affection toward me shine through.

When I remained rooted to my spot, he shook his head at me, a side of his mouth edging up in a tired smile.

"What was the first thing I taught you when I started taking you on missions with me?" he asked.

I swallowed down the argument I'd been building. Nearly choked on it. "Live to fight another day," I answered.

"Exactly. Because you can't further *any* cause..."

"If I'm dead."

He nodded. We had become a mentor and mentee once more, if only for the span of a few painful heartbeats. It couldn't last. I was not the same child I'd once been, eager to follow his lead—I was prepared to stand my ground, to argue against him in a way I never had before.

At least until something odd caught my attention.

Turning away from Cillian, I stepped closer to the entrance of the tent, listening for the roar of chaos outside, and I heard...

Nothing.

The night had gone completely silent.

CHAPTER 22

Karys

I raced outside, sprinting to the top of the hill that overlooked the main camp.

The chaos created by Valas had dispersed.

There were still people moving quickly about, but they exchanged nothing more than an occasional whisper, completely focused on organizing themselves with an unflinching resoluteness that was almost eerie.

Most of them were looking toward the east, where two figures loomed on an adjacent hilltop, looking down on them. These figures were the only ones speaking above a hushed tone. Calling out orders, it sounded like; I could make out their imposing voices, but individual words were difficult to decipher over the distance and the sound of my own pounding heart.

Who were they?

I started toward them to get a closer look, but an arm closed around my waist and pulled me backward.

I nearly cried out. Dravyn clamped his hand over my mouth before I could. I immediately recognized his scent along with his energy... I would have recognized him sooner, but something about those distant figures had me entirely too rattled to focus my senses.

Dravyn dragged me away from the tents and the camp, far away from the dark figures and everything else, waiting until we reached the cover of a shallow cave before he spoke.

"There are already more elves here than we expected. Mai's gone above to get a clearer picture of things." He cast a worried glance skyward.

I followed his lead, searching the moonlit clouds for flashing scales or other signs of her favored serpentine dragon form.

"They seem to be stealing their way in from all directions," Dravyn continued. "It looks like tonight is going to be more than just a small, strategic strike."

I settled my rattled nerves and told him what Cillian had said—though I still didn't understand what he'd meant by tonight being about more than just blowing things up. How much more? And what other rebels were coming?

Was Andrel here?

Was my sister here?

"What should we do?" I wondered aloud.

"Valas is already moving toward the outer defenses of Mindoth. Whatever the planned attack against this keep is, we're going to try and soften it. Maybe warn the humans who will listen. Hopefully, we can prevent a complete massacre."

I nodded, but I didn't follow him as he started toward what I presumed were those outer defenses. I was frozen, looking in the direction of Cillian's tent.

I don't know why.

What was I hoping for? That Cillian would come racing over the hill, begging me to stop, telling me he was sorry and that he wanted to find a way to secure peace after all?

I stared at my boots, feeling foolish for even letting such a thought enter my mind.

"Are you all right?" Dravyn asked, softly.

No.

I lifted my head and set off at a brisk pace. "Let's keep moving."

I could sense his concern—it settled like a second layer over my own thoughts—but he didn't ask for any more details. Later, maybe.

After we survived this night that was spiraling rapidly into our worst-imagined scenarios.

We raced through the forest, eventually making our way out of the trees and onto a plain covered in long, swaying grass that appeared pale blue in the moonlight.

Here, I got my first clear look at Mindoth's Keep in the distance.

With no trees or hills obscuring the view, I could see just how impressively wide its footprint sprawled. More buildings than I could count crowded the peninsula. High stone walls cut the compound off from the rest of the kingdom, their wide tops lined with torches and flags that fluttered in the humid breeze. The air smelled of salty sea and smoking chimneys. A warning bell was ringing somewhere deep within the heart of the training grounds, each of its echoing peals urging my pulse to skip a little faster.

I looked skyward again. This time, I caught a glimpse of gold weaving in-between the clouds.

Mairu shifted her scales to a mixture of pale amethyst and deep blue —blending better with the night sky above—as she descended to earth. The ground trembled as she touched down.

By the time we made our way over to her, she was sliding out of her dragon form and back into her humanoid one, though parts of her skin retained shimmering scales of purple and blue. Like armor. Like she was preparing for war, even though we'd all agreed to avoid it by any means necessary.

"We have a decision to make," she told us, frowning as she caught me staring at the beautiful patch of violet scales along her throat. "The situation is escalating beyond what we expected. If we intervene, we'll be committing to a bloody battle, it looks like."

Shades of fiery red flashed in my vision as Cillian's question whispered through my thoughts.

Whose side are you on?

I still wasn't sure what the right answer was.

I only knew I didn't want a bloody battle for *either* side.

"Can we focus on simply keeping them apart?" I wondered. "We could use magic to drive back the invasion. The main entry into Mindoth is relatively narrow, already cut off by high walls...if we help fortify it even further, maybe we can get the elves to turn around? At least for now."

"The tunnels underneath are still a vulnerability," Mai reminded me. "One that will be difficult to keep in check by any kind of barrier, magic or otherwise. There are too many entry-points, and we don't know how well the elves have mapped out the underground cave network. They may already be worming their way inside and planting weapons as we speak. Speaking of which, did you get anything useful out of Cillian?"

"He didn't deny that there were weapons planted, and more to come. He wouldn't tell me the number, though." I took a deep breath. It seemed to echo in my chest, like there was too much space inside of me—like my heart had finished the shriveling it had started in Cillian's tent. "Which makes me think that number is...high. He wouldn't try to hide it from me, otherwise."

She sighed, gaze lifting upward as if she was considering retreating back to the divine realm above.

"I believe we're beyond the point of not intervening in some way," Dravyn said, pointedly.

No one disagreed with this.

After a brief discussion, it was decided—Dravyn and I would try to at least reinforce the defenses of the main gates of Mindoth.

Meanwhile, Mai would find Valas, and the two of them would focus on sniffing out any weapons that had already been planted, as well as any smaller entry-points that had already been breached.

We wasted little time fussing over details beyond this.

Dravyn and I decided on a direct approach, strolling straight for the main entrance of the keep.

As we drew closer, I realized the outer wall was the first of many. More were stacked behind it, and each seemed to be a different height, length, and thickness. A maze of barriers with narrow corridors and gates in-between—so even if you managed to scale one wall, there was no telling what new challenge awaited you on the other side of it.

"Another wall—one of flame—could add to the frustration of trying to march into this place," I thought aloud.

Dravyn agreed, and we made our way to the outermost rampart with plans to create parallel barriers of magic in front of it.

That outer wall was actually made up of two stretches of stone with an elaborate metal gate between them. Both were wide enough to have multiple guards patrolling along their tops, and tall enough that staring up from the bottom strained my neck and made me dizzy.

Dravyn took the one to the left, summiting it with a running start, a few inhumanly powerful vertical strides, and the brief help of wings— flashes of fire-tinged feathers that were there one moment, gone the next.

As he disappeared from view, I scaled the outermost wall to the right, not with wings, but with a combination of my claws and my divine speed and strength. As I hurdled over the parapet and landed in a crouch, two guards immediately caught sight of me.

I straightened slowly, lifting my hands in a gesture of peace.

The one closest to me drew his sword.

My magic responded reflexively before I could even think of stopping it. Faint symbols glowed to life on my skin. Smoke and embers lifted from my pores. The torches all along the rooftop went out, their flames whisking toward me and swirling around my body.

In the suddenly darker surroundings, the fire building around me seemed even brighter, and the second guard—whose weapon remained in its sheath at his side—let out a gasp, blinking in disbelief.

"A divine being," he whispered, taking a step backward, his expression shifting to a mixture of awe and terror.

The sword-wielding man's eyes darted from his companion back to me, widening as if he was taking in the sight of me for the first time. He dropped his weapon and held up his hands.

Then both men knelt before me.

That's new.

It was also uncomfortable.

The one who'd dropped the sword fumbled with his sleeve, nervous fingers rolling it up to reveal a divine mark on his wrist—one that resembled a lightning bolt.

Wrong court, I thought wryly. But he was clearly hoping it would still gain him some kind of favor with me. Enough to keep me from smiting him, or whatever other horrible thing he imagined I was contemplating.

"I'm here to help," I assured him.

More gasps and trembling followed this pronouncement. The guards exchanged a wide-eyed look, clearly unable to believe I was actually *speaking* to them.

I didn't have time to deal with their unnecessary reverence on top of everything else.

"Leave the wall to me," I ordered, in what was hopefully a tone that rang with divine authority. "Move deeper into the training compound and bring the ones there a warning: There are enemies at your gates. More elves than I believe you're prepared for, coming from both over the ground and below it."

They hesitated only a moment before nodding. With his eyes downcast, the Storm-marked human spoke: "The gods show us favor by sending you to us in this hour of need, protecting us from the Fallen and wicked ones."

I was suddenly glad for his downcast gaze, as it meant he couldn't see me flinch at his last words.

Whose side are you on?

As the man chanced a quick glance up at me, I gave him a single, curt nod. He reacted as if I had promised to bless him and the rest of his bloodline for all eternity, his hands clasping together in prayer before he dropped into another bow along with his fellow guard.

I fought the urge to cringe. I waited until they had risen, hurried away, and fled down a nearby ladder, before I let any discomfort show.

A strange sense of power itched through my veins as I watched them disappear. A different sort of power than the one that came with controlling fire—and one I had no real interest in learning how to wield.

I thought again of my conversation with Cillian.

Have you already forgotten what it was like to live in this realm?

No human had ever bowed to an elf. Not even in the earliest days, when some of the most powerful elven houses were still clinging to some of their authority.

And contrary to what Cillian thought, I *hadn't* forgotten about the frustrating trips I used to take into human villages, desperate to find someone who would sell me the basic goods we needed to survive. Even on the rare occasions when I had plenty of coin to spend, the human merchants would take one look at my pointed ears and send me on my way with nothing but curses for my efforts.

My scarred face and clawed fingers often earned me even more violent reactions.

But the two guards hadn't seemed to notice any of those things. As soon as the divine fire appeared, they'd seen me as a higher being. One worthy of respect and awe.

"Fools," I muttered to no one.

I paced the top of the wall, letting the fire around me continue to build. Uncomfortable as I might have been with it, I still preferred pouring my energy into magic rather than thinking about those guards and their ridiculous worshipping.

When the flames around me became too large and wild to hold on to, I paused in the center of the wall. I picked two points on the ground below, then guided the flames between these points, stretching the inferno along my chosen path with steady, determined hands.

The two guards were still close—I heard them below me, in between the walls, shouting at their fellow soldiers. Telling them not to panic at the sight of the flames. Assuring them that the divine were here to help them.

And I was.

I wasn't going to go back on what I'd told them.

But how strange it felt to help, when I'd spent so many years cursing the gods for the lack of help they'd given *me*.

I wiped beads of sweat from my forehead and summoned even more flames, guiding them into the wall I'd created until it roared to a terrifying height. A blistering hot wind kicked up all around it, driving back anyone who dared to approach it.

It was eye-wateringly bright and uncomfortably hot, even to me. Even from a distance. I didn't care. I just kept building it brighter. Taller. It was fast becoming a compulsion. I couldn't stop adding to it because it was the only thing I felt in control of just then.

Out of the corner of my eye, I saw Dravyn's wall rising as well. I told myself I needed to build higher than even he could. I lost myself in the competition. Or tried to.

In truth, I was trying to *find* myself, to find something like solace and certainty in the flames I was creating—something that would make me feel like I was giving myself to the right cause. The right side.

I gave until I was out of breath. My head pounded. My chest ached. I made myself stay upright, narrowing my gaze on what little I could see of the other side of my fiery barricade.

Nothing there...at least, not that I could make out.

The voices directly below me had ceased as well, the guards having moved inward as I'd instructed them to. More and more followed them as I watched.

Good.

They could focus on dealing with any enemies who had already slipped inside or made their way into the tunnels. Dravyn and I could keep any more from attempting to breach the gates.

I breathed a sigh, glad to have a clear purpose and—

A terrifying rumble sounded from somewhere behind me.

I spun toward it, nearly losing my balance in the process.

It sounded far away, yet it was violent and powerful enough that the wall beneath me—and the ones behind me—trembled. A few tiny cracks appeared in them. The few remaining guards in the gatehouses rushed outside, surveying the damage.

Dravyn was by my side a minute later. I grabbed his arm, steadying myself as another tremor rocked the walls.

As soon as the shaking stopped, he took my hand. Together, we leapt to the second wall. Then the third. Then the fourth and still onward, racing from one to the next without stopping, dashing across their tops at an increasingly dizzying pace, occasionally aided by his wings.

Finally, we came to the last of the outer defenses—a short, narrow wall with sharp spikes all along its edge.

Just as we started to leap over this final barrier, another tremor shook the world, sending us pitching forward and nearly tumbling over the edge.

We caught ourselves and crouched in place, waiting for the shaking to subside.

It took a long time.

Long enough for us to get a good look at the spikes we still had to cross over, and see just how wickedly sharp they were.

And long enough to see that some of those spikes had severed elven heads impaled upon them.

CHAPTER 23

Dravyn averted his eyes.

I wanted to look away, too, but couldn't.

The blood oozing from the nearest heads still glistened in the moonlight.

"It looks...fresh," I said softly.

"More proof that some have already managed to breach the defenses tonight, as we feared," Dravyn said.

And as a reward they had become a gruesome warning to anyone who might think they could do the same.

Dravyn and I continued without another word. Words would only weigh us down, and we couldn't risk being anchored to this spot.

We vaulted over the blood-soaked spikes, bounced against the narrow top of the wall, and soared down the other side in a flurry of fire and feathers.

I stared straight ahead as we landed, bracing myself for whatever awaited us, refusing to look toward the spikes again.

We were properly inside the sprawling compound of Mindoth's Keep, now. It was almost empty where we landed, most of the soldiers either focused on fortifying the walls at our backs, or else running toward the sounds of explosions and rumblings in the distance—sounds that were becoming more violent and more numerous every moment.

We joined the ones racing toward the explosions.

Soon, we came upon a larger crowd, most of them gathered on the docks along the area's edge, working to unload things from several different vessels and then helping to evacuate the ones manning them. The sea churned restlessly against their efforts—a side effect of the underground rumblings that continued to regularly rock the area.

There were pockets of damage scattered about; cracked ground and shattered windows; broken cargo boxes and spilled goods; a few completely still, cloth-draped heaps—covered bodies, I suspected. The stench of death was nearly buried beneath the tang of sea salt, but it was unmistakable.

And it was growing stronger.

Aside from these things, however, the scene was less horrific than I'd anticipated. A sense of impending catastrophe hovered, yet something seemed to be holding it back—like a rabid, snarling dog held taut on a chain.

"I expected much worse," I admitted to Dravyn, despite the prickling unease shooting down my spine. "More fighting, more elven infiltration. But it seems relatively under control here, doesn't it?"

He didn't answer right away, too busy watching the sea. Another unnaturally high wave was building, rocking the ships perilously about. The soldiers on the docks scrambled backward, abandoning their efforts to finish unloading things.

"These explosions..." Dravyn finally replied, "...they feel more like distractions than anything."

Unease dug its claws more deeply into my heart.

Looking around, I realized how the scene felt unnervingly similar to the attack we'd faced in the middle-heavens weeks ago. We'd fought off group after group of invaders, only to realize—almost too late—that their true, larger target had been the Tower of Ascension.

So what were they truly attempting to destroy tonight?

"I assumed they were here to claim lives and deal a moral blow to the rising recruits," Dravyn said, voicing my own thoughts. "They have the numbers to stage a full-scale attack...why aren't they doing so? Too many of them are hanging back in the shadows for some reason. I don't like it."

"What else would be their end goal in this place, if not a massacre?"

He shook his head. "I don't know. There isn't anything of particular value here, aside from those budding army regiments. There are much larger ports of commerce elsewhere, and more important infrastructure they could target if they truly wanted to make a declaration of war. Why go to the trouble of setting off a bunch of small bombs that are an inconvenience, at worst?"

"Maybe there's a larger one somewhere?"

"Maybe. But they've drawn attention to the weapons now, so they would be jeopardizing their own plans by setting off warning explosions. It just doesn't seem smart. We're missing something."

We moved discreetly through the shadows, watching the growing unrest, trying to make sense of it.

Skirmishes continued to break out. Small explosions rumbled on, the sound echoing in the humid, heavy air like far-off thunder. It added to the other noise that was slowly building to a deafening level all around us—clamoring voices, pounding boots, clanging weapons.

Approaching a fork in the road, we hesitated, debating where to search next.

"We should split up and keep looking for whatever their true target is," I suggested.

Worry rippled through the connection we shared.

I had already latched on to this plan, though; I didn't want leave his side, but each of my heartbeats felt like it might be the last before everything exploded into pandemonium. Time was not on our side, and we could cover more ground apart than together.

"I can find my way back to you through the chaos easily enough," I assured him. "I always do."

Though the feeling of worry didn't ease, he agreed with a reluctant nod. "Be careful."

"When am I not?"

He arched a brow. "You spent yesterday jumping repeatedly from the tallest tower on our palace grounds, didn't you?"

"Yes, but I'm still in one piece," I pointed out.

He returned the smile I gave him, though the amusement didn't reach his eyes; his gaze was elsewhere, distracted as he scanned our surroundings for immediate threats.

"I promise I'll refrain from jumping off buildings," I said, "and I'll see you soon."

He responded with magic rather than words, sending a wave of warmth flooding through me with little more than a deliberate look. I wasn't entirely sure what he'd done—only that my own magic responded to it, and the fire that surged through my veins made me feel briefly invincible.

As we'd done when placing our walls of flames earlier, he went left while I went right. I moved quickly, my cloak drawn even tighter around my head than before.

Invincible or not, I was in a hurry.

I avoided making eye contact or lingering too long in any spot. I noted the numbers of both elves and humans, mapping out where and how they were gathering, trying to discern some sort of pattern. Something that would give me a clue about what points they were converging toward.

After several minutes of observing and searching, my attention snagged on a tall fire roaring in the distance. I drew to a stop as I stared at it, my sensitive nose picking up a nauseating smell. One I'd become far too familiar with over the past months: burning flesh.

The soldiers here wouldn't have incinerated their own so hastily; their customs surrounding death wouldn't have allowed it. But this seemed like precisely the way they would have disposed of any elvish enemy they'd killed.

The thought threatened to turn my stomach even more than the smell. I couldn't bring myself to move closer to the bonfire, so I turned around and started to make my way back toward the place I'd left Dravyn.

I could feel him through the chaos, as usual—like an unusually warm breeze in the dead of winter, bolstering my own magic whenever I reached for it. It was usually a powerful yet subtle feeling.

But this time, the gentleness soon became searing, and the faint breeze turned to a howling wind that suggested a wild, unsettling amount of magic use.

Why was he using so much magic?

Who was he fighting?

I broke into a run.

But I didn't find him.

Something else caught my eye first: A large crowd rushing down the street parallel to the one I currently raced along.

Curiosity carried me through a narrow alleyway and closer to this crowd. Before I realized what was happening, the group was growing larger, dozens of soldiers filing in from seemingly nowhere and sweeping me along with them. Galithian soldiers. They clearly had a destination in mind, and they were moving as a single unit toward it.

I stood out in this uniformed group; it wasn't long before one of the regiment looked my way. His face scrunched in confusion. Then widened in alarm. He opened his mouth to question me, snatching for my arm as he did.

I side-stepped his reach, averted my eyes, and slowed my pace as inconspicuously as possible.

My would-be questioner was swept out of sight by the surging crowd.

Keeping my face tilted away, I ducked back into the alley I'd passed through and pressed against a building, covertly peering around the edge to see where the crowd would end up.

As I leaned against the cool brick, I thought I heard someone say my name.

It sounded faint, from somewhere far-off to my right. When I chanced a glance in that direction, I saw no one I recognized, nor anyone who seemed to recognize *me*.

The last members of the marching group were mere dots in the distance. The street became eerily quiet. A shiver of warning crawled through my bones. I shrugged it off and focused on watching, determined not to lose track of that distant group. They seemed to be heading toward a large gray building on the far side of the main docks—a storehouse of some sort, maybe.

As I debated moving in for a closer look, I heard my name again.

I stepped out of the alley once more, drifting toward the sound in a confused sort of daze. I still kept my eyes trained in the direction of the storehouse, but my feet were carrying me towards whoever was calling for me—towards a narrow, rocky road that ran along the sea, and docks that looked old and ill-used.

"*Karys!*"

This time the voice was loud enough to turn several heads, mine included. I forgot about the soldiers and the storehouse I was watching. I forgot about *everything*. My name had been so clear this time, and that voice...

I followed it, maneuvering my way around jostling bodies and broken things, finding a wall and scaling it before leaping to the rooftop of the house it surrounded. From this higher vantage point, I could finally see the person who had been calling my name.

It was her.

I hadn't imagined it.

For over five years, I had been desperately wishing I could hear that voice again. And now it had happened. Just like that, my sister had seen me.

Recognized me.

Called out to me.

It felt like a dream. Or maybe the beginning of another one of my countless nightmares. Either way, it was not real. I would have to wake, soon, and face the fact that the sister I loved wasn't truly here at all.

She called my name again—no, *screamed* it. She was desperate for me to hear it, for me to see her. To answer her.

Desperate for my help, I realized.

Because she was surrounded. Backed into a corner, soldiers converging toward her, swords in hand.

I have to get to her.

I thought of nothing else. Power surged in my veins, a magic waking inside of me that was unlike anything I'd felt since my ascension. Like all of my potential had suddenly unleashed at once, fueled by the sight of her. By five years of *needing* to see her.

I had yet to manage actual flight, but suddenly I was willing to try again. I was willing to try anything if it meant finally closing the space between my sister and me.

Just give me the strength I need to reach her.

I leapt from the wall. I wasn't thinking of falling. I refused to believe I couldn't reach her now that she was so close. I saw only her. I *thought* of only her—and maybe that was why my wings worked better than they ever had before.

I soared the span of several buildings and landed directly in front of my sister, my momentum sending me tripping forward into her chest.

She caught me, hands bracing against my arms. Helping me find my footing, just as she'd done over and over again when we were younger.

For a long moment, she couldn't seem to take her eyes off the fading glow of my wings and the bits of fire rippling around me. Then, slowly, she turned her face to mine. Her fingers lifted as she did, tentatively tracing my scarred face. And my sister...

My sister was looking directly into my eyes.

"You're here." Her voice was hushed, like she was afraid of scaring me away. "You're actually here."

I started to reply, but I was distracted by the bodies drawing closer to us. I reached for the short blade at my hip. Fire wrapped around my hand as I took hold of the grip. I was prepared to defend my sister against this entire kingdom and all its armies if need be—

But she put a hand on my arm once more, holding it in a tight grasp, preventing me from even drawing my sword.

An instant later, I realized why: The ones drawing closer weren't the human soldiers I was expecting.

They were elves.

"Don't worry about them," my sister said. "They're here to help."

"...Help?"

No, that didn't make any sense.

I was here to help—I was here to save her.

"Don't worry," she repeated, her grip tightening even further. "You're safe, now, okay?"

The world reeled. I couldn't breathe. A thousand questions swirled in my mind. Savna's hand moved from my arm, digging something from the leather bag at her hip before shooting toward my neck. It happened so quickly I didn't have a chance to ask even the simplest of my questions—

Why?

Something sharp punctured my skin. A burning sensation followed seconds later—not the comforting smolder of my divine fire, but something terribly acidic that tingled its way through my veins, eating away at my insides.

Poison.

My sister poisoned me.

The knowledge plunged through me, sharp and aching, like a dagger through my chest. My legs buckled with the impact, and I collapsed into my sister's waiting arms.

CHAPTER 24

Dravyn

It was like a candle being snuffed out by a sudden gust of wind—one moment I felt Karys's magic burning more fiercely than it had all evening; the next, it was gone.

Distracted by the sudden shift, I pitched to a stop mid-swing. The elven soldier I'd been fighting took advantage of my distraction, nearly impaling me in the chest before I twisted away at the last possible second.

His blade clipped my arm, cutting through layers of clothing and leaving a shallow scrape across my bicep. Blood seeped out. Smoke joined it as my temper rose and a combination of fury, fear, and impatience ignited the fire that was forever simmering just beneath my skin.

The soldier's eyes grew large as he watched the smoke rising from my blood. I'd been holding back up to this point, so perhaps the fool didn't realize he'd risen his weapon against an actual *god*.

When the idiot dared to lift his blade once more, I made sure he went to his death without any doubt about the matter.

Curls of smoke turned to ribbons of flame, snaking from my

wounded arm and wrapping around the sword I held. In a few blinks, the steel was searing hot. His eyes grew even wider at the sight.

"Wait! Have mer—"

I plunged the sword into his throat.

The scent of the soldier's blood and burning flesh filled the air. I gripped his arm, yanked my sword free and wiped it on his coat, then threw him to the ground.

Without sparing him another glance, I turned and resumed my search for Karys.

I'd seen her only minutes ago. She couldn't have gone far. Unless… had she transported herself somehow? It seemed unlikely she would manage to carry herself far enough away that I couldn't feel her at all. Which only left a few other explanations, and—

No. The word formed on my lips even though I still didn't understand what had happened. *No, no, no.*

A cold wind washed over me. Valas appeared at my side a moment later, took one look at my face and immediately reached for his sword. "What's wrong?" His gaze snapped back and forth, searching. "Where is Karys?"

I didn't—couldn't—answer.

Instead, I started to run, racing in the direction where I'd last felt her energy radiating from. Maybe there would be a clue there. Maybe she would still be there, still fighting. We didn't fully understand the connection we shared; wasn't it possible that it had snapped for some reason, but that she was otherwise fine?

I reached a more narrow street that appeared to dead-end at an older, broken-down docking yard. This was the direction she'd traveled in, I was certain.

Yet she was nowhere to be found.

I tried listening for her. Picking out her scent. Anything, everything —but there were too many bodies in my way. Too many distractions. The sea roared its restless song and slammed its dark, foamy fists against the shoreline, turning boats on their sides and occasionally popping them up out of the waves altogether.

My gaze lingered briefly on the tossing and tumbling water. I had a horrible vision of Karys plunging over the edge of the rickety docks, sinking out of sight faster than I could call her name, and—

No.

I refused to believe it. Even if she'd fallen in—or worse, been *thrown* in—the sea would not have silenced her so quickly. She would have fought back against the waves no matter how high they rose or how viciously they churned. I would have felt her energy dwindling, maybe, but not extinguishing as instantaneously as it had.

So where the hell was she?

I turned around to find Mairu and Valas running toward me, their faces reflecting the same confusion I felt—a confusion that was inching quickly toward despair.

"No sign of her anywhere." Valas's usual carefree smile clenched into a tight baring of teeth as he fixed his eyes on me. "Why didn't you two stay together?"

The challenge stoked the embers of fury smoldering in my gut. He was not the one I was truly mad at, but I briefly considered taking it out on him all the same.

Before I could, Mairu stepped between us. "Many of the elves seem to be retreating," she said, pointing our attention to a spot far in the distance, where the road gave way to a large expanse of brittle, brown grass. Farther on, grassy hills sloped upward toward a rocky crest, a natural barrier that had been reinforced with spiked iron fencing across its top.

A section of that fencing had been blown away. Dark scraps of it littered the hills, shining faintly in the moonlight. Elven soldiers stood watch by the opening, shouting orders for a faster, more organized retreat.

"Because they've realized they're outnumbered, or because they've already succeeded in whatever they came here to do?" Valas wondered.

All the questions seemed irrelevant, now. I no longer cared about what their motives had been or what bombs they'd placed. Or about their successes. Or failures. I no longer cared about our own goal of keeping the war in this realm from escalating, either.

I would have started a thousand wars if that was what it took to find Karys and keep her safe.

I didn't care if any or all of them were retreating, either—at least not until I spotted one I recognized climbing into the saddle of a ghostly pale horse.

Andrel.

Mairu said my name in warning.

But I was already moving.

I shifted my form, flames engulfing my body and burning away the limits of my human shape. As I passed beyond the edge of the training grounds and into the hills beyond, I was fully changed—a great, winged beast spiraling through the air like a flaming arrow shot by a divinely powerful, impossibly accurate archer.

People screamed. Chaos and confusion roared at my back. I was making a messy situation messier by revealing this form, this power. But I didn't look back to witness what turmoil I'd stirred up—only ahead, my gaze fixed on the pale horse Andrel rode as he dragged it to a stop and jerked it around to see what everyone was shouting about.

I soared directly at them, fiery claws lashing out and scraping against the horse's sweat-slicked body, causing the creature to rear and throw its rider to the ground. It shot off into the night as Andrel rolled onto his back, gasping for breath.

I landed directly in front of him, bringing a swirling vortex of wind and fire crashing down with me. My claws dug into the earth. The dry grass ignited all around me, cutting us off from the rest of the world.

A few of Andrel's fellow soldiers attempted to push through the flames and reach him.

I focused my power and the fence of fire roared higher.

We would not be interrupted.

As Andrel tried to push himself upright, I began to change.

I could have stayed in my beastly form. Could have wrapped my wings around him and set him alight, easy as that. The fires of my body would have swallowed him entirely within seconds, easily burning his worthless body until nothing but ash remained.

But it would not have been nearly as satisfying as drawing his blood. As watching him squirm. When I went into more beastly shapes, much of my awareness went with it. Submitting to a more primal version of me and my power served a purpose occasionally, but for this...I was going to remain fully conscious for this so I could enjoy it.

Andrel's eyes met mine as my human-like features took shape once more. He stopped attempting to sit up. He stayed on his back, one hand over his heart, the other stretched out beside him.

I took the small knife from my ankle sheath. My gaze swept over him, fixing on the hand outstretched to his right.

I stabbed my knife into the center of his palm, all the way through, pinning him to the ground.

His body convulsed. Curled up with pain. Shock blanched his face. His eyes squeezed tight, then opened and stared wide-eyed at nothing, clearly trying but failing to register his surroundings.

It took several more gasping breaths and slow, dazed blinks before he returned to something like awareness. He managed a breath. Recognized me more fully. Went very still. His fingers twitched as blood oozed from around my impaled knife.

But eventually—as I probably should have expected—a slight, mocking smile stretched across his pale face. "Oh, great and powerful God of Fire," he mumbled, "show *mercy*."

"You are praying to the wrong fucking god for mercy," I informed him.

He closed his eyes. Pain clenched them tighter and tighter. "Please."

I pushed the knife deeper. Twisted it until I drew another satisfying, desperate gasp from him.

"*Please*," he said through another choking breath.

"You'd like for me to free you from this knife, would you?"

He went deathly still. His lips moved as if to form words, but then he merely breathed in a deep, shaking inhale—swallowing what I was certain was a foolish, mocking statement to go along with his foolish, mocking smile. Sweat dripped from his forehead. His eyes crinkled around the edges.

"Yes," he said.

Scarlet edged my vision. Divine strength surged through me, sending more tendrils of fire rolling out from my body. I pulled the knife from his palm, only to strike toward his wrist instead, guiding the blade deep into flesh and bone alike, severing his hand with a single quick, calculated motion.

Once I'd finished, I wiped his blood from my knife and rose to my full height. "Consider yourself *freed*."

I stood over him, perfectly still, watching as he writhed about and cradled the bloodied stump to his chest. His pain was music to my ears. Little stuttering breaths. Occasional whimpers. Gasping dry heaves as he clenched his remaining hand around his stomach and tried not to vomit from pain.

A human would have likely already succumbed to shock, and there would have been nothing left to do but watch him bleed out. But the elf showed a bit more vitality than this, staying conscious despite the lack of color in his face.

He went silent disappointingly quickly as well, gritting his teeth and closing his eyes against the pain until he managed to collect himself.

His eyes flashed open again. Another cry started to rise in his throat, but he strangled it down, twisting his teeth into a vicious smile and shaking his head. He rose to his knees, pressing his wrist hard against his body, trying to stem the bleeding. He looked up at me without lifting his head. His pupils were fully dilated, his eyes like two cavernous pits.

"And here I thought you gods always aimed to kill," he rasped.

"I am not finished," I assured him, withdrawing my sword and planting the tip of it against the hollow of his throat. "I was simply making good on the promise I made the first time we spoke—to remove your hand if you touched her again. And you have. Several times, now."

"Yes; I was beginning to wonder when we'd have a chance to catch up on these things."

I pressed the sword deeper into his throat, drawing trails of blood to mingle with the sweat coating his skin. "Apologies for the delayed reply. I'm a busy god."

"Still—a man of his word. I appreciate that." He watched the embers flying around my body as he added, "Though I do believe you also said you'd cauterize the wound for me."

I summoned more fire to my palm. Without a word, I shaped it into a blade to match the one I held in my right hand.

I swung this second sword toward the bloodied stump he cradled to his chest, but I didn't let it actually touch anything; I merely let the flames hover over his wound, increasing the heat with every breath I took.

"You'll be dead soon," I said. "So I don't think it's worth the effort to stop the bleeding."

Blood had already soaked the entire bottom half of his coat. His smile finally disappeared, his face twisting in a way that seemed beyond his control, his pain too great to continue to mock me.

He might have been more resilient than a human, but he was still not long for this world if he continued to bleed at the rate he was.

And I needed to pry whatever useful information I could from him before I finished him off.

"Am I right to assume you know where Karys has gone?"

"You might be." He looked close to smiling again. Then he thought better of it—a rare intelligent decision from this fool.

"Tell me what they've done to her and where they've taken her," I demanded, "so I can end your worthless life and be on my way."

"Help you, just so you can kill me?" His words were just above a whisper. They were beginning to slur together. "That's quite the offer, but I'm afraid I don't accept."

"Then I'll find someone else who will tell me." I pressed the metal sword more fully to his neck. Heated the other, fiery one to the point that the scent of singed flesh engulfed us. "Which means your usefulness to me has ended."

"You're going to kill me? *Really*?" He coughed. The motion made my blade slip against his skin, drawing another trail of crimson to the surface. He didn't flinch. His eyes never left my face. "You would make me a martyr?"

I hesitated for a beat, considering his words. It was a short debate. I quickly decided his death was worth any consequence that might follow—

But it didn't matter.

Because in the next moment—before I could properly end him—several things happened all at once: The ground shook with a sudden tremor that lasted for several seconds; the shield of fire I'd created wavered; an arrow screamed through the smoke and heat-hazed air, striking me in the shoulder.

The arrow didn't sink in very deeply, but it distracted me enough that my sword of fire lost its shape. As I rebalanced my remaining sword, while simultaneously inspecting the arrow's head, Andrel scrambled to his feet.

"I wouldn't be so concerned about Karys right now," he said, taking a few shaky steps away from me. "She was not the main target tonight. Collecting her was merely a bonus objective that happened to work out for us. One of many victories we'll be celebrating later."

I yanked the arrow from my shoulder. "I'm sure it will be a wonderful celebration," I snarled. "Right up until I send fire raining down over it."

"And over her, too, I presume? Since she'll be among us."

I placed a hand on my shoulder and summoned a small flame, searing the wound closed. "She isn't as weak as you," I said. "She can withstand the heat."

"Unlikely, given her current condition."

The grip on my sword burned red hot from the heat of my palm. A blistering wind rose as I closed the space he'd tried to put between us. "Where. Is. She?"

The barest hint of a smirk curled his lips. "Some place safe. And don't worry: I'm going to take good care of her."

I swung.

Clearly anticipating it, Andrel leapt aside as my sword slashed forward—but he wasn't fast enough. The still blade caught him in the chest.

Blood showered the singed ground.

I adjusted my grip on the weapon and stormed forward again.

He staggered backward.

Every sword-fighting lesson I'd ever had was forgotten—I was wild, formless, thinking of nothing except running the blade through his body in the most painful way possible. I didn't merely want to kill him. I wanted to *gut* him and leave the pieces of him in an unrecognizable heap on the ground.

But just as I stabbed, another arrow pierced my shoulder, striking right below the mark the first one left.

I looked toward it for a fraction of a second. Enough time for Andrel to twist aside and avoid a fatal blow from my sword—though I did draw more blood, cutting a shallow gash into his lower stomach.

He dropped to one knee, breathing hard.

I stalked toward him, sword at the ready, but he didn't attempt to back away this time.

He didn't need to.

He was no longer alone.

I realized then that he'd been trying—successfully—to draw my attention away from everything else happening around us. An entire section of my fiery wall had collapsed while I was distracted. Soldiers poured through it, racing to his aid.

I considered gutting every last one of them as well.

Something stopped me, however—a sharp prickling sensation sweeping down my arm, which soon turned to a burning I had no control over. I shifted my sword to my other hand and reached to put pressure against my shoulder; the discomfort was radiating from the spot where the first arrow had struck.

What had that arrow been laced with?

This question quickly became the least of my worries.

The ground was shaking again. Not from an explosion, this time, but from a rush of pounding hooves and boots. What appeared to be the rest of the elven army was thundering our direction, their retreat more frenzied than ever, whatever disaster they were trying to get ahead of clearly imminent.

Andrel paid the fleeing crowd no mind as two soldiers helped him back to his feet. He remained surprisingly steady once upright—steady enough that he managed to meet my gaze and hold it as he asked, "Did you even wonder why we decided to target these training grounds, of all places?"

Something in his voice made me forget about our personal battle for a moment. I clenched my shoulder more tightly as I looked back toward those grounds, pulse quickening. Another rumble echoed in the distance. Frantic shouts followed soon after—the cries of countless soldiers running toward a large grey building near the main docks.

"Because an honored guest is visiting the grounds this very night," Andrel said, answering his own question. "The King of Galizur, himself. I believe you know him?"

My hand fell to my side, wounds momentarily forgotten. "You lie."

"Afraid not. I *do* hope he's not in that building there in the distance," he said, gesturing flippantly at the one I'd just been staring at. "Would be a shame if he was there when our main bombs ignited."

The itching and burning in my arm grew more intense than ever. I was certain of it, now: It had not been a normal arrow that pierced it, but likely one dipped in whatever disgusting sort of anti-divine poison they'd come up with...and I'd sealed that poison inside my body with my hasty attempts to stop the bleeding.

Fuck.

A crowd of elven warriors appeared behind Andrel, their movements as silent as fog rolling in. Several carried bows. Arrow tips glistened in the moonlight as they were nocked and pointed my direction.

How many of those arrows were laced with poison? How much could I withstand before I collapsed?

I would not find out.

I calmly sheathed my sword. Then, with a furious roar, I swung my hand forward, throwing fire to the ground before the elves, setting the grass around them ablaze.

A few attempted to skirt around the flames and challenge me, while others took aim at me through the fires themselves, rapidly unleashing arrows from all directions. A few grazed my skin, but most I ignited in mid-air, turning them to ash that drifted harmlessly to the ground.

The chaotic battle was soon interrupted by a falling blanket of ice, followed by the screech of a dragon. As Mai and Valas descended over us, I caught sight of someone helping Andrel onto the back of a new horse.

I didn't chase him this time. While my fellow court members dealt with the remaining elven soldiers who dared to continue trying to challenge and distract us, my attention fixed in the direction of the grey building.

I couldn't fight off the pull that carried me toward it, first at a slow, slightly dazed jog, then a full sprint.

I was halfway to it when an explosion unlike anything I'd ever witnessed rocked the ground all the way out to where I stood—and beyond.

Light flared. The sound of shattering glass and breaking stone pierced the night. Cracks zigzagged out from the building's foundations, and in the next breath, the stone walls were crumbling upon that foundation, buckling precariously before collapsing completely.

The world continued to spin while I froze in place. The arrow's poison flared in my veins.

Breathless, I stared as that distant building came crashing down, hoping with every ounce of my being that my brother was not inside of it.

CHAPTER 25

Dravyn

I RAN, SHOVING MY WAY THROUGH HORDES OF BODIES, leaping over fallen debris, dodging fractured ground. It didn't occur to me—not until I'd nearly reached the imploding building—that magic could have carried me to my destination much faster.

I did not feel like a god in that moment; I was merely a brother racing to save the only family he had left.

And this time, I would be quick enough.

The closer I came to the fallen building, the thicker the dust in the air became, until I could no longer see more than a few feet ahead. I summoned a fiery wind to push aside what haze I could, as well as to better light my way through what remained. The magic came alarmingly slowly. Between the poisoned arrows and my separation from Karys and her magic, I feared what might have been happening to my power—but I didn't have time to think about it beyond that.

I pressed on until I found what looked like it might have been the main door to the fallen building. It lay on the ground, its metal shape crumpled as if it been made of mere paper.

Past it, there had clearly been a wide corridor; most of the debris seemed to have landed outside this hall, save for a few large slabs of the roof, so I was able to pick my way deeper into the mess with relative ease.

I heard shouting coming from my right. A frantic cry for help and—*The king! The king is here!*

I followed the noise, eventually stumbling upon a trio of distraught looking soldiers. One was injured, his leg bent at an odd angle. It appeared as though the three had been digging, trying to make their way into an adjacent room, and something had shifted free and landed on that leg.

The other two soldiers appeared torn between tending to their companion or continuing to dig.

"We think the king is inside this room here," one of them explained to me, breathless, while the other eyed me warily.

I nodded, stepping toward the pile of splintered wood and dusty stone blocking the entrance.

The wary soldier started to follow—whether to aid me or protect his king from me, I didn't know—but the sound of wood creaking, cracking, and shifting somewhere above stopped him in his tracks. His gaze shifted restlessly between me and the ceiling before finally settling on his injured companion.

"You should get him to safety," I urged.

The man didn't budge.

I didn't say anything else. I merely looked back in the direction I'd arrived from and, with a stiff, somewhat painful wave of my hand, I summoned another gust of fiery wind. This time I poured some sentience into the spell, so that the embers within it turned into living creatures who would be able to find the path of least resistance into clearer air. A trail of them swept around the three soldiers before shooting away, winding through the wreckage and beckoning them to follow.

"*Will o' wisps,*" I heard the one with the mangled leg whisper. "Following them leads to good luck."

"Not always," muttered the wary one, his eyes darting briefly to me once more, his expression dancing between skepticism and reluctant awe.

The third looked somewhat skeptical, too. All the same, they both helped their injured ally upright and dragged him along, following the lights and leaving me to the task of digging out my brother.

I wasted no time. My shoulder ached and itched to the point that I was beginning to lose the feeling in it. I had to move quickly, before it became entirely useless.

This time, I will be quick enough.

I found a spot that looked disturbed, as if the three soldiers had already started digging into it. I listened for movement and heard nothing. Scent was more helpful—I picked up the salt and metallic tang of human blood.

A large concentration of it.

I tracked that scent and, little by little, worked to uncover the source, watching carefully for signs of life, until finally—

There.

More slowly, taking care not to let anything else shift and fall onto him, I went back to digging. I pushed away the stone and broken glass around his head, first, making sure he had plenty of space to breathe.

And—thank the Creators—he *was* breathing, though each breath was more ragged and shallow than the last.

His face was a wreck of terrible colors: green and purple bruising across his cheeks, one eye swollen shut and circled in black, all of it streaked with dust and blood.

"Fallon."

He blinked at the sound of my voice. His eyes darted wildly around before finally settling on my face. Green eyes rimmed in gold, just like our mother's. They flashed with a whole range of emotions in the span of a few heartbeats. Confusion. Shock. Disbelief. And then they closed again, as if the sight of me was too great a burden to bear.

I didn't know what to say, so I just kept digging.

Eventually, I'd freed enough of him to manage a solid grip on his torso. I wrapped my arms around him and heaved his limp body the rest of the way out.

Dislodging him triggered an avalanche of debris, each shifting piece knocking another piece free. As a large section of the wall came crashing toward us, I swiftly repositioned myself so I caught the brunt of it with my back.

The avalanche settled with me hovering over my brother's still body. Several boards rested upon my shoulder blades. My palms were braced against ground that was covered in slivers of wood and glass, and several of those slivers had slid into my skin. Part of the ceiling had fallen away, allowing moonlight to illuminate the swirling dust all around us.

With a grunt, I shoved the fallen pieces away from Fallon and myself before rising to a crouched position.

When I looked to my brother once more, his eyes were open again, staring at me with a dazed mixture of horror and wonder.

"So it ends in dust and rubble," he mumbled through dry, cracked and bleeding lips, his eyes fluttering shut, "and my brother, the god, comes to see me at last, here at the gateway to the heavens."

"You aren't dead, you dramatic idiot. Not yet."

He blinked again, disbelief flooding his features—but this time he kept his eyes open. Kept them on me.

With some effort, I managed to maintain my balance as I scooped him carefully into my arms and rose back to my feet.

"Dravyn—"

"Don't talk. Save your strength."

Throughout our entire childhood, I don't think he'd ever listened to any command I'd given. But he listened now. His body went disturbingly limp. His head lolled against my chest.

I carried him out of the dust, occasionally stumbling over bits of scattered stone and splintered wood. My own condition seemed to be deteriorating with every step. I was forced to reach deep into the wells of my power, bracing myself with all the magic I could muster just to stay on my feet.

A small company of soldiers met us outside, drawing up short as they caught sight of me.

They stared. At first, none of them spoke. Or moved.

I wouldn't have dared to approach me, either; I must have been an interesting sight. A frightening one. Divine symbols blazed on my skin, growing brighter every time I accessed my power in a desperate grab for strength. My vision was tinged in red and orange, which likely meant my eyes had taken on a glowing appearance—a powerful gaze of fury and hellfire.

But I still felt alarmingly weak. Far too aware of the blood and dust coating me. Of the poison emanating from the wounds in my shoulder. A ragged, angry god, bristling from too many losses and too many mistakes.

Yet their king was unconscious in my arms—and, to their credit, the humans didn't shy away, despite whatever terror my appearance invoked.

After several attempts to gather his courage, one particularly brave soul even stepped forward to meet me, his hands outstretched and shaking only slightly as he reached to pull the lifeless body away from my chest.

Others followed his lead. Soon, I was swarmed by humans, all of them reaching, trying to support their leader as best they could while also keeping one wary eye on me.

Part of me didn't want to let Fallon go.

The other part wondered if it would do more harm than good holding on to him.

With reluctance, I relinquished my burden. As he was carried away, a few of the soldiers lingered, watching me. They bowed hastily before they finally turned and hurried away, several of them calling for the attention of healers as they went.

I felt oddly unbalanced without my brother's weight in my arms. I started to follow him in a daze, but a sudden power overtook me after only a few steps, paralyzing my limbs and rooting me to the spot.

"Dravyn." Mairu's voice snapped like a whip, another force wrapping around me, holding me back. "Where do you think you're going?"

I shot her a cursory glance before shrugging off her power and returning to my walk. "The king must live." He was almost out of sight. "I have to make sure—"

"Never mind the king," Mai hissed, jogging after me. "He's in the hands of his subjects, now, and I'm sure every healer in the kingdom will be rushing to his side before the night is over with. You need to get back to the divine realm and deal with your own problems. That wound on your shoulder looks horrific."

I ignored her and kept walking.

She sent another wave of magic over me, stronger this time. It sank its claws fully into my legs, and then it was pulling, trying to drag me back rather than just holding me still.

I responded with a flare of my own magic, heat exploding backward and swallowing her up until she lost her focus—and with it, her hold on me.

She stumbled, cursing my name.

But that was the extent of our battle.

Valas dropped to her side an instant later, tucking his wings away, grabbing her arm and holding her back as she started to take aim at me once more.

He needn't have interfered; I was already done. The burst of magic had required too much of me. The sharp, needling pain in my wounded shoulder was now a hundred times worse. I didn't want to try summoning more magic.

I didn't even want to *move.*

So I merely watched.

And as my brother disappeared from sight, my thoughts expanded back to the bigger picture.

The whole bloody, massively fucked up picture.

I tentatively touched my wound. More daggers of white-hot pain stabbed through me. As they subsided, I couldn't help noticing I felt even weaker than before. Like I couldn't have summoned more magic even if I'd wanted to. It was as if every pulse of pain and every too-quick beat of my heart further activated the arrow's poison. And that poison was eating up my magic. Draining it.

Draining it.

Whatever they'd used against me...had they used it against Karys, too?

Was that why I couldn't sense her energy?

I didn't think I could feel any more sick than I already did, but the thought of Karys in the hands of our enemies, without even her magic to protect herself...

I never should have let her out of my sight.

I'd failed to protect her, just like I'd failed—

"We need to get you back to Nerithyl," Mai insisted once more, cutting into my thoughts as she reached my side, her eyes narrowing on my injury. "Armaros needs to look at that. Hopefully the Healing God can—"

"No. We aren't going back without Karys." I started walking again. I didn't even know where I was going. Moving might have been hell, but the thought of going back to the middle-heavens without her beside me was worse.

The Serpent Goddess followed once more. It obviously pained her to speak the words she wanted to—*needed* to—but after a pause she quietly managed to say: "You can't save her right now. Not in the state you're in."

"I'm fine."

"You're a fucking liar is what you are."

I would have argued, but for the sharp pain that shot through my injury at that exact moment, stealing my breath. It was soon spreading across my entire back—like someone was using my shoulder blades to sharpen their knives, scraping right down to the godsdamn bone.

The urge to drop to my knees overcame me. I somehow fought it off. But the dizzying pressure that had settled over me persisted.

Mai drew closer once more, but I ignored her, looking instead to the sky, losing myself in thoughts of soaring through it and getting a better view of the world below. I could transform entirely. Become a beast, ignorant of whatever damage this human form had sustained. It might not rid me of that damage—there was a chance it could aggravate it further—but as long as I could find out where Karys had been taken before the injuries overwhelmed...

Valas stepped in front of me, his expression serious for once, as if he could sense the mad, desperate plan half-forming in my mind.

"I'll stay in this realm and keep searching for Karys," he said.

Before I could answer, Mai added, "And you and I are going back to the divine realm, in the meantime."

Even when I wasn't gravely wounded, she was still a formidable opponent. With the poison continuing to spread and drain me, I had almost no chance of fighting off her magic. She knew it, too, and she showed no mercy; a tendril of controlling power wove its way around my chest, crisscrossing it like a heavy set of chains.

"Release me, you witch," I half-mumbled, half-snarled.

"Be quiet," she snarled back, taking a physical hold of my arm while her magic continued to bind me. "And don't fight me, or who knows where we'll end up transporting ourselves to."

Her grip on my arm tightened. Before I could utter another syllable of protest, the scenery blurred around us. Then we were moving, lifted by unseen hands, pulled into the space between realms.

I closed my eyes. Kept them closed long after we touched down in the divine realm once more. I didn't want to be here without Karys. I wanted to go back. To her, to my brother; back to the beginning of this night so I could fix all the mistakes we'd made and somehow make a new ending.

I heard Mairu say, "She'll be okay, Dravyn. Even if you can't feel her, she's strong enough to endure. I...I'm certain of it."

I didn't answer. Or maybe I did. I was no longer entirely aware of what my body was doing. Her words had triggered a memory of a conversation, and now it was all I could think about.

I know a wildfire when I see one, I'd once told Karys. *And I don't think they would have put you out so easily.*

As I opened my eyes and took in the divine landscape before me, I tried one last time to sense her energy. We'd reached across realms to one another before. Even when doing so should have been impossible, I'd felt her through whatever fire and chaos surrounded or separated us.

But this time, nothing but my own pain and exhaustion answered my reaching.

It felt as if every fire inside of me had gone out, and the middle-heavens loomed darker and colder than I ever remembered them being before.

CHAPTER 26

Karys

AT FIRST, THE ONLY THING I NOTICED WERE SMELLS. Woodsmoke and dust. Melted candle wax and warm earth.

Then, the sensation of touch. Little by little, I managed to move my hands, fingers feeling across numb, tingling skin, trying to assess any damage I'd sustained.

Once I'd confirmed I was in one piece, with all limbs accounted for, I slid my hands down to the lumpy surface I rested upon—an old mattress? The sheets beneath me were worn and scratchy, but...familiar. Comforting. Warm.

All at once I realized: *This smelled like my old house.*

This felt like my old bed.

My old room.

And when I opened my eyes to confirm it, I realized I was not alone.

My sister sat in a rocking chair at the foot of the bed. A chair I recognized. One my father had made many years ago, before I was even born. It used to sit on the front porch.

But now it was here, cradling the unmistakable form of my sister.

My sister.

Her eyelids fluttered with restless sleep while her legs slowly pushed the chair back and forth.

Creeeeak.

Creeeeak.

I sat up. As the bed groaned under my weight, Savna's breath caught. Then it stopped altogether. Her heart still raced, though, pounding a frantic rhythm as she opened her eyes and fixed them on me.

We stared at one another for what felt like a lifetime.

My hand went to my neck, feeling for the spot where she'd stabbed me with...well, whatever the hell she'd stabbed me with. Something that had allowed her to carry me away from Mindoth, and then all the way back to our childhood home.

How long had I been asleep?

What had happened during that time?

And why had she brought me *here*, of all places?

She swallowed hard. "Karys, I can explain. I—"

"No," I whispered. "No, I don't think you can."

She got to her feet.

I did the same.

We stared for a second lifetime, our breaths growing scarce once more, our hearts both chanting to wrecked, uneven beats.

I backed up until my legs were flush against the bed. Pressed to the mattress, I realized how violently I was shaking.

Savna started to reach for me but drew her hand back just before it closed over mine. She pulled it into a fist and clutched it like a shield over her heart, watching me. Giving me space to speak, I guessed.

Where the hell was I supposed to start?

Inside, I was screaming. My questions, my accusations, my pain and uncertainty—all of it was so, so *loud*. All I wanted to do was get these things out of my head. I wanted to corner her, to shout until my lungs were sore and she was cowering, shrinking into nothing the way I'd wanted to do so many times since losing her.

But when words finally made it out, they were quiet. Broken. Spoken in the voice of a younger me—the me she'd left behind five years ago.

"You're...*alive.*"

Her hand fell from her chest. She took a step toward me. I was still backed against the bed with nowhere to go, so I simply stood, stiff and uncomfortable, as she wrapped her arms around me.

I couldn't bring myself to hug her back.

For so many years, I would have given *anything* for the chance to embrace her again. But now my arms wouldn't even move. No part of me would move, save for my mouth.

"You've been alive this entire time," I whispered, still in disbelief.

A long, awful pause, and then she gave the barest of nods. Her dark hair brushed against my cheek as she did, sending her familiar fragrance washing over me. Little had changed about it, even after all this time. She was still soft earth and overgrown grass, because she was never inside long enough to fully shed these wild scents from her skin. There was a hint of something woodsy, too, along with subtle notes of flowers and herbs from the tea she was always drinking or making for someone else.

She was still so close. I couldn't breathe without inhaling all these reminders of her. I felt like I was suffocating.

Finally, she took a step back.

Still staring.

Still not speaking.

"Savna...*how could you?*"

She flinched as though I was speaking much louder, only to quickly collect herself and step farther away from me. Smoothing a wrinkle from the hem of her shirt, her eyes on it instead of my face, she calmly replied, "How could I what?"

Again, I didn't know where to start.

"How could I not have told you about the trip I took to the divine realm, you mean?" She continued to back away, hitting the chair in the process and sending it toppling to the ground. She left it overturned as she walked to the window, hands tapping together with soft, rhythmic claps. She always used to do that when she was anxious or agitated.

Such a small movement, but for some reason it made the whole scene that much more impossible to deny—because here was more painful proof that this was Savna, not some cruel imposter.

Clap.

Clap.

Clap.

"How could I have abandoned you?" She turned my way but still didn't meet my gaze. She looked everywhere, anywhere else—to the faded red rug; the shelves filled with books and stacks of recipes I'd planned to try; the tattered curtains glowing soft and pink in the sunlight.

Her beautiful blue eyes were wide and haunted, as if she was watching the ghosts of our past flicker around us. She couldn't seem to look away from them.

"How could I have let you believe I was dead for so long?" she whispered, more to herself than me.

I braced a hand against one of the bed's posts.

"*How could I?*" Her gaze finally alighted on mine. She inhaled, shoulders shaking from the effort of it, and said, "Because it wouldn't have been safe for me to come back to you. *I* wasn't safe. Not after what I'd done."

I gripped the post so tightly I lost feeling in my hand.

"For years, I have been hiding from more than just you. I've been underground, building a movement, sharing what I'd taken from the gods and spinning it into something like hope for our kind. And now, we have enough power for us to take a stand, to rise up from the ashes..." She spoke quickly, face flushed, the way she'd always talked of her grand, rebellious dreams. It was easy to get caught up in the passion she exuded. Or it had been, once upon a time.

So little had changed on the surface. But underneath...

Underneath, it felt like everything had.

"But now," she continued, "I felt as though I could *finally* make myself known, and one of the first things I set out to do was find you. My life—and my plans for it—are still not safe, but the future is finally clear, and I knew you would want to fight alongside me to help secure that future."

She walked slowly back to my bed. Picked up the chair she'd knocked over and carefully placed it upright, bracing her hands against its backing as she continued, "But what did I find upon resurfacing? That I was very nearly too late. That the gods had taken you hostage."

"I...I wasn't a hostage. I went to the divine realm willingly, same as you did. And I—"

"I've heard the story."

"I doubt it was the *whole* story."

She continued as though I hadn't spoken: "I regret not intervening sooner. I should have known you'd follow in my footsteps. You always did, didn't you? Even when I made you swear you wouldn't." Her smile was fond. Genuine.

For some reason, the sight of it made me feel like I'd been kicked in the stomach.

"I went to Nerithyl like you did, that's true, but..." My eyes strayed to the curtains and stayed there. Their rosy glow reminded me of the way the forgelights diffused into the middle-heaven sky.

"But what?"

I forced my attention back to her. "But we didn't find the same things in that place."

She studied me for a long time. Folded her arms across her chest and walked to the window I'd been staring at, leaning against the wall next to it and studying it closely, as if trying to see what I'd been seeing.

Her brow furrowed. Her voice was strained as she said, "Right. I heard you were using magic against some of our soldiers in Ederis—and then you used it in Mindoth, too. The gods gave it to you, of course. And I'm guessing they forced you to do their bidding with it. The hierarchy of divine power, still alive and well."

Anger heated my skin. Not just anger at her, but at myself—because she was saying exactly what I would have said months ago. How could I convincingly argue against something I'd spent most of my life believing?

I didn't know.

But I had to try.

"They didn't force me to take anything, or to become anything I didn't want to be," I told her. "The God of Fire gave me the powers I have to save my life. More than once, the Marr saved my life, in fact, and they—"

"The gods don't save lives. They only destroy them."

Her voice was so cold—so unlike the sister I remembered—that I was too shocked to respond right away.

"It may look like the former, at first," she went on, "but there is always a catch. Some price they don't tell you up front." Her voice softened. "Come on, Karys. You're smarter than this."

The softer tone made me even angrier; she was speaking to me as if I was the same person she'd abandoned all those years ago. Like I was a child, not a goddess with fire in my veins.

That fire was starting to get restless, eager to make itself known.

As it rose to the surface, however, I noticed something felt...*off* about it.

The lingering effects of whatever she'd injected into my neck, maybe, combined with my separation from Dravyn. Effects that could very well become more debilitating with each moment I spent trapped here, away from the rest of my divine family.

"Why did you bring me to this place?" I demanded.

"Because." She sucked in a deep breath. "I thought it might be... soothing, for us to return to a simpler time. And to a place where we wouldn't be interrupted. This smaller area was easier to wrap in protection, too."

It took a moment for the meaning behind her words to sink into my overwhelmed mind. "So there are wards of some kind around this house and its boundaries, too?"

"Of course there are." Her tone was perfectly even. Perfectly unapologetic. "I've witnessed enough destruction from the gods—I didn't want them or their monsters crashing in and destroying my chance to actually speak with you after all these years."

"You're worried about the destruction the *gods* have caused?" Seething, I asked, "And what about the lives *you've* destroyed? The humans you've killed? The damage you did to Mindoth with your bombs, and the ones you killed in Ederis before that—I saw you playing executioner for those men on the platform, you know."

I swallowed several times, trying to keep my throat open as it threatened to swell shut. I licked my painfully cracked and dry lips, took several deep, steadying breaths—but nothing I did helped the words I wanted to say make it out.

Savna's voice softened again as she said, "What do you know of the ones we put to death in Ederis?"

She waited patiently, until I finally managed to cough up a response. "I know you smiled when you swung the blade."

"Because the people of Ederis needed to see a confident leader."

"They needed to see you murder humans? People who likely had families and—"

"They stole from our storehouses. And what they couldn't steal, they destroyed through fire and poison. They also murdered three guards in the process. So hardly what I would call *innocent souls*. I didn't enjoy putting my blade through their necks, but I know how to put on an act when needed. And our followers needed that show of confidence after weeks of dealing with losses at the hands of human-kind."

My throat closed up even tighter than before.

"We're just trying to survive, Ryssy."

"Don't call me that." The words hissed out of me before I could stop them. "I'm not a child. I don't need a childish nickname."

"Right. Sorry." She started to brush her hands together but stopped herself, clenching them into fists instead. "You understand, though, don't you? We have a right to fight back. To survive. To maybe, some-day, find a way back to an existence that's *more* than just surviving. And I thought that you and I...that together we could..."

The trailing hint of hope in her voice was the most painful part of this ordeal yet. To know that I couldn't share the weight of that hope, no matter how badly she wanted me to. No matter how badly *I'd* wanted to, once upon a time.

The words hurt, like they were wrapped in thorns that caught on the swollen walls of my throat, but I forced a reply out: "I'm not inter-ested in fighting that war with you anymore."

"...I see," was all she said.

But the question lingering in her gaze was easy enough to read: *Whose side are you on?*

I still didn't know how to answer that.

I just knew I couldn't think clearly in this house. Even if the wards had not been wrapped around it. Even if she hadn't poisoned me. Even if Dravyn and his magic had not been so far away. Even then, I suspected I wouldn't have been able to.

Because I no longer belonged here.

And the longer I stayed, the more unbalanced I feared I would become—and what would happen if I remained trapped here? I didn't know what Dravyn would do to get back to me. What fires he would set or what battles he would wage.

Nothing that would help settle the wars building around us, I guessed.

"You have to let me go," I said. "I have to return to the divine realm. I have to let the rest of my court know that I'm safe, or else…"

Her expression hardened so swiftly, so violently, that it made my heart skip several beats. "Or else *what*?"

"It's just—"

"What have they told you?" she asked. "That you'll be punished if you don't come back to them when they call? Like a dog, beaten for refusing to heel?"

"It's not like that. You've got it all wrong, again."

"Or maybe they'll take out their disappointment on the mortal realm instead? How very like our revered *gods*, to throw a fit when they aren't the ones controlling the show."

I couldn't refute this point, I realized, so I simply sank back onto the bed, clenching my hands into the scratchy sheets.

Savna turned away, muttering, "Let them come get you if they value you so much."

Who's holding who hostage, now? I wanted to snap.

It wouldn't have solved anything between us, though, so I held my tongue.

Her back remained to me. I noticed then that the door to the hallway was open. It would have been easy enough to make a run for it. But how far could I get in my current state? And how dangerous were the wards wrapped around the perimeters of this house?

Before I could decide whether or not to chance it, she spoke again: "Do you know what I risked to go to Mindoth and find you? All the others were against it. We had other things, bigger things, to focus on, aside from you. But when I realized you would be there, I could think only of *rescuing you*.

"And I'm sorry I didn't find a way to reach you sooner, but that doesn't change the fact that we're finally together, now. That's what matters. You're safe. Whatever it takes to heal you from whatever the gods have done to you, whatever you need—I'm right here. I'm not going anywhere."

I held more tightly to the sheets in my fists, trying to breathe normally over the massive lump that had formed in my throat.

I'm right here.

I'd had dreams like this.

In between my many, many nightmares, occasionally there would be one like this, where my sister found me. There was light. Warmth. Her voice comforting me as I trembled. These were the *good* dreams, I'd always thought—the kind I held on to for strength, for hope, for clarity.

But now I was living one such dream, and there was no denying it felt more like a nightmare.

Quietly, I said, "I didn't need rescuing." She opened her mouth to argue, but I continued without giving her the chance: "And just because we're together again doesn't mean we're a family again."

Though they were true, I wanted to take the words back the instant they slipped past my lips.

But the damage had already been done.

Savna's face fell, whatever argument she'd been preparing dying a cold, silent death. Her face paled, her expression turned stony. Like a gravestone marking yet another loss between us. She muttered something about needing to go send a message to someone. Then she was gone again, tapping her hands softly together as she left.

Clap.

Clap.

Clap.

And just like that, I was alone.

I sank down to the floor and cried until I ran out of breath.

At some point, I must have drifted off, because I opened my eyes to the sight of moonbeams spilling across my bedroom, reaching toward my outstretched hand, but not quite touching it.

I was still on the floor. I'd pulled my sheets from the bed. They were tangled around me, cocooning me in a feeling of safety. I'd often slept that way as a child—wrapped so tightly I could hardly move—and some part of my mind must have longed for that safe surrender.

Foolish mind.

I fought my way upright and peeled the sheets from my body. Rubbing my eyes, I took in my surroundings. The shelves and curtains and the few meager trinkets my younger self had prized were reduced to figures casting strange, jumbled shadows against the walls.

As I stared at them, a flood of emotions rose in my chest, choking the breath from my lungs.

I couldn't stay in this room for another second.

After grabbing my coat and boots from the corner chair and pulling them on, I silently made my way into the narrow hallway. What had felt so small and cozy when I was younger now felt massive—a cold, yawning abyss that seemed unending.

But I could traverse it easily enough. Quietly enough. I was out of tears to cry, so the ache in my chest and the burning in my lungs could proceed in silence.

As I'd done so often when growing up, I would make no noise, alert no one to my presence.

I knew all the places the floor would creak. The layout of things was still familiar, too, as large and twisting as it all felt in this moment. I could navigate even as my mind battled with other things.

I sensed my sister in her familiar place, too—in the small study beside the kitchen.

After our father died and our mother left, Savna had taken to sitting in that room most nights, hunched over the desk making lists and notes, counting what little money we had and devising the smartest ways to spend it. Praying to the gods for more. Cursing at them when they didn't answer. Trying to figure out how we were going to make ends meet. Some nights she didn't leave that room at all and I would wake the next morning to find her passed out in the tattered armchair in the corner, often clutching a wineskin to her chest.

I couldn't resist peeking inside that room as I passed it now.

And there she was, asleep in the expected chair.

I eyed the blanket that had fallen into a dark pile at her feet. When I was younger, that was part of my ritual on those cold, lonely mornings: I would cover her up and let her sleep in while I quietly did my best to create breakfast out of whatever scraps I could find in our kitchen.

Tonight I walked on, even though my knees threatened to buckle as I did.

The wind howled outside, rattling the walls. Though the old house was relatively well-insulated, I felt as if *I* wasn't—like I'd been left hollowed after all the tears I'd cried, and now the cold cut straight through even the fine coat Rieta had made for me, driving right into my bones.

I couldn't stop shaking.

None of the fireplaces I passed were lit. Firewood had not been particularly easy to come by when I was growing up, and we had always used it sparingly, even on the coldest nights; I could still hear my mother's voice demanding us not to waste it. I wondered what my family would think if they were all here now, confronting the goddess I'd become. I wasn't thinking of the complications of my existence in that moment—only the fact that my magic could have kept us all warm.

As I made my way toward the back door, guided by memory more than sight, I half-expected to hear more familiar voices from my childhood echoing around me. I paused on the threshold, listening for them. Whether hoping for or dreading the sound...I wasn't sure.

I heard nothing, either way. It was just me and my sister here, I was certain—at least until I stepped outside for a breath of fresh air, caught a familiar scent, and realized I was wrong.

I was not alone.

CHAPTER 27

Karys

"Andrel." Just speaking his name made my stomach curl.

"Hello, Karys."

I resisted the urge to back away as he drew closer. Beneath his familiar spice and sandalwood scent, he smelled strongly of blood and burned flesh. He looked poised and perfectly put together, though—as if he'd had time to clean himself up between the battle at Mindoth and now, yet was unable to fully wash the proof of it from his skin. As he came to a stop before me, I saw part of that proof more clearly: Thick bandages covered one of his hands.

Or what was left of it, at least.

Perhaps it was a trick of the moonlight, but it looked as though part of that hand was entirely...*gone*.

I swallowed hard. "Missing something, aren't we?"

"Ah. Yes. This." His expression remained unbothered—the practiced indifference I expected from him—as he lifted the injury so I could better inspect it. "Your other half took himself a souvenir, I'm afraid."

My heart clenched at the mention of Dravyn, but I didn't let any emotion show. "You're lucky he only took your hand."

Andrel chuckled at this, though the sound was disturbingly without humor. His eyes seemed to darken as he said, "I would ask what you see in that barbaric, brutish monster, but I think I'm past trying to understand it."

I looked away from his injury, focusing on the small garden in the corner of the yard instead.

With our mother's help, my sister and I had planted the golden blooms within that garden when we were children; it was one of the last memories I had of the three of us. To my surprise, the flowers were still neatly intact, with no weeds to be seen between them. Had Savna been tending to them?

A chill crept down my spine. I couldn't decide which was worse to look at: The flowers—painful reminders of the family I once had—or Andrel.

I eventually settled on him, though meeting his eyes made the rage swirling in my gut rise up and settle uncomfortably tight in my chest. "Why are you here?"

"Because I wanted to be a part of the reunion, of course. Why else? Your sister has been looking forward to seeing you again for a very long time."

"And you thought we would want you here to witness things?"

"Not you, perhaps. But Savna and I have gotten very close, as of late. So I'm here as her partner and supporter."

I shoved past him, heading for the bed of flowers.

I needed space.

"Partner," I hissed. "Does your *partner* know what you did to me after we fought in the middle-heavens, by chance? Does she know you essentially killed me?"

"No one knows what happened except for you and me. I wouldn't betray you like that."

I couldn't keep the heated emotion from my voice this time. "What the hell are you talking about?"

"Oh, did you *want* me to tell your sister how many of our kind you killed that day in Nerithyl? How you stole our prized weapon and ruined what should have been our most successful attack against the gods to date? It might put a damper on your heartwarming reunion, don't you think? If she realizes all the *disappointing* decisions you made that day, well..."

I started to reply, but the words died in my throat. I was spiraling into that awful memory once more. Back on the shores of the river with his knife, his betrayal, his words slithering over my skin—

Your sister will be so disappointed in you.

"That's what I thought," he said, mistaking my silence for agreement. "So we can keep it our little secret. No one but me needs to know the depths of your traitorous behavior, Kare."

I glared at him over my shoulder. "I am not the traitorous one between us."

"You don't think so?" He held up his bandaged hand, studying the misshapen end as though seriously considering my words, only to dismiss them with another cruel, hollow laugh. "Well. I am not the one fucking a god whose hands are drenched in the blood of our kind, now am I?"

Streaks of red blurred my vision.

The wards surrounding the yard were clearly even more powerful than I'd feared—because if they hadn't been, fire would have engulfed everything around us with my next breath.

Whatever was caging me in was enough to reduce my magic to mere flickers.

I tried the same trick I'd used against the Sun Court goddesses, gathering those flickers and shaping them into something sharp that I might wield. But the resulting weapon was not nearly as impressive this time— a mere dagger of fading firelight that wouldn't hold its shape.

"Relax," Andrel said, stepping closer. "I'm not going to tell anyone about that part, either. Most of them still think you're a victim of the God of Fire, being forced to do his bidding."

Lies. So many lies it made my head spin just trying to keep track of them. I tossed the dagger of fire away and knelt down, picking one of the flowers. The bloom of pale gold felt velvety and cold beneath my fingertips—something tangible to focus on.

"You have an opportunity before you, you know."

I didn't reply, but he continued all the same.

"You could start over here as though what our followers believe is true. You could be an inspiration to them—a victim, but one who escaped the chains the gods attempted to bind you with."

I crushed the flower against my palm, staring at the bright yellow stain it left behind as I said, "Start over with you holding those chains instead, I assume?"

I kept my back to him, but I could hear the smile in his voice as he said, "I've always held your chains, Karys. Nothing has really changed about that."

I straightened, unclenching my fist and letting the bits of flower fall from it as I replied in a low, furious voice: "*I've* changed. And I am more than just a victim."

He cocked his head, eyes dancing between darkness and amusement. "Your time among the gods really has made you delusional, hasn't it?"

I flexed my fingers as claws extended.

"You don't belong among them," he said. "You don't belong with *him*. And the sooner you admit that to yourself and come back to your true home, the happier you'll be. You were happy before, weren't you? Before he stole you away from us."

"You think he stole me from you? Is that why you and my sister attacked his kingdom?"

He laughed the idea off, but there was violence in the sound, which made me think I'd struck somewhere close to a truth he was trying to keep buried.

"I wasn't taken from you," I said, turning to face him more fully. "I was never yours."

I held my ground even as he closed the space between us, tilted his face uncomfortably close to mine, and said, "I must be misremembering all the times you and I laid together, then. And all the times you swore your loyalty to me, among other promises."

My claws twitched. I wanted to rake them across his mouth to shut him up. I hated his words. I hated myself for not being able to deny them. I wanted to set fire to us both—turn it all to ashes that I could rise up from, reborn into something entirely new. Something he had never touched.

He stepped past me before I could do any of these things, however, moving to study something in the distance. His boots crushed a few stray flowers along the garden's edge as he went. He paid them no mind.

"But to answer your question," he continued, matter-of-factly, "No. I'm not orchestrating a war merely because I'm some pathetic jilted lover. Galizur is a strategic target for us, and one that had it coming long before you ran off and started fraternizing with the gods.

"And they're only the start of our plans—we have other kingdoms on our list, of course. Other operations that have already started elsewhere. The fact that targeting Galizur *also* gets under the God of Fire's skin is really just a lovely coincidence. You should have seen his face when he realized his brother was our true target in Mindoth."

"...Your true target?"

Had they succeeded in killing the king?

Fresh horror and rage tore through me as I pictured Dravyn losing the only family he had left, and that rage carried me forward before I could stop myself.

I swiped my claws toward Andrel's neck. My first strike grazed skin. He spun around and quickly blocked the second, catching me by the elbow and twisting my arm painfully away from his body, his beastly, inhuman strength surging to meet my own divine vigor.

"Looking rather weak for the *goddess* he claimed you were," he sneered.

I jerked free of his hold. Embers flew out from my body. Suppressed, but still there, bristling beneath the surface. Maybe I could still summon more if I tried harder...

Or maybe trying to force it while within this oppressive space would result in me passing out—or worse.

The debate distracted me. My magic dimmed.

Overthinking it, again, I silently chastised myself.

"Your new divine skills aren't worth much in this place, are they?" Andrel mused.

I swept a cold, calculating look around the yard's perimeter, studying the way the air around it wavered and occasionally shimmered. "The ward around this yard is stronger than what I encountered around Ederis."

"Yes." He looked entirely too pleased with himself. "We actually have your visit to Ederis to thank for that; it helped us realize some of the weaknesses in our previous designs. Your sister thought this location would be a nice, confined place to visit with you *and* test out new spells."

"A nice, confined place to imprison me, you mean."

He shrugged. "Or keep you safe. It depends on your perspective."

I took a step closer to the boundary, even though drawing nearer made my skin tingle with warning.

I couldn't be trapped here.

I *wouldn't* be trapped here.

Another rush of anger overcame me and sent me charging forward once more—this time, toward escape.

Andrel didn't attempt to stop me.

He didn't need to.

Running into the ward was like running into an invisible, electrified wall—it sent a jolt of uncomfortable energy hissing through me, stealing my breath away.

Stranger sensations followed.

The buzzing current settled, but the discomfort continued as I tried to keep moving; it was like the very air was sticking to my skin, threatening to peel it from my bones if I didn't hold still.

Even after I'd stopped, I felt like parts of me were being pulled in different directions. The world twisted and turned. I stared at my boots as I attempted to keep my balance, and it was then that I noticed the runes that had been sketched along the ground.

The source of these ward spells?

They must have been.

Similar symbols likely covered the landscape in the Hollowlands, near the barriers I'd crossed before entering Ederis. Though they must have been better hidden there; I hadn't noticed anything when passing through.

The analytical side of my brain longed to sit with these marks and try to sort out their magic. My gaze swept over all the ones I could see, doing my best to commit them to memory. Later, I would try to recreate them and search for patterns and meanings.

In the meantime, I needed to escape their hold before it destroyed me.

The more I tried to move through the barrier, the more it felt like I was being torn apart. Trying to push forward made things worse, leaving me with no choice but to stumble backward into the yard instead. I lost my balance as I did.

Andrel caught me as I fell.

I was too stunned by the ward's power to immediately fight my way free of his hold. My limbs dangled uselessly as he carried me toward the cracked, moss-covered bench of stone near the center of the yard.

"Put me *down*," I snarled.

He did—placing me on the bench—but he stayed entirely too close. I longed to shut my eyes to try and fight off the spinning, but I didn't dare. Not when he could so easily reach out and touch me.

"I wish Dravyn had ripped both your hands off," I muttered.

Andrel expelled another low, humorless laugh. He settled down on the bench beside me, leaning forward and resting his elbows against his knees.

How many times had we sat together on this very bench, just like this, dreaming and plotting and chatting together? It had always felt like a place of infinite possibilities to my younger, more naive self.

Stupid, stupid, stupid *younger self.*

Thinking about it made the spinning in my vision and the churning in my stomach worse.

Quietly, Andrel said, "I'm sure he wishes he'd ripped them both off, too. Too bad. And now he won't be able to find us, either—yet another tragedy."

"You underestimate how connected we are." I risked closing my eyes just for a moment. "There is no ward you could create that would stop him from finding me."

"Hmm."

I looked over to find him watching me as though I was an experiment of some sort, making me regret opening my mouth.

"I *have* heard that the gods can connect with one another without the need for speech, or even proximity," he said. "That within their own court and the line of their hierarchy, the ability to communicate is even stronger…"

I averted my gaze so he couldn't see the confirmation in it.

"It could be useful to know more about how this power works."

I attempted to put more space between us. Trying to properly sit up and move made my dizziness worse, but I still managed to drag myself all the way to the end of the bench, gripping the corner of the backrest for support.

"In fact, I'm sure you have *lots* of useful information about the gods that you could pass along to us," Andrel continued, his arms still resting casually against his knees, his tone still easygoing—still eerily similar to the countless bench chats we'd shared in the past.

"What makes you believe I would give you any of that information?"

"It would be easier than making me force it out of you."

"You won't force anything out of me."

He cut me a sidelong glance that made the hairs on the back of my neck stand on end. "Maybe not," he said with a shrug. "But I'm still willing to try."

I gripped the back of the bench harder. Pulled myself up taller.

"I wonder…how much would it take to catch his attention through the impressive wards we've created?" His appraising gaze drifted between me and those wards. "My theory is it would take *quite* a bit of pain for the sensation to pass through and reach him. Shall we experiment?" He leaned back, propping a foot upon the opposite knee and reaching for the knife sheathed at his ankle.

I stood, still holding onto the bench as I tested my balance. "Stay away from me."

"I *want* to," he said, holding up his bandaged, crudely amputated hand, "but I do owe him for this." He got to his feet, stretching, the knife clutched loosely in his hand.

I held my ground as he turned to me. Heat swirled in my gut, my magic still fighting for a chance to rise up and confront him regardless of all the different things trying to shove it down.

He twisted the knife around in his hand, speaking more to the blade than me as he said, "What torture it would be to him, to feel your pain but not be able to reach you."

His eyes flashed to mine.

He lunged.

I swung my fist forward and flames exploded from it, forcing him to a stop. He took a step back, throwing his arm up to block the scorching air from his smiling face. "A bit of a goddess in you after all, it seems."

"If you take one more step toward me, it's a demon you're going to encounter, not a goddess."

He smirked at the challenge. "One in the same, as far as I'm concerned."

In the next breath he was darting forward again, sidestepping more flames I managed to summon, then curving around behind me.

I sensed his arm falling toward my shoulder. I ducked and dove out of the way of his first slash, but the evasion triggered another wave of dizziness that slowed me down. He took advantage when I stumbled, immediately following up his first swipe with another.

Still half-unbalanced, I parried wildly with all the unbridled divine strength I could summon. My fist struck his forearm, forcing his grip on the knife to unclench for an instant. As his hold faltered, I hooked another, more accurate punch into his wrist. The knife slipped free and thudded against the dirt.

His hand caught me by the throat as I focused on kicking the blade away. He jerked me back against him, trapping me in a close embrace that was worse than any knife trailing across my skin.

"Just like old times," he murmured in my ear. "I miss training with you."

I slammed my hand into his thigh. Claws sprang forth as I did, accompanied by a rush of heat—enough fire and sharpness to make him curse and send him staggering backward once more.

"And all those training sessions we had together seem to be paying off now," he said. "Well done."

"Trying to take credit for my strength, even now," I growled. "What a fucking delusional bastard you are."

"Maybe I'm not the one responsible for your strength," he countered, "but let's not forget that I do know your *weaknesses.*"

He proved this an instant later by striking forward again without restraint, aiming for my face. For my scars. He knew my tendency to flinch whenever anybody focused on those scars.

I knew it, too, yet I couldn't stop myself from twisting frantically away, leaving my shoulder vulnerable to a blow that sent me sprawling across the ground.

Countless times, he'd used this same move during all those training sessions we'd endured together—and almost every time, it ended with me on the ground. It was usually the move that signaled the end of our practice.

It would not be the end of me this time.

Despite my awkward landing, I recovered quickly and sprang back to my feet. My skin was burning, my magic glowing faintly, lighting symbols over my body and illuminating the old scars along my face and neck.

Proof of my power, not my mistakes, I reminded myself, fiercely.

My claws came to rest against Andrel's chest in the same instant his fingers wrapped once more around my throat.

For every bit of pressure I inflicted against him, he countered with a tighter hold, crushing my windpipe and threatening to choke the breath from my lungs.

We remained in this stalemate for a long, tense moment, until a lantern flickered to life in the house and briefly drew our gazes toward it.

"I wonder what your sister will say if she finds us like this?" Andrel mused.

"I have no problems explaining myself to her."

"You think she would listen to you?"

"Of course, she—"

"Are you sure about that?"

I inhaled a little too sharply, a little too painfully, as I realized: I *wasn't* sure.

Who would she side with? The one she had apparently spent years plotting a revolution with? Or me? Me—who she believed was deliriously confused, a victim of the gods being forced to attack my own kind against my will.

"For her sake, let's hope she *doesn't* listen to you," Andrel said. "I'm running out of patience for those who test my loyalty. So keep that in mind if you're going to try and win her over to your side."

"My sister is not a fool. She'll realize the truth about you before the end. I am going to make certain of that."

"The truth can be a tricky thing," he replied, relaxing his stance and calmly stepping away as though we hadn't just been locked in a deadly embrace.

I remained tense, claws extended, even once he'd put considerable space between us.

He eyed those claws for a long moment before he said, "Stop this. Stop fighting and come home for good. Stop breaking your sister's heart."

What about my *heart?*

It was a question I wouldn't have been able to ask months ago, but now it was all I could think in response.

"You don't belong with the gods," he said. "You belong with us."

It was almost refreshing compared to my conversations with Cillian and my sister—because Andrel was not asking me whose side I was on.

He was *telling* me.

Which made it so much easier to lift my head up and say, "No. I don't."

I might not have known exactly who I was yet, but I was beginning to understand who I *wasn't*.

The light in the house brightened. Beckoning me. Andrel's gaze followed me as I started toward it, though he remained perfectly still, holding like a predator tensing and waiting for the exact moment to pounce on its prey.

"I have worked very hard to prepare for the grand ending we're now approaching," he called after me. "Your sister is a large part my plans, and I will be watching both of you more closely, now, making sure neither of you does anything to derail things."

I paused, one foot on the porch steps, and tilted my head just enough to keep him in my sight.

"So if I were you," he said, "I would rethink my loyalty one more time, and I would choose my next steps very carefully. For Savna's sake, if nothing else." His gaze finally left me, sliding instead to where my sister's silhouette had appeared in the kitchen window.

I couldn't reply over the lump forming in my throat.

"You've already lost enough," he said. "I would so *hate* for you to lose anything else."

CHAPTER 28

Dravyn

THE SOUND OF A DISTANT DOOR OPENING VAULTED ME FROM my restless, reluctant attempt at sleep.

I sat at the desk in my usual study. Rieta had badgered me for hours about going to my bed, but I hadn't been able to bring myself to lie in it alone.

So instead, I'd tried to find things to distract myself with in here. And at some point, I must have laid my head on the desk and drifted off, clutching the thick book that was still in my hand.

Several of the tome's yellowed pages were marked by scraps of parchment—yet I didn't remember what I'd been looking for. The hours were running together, each darker and more pointless than the last.

What did it matter what else I was looking for when Karys was still nowhere to be found?

My shoulder throbbed dully. The Healing God's magic had driven out the poison, but a mark remained, similar to a bruise made up of various, sickly shades of grey. It spilled around to the center of my back, and it had not faded in the slightest, even as the hours passed. Weakness lingered in that shoulder as well.

The longer Karys and I spent apart, the more noticeable the weakness was becoming, as per usual—and the fatigue was not limited only to my latest injury. It was spreading to every part of me.

I did not regret giving her so much of my magic—I would never regret it—but the complications were compounding. Physically, magically, mentally. Combined with the lingering effects of the elven poison, those complications were...concerning. Almost too much to bear.

I rose slowly to my feet, flexing my hand and calling a small flame to it. I was stronger when she was close to me, yes, but I was still powerful on my own. Powerful enough to keep moving. To find her. To fix everything that had gone wrong.

Moth rested upon his back on one corner of the desk before me, perilously close to rolling off the edge. The room was deathly quiet save for his breathing and occasional snores.

The door to the study remained closed, but I heard footsteps drawing closer to it. I sensed the Winter God's energy along with those steps, and suddenly, I was wide awake, my magical troubles entirely forgotten.

Valas let himself inside without knocking.

His face was grim.

I steeled myself for bad news.

"No sign of her," he said, shrugging off his coat and tossing it onto the chair in the corner. He sank down into the same chair, raking a hand through his hair, clenching the pale locks tightly in frustration.

I braced my arms against my desk. "What are you doing back here, then?"

He darted a glance my way without moving.

"There are more places that need searching," I insisted. "The realms are vast, as are the spaces in-between them. I was thinking...she could have tried to escape, and if she wasn't able to focus enough to properly use magic to transport herself, there's no telling where she might have ended up by mistake. Have you really checked *everywhere*?"

"Everywhere..." Valas settled more fully into the chair, clasping his hands behind his head with a sigh. "In three days? No. Afraid I didn't manage to search the entirety of the realms—and everything in between them—*in three fucking days*. My sincerest apologies."

I ignored his droll tone, shoving my chair under the desk with enough force to rattle everything on top of it.

Moth stirred with the shaking, rolling closer to the edge and letting out an irritable yawn without opening his eyes. I caught him by the leg and pulled him back toward safety.

He slept on in the center of the desk while I went to one of the many shelves lining the room and ran my hands along the rows of books and other things stacked upon them.

Again, I didn't really know what I was looking for.

But Karys had re-arranged these shelves the last time she was in here. I couldn't help being drawn to the things she'd touched, even in spite of the painful memories they invoked.

In between the rows of books were stacks of notes she'd made on countless subjects; everything from magic to divine politics to realm layouts to recipes. I could still picture her taking these notes—the grumpy looks she would give me when I interrupted her; the quill flashing with her obsessive scribbling; her voice, mumbling under her breath while she worked things out...

I felt unbalanced without these small pieces of her surrounding me. They'd become like guideposts over the past months, keeping me on the right path even when everything else was going to hell.

I picked up one of the notes. On it, she'd drawn a symbol for each of the three Creators; four more symbols underneath each one, representing the Marr; and still more symbols along the very bottom, representing some of the Miratar spirits—a more or less complete diagram of the current divine beings.

The symbol of Fire appeared to have been reworked several times. The parchment under it was worn through and streaked with stray marks, as if she hadn't been able to decide how to represent the two of us. And the twin flames she'd settled on were faint compared to the rest of the symbols she'd drawn.

The longer I stared at it, the faster the room seemed to spin.

"What are you doing over there?" Valas asked.

I didn't answer right away.

What the hell *was* I doing here?

The Winter God cleared his throat.

"We have work to do," I finally replied, gripping the shelf in front of me. "I need you to tell me every place you searched. We need to be methodical about this—"

"She's still in the mortal realm."

The certainty in his tone made me pause.

"I didn't find *her*," he said, "but I did find witnesses...people who saw someone attack her. An assailant who apparently looked very similar to Karys herself."

I clenched the shelf's edge hard enough that I lost the feeling in my fingers. "Her sister?"

"That would be my guess. Where she took Karys to, no one could say. Or *would* say. But there may be more answers in your old kingdom. In the palace you once called home, to be specific."

I tensed, crumpling the paper in my hand before I realized what I was doing. "Why there?"

"Because apparently several members of the elven army were taken captive in the aftermath of the attack on Mindoth's Keep. Cillian was among them. If they haven't executed him yet, then he could prove helpful to us." He frowned, looking suddenly doubtful as he added, "Although he wasn't particularly helpful to Karys before, was he?"

"No. But I can be more persuasive than she was." I hastily placed the diagram she'd made back on the shelf just as fire ignited in my palm once more. The flames snaked all the way up my forearm before I settled them and turned them to smoke.

I didn't have the same desire to dismember him as I did Andrel, maybe—but if Cillian was not willing to cooperate with me, I would do much worse.

Valas stretched his legs out in front of him and tilted his head back, staring up at the ceiling in thought. "The question, then, is how willing your brother will be to let you interview his prisoners."

"I'd keep my expectations low."

"You did pull him out of that collapsing building, didn't you? I'd say he owes you."

"He isn't really the type to return favors, unfortunately."

"Still worth a try." He fixed his stare on me.

For once, he wasn't goading.

Concerned, more like—which was a strange expression on his face.

He and Mairu didn't know all the details of my past life, but they knew better than to push me about matters concerning my brother. And it was clear Valas expected me to disagree with his plan.

I didn't.

Despite the dread that filled me at the thought of paying Fallon a face-to-face visit, there was no real question in the end. He could bring me a step closer to Karys.

And for her, I would have faced every demon of my past, and then some.

"It's the only real lead we have," Valas said, almost apologetically.

I reached for Karys's drawing again, smoothing it out before stacking it once more with the other notes. I made sure to put it back precisely as I'd found it, knowing she'd give me hell if I didn't.

"Then it's the lead I will follow," I said.

I TOOK the path through Eligas, making my way into the mortal river that bordered the royal city of Altis, just as before. Because it was the less taxing method of travel, and because I'd already taken this path such a short time ago—so I could follow it unconsciously and not truly think about what I was doing.

I'd tried to come up with a different plan to get to Cillian and the other prisoners who might prove useful, concocting increasingly elaborate—and admittedly foolish—plots that would have potentially gotten me in and out of the palace dungeon without having to speak with Fallon.

But facing my brother—truly talking to him—would be the quickest option. The quietest. And, relatively speaking, the easiest.

I would just have to ignore the weight in my chest growing heavier with every step I took toward my old home.

Mairu accompanied me into the city. Once there, however, I moved alone in the direction of the palace. I traveled around the outskirts of Altis, this time, not bothering to hide my appearance with the Serpent

Goddess's magic, or otherwise, but not wanting to draw any extra attention, either.

It was late enough that I passed almost no one. I still kept my hood drawn. Stares followed me around most corners, but the paranoia likely had more to do with the unease after the attack on Mindoth than anything.

If any of the few I passed recognized me as a god who bared a striking resemblance to their former prince, they gave no indication of it.

Most of them knew what had become of that prince, of course. Or had at least heard rumors about it. And years ago, perhaps they would have been anticipating a visit from me—especially after all that had happened in Mindoth.

But it had been so long since I'd walked these streets in a recognizable form that there were no eager bows or other greetings to welcome me; only wariness. Which was just as well.

Yet, as I arrived at the palace gates, I found myself *hoping* to be recognized. Because I'd decided on my plan by this point: The quickest way to get inside and speak with the king would be to reveal my true identity and dare anyone to deny me entry.

A pair of alert guards flanked the main door, hands resting on their swords.

I rolled the tension from my shoulders—sending a slight throb of pain through my still-healing injury in the process—and lowered my hood.

The lanterns around the door burned low, their light barely enough to illuminate the mosaic of my family's crest that featured on the ground before the double doors. As I stepped onto that crest, pausing in the center of the eagle's outstretched wings, the guard on the left snapped his gaze to me.

The guard on the right froze mid-way through unsheathing his weapon, his gaze sweeping over me, stalling on my face as he clearly tried to place it.

It took more effort than usual, but I breathed in deep and called magic to the surface on the exhale, lighting fiery patterns across my forearms and up around my neck. The lanterns brightened as well. The gold and ivory mosaic glittered beneath me.

"You..."

"Yes. Me." I kept my voice low and controlled, the barest hint of a threat under the words. "I am here to speak with the king."

I watched their eyes, the swift calculations and questions tumbling behind them.

"I'm afraid we can't—"

"Yes," I corrected, "I assure you, you *can*."

They both swallowed down whatever objections they'd been considering, though their eyes continued to dart restlessly about, looking for some other solution to the problem I presented.

Finally, the left one gave in, relaxing somewhat. He gave a small bow of his head, then opened the door and called for another guard stationed farther inside.

This new guard served as my escort—after some coaxing and several harsh commands from the door guard—and he cautiously led me up the second set of stairs we came to.

His eyes grew a little wider every time we passed one of the evenly-spaced torches along the hallways; the fires in them reacted automatically—even to my weakened, unconscious magic—dancing a little brighter as I passed. My escort winced with every shift in the lighting, as though he worried I would wield the flames against him, next.

We walked in silence until we reached the third floor.

"The king is likely still in his eastern study, despite the late hour." His voice shook slightly. "He passes the majority of his nights within it, as of late. Sleep eludes him often."

I know the feeling.

So at least we still had *something* in common, even now, after years and realms apart.

Our destination stood at the very end of a dark hallway lined with maps of various kingdoms and the regions within them. I'd never paid much attention to them as a child, but now I found myself falling behind as I took them in, thinking of how Karys would have been completely absorbed in the wealth of information they depicted.

Two more guards waited for us at the door to the eastern study.

"Captain Garn's orders," my escort said to them, voice still wavering a bit. "He's to be allowed in to see the king without any more questions."

Confusion flashed across the guards' faces, but they slowly stepped aside without argument.

I hesitated only a moment before pushing the heavy door open and walking inside.

I'd been granted access to this room on very few occasions growing up. And usually only when I was in trouble, being dragged before my father to face punishment—so the memories of this space were mostly unpleasant ones.

It still looked more or less the same as the image seared into my mind. Towering shelves filled with bland record books on one wall. Rows of ornate shields, swords, knives, and other gleaming weapons hanging on the other—just a small sampling of the impressive collection the former king possessed.

Torches like the ones in the halls lined these walls, as well, but they did little to warm things, even after I purposely directed more energy into them to make them burn brighter.

The room smelled as I remembered it, too—like leather and ink and metal, with a hint of the oils used to clean blades. Father had often polished those blades while listening to reports and holding small council meetings in this space. Gripping a sword kept him weighted and grounded in his decision making, he'd claimed.

Tonight, yet more guards were currently stationed in the corners. All these sentries...were they expecting another attempt on my brother's life, so soon after the last?

Fallon sat at the table, looking calm and unworried about any would-be assassins. An untouched plate of food and a goblet of what smelled like spiced wine sat beside him.

Despite my escort's claim about his lack of sleep, the king looked wide awake, a pen clutched in his hand and moving urgently over an already impressively-long letter.

He seemed mostly intact despite the injuries he'd sustained, though his movements were stiff and occasionally accompanied by wincing. His face remained a canvas of bruises, most of them now faded to a mottled shade of greenish brown. A fresh scar covered the left side of his face, the edges of it still an angry shade of red.

It reminded me of another scarred face, which made the heavy feeling in my chest grow worse.

"Why are you here?" Fallon didn't look up from the desk as he spoke, continuing his writing. Even once he placed his pen aside, he kept his gaze on the paper, lifting it more fully into the lamp light and reading it to himself over and over again.

He reminded me of our father in that moment—so desperate to seem busy because it meant he didn't have to look me in the eyes.

"I want to discuss what happened in Mindoth," I said, "and the ones you took captive after the ordeal."

He grunted. "I'm still recovering, but my prognosis is good enough. The attack was a grave mistake on the part of the elves, however, and they will pay dearly for it—through those captives and otherwise. What else is there to discuss?"

"That attack was only the beginning. The situation is fragile. Complicated."

"And you think I'm unaware of this?"

I held my tongue. I hadn't really come here to provide counsel for his war efforts. I had only one true goal tonight, and it was to get closer to finding Karys.

My brother clearly had other things on his mind.

"I didn't think you'd ever show your face in the halls of this palace again," he said after a weighted pause. "Because, after all, you are part of the *reason* the situation is so fragile and complicated, aren't you?"

Again, I said nothing. It felt like we were walking through a forest on the darkest of nights; so many rocks and roots hidden and waiting to trip us, each as likely to derail this conversation as the next.

"You started this years ago," he continued, "when you answered the attack on our family with divine fire, and then left us to clean up the mess."

I stared at the sword hanging on the wall behind him—once our father's favorite one—as I said, "And you've done nothing to keep the fire going over the years, I suppose? No attacks or unfair sanctions against the elven-kind? No thirst for vengeance of your own?"

I could feel his glare settling on me, though I kept my eyes on the sword. The blade was wide enough that I could see my distorted reflection in it—my unnaturally bright eyes, the softly-glowing edges of the symbols on my skin.

I made a conscious effort to try and settle these things; I wanted to go back to a time when we were both powerless mortals, if only for a moment.

"I've simply been trying to hold the line," Fallon said. "I would welcome peace if I thought they were capable of it."

I thought of the many, many conversations I'd had with Karys about what the elves had endured as the humans' population soared and stretched across the kingdoms. Her kind claimed they would welcome a ceasefire, too, if only the humans were capable of it.

Such a messy thing, this idea of *peace*—especially when no one could agree on who had started the war.

"And what would you know of mortal politics?" my brother asked. "How well can you really see our troubles from your divine throne?"

"I am not oblivious to them. I'm intimately familiar with the battles you face—now, more than ever."

"And why is that?" He fixed a commanding glare on me.

When I didn't answer immediately, his eyes shifted toward the guards in the corners of the room, as if considering ordering them to drag me away.

So much like our father.

Answer me, or get out of my sight.

I sighed. I'd hoped to avoid this complicated conversation—but if it was the only way to get him to understand where I was coming from, then perhaps I didn't have a choice.

"If you can be silent and listen for once in your life," I said, settling down in the chair on the other side of his desk, "then I'll explain some things."

He continued to glare for several beats before finally giving in with a slight nod.

I spent the better part of the next half hour explaining as much as I could bring myself to share about Karys, the world she came from, and the way we had collided, for better or worse.

To my surprise, Fallon didn't interrupt, except to take a moment partway through to dismiss the guards so we could continue our discussion in private. It felt like a small victory to be left alone with him. Although plenty of guards continued to linger outside, my brother didn't seem to think I was an *immediate* threat to his life, at least.

When I had finished speaking, however, he merely leaned back in his chair, crossing his arms over his chest while grooves of skepticism furrowed his brow. "And you think I should accept your stories—and counsel—without question, I assume?"

"Do you have other allies in a better position to give you information about all of these things?"

"*Allies*," he repeated with a snort. "Why should I believe you're truly an ally? The divine are known to play tricks. How do I know if everything you've said is true?"

"I'm more than just a divine being. You and I are—"

"You left," he interrupted, rising to his feet. "Ascended. Whatever you and I *were* is no longer what we *are*. There is no returning to it, either. You became a god. Powerful, worshipped, invincible. I became a king. Worshipped and powerful to some, maybe, but also targeted and alone in a way you could never comprehend. I've a reason to be guarded against outsiders, haven't I? Divine or otherwise. And *you*..." He trailed off with a hiss-like sound, one that reminded me of water trying to extinguish a fire.

He walked to the window. The curtains were open, revealing a dark stretch of land—the side of the palace that faced away from Altis. "How many years has it been since we've spoken?"

Too many.

"And you come back *now*, acting as if nothing has changed."

I rose to my feet as well, following him across the room.

"I know there are many kings who like to think of themselves as gods," he said without turning around, "but I'm not one of them. I'm afraid we have little in common these days, my divine, invincible little brother."

It was difficult to keep the frustration from my tone. "I am not invincible."

I watched the reflection of his face in the window. His expression was unreadable and unchanging, even as I drew closer and the space heated with my growing impatience.

"And I have a weakness," I said. "Weren't you listening to me earlier?"

He glanced over his shoulder. For a fraction of a second, he regarded me with something more than contempt—with something more like the exasperated but concerned looks he'd occasionally thrown my way when we were children.

He looked back out the window and said, "You mean the elven woman you spoke of."

"Yes."

His back remained to me, not inviting further conversation.

Months ago, I wouldn't have pressed this conversation. I would have accepted the silence between us—welcomed it, even. It was easier. More comfortable to just let it be.

But I'd changed.

I had something more important than my own comfort, now. Something that drew forth words I never thought I would say to my brother: "I need your help."

Fallon huffed out a laugh as he closed the curtains and went back to his desk, shaking his head. "Well, *this* is not how I imagined our reunion would ultimately go."

"I have to find her," I pressed. "And your prison hold is currently full of beings who might help me do that."

He busied himself again with his letter, ignoring me as he read whatever he'd written for what must have been the tenth time. His gaze was cold. Calculating. Unyielding. It reminded me of the nights I would follow him into the city and watch from the shadows as he tossed dice or counted cards—the icy calm demeanor of a gambler.

One who didn't seem likely to take a chance on me.

I started to once again consider the elaborate, more complicated plans I'd made on the way here; it was looking as if I might need one of those schemes to actually make my way into the dungeons...

Then he slowly, quietly said, "You pulled me from the rubble in Mindoth. I owe you a debt. And if there is one thing I have learned since picking up this crown, it is that debts make it even heavier to bear."

I stared without speaking as he made one last edit to his letter before finally folding it up and preparing to seal it closed.

"I'll grant you clearance to enter my prison holds," he said. "Speak to whomever you wish, but once your business is done, you will leave the palace as quickly and quietly as possible. I have enough complicated meetings ahead of me without having to explain to my advisors why I'm letting you do this."

I nodded my thanks and immediately turned to leave, not wanting to give him an opportunity to change his mind.

"One last thing."

I paused in the doorway and turned to face him, listening.

"I don't know what obligations you middle-gods have to this realm, but...if you find the one you're looking for, you should take her back to your heavens and keep her there," he said. "Leave the mortal wars to mortals. We don't need any more meddling deities." He busied himself with stamping his seal onto his folded letter as he added, "And don't worry—the elves will not threaten your power or the hierarchy of gods for much longer."

Those last words settled heavily over me, making me hesitate longer than I should have. "It sounds like you're underestimating them," I said.

Like a disaster waiting to happen.

He gave a dismissive snort.

"Fallon—"

"You are not welcome here any longer." His face flushed brighter from the effort of keeping his words calm. "Get out. Now. Before I change my mind about letting you into my dungeons." His eyes flashed up to mine, shining with impatience. With warning.

So I went.

I had come here with only one real purpose—I would not be diverted from it now.

But as I stepped from the room, into the dark halls filled with grim-faced guards and anxious whispers, the sense of foreboding in my chest became so heavy I could scarcely breathe.

CHAPTER 29

Karys

I SAT ON THE FLOOR OF MY OLD BEDROOM, USING A STUBBY
pencil and the few scraps of paper I'd scrounged up to create a series of
drawings.

One after the other, I was recreating the runes I'd noted along the
yard's edge, rendering each one in painstaking detail.

I was determined to memorize them. To figure out the patterns
they'd been set in. To make some sort of sense out of this power the
elven-kind had created.

After Andrel's visit last night, I'd tried several more times to walk
through the rune-powered wards. Each time had left me more dazed and
drained than before. My magic—and alongside it, my divine strength—
seemed to be dwindling more with every passing hour, as I'd feared it
would.

Being separated from Dravyn wasn't helping, either.

I didn't know how much longer I could withstand it all; I needed to
be smarter about plotting my escape.

So I was done with reckless charging. I was calmer, now, and
approaching things in my usual methodical way. I had stacks of papers

hidden under my bed already. I snuck out every chance I could, creeping my way along the edges of my prison—close enough to make the symbols on the ground flare more brightly, but not close enough to subject myself to the full extent of the ward's draining power.

If I could figure out what patterns had created that power, then I could find a way to undo it, I reasoned.

As I finished filling another page with a recreation of the last symbols I'd seen, my ears twitched, picking up the sound of my sister coming in from outside.

Even after years spent apart, I could still recognize her steps. Her tendency to tap her feet. To sway in place. She rarely moved quietly, and this evening was no exception; she fumbled around in the kitchen for a few minutes, banging pots and clinking glasses, before making her way toward my room.

I hastily shoved my newest drawings under my bed and stood, walking to the window.

It was a dreary evening. Fog blanketed the yard, making the already secluded house feel even more cut off from the world beyond it.

Savna appeared in the doorway of my room a moment later, clutching a steaming cup in her hands.

"A peace offering," she said, lifting it toward me.

I stared at the steaming cup. I recognized its scent and instantly knew what it was—a drink we'd indulged in on special occasions and on the difficult days we'd shared growing up.

"Cinnamon milk." I made myself hold still as she approached and offered it to me. "It's been a long time since I've had this."

"I thought it might've been."

I accepted it but didn't drink right away, as my throat had developed a habit of swelling up every time my sister drew near.

She suddenly seemed eager to look everywhere but my face. As I inhaled the creamy, spicy scent wafting up from the mug, her eyes fell to the floor near my bed.

I sucked in a breath as I spotted my mistake: One of the charts I'd been working on was still sticking out.

"What were you drawing?" she asked.

"I wasn't," I croaked out. "It's just...it's nothing."

She gave me a curious look before walking over to pick up the stray paper. "I find that hard to believe. Even when we were kids, you were always drawing *something*."

I thought about stopping her, maybe stomping over and ripping the page from her hands.

I couldn't get my feet to move.

"I remember all your lists," she said, distractedly, smoothing out the paper and studying it closer. "Your diagrams, your charts, your maps. You had a gift for remembering details." She was quiet for several minutes, eyes still on my work, before eventually saying, "You've gotten even better."

I swallowed. Or tried to. The swelling in my throat was becoming painful.

She sighed. Her voice trembled a bit as she asked, "So tell me...is there a map for *us*?"

The question caught me off guard.

"I don't think so," I said. "Not one I've managed to draw, anyway." I clutched the mug more tightly. It might have burned my palms if not for the command I now had over fire; as it was, I found the blistering heat comforting.

With a sigh, Savna placed the paper on my nightstand. Her eyes lingered on it for a moment longer, and then she said, "Those are the runes I set along the edges of our yard, aren't they?"

There was no use in denying it. "Yes."

"You want to know how they work?" There was a painful hint of hope in her tone. "I could teach you to create them if you wanted me to."

Her last sentence slid like needles under my skin. "I don't want to create more of those wards."

She visibly braced herself, as if I'd drawn back a sword and prepared to stab her with it.

"I want to break them," I continued, quietly. "I want to leave this place."

She stared at me for a long moment before hastily dropping her gaze back to the runes I'd sketched. "Andrel warned me you would try everything you could to get back to the gods. I'd hoped he was wrong—

hoped that you'd want to stay as long as I was here, and maybe we could…" She trailed off, shaking her head.

"What else did he warn you about?" I demanded, temper flaring at the mere mention of his name. "I would love to know the extent of the lies he's told about me."

She gave me an exasperated look. For a moment I thought she might throw up her hands in defeat and storm away, but she stood her ground, her exasperation turning to the calm fierceness I'd always admired in her as she said, "I don't know what's happened between the two of you. All I know is he's helped me hide all these years. Helped me stay safe, and helped me build an army worthy of the cause I'd envisioned—a cause our ancestors would have been thrilled about."

"An army he wanted me to serve without question."

"Of course. And I did, too, because—"

"But has he told you what he tried to do once I *opposed* him and that army?"

Her fierceness faltered for an instant, and I blurted out more words before I could lose my nerve: "The gods are not blameless, no. But he's more of a villain in this story than they ever were."

My voice shook, as did my hands, but it didn't matter. I'd gotten the words out. And speaking them made me feel more powerful than I had when gripping a blade of pure fire.

I didn't regret them or doubt them, even as the silence between us became unbearably tense, like a bowstring drawn as far back as it could go while I braced for the arrow to pierce my heart.

"We have a lot of things to work out," Savna finally said. "I am trying to make sense of so many of them, and you and me, we…"

"We always made sense," I reminded her, breathlessly. "Even when *nothing* else did, there was still you and me. Why is that so different now? Why can't you just believe what I'm telling you?"

She hugged her arms around herself and slowly circled the room, taking in the sight of my old things, clearly losing herself in memory instead of answering me.

"Savna. *Please*."

Her gaze flickered back to me. "I was surprised to find this place so intact," she said, changing the subject.

"...There was little worth stealing here," I said. "And the humans started avoiding this place more than ever after the rumors about your disappearance and the divine creatures and curses surrounding it began to spread."

"Right. But I thought you would have taken more of your belongings with you when you moved out."

I'd considered it.

In the end, it proved easier to leave most of it behind. Almost all that I *had* taken were things that belonged to—or reminded me of—her.

Everything else had been left to rot and gather dust, a decaying monument to all we'd once been.

I'd dusted a few things off since my arrival, and Savna continued to absently swipe at cobwebs and shake the staleness from throw pillows and other decor as she circled the space now.

But no matter how much we cleaned, I knew we would never again uncover the place where we'd once lived.

I still watched her as I had when we were younger. Wanting to follow her lead, to take my next cue from the big sister I worshipped. I'd been so eager to exist in her wake for most of my life that it was what I defaulted to even after everything that had happened.

But I didn't actually move to follow her this time.

And soon I realized *why* I couldn't move: Because I'd grown. I'd changed. I'd stepped outside of her and this house and all it represented, and now, I burned too brightly to be confined to my sister's shadow.

I finally lifted the drink she'd brought to my lips; I wanted to focus on the taste of it one last time, and not on the bitter uncertainty lingering between me and her. The milk was sweet but burning, much like the memories it invoked.

"This makes me miss Mother," I whispered, the words cracking as they escaped my swollen and aching throat. The drink had been her own mother's original recipe, and sipping it alongside her was one of the few pleasant memories I had of the two of us.

Savna nodded in agreement. Her eyes glassed over as they settled on the window, her mind clearly overtaken by some thought she didn't want to share with me.

"What is it?" I pressed.

Hesitantly, she said, "I found her, you know. Several years ago."

I froze mid-sip.

My sister hesitated a moment longer, bright eyes watching me closely. Silently searching my expression, wondering if I truly wanted the knowledge she had been carrying for all these years.

My heart had endured so much pain at this point that it almost felt wrong not to invite more. What did it matter, when it was already so used to aching?

I asked, "Where?"

"Olithia."

"That far south? Why were you there?"

She shrugged. "I was doing my best to keep the gods and all the other troubles trailing me as far away from you as possible."

Protecting me.

Or hiding from me?

Maybe both.

I took another sip of the milk to avoid having to speak.

"The temples to the divine in the capital city of the Olithian Kingdom are said to be the most splendid on the southern continent, and I was drawn to them out of curiosity...and disgust." She stared at the ceiling as she spoke. "Those temples have keepers. The Heart of the Divine, they call themselves. And Mother took up their garb and their oaths years ago. She wouldn't speak to me when I saw her. Wouldn't even acknowledge her own daughter. It's common practice in the Heart's circle, from what I gathered, to not associate with non-believers."

"You couldn't have pretended to believe for a minute, just to have a chance to speak with her?"

"Why should I have pretended? She was the one who abandoned us. The effort was hers to make, not mine."

I sighed.

Savna went back to staring out the window. Even though she didn't say it out loud, I could guess what she was thinking; she was comparing the loss of our mother to the loss she felt whenever she looked at me. Because she thought I was the same—a fool taken in by the gods, worshipping them blindly, turning my back on all the ones I'd loved before.

"She would be thrilled to know that at least one of her daughters is so closely connected to the divine world, now." There was a bitterness in my sister's tone that made my hackles lift.

I sat the mug down next to my drawing on the nightstand, no longer thirsty, nor eager for the memories the drink brought with it.

"I felt abandoned by you, too, you know." I tried, unsuccessfully, to keep the bitterness from rising in my own voice as I continued: "Do you have any idea what it's been like for *me*, living without you all these years?"

We glared at one another, on our way to yet another deadlock. Or so I thought—until she unexpectedly broke, and the fierce lines on her face began to soften.

I was even more shocked when she said, in a slightly uneven voice, "Well...why don't you tell me what it was like?"

I took a deep breath, unsure if I could truly put it into words—even though I'd done it before. Not for her, but for Dravyn and the rest of the divine court that took me in. They'd listened to my story countless times over these past months, patient with me even as I stumbled over the words and held back the more painful parts.

Thinking of them now brought me strength; I didn't realize how much they'd helped me heal until this moment, back in this place, surrounded by all the things that had made me sick.

My sister remained silent, her gaze heavy and conflicted.

"It was like...a tightness," I finally said. "Like being encased in rock, unable to move unless I chiseled my way out, bit by bit. Over and over. Nearly every single morning for over five years, I had to start each day by scraping away the heavy weight of stone or else I couldn't even get out of bed. And then, when I finally did make it out, I was just...*angry*."

Savna frowned, lips parting with questions she didn't manage to get out.

"Furious at you, but also at *me*," I went on, "because how *weak*, to not even be able to get out of bed. How maddening to have to carry this weight around, to not be able to throw it off. I wanted to be rid of you so many times, yet I clung to you tighter than I've ever clung to anything. I knew it made no sense. But I couldn't stop. Until I..."

Until I replaced you.

My sister kept her lips pressed tightly together this time, her eyes shining with emotion, urging me on.

But I couldn't bring myself to tell her I had become someone powerful and new—someone who existed outside of *her.*

It was true, yet knowing this didn't stop the guilt or the pain that came from letting go. She had been my comfort for so long, even in her absence. I'd grown used to the grief of that absence. I'd built my life around it.

Grieving the loss of her while she stood directly in front of me was a different challenge, all together.

I looked past her, to the same window she'd been staring through. My thoughts again turned to escaping. To running out into the fog, putting as much space between us as I possibly could, attempting to shove my way through the wards at whatever the cost.

"I understand why it made you feel weak," Savna began before I could convince myself to move. "How tired it must have made you, clinging to our old life. But..."

My gaze darted back to her. It seemed to startle her, my sudden, rapt attention—or maybe just the fact that I was still listening at all.

She calmed her breathing and quietly finished: "But how strong you must be at this point, to have managed to claw and push your way through the heaviness so many times."

I bit my lip. Hard. Trying to cause pain, to draw blood that I could focus on instead of her voice.

"I mean it. You really have grown strong."

She didn't move.

Neither did I.

But the space between us felt like it was shrinking, forcing us closer and closer.

Why did I let myself get so close to her again?

"I'm sorry you had to be so strong, Karys."

"It doesn't matter anymore."

"Yes, it does."

I shoved past her, heading for the door.

She caught my hand. Held it gently, uncertainly—it would have been easy to pull away from the timid grip.

But I didn't.

"I'm so, so sorry," she whispered. "For everything."

Her grip on me tightened. Something inside of me crumbled—one of the countless walls I'd built around my heart breaking apart, parts of it settling like actual bricks in the pit of my stomach.

And I forgot, just for a moment, about leaving.

CHAPTER 30

Dravyn

The stairs that led into the prison hold reeked of sewage and sweat.

The same escort who had brought me to my brother also accompanied me now, announcing my presence and purpose to every other guard we passed—of which there were dozens. He trailed me to the lowest point, falling farther and farther behind as we descended, as though reluctant to venture so deep underground.

Fresh air soon became a distant memory, warmth along with it, and the foul stench grew so overpowering it nearly took my breath away.

At the bottom of the stone steps, my escort rallied his courage and soldiered ahead once more, leading me to the very last of several barred cells.

A single torch flickered on the wall outside of this last cell, enough to light a path into the dismal chamber yet illuminating nothing inside of it. My vision adjusted well enough to the dark, however, allowing me to make out Cillian's shape huddled against the far back wall.

He stirred at the sound of the guard's keys clinking and rattling against the lock, lifting his head in a slow, dazed motion.

I commanded the torch beside me to glow brighter, until the firelight reached nearly to Cillian's boots. The divine symbols blazing on my body brightened the area even further with every breath I took and every bit of power I exhaled. My escort backed away as light and heat rolled off me, nearly tripping in his haste to put space between us.

Cillian stood, hand grappling against the wall for balance as he watched me approach.

"You're alone." His voice cracked out of him, brittle and dry, as though it had been some time since his last sip of water. "Karys was not interested in another chat with me, I take it?"

"I'm sure she would be, if such a thing were possible."

"...What do you mean?" There was a touch of genuine concern in his tone. It tempered the irritation that had been smoldering in my veins since I'd stepped foot into this city; despite his mistakes, he'd always seemed to be one of the few whose affection towards Karys rang true.

Hopefully, he was feeling affectionate enough that this next part would not require force.

"Where is she?" he asked.

"That's what you're going to tell *me*," I said, slipping inside the cell and dragging the barred door shut behind me. My escort was no longer anywhere to be seen. *Coward.*

Cillian blinked rapidly as I stalked closer, trying to find my face in the sudden onslaught of light and shadows.

"She disappeared in the chaos at Mindoth," I informed him.

"Many were lost in that chaos."

"She didn't get lost. She was taken. By one of *your* allies."

He leaned more fully against the wall, dragging the shackles binding his wrists and ankles into view. The sound of scraping metal echoed in the emptiness around us.

"You must have at least some idea of where they could have taken her. And why."

A shuddering breath slipped through his parched lips. "The why is obvious enough, isn't it?" he muttered.

I narrowed my gaze, silently ordering him to keep speaking.

"She's a threat."

"Why? Because she's found favor with the gods, whereas most of your kind continue to do all they can to stoke the hostility between us?"

"Most of our leaders see her as a traitor. One who might be able to convince too many of us to stop fighting for power and status. A few have held out hope that we might be able to turn her back to our side—myself, Andrel, her sister—but others grow tired of the wrinkles she's put in our plans. Her sister wanted a chance to prove that Karys was still loyal to us. So when Karys appeared on the edge of the Galithian Training Grounds the other night, I..." He hesitated.

"You told her sister she was there." My jaw clenched. "You helped them set a trap for her, didn't you?"

He stood up straighter, the metal around his ankles grating harshly against the stone. "Savna truly wanted to protect her. From the destruction happening in Mindoth, and from the grumblings and increasing vitriol our kind had started to spit toward her."

"And do you think her sister will succeed in changing those grumbling minds?"

He considered the question as he shifted his hands, twisting his wrists around and trying to redistribute the weight of his chains. "I want her to, if only because the alternative would be..."

I stepped even closer, heat flaring around me and making him wince. "The alternative would be *what*?"

I expected him to wither as I pressed nearer. But he looked me directly in the eyes and said, "Our kind have never been lenient with traitors."

"*Traitors*," I growled. "Because if she does not conform exactly to your ideals, then she must be a traitor and a grave threat to your kind. There is no in-between."

He smiled grimly. "We understand one another, at last."

We fell silent.

The quiet deepened as the seconds passed, until I became unnervingly aware of every sound—from the pitter-patter of scurrying rat feet to the distant, nervous heartbeats of the guard who continued to keep out of my sight.

The torch outside settled as I contemplated my next words and studied Cillian. Now that I stood so close, his dire state was even more apparent.

I was not sure what my brother's soldiers had put him through, but he looked as though he had barely survived it.

His body sagged under the weight of his shackles. His breathing was ragged and uneven. His face seemed to be growing more pallid with every passing second. And all the violence I was capable of suddenly seemed useless, as did coercing with threats.

In my experience, it was difficult to threaten people who had little left to lose.

"Karys told me you were always the voice of reason amongst her old friends," I tried instead.

He didn't reply, too busy staring at his reflection in the tarnished metal cup that lay at his feet. "This isn't about me."

"No, it's about her. And you helped her escape once before. So clearly you have not forgotten about the friendship you once shared. Which is why you will tell me where she is."

He kept his eyes on his tarnished reflection, but I saw them flash with brief awareness and concern—a break in his stubbornness.

"What will it take?"

His gaze flickered to me, questioning.

"You must have a price in mind."

He lifted his hands, studying the chains attached to them as if seeing them for the first time. I expected him to barter for his freedom. It would have been easy enough for me to break him out; however impressively deep these palace depths might have been, everything around us had still been built by mortals. And I had strength enough to destroy it all, even though I was currently weaker than normal.

"Your price," I growled.

"Answers."

This was unexpected.

I swept my gaze around every corner of the cell, expecting a trick.

Cillian's face was perfectly impassive when I looked back at him.

"...Fine," I relented. "Though I warn you: What little patience I possess is very close to being used up." I rolled the tension from my shoulders and asked, "What do you wish to know?"

He hesitated an instant before deciding on his first question: "Is it true that she wields the same divine fire as you?"

"Yes."

"A goddess, then?"

"In every sense of the word."

"So what does that make you?"

I regarded him calmly despite the heat that surged through my veins.

"The gods do not share their specific powers, do they?" he pressed. "I've never heard of such a thing."

"There's more to her powers than what I gave her. What she ultimately becomes remains to be seen."

"So she doesn't truly *serve* you, as so many of our kind fear?"

The heat surged into my palm. I clenched my fist, preventing a flame from igniting. "I poured my magic into her in order to convince the Moraki to spare her after Andrel nearly killed her—to let her ascend rather than perish. And I wanted her to be my equal, so I gave more than what one of the Marr would typically use to create a servant spirit. Her power is equal to mine, even if it hasn't fully taken shape."

He was quiet for a time, seemingly struggling to wrap his mind around all of this information. "She explained it to me, once. The way the divine courts are structured and balanced. I didn't think adding another goddess—another equal—would allow them to maintain that balance."

"The Moraki had their reasons for allowing her to become what she did. I can't say what those reasons are. Or what will ultimately become of either of us."

His eyes darted up to mine, more awake, more calculating than they had been since the beginning of our conversation. "She could very well be a pawn in some great and terrible scheme of theirs. Both of you could be."

The idea was not new, and it had brought dread with it every time it crossed my mind; it was no better hearing it out loud, spoken by another.

He let the statement hang in the air, staring at the ceiling, unblinking.

"If I had to guess," he said after a long pause, "I'd say you'll find her somewhere near her old home. About twenty miles southeast of the Nightvale Wood. Her sister has been returning to it often, lately..."

He trailed off as though he intended to say more.

Before he could, his breath seized in a violent cough that lasted several seconds.

The movement sapped more of what little energy he possessed, leaving him slumping against the wall by the time he was finished, pulling the chains of his shackles taut.

Silence overtook us once again, lasting for several beats before I finally cleared my throat and offered my thanks.

Another coughing fit was his only reply at first.

Something about the sound and suddenness of that hacking set off alarm bells in the back of my mind.

After several seconds, he settled enough to mumble out more information. "I know Savna and some of her inner circle have been experimenting with different types of wards, but I can't say what they've put around that old home of hers, or how they'll try to keep you from reaching Karys if that *is* where she was taken to."

"Whatever they've done won't stop me. If that's where she is, I'll find a way to reach her."

With some effort, he met my gaze again and gave a slow nod. His eyes brightened for just a moment, back to their usual, otherworldly green, glistening with an emotion I couldn't readily name.

An unspoken understanding felt as if it was passing between us.

He stifled another cough—or was perhaps too weak to expel it. Over and over this happened: deep, ragged, would-be coughs rocking his body until he was forced to slump fully against the wall, to sink to the ground before losing his balance.

"Are you all right?"

Commotion outside his cell answered me before he could.

I ran for the door and peered out.

Countless guards raced down the steps in the distance, pouring into the hallways and darting from cell to cell, shouting questions and commands at one another.

More coughing that sounded eerily similar to Cillian's began to echo throughout the dungeon, occasionally pierced by moans and groans and agonized cries.

Then, somewhere far in the distance, I heard a guard shout, "The water! There's poison in the water!"

I turned around to find Cillian clutching the same metal cup he'd been using to study his reflection. Turning it upside down. Watching a single drop of water fall to the cold stone.

Realization sank into me, the weight of it threatening my balance.

Cillian only laughed, shaking his head. "I should have known he would take measures to make certain no captives could spill secrets." He bared his teeth in an uncharacteristically wild, rebellious expression. "He'll be furious about even the little bit of information I've managed to give you tonight."

I didn't have to ask who he was referring to; it was becoming more and more clear who the greatest source of poison among their kind was.

I stepped back to his side, kneeling to pick up the metal cup, lifting it toward my face and inhaling. A faint scent of something earthy and bitter clung to it.

"Do me a favor, won't you?" Cillian asked, back to his usual stoic appearance.

I remained crouched before him, listening, watching sweat bead on his face and trying to ignore the disaster steadily building behind me.

"Tell her...tell her I'm sorry." As the words finished slurring from his mouth, he slumped forward. I tried to prop him back upright. Breaths still trembled through his lips, but his eyes were turning empty, unseeing.

My thoughts raced. He had helped Karys in the past. He had also betrayed her in Mindoth. But now he had told me where to find her...

He was, like so many caught up in all the wars building around us, neither good nor bad. Perhaps poison was a fitting end for him. Perhaps it wasn't. Weighing souls and their endings wasn't really within my dominion.

The only thing I was certain of was that Karys would be devastated by news of his death.

I didn't think beyond this.

I grabbed his arm and poured all the energy I had into summoning a ribbon of fire that circled around both our bodies, binding us together. As the guard who had led me to the cell came rushing back into view, the ribbon of fire split into multiple strands, engulfing Cillian and me more completely, lifting us off our feet.

The guard watched helplessly as I rose from the ground. He yelled something, but it was lost in the roar of wind and flame. It didn't matter, anyway.

I was leaving.

And I was taking Cillian with me.

We traveled as fire, then smoke, then nothingness through the aether, eventually reappearing near the spot on the shoreline where I'd emerged into this realm. The concentration of my own magic in this spot helped pull me back, as did the pull of Mairu and her magic. The goddess had returned here some hours ago, as planned, waiting and watching in case I needed backup.

Even though these things made our travel relatively easy, Cillian still looked far worse by the time we fully materialized beside the river.

His face was a putrid shade of yellow. Foam dribbled from one corner of his mouth. His fingers clenched and unclenched slowly, desperately, as if trying to grab hold of something that would tether him to this living world. The prison shackles still encircled his wrists and ankles, tight enough that the magic had carried them as if they were a part of his attire —though the chains had been seared off during the process.

I was feeling only marginally better. I'd had no choice but to use magic to get us here, but now I paid for it with a disorienting rush of weakness—a reminder that I was still recovering, still separated from Karys, still not at my full power.

Nevertheless, I kept moving, carrying Cillian's limp body along the river's edge, trying to decide where I would take him—and what the hell I could possibly do for him—next.

Mairu caught sight of us and stormed over, her eyes wide and nostrils flaring. "What do you think you're doing?"

"He's dying. Poisoned by his own kind."

"And that's our problem?"

"I'm afraid it is."

"He turned Karys away when she asked for his help at Mindoth. Have you forgotten that?"

"No. Nor have I forgotten how he helped her before. And he's given me information tonight. We owe him a debt."

She pursed her lips.

"Karys would not want him to die."

Her mouth opened. Closed. She gave a curt nod. "Maybe Zachar can help," she suggested, begrudgingly. "He could put him in suspension until we figure out an antidote, and he might even be able to identify the poison they used. He's good at that sort of thing. I could go fetch him from Nerithyl. It might take some coaxing to get him here, but he's more likely to come than Armaros. I think the Healing God is growing tired of us..."

As she continued to rattle off thoughts and potential plans, I looked down at the burden draped in my arms.

His body had gone very still.

I jostled him until his eyes finally shot open and words trembled out: "Tell her...make sure you tell her..."

No less than a full minute passed, the seconds marked by shallow breath after shallow breath. Warmth seeped from his skin. His fingers continued clenching, unclenching, clenching, unclenching...

"That you're sorry?" I finished for him.

He blinked once, then shut his eyes with a small sigh.

Carefully, I knelt and laid him in the damp grass at the riverside. Even when I tried to infuse warmth into his body, his skin remained pale. Cold.

The wind rattled the trees around us. The city in the distance slept on, still and dark, seemingly oblivious to its restless leaders and budding wars and palace dungeons filled with death.

Were others outside the dungeon at risk as well?

I thought of my brother, alone in his study save for his countless guards. Could all of those guards be trusted?

Who had poisoned the water?

The world felt balanced on the cusp of disaster, like one more gust of wind might tip it into catastrophe.

Mairu had fallen silent, I realized. The plans she'd been making hung unfinished in the air as she stepped closer.

"Dravyn? Is he..." She trailed off with a sharp inhale—a sound that confirmed the fear already digging its roots into my chest.

It was part of her magic, to be able to sense even the faintest energies of living things...and her expression told me she no longer felt anything from Cillian.

I tried to jostle him awake once more, but there was no response this time.

He was gone.

CHAPTER 31

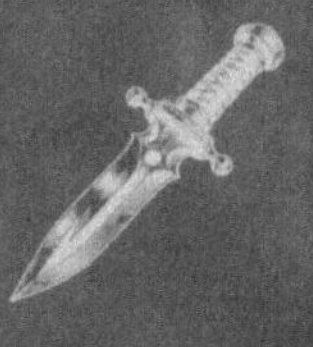

Karys

I had a plan.

I'd spent the past two days making up my mind about it, pacing the edges of the yard, double-checking every square inch of rune-inscribed ground as I continued to try and make sense of the power those symbols invoked.

My sister came and went throughout the days. Whenever she was with me, I stayed away from the edges, pretending to be centering myself once more within my old life.

This was only a ruse, of course.

A way of hiding my actual intentions from her.

That's what I told myself. But truthfully, it was alarmingly tempting to fall for my own lies. It was fast becoming too easy to talk to her again. To laugh and reminisce about our old life in between the painful questions and awkward silences.

I should have known better by now, yet something like hope threatened to bloom inside of me every time my sister returned.

Until she left again, anyway, and I found myself wondering—as I had so often throughout my life—where she'd gone.

True to form, she left me in the dark about most of the details. Only now I had things to fill those dark spaces with—the ugly, bloody, complicated things that I'd witnessed her doing.

So though I could fool myself into believing I had my sister back whenever she was here, every time she left it was like dropping on a pair of glasses that instantly made the truth perfectly, painfully clear once again.

It was approaching twilight. Savna had been gone for most of the day. Long enough that a familiar question had time to worm its way into my thoughts.

Is she coming back this time?

My chest always became painfully tight in the minutes following her departure, my heart instantly hardening in preparation for being abandoned again. The pressure had eased throughout the day as I focused on other things—more important things, like escape—but now it was growing tense yet again; this was the longest she'd been gone over these past few days.

"All the more reason to focus on my plans and not her," I said aloud to no one.

And I continued to do just that, telling myself it didn't matter if I ever saw my sister again.

If she stayed away, it would just make my plotting easier to carry out.

My plan was this: I didn't need to destroy the barriers keeping me in. I only needed to be strong enough to destroy the runes holding them in place. And after diligent note taking and hours spent deciphering those notes, I was reasonably certain I knew which of the runes to aim for first —where I might be able to do the most damage. Enough damage to open a passageway that I could slip through.

I would set fire to the symbols holding me hostage, and then I would be free.

After I slipped away, I would just have to hope I could remain conscious enough to follow up my destructive spell with one that would carry me back to the middle-heavens. Back to Dravyn.

Just thinking about it—about him—made my heart pound faster.

The effects of the poison my sister had used to get me here still lingered, even all these days later. Drawing closer to the yard's edges still made me feel like I was in danger of being peeled apart.

I needed to get as far away from the barrier as I could, I decided, to make sure I had an entirely clear head before I made my move. That farthest point, after some quick calculations, ended up being in my parents' old room.

Which was how I ended up inside of this room, sitting next to the same shrine table my mother had once knelt and prayed before on a daily basis.

The space underneath was where I had set my first fire—an accident that all but destroyed the small table.

Mother had repaired and repainted the damaged parts, but it still carried the faint scent of smoke. In some places, scorch marks could be seen bleeding through the newer coats of stain.

The statues that had once adorned the table were all gone. They were the first things my mother packed before leaving us.

If they had still been there, would I have been tempted to set them ablaze? It would have been easier, now. Even in my weakened state, I could still summon enough power to set small things on fire.

Yet it also would have been harder, as I no longer believed all the gods should burn.

I was still debating which deities deserved my flames when my sister finally returned. I tried to collect myself, the notes I'd been studying, and to escape our parents' room before she found me there, but I wasn't quick enough.

She walked inside without saying a word, pausing in front of the table and kneeling as Mother used to do.

She wasn't praying. She never prayed. She only ran her hands over the faded, stained wood, tapping thoughtfully in the places where the burn marks bled through.

Finally, she glanced at me and said, "Sorry I was gone so long. Have you eaten dinner?"

I shook my head.

I didn't protest when she led me to the kitchen, sat me at the table, and plopped a plate of food down in front of me. I picked at piles of vegetables and the heavily-spiced and roasted meat. My sister was an excellent cook—naturally gifted in ways I could only mimic after years of practice—but mortal food didn't taste as good as it once had to me. Not even hers.

Or maybe it was just this house, its wards, this whole situation making everything unappetizing.

Savna settled down in the chair across from me, carrying a plate of her own. "How are you feeling?"

My head felt the clearest it had since my arrival...and the downside of this was that it left too much room for anger to fester and turn my tone venomous.

"Relatively healthy," I spat, "for a prisoner on her—what is this, the fourth day?—of being tortured by the remnants of her past."

She arched a brow. "Well, I pride myself on pristine prison conditions and relatively healthy torture practices. I'm glad you approve of my methods."

I bit back a laugh, hating that we still shared the same sense of humor.

The next few minutes passed in silence, but we eventually found a way to maneuver around the tense and sharp uncertainties, making more small talk and the occasional sarcastic jab at one another.

Jabs that soon led to glimmers of real laughter.

I was falling for her. Again. I could feel myself tumbling down, and I again hated myself for it, but I felt powerless to stop.

I stared at my hands as she chattered on about some game we used to play as children. I was half-expecting to find that she'd carved runes into my palms like she had in the ground outside—proof of whatever strange spell she'd woven over me. Because surely that was the only explanation for why I kept getting caught up in the possibility of us again and again and again.

The spell broke several minutes later, but only because she released it; she fell silent, the laughter fading from her eyes as her mouth pressed into a thin line. The abrupt shift in tone was jarring.

"What's wrong?" I asked.

A long pause.

A chill of uncertainty swept over me, raising bumps along my arms.

Savna gripped her drink more tightly and said, "I need to tell you something."

She was silent for such a long time after that I began to think she'd forgotten what that *something* was. Maybe she was trying to forget it.

"Well?" I prompted.

She looked up, gaze focusing on the wall behind me—on a peeling painting of our family's ancient coat-of-arms—rather than on my face as she said, "Andrel is coming here later tonight."

I put my fork down. "Why?"

"Because I asked him to."

I dug my fingers into the edge of the table. There were already scratch marks in the wood from heated dinner conversations of the past, back when I was still a child and my claws were harder to control.

I kept those claws retracted, now.

At least for the moment.

Savna abandoned her food, her hands moving instead to her napkin, which she continuously twisted and untwisted as she spoke. "I knew you would be upset."

"Then why did you arrange it?"

"Because I think we all need to clear up some things between us."

"There is nothing to *clear up*. He's a monster. He's poisoned your mind. He tried to do the same to me, and when I didn't swallow that poison without complaining, *he tried to kill me*."

She ripped the napkin in two, letting the pieces of it flutter to the floor. Her eyes locked on those pieces and stayed there, her expression pained as I continued.

"I haven't told you the half of what he's done because I...I...couldn't bring myself to speak of it. Just believe me when I tell you the war he's trying to wage is *wrong*, and it will end in disaster for every side involved—humans, elves, and gods, alike."

"The alternative is disaster reserved solely for elven-kind—do you honestly think that's better?"

"That isn't the only alternative."

"What else is there?"

"Compromise. Peace."

She scoffed, shifting her weight from side to side, stretching and rearranging her limbs as if the dinner table suddenly felt too small for the conversation we were having.

Yet we were still *having* it, I realized.

She wasn't leaving for once, and, despite her discomfort, she looked prepared to actually listen to me.

Astonishment rendered me momentarily speechless.

"He lost everything because of the humans, and the gods that enable and protect those humans," she said, slowly, before I could find my voice. "And you and I have lost more than our share of things as well, we deserve a chance to—"

"I am tired of being defined by loss. And I don't want to hear any more excuses for him or anyone else."

She took a deep breath. Frustration lined her tired face, but she fell silent again, watching me closely, as if still genuinely trying to understand where I was coming from for the first time.

A sudden burst of hope—and courage—seized me. I still didn't know the exact words I needed to say, but I stood and went to her side, pulling the collar of my shirt down so she could see the scar left by Andrel's knife.

Her lips parted with a soft gasp.

I often wondered why the Moraki—with all the magic and power at their disposal—had insisted on leaving this ugly marking of my mortal life even after granting me divinity. Both this scar and the ones on my face. Why had they not made me as flawlessly beautiful as almost all the other goddesses?

Now I believed I understood the reason.

Because I needed to show my scars to others. To speak of them. To not hide from them.

My sister didn't flinch as she stared at the one near my heart. Tentatively, her hands moved as they had when we'd first reunited, her fingertips tracing my ruined skin before drawing back into a fist.

One minute passed.

Then another.

I realized I was holding my breath, my entire body tensed as if anticipating a punch from her clenched hand, even though my sister had never physically struck me.

She never moved.

The weight of all the unspoken things between us threatened to buckle my knees. I backed up a few steps and sank into the chair closest to her.

Quietly, she said, "I just wanted us to be on the same side again."

"I wanted that, too." I inhaled deeply, trying to take in more of the courage that had enveloped me a moment ago. "But things are different, now. And if you are on my side, then you have to keep listening when I speak my truth. Even when it's not what you want to hear. Even if it's not the same as your truth anymore."

Her eyes narrowed at first—the reflexive, defensive anger I'd mirrored so well for so long—but it burned up quickly, this time, leaving behind nothing but a deep, aching sadness in her gaze as she said, "You're still my little sister."

I couldn't speak over the thickness in my throat, so I merely nodded. There was no changing where I'd come from. No changing what I was, or where I'd been.

Savna clenched her other hand into a fist and fell into her habit of knocking them against one another.

Clap.

Clap.

Clap.

I averted my gaze. It eventually caught on the painting on the back wall. A myriad of conflicting feelings overcame me at the sight of the cracked and peeling mural of my ancestral house's symbol. I'd always debated what to do with this wall; the art had been fading long before this home was abandoned. Should I repaint the symbols—sharpen the edges of the feather-wrapped sword, add shades of color back to the jeweled goblet?

Or simply paint over it all?

Or maybe just ignore it?

I still didn't know.

When I looked back to my sister, something had hardened in her expression. Another defensive tactic I'd learned from her, that specific way of setting our jaw and silencing our emotions—like a steel barrier dropping down, cutting off the air so it couldn't feed the flames inside.

"I am listening to your truth," she said evenly. "But Karys, I think maybe you're being—"

"No."

I didn't realize I'd managed to say the word out loud until the surprise registered on my sister's face.

My heart pounded painfully fast, but I didn't take the word back. For once, I was not going to let someone else tell me what or who I was. For once, I didn't feel the need to keep explaining myself.

For once, 'No' felt like a complete sentence.

And I realized, with a mixture of pain and relief, that it was all I had left to say.

I'd started the day with a plan, and in that moment, I made up my mind to follow it—I would be gone from this place before the night was over.

Even if it meant saying goodbye to my sister and everything else I had been holding on to for so long.

CHAPTER 32

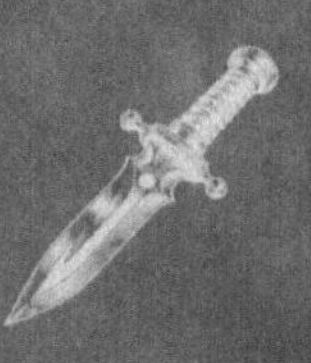

Karys

Hours later, I bolted upright in my bed, awakened by warmth flooding my body.

I thought I was dreaming at first.

Then, I felt it again. Not merely a nudging, dreamy warmth this time—but true *fire* shooting through my veins. Heavenly heat ballooning in my chest, lifting me onto my feet.

I'd fallen asleep with a hope that I would wake up alone, my sister long gone. Something I don't think I'd ever hoped for.

My wish had come true.

She was nowhere to be found.

I was burning, but the house around me sat as cold and empty as an expectant tomb, and I saw, now, that this was what it was—a place to bury things that no longer served me.

The God of Death had called it weeks ago, hadn't he?

If I was going to move forward, I would have to lay some things to rest. Those things could stay in this house, this grave.

But I couldn't.

So I made myself breathe and I made myself move, one foot in front of the other, heading for the door without looking back.

The burning in my veins became more powerful as I stepped into the yard and faced the walls of anti-divine wards caging me in. This burning went beyond my own power, I thought—like something building just beyond the wards, trying to reach through, just waiting for me to reach back.

Dravyn?

My pulse quickened.

I hurried to the edge of the yard before I could lose my nerve.

The grass along this edge was dead and gone, so there was no kindling to speak of—only the dirt and the rune symbols cutting deeply into it. All of the fire that would burn away those runes would have to come from, and be sustained by, me and me alone.

I recalled the notes I'd taken over the past days, sidestepping my way around the perimeter until I found one of the precise patterns of symbols I was looking for—a grouping I believed to be the most powerful.

The foundational pattern.

"Three rows of four triangles," I mumbled, trying to keep my mind focused. "Each with a cross in the center..."

This pattern was the only one that repeated multiple times along the entire encircling ward. It also did so with measured, equal spacing— much like the footings of a house.

My skin was already drenched in sweat as I knelt before one of these foundational points and summoned fire into my palm.

The familiar pulling sensation from the runes' power attacked immediately, making my surroundings spin and my balance sway.

My eyes watered from the growing intensity of it, but I pushed through the discomfort, thinking only of the other side. Of the warmth that had woken me up. Warmth that continued to reach for me in spite of the spinning pressure trying to hold me down.

The embers in my hand sparked brighter, forming a chain that wove deeper into the barrier. The links started to disintegrate as they pushed into the ward's magic, but I concentrated with all the strength I could summon, pulling the flames back into a line and sending it shooting toward the symbols at my feet.

Like the wick of a candle it burned down, down, down into the ground before surging back up and filling the grooves of the runes with a fiery glow.

The two powers battled, pressure and fire colliding and erupting, strange energy and smoke billowing wildly around me.

The world seemed to close in as I dropped to one knee, bracing an arm against the warm dirt. I bowed my head, focusing my weary, divine power into a more precise strike.

The pressure against my body grew so immense, I felt like I was sinking, the ground caving in beneath me.

But when I lifted my head a moment later, that ground was perfectly level, burned black—and scoured clean of runes and everything else.

Clean.

Tears welled in the corners of my eyes at the sight. I wiped them away, pushed back to my feet, and kept moving.

The opening I'd created was not much wider than my body. I could still see un-burned runes in my peripheral vision, and the anti-magic on either side of the opening felt as if it was pouring in, faster and faster, threatening to collapse in on me.

I pushed onward.

I refused to be denied at this point, even though it was like running through thick mud while thorn-covered vines caught at my body and tried to rip off pieces to keep. Several times it felt like I'd been caught— like I was suspended in place even as my legs continued moving.

But I kept going.

I kept running until, finally, I fought my way through the last of the barrier.

Blinding flashes of red and orange greeted me on the other side.

Fire.

The fields all around my former home were entirely ablaze.

My mouth grew dry, both terror and wonder battling for dominance in my pounding heart. These were not regular flames. They rippled and crackled with divine energy—energy I had not summoned.

As I staggered over the scorched and smoking ground, a warm wind swirled up around me, circling my body in a tight embrace as if eager to greet me. As if it had been looking for me.

Waiting for me.

I didn't see Dravyn, but I felt him in every lash of heat and spiral of smoke that caressed my skin.

The longer I stood among his wind and fire, the more I felt myself regaining my balance. My power. Power that was almost overwhelming after so many days of weakness, but still welcome—it would be much easier to carry myself back to the middle-heavens while wrapped up in this divine magic.

I walked until my old house and its memories were no longer in sight, letting more Fire magic seep into my body, my breaths, my very soul. Wind whipped my hair and clothing around. Symbols of power appeared on my skin. I stared at them, thinking of all the places in the Palace of Fire where I had seen corresponding symbols.

A little more concentration would bring me back to that palace.

I could do this.

My physical body began to fade, to move toward the path between realms. My fingertips went first, as they usually did, turning to smoke that trailed behind me like ribbons caught in the breeze. The sight still unsettled me a bit, so I closed my eyes and focused on what I could feel rather than see.

"All. These. Flames. And I wonder…what else do you suppose he's burned in his fury?"

My eyes flashed open as I spun toward the sound of Andrel's voice.

The transporting spell broke with the motion, thrusting me back into a solid form with jarring speed.

I rebalanced and braced myself, listening for his footsteps, trying to pinpoint him within the haze of smoke and magic.

I could only just make out his shape as he approached, his edges wavy and blurred by the fires between us.

A blistering wind rose to my right, lifting a smattering of embers from the ground and curving them into a whip-like line. I focused on it, taking a determined command of it, ready to wield it however I needed to.

"This is but a taste of what he's been doing since we took his trophy away from him," Andrel said as he approached. "The gods are benevolent until something angers them. Then all they know is destruction."

Destruction.

It was hard to deny this when everything was burning in every direction, for as far as I could see.

There was a village just beyond the borders of our land in one direction, and a beautiful forest lay in the other...were they on fire too?

Where did this end?

I knew Andrel was trying to plant that question—that fear—in my mind. I also knew there might have been some truth to what he claimed.

I would not listen to him, either way.

"You provoked his anger," I said, lifting my chin, "and now you're crying because he unleashed it. Make up your mind—are you prepared to wage a war against us or not?"

He didn't answer right away, too busy eyeing the whip of fire hovering in my control. Though I didn't actually grip any of the flames, they shifted about as if I had them by a handle, snaking back and forth in time with the movements of my clenched fist.

He continued to watch these movements with cold, calculating eyes until I cracked the makeshift lash, sending a line of fire across the ground between us. A deliberate breath and twist of my hand sent it shooting upwards into the beginnings of a shield.

Andrel leapt straight through it before it could reach its full intensity.

I stumbled back, surprised by his lack of hesitation. I clenched my fist tighter, holding my fiery whip ready but not yet striking. My emotions warred, torn between the desire to flee to safety and the desire to end him right then and there.

He brushed a few dying embers and ashes from his shoulder and said, "Last chance to choose the right side."

"I've already chosen."

"Yes, but I am a generous being...so I'm giving you yet another opportunity to change your mind."

"I will *never* be on your side again."

His gaze swept around us, taking in the roaring, destructive magic that now seemed brighter and hotter than ever before.

It was hard not to let my eyes be drawn to it all as well. Hard not to wonder, again, about what sort of fire and fury Dravyn had rained down upon this realm during his search for me.

But I couldn't let my mind wander over such dangerous territory. I just needed to get away from this place and back to a realm where I could think more clearly about everything.

I put more space between myself and Andrel, breathing in as calmly and deeply as I could, drawing my magic to the surface as I exhaled.

"You're prepared to fully walk away from your entire life?" he called, not moving from where he stood. "Away from your past, your kind, your home? Your *sister*?"

My pulse skipped a beat.

My magic didn't.

I'd made my choice, and the divine power followed through where my aching heart could not, building up the fires around us while simultaneously pulling at my solid form, preparing to unravel it and whisk me away to the heavens.

"How disappointing," Andrel drawled. "I suppose you are nothing but a stubborn coward in the end."

I paused my spell casting long enough to fix my gaze on his one last time. "And you are nothing but a foolish little boy who never learned not to play with fire."

A throwing knife was in his hand before I'd finished speaking.

He flung it with no more warning than this. It spun from his fingers with blazing speed, grazing the sleeve of my coat as I dove out of its path.

As it soared through the air and struck the ground beside me, it left a trail of shadowy purple energy in its wake. That energy carved through my divine fire, devouring the flames with alarming ferocity.

A memory flashed into my mind: One from months ago, when Cillian had first shown me the true weapons they'd been creating for their wars. I still remembered the dark, rotting energy radiating from the anti-divine knife he'd handed me, and the way that energy shriveled up the stone I stabbed with it...

More throwing knives were strapped to Andrel's leg.

More sharp edges to cut through and extinguish my fires—and *me.*

I dodged a second throw that came as quickly as the first, leaping backward just as a fresh, warm wind stormed to life around me. Fiery wings exploded from my back to catch that wind, carrying me further toward safety.

I landed lightly on my feet. A whip of embers reformed and floated by my side, awaiting my command. My wings rose and fell with each flutter of wind, feeling surprisingly heavy and formidable against my back—like an extension of me.

I'd finally managed to shape them into something truly magnificent and capable.

I had little time to celebrate, however, as Andrel was closing the space between us with poised, confident steps, his hand resting on the sheath of his knives.

I braced myself, but he didn't draw a third knife out.

Instead, he stopped a short distance away and inclined his head—a tiny, barely perceptible nod.

A signal.

I rolled aside just as an arrow flew in from somewhere above, from a perch I couldn't see through the smoke and brightness. It didn't cut a path through the flames as the knife had, but I remained wary, watching for more projectiles; the arrowhead was almost certainly laced with *something,* whether runes or poison or who knew what else.

While I was frantically trying to spot the person from which the first arrow had flown, a second one streaked in from my left and struck a wing, cutting a clean path through it before impaling itself in the other.

Gritting my teeth, I jerked it out and tossed it aside. As it hit the ground, a stinging pain radiated from the marks it had left behind. A faint, mildly numbing sensation swept from my wings toward my spine, my shoulders, my arms.

Was this the same poison I'd been injected with in Mindoth?

Was my sister behind this attack, too?

I was stronger now. More certain of my magic and where I was going, and surrounded by divine fire that I continued to siphon power from—all things that better shielded me—yet I could still feel the toxin working, itching through my veins, slowly but surely.

More arrows showered down. I dodged some, incinerated others, knocked at least three aside with precise shifts of my wings. All in the span of a few chaotic moments.

But I couldn't keep this up indefinitely.

Couldn't risk even a little more poison slipping in, dulling my magic, threatening my ability to transport myself back to Nerithyl.

I needed to leave before I ended up right back in the prison I'd just escaped from—or someplace worse.

Another arrow flew in, distracting me. I knocked it away just in time to look up and see Andrel racing toward me, a knife flashing in his hand.

I tried to leap, to let my wings catch the wind and carry me away as before. But the numbing poison pumping through them was starting to eat more viciously at their shape and solidness, turning them into more of a hinderance than a help. The right one crumpled when I tried to beat it, showering me in ash and glowing feathers, making me stumble.

As Andrel charged toward me, I struggled for balance, trying to decide how to stave him off long enough to make my escape.

My sister appeared before I was forced to make a decision, bursting through a wall of smoke and flame, a sword in her hand and a wild expression on her face.

She sprinted straight toward me.

But at the last moment she veered, slamming into Andrel, instead, knocking him aside.

He landed in a crouch, somehow still graceful despite only having one hand to catch himself. He stared at Savna for a long, tense moment, clearly stunned.

I was equally stunned, desperately trying to reconcile what I knew in my head with what I felt in my heart.

"*Run!*" she shouted at me.

I had to run.

I *meant* to run.

Then Andrel leapt back to his feet and grabbed hold of my sister's arm.

His gaze was livid as he jerked her closer, words falling furiously from his lips. Whatever he was saying was lost in the cacophony of howling wind and crackling fire and my own raging heartbeat.

They scuffled, both struggling to throw the other to the ground.

He knocked the sword from her grasp, but she disarmed him a few seconds later. Neither seemed to have the upper hand, but Savna eventually managed to throw him aside long enough to look my direction, to see me still standing in the same place as before.

"RUN!" she bellowed. "NOW!"

Protecting me. Letting me go.

But at what cost?

So many of my questions had been answered in the days we'd spent together, but now I had a hundred more.

Will she be safe?

Will I see her again?

Does it matter?

How can I leave her with him?

This last one was answered for me—I was already transcending into a smokier, less solid version of myself, some part of me still aware of what I needed to do, despite all my questions.

As the last of my body disappeared, my sister broke free of Andrel's hold and spun toward me, meeting my gaze one last time.

Of all the things I wanted to say, I only managed to mouth one of them: *I'm sorry.*

Divine fire engulfed all that remained of me an instant later, cutting me off from her response.

I tumbled through the aether, weightless and directionless, for what felt like a lifetime before finally landing on my back in one of the fields outside of the Palace of Fire.

My wings were gone, yet a strange heaviness and an alarming tingling persisted between my shoulder blades. I fought my way to my feet and staggered forward.

The palace didn't seem to get any closer no matter how many steps I took.

Was I even moving at all?

I couldn't feel my steps, my feet, yet I remained upright—*somehow* —until I heard someone shouting my name.

I looked toward the sound.

Streaks of fire and gold rushed in my direction, occasionally, briefly shifting into the shape of a horse-like creature and its rider. A familiar feeling of warmth overtook me as that rider drew closer, almost driving away the horrors of my escape from the mortal realm.

Almost.

But the last glimpse of my sister's face stayed with me long after I collapsed to the ground and everything else burned away.

CHAPTER 33

Dravyn

"I'm not sure which is more annoying," Valas muttered, gaze sliding between me and Mairu, "your pacing or her magic tricks."

The Serpent Goddess stopped midway through the spell she'd been absently performing, causing the book she was controlling to tumble toward the ground. She caught it with another flex of her magic just before it hit.

With a flourish of her wrist, she lifted it back into the air, directing it to the top of the castle she'd already built from dozens of other books. As this latest tome settled into place on top of one of the 'towers,' her gaze narrowed on the Winter God, daring him to make another comment.

"It's very distracting," he told her with a shrug.

"You can leave if you're annoyed," she replied. "No one here is desperate for your company."

He smirked.

She flicked the book back into her control and aimed it at his head.

He remained perfectly still, unconcerned about the threat.

Their standoff eventually gave way to harsh whispers, a hushed argument—not their first of the night, and unlikely their last.

But neither of them left.

Because just like me, they were waiting; Karys still had not woken since she'd collapsed upon her return to the middle-heavens.

I'd felt her coming back long before she appeared in this realm. I'd sensed her power fluctuating and fading, too, and I'd tried—unsuccessfully—to reach her before she fell. It seemed she'd fled too quickly, too recklessly...but from *what* I didn't know.

What had she endured these past days?

What had she been so desperate to escape?

Too much time had already passed since we'd last spoken, making every additional second of her unconsciousness feel that much longer. We were all on edge as a result, our combined feelings of helplessness and uncertainty bristling like a living, snarling beast between us.

I continued to pace in front of the window despite Valas's objections. I was watching for changes in the darkness outside, for any sign of movement—my senses were on high alert, because I'd witnessed something earlier that I hadn't in some time: A *tellesk*. A shadow servant of one of the Moraki, sent down from Valla, the upper-heavens, to silently spy and collect information.

They never interacted with me or anything else, but they absorbed everything they encountered—even the very thoughts and emotions of the ones they were observing. It was always unsettling, being watched by one. Its presence felt like an omen. A sign that the powers above us were growing impatient, and perhaps tired of our mistakes and missteps in the mortal realm. I was hardly surprised by this.

Everything was such a fucking *mess*.

Another hour passed.

Valas and Mairu eventually struck up a new conversation, their tones still hushed but slightly more cordial now. Moth joined us, as well, leaving Karys for the first time since I'd carried her to bed.

The griffin was restless, but eventually settled near me, mirroring my attentive stare into the garden on the other side of the window.

After a few minutes, his tufted ears perked up and his tail twitched, a low growl rumbling in his throat. He slipped away, reappearing outside a few minutes later.

Chasing something, it looked like.

The flaming tip of his tail made him easy to track. I watched as he drove a small creature from the bushes: A shadowy, spider-like beast that scurried haphazardly about before leaping into the air and sprouting veiny, iridescent wings. It disappeared an instant later, thwarting Moth's attempts to grab it between his paws.

As I stared at the streaks of dark, shining residue it had left behind, a prickling sensation of higher, otherworldly power overcame me. The others had fallen silent behind me, likely noticing the twinge of power as well.

Valas rose from his place by the dying fire, coming to stand by my side and staring at what remained of the tellesk's residue. "The God of the Shade is monitoring this palace."

I sighed. "With great interest. That was not the first spy he's sent today. I suspect he's been sending them for weeks now; Karys has noticed their presence as well, I think."

He folded his arms across his chest, bending toward the window and trying to get a closer look. "Do you think what Cillian suggested to you is true? That Karys is a pawn in some grand scheme they haven't told us about?"

I didn't reply.

I didn't want to think about it. Doing so would only trigger an avalanche of yet more questions I didn't have answers to.

"What could they possibly want from her?" Mairu wondered. "And why not just be forthcoming about whatever it is?"

Valas snorted at this. "Have you ever known the Creators to be forthcoming about anything?"

She mumbled something in response. The Winter God turned and fired back an equally disgruntled response, and the two of them resumed their arguing.

I moved toward the door, finished with both of them. With the talking, the waiting—all of it.

I left without a word, wandering throughout the palace and its grounds, trying to pretend everything was normal.

I tended to Moth, who—in the short time between chasing the tellesk and now—had somehow managed to trap himself in one of the supply closets in the kitchen. Likely while he was looking for something sweet to steal.

After freeing him, I lingered in the closet for several minutes, taking note of the contents and wondering if it was stocked well enough. Karys had a habit of locking herself in the kitchen and testing every recipe she could whenever she was stressed or upset; whatever she needed to make when she woke up, I wanted to be certain she had the supplies for it.

While taking inventory, my hands fell upon a batch of treats meant for a selakir. It was a recipe Karys had created herself, featuring the dried savos fruit Zell loved so much. They would only last a short time on the shelf, I remembered her saying—and these looked close to expiring.

Glad to have a simple task that needed doing, I took the jar and went to summon Zell.

I found him quickly; he'd witnessed me taking Karys back to the palace earlier, and he hadn't strayed far from the grounds ever since.

He bumped the jar of treats aggressively with his nose—clearly recognizing what was inside it—but he didn't take the one I offered him. Not at first. He only stamped his feet and tossed his head anxiously before trotting behind me, sniffing the air and twitching his ears. Searching. Looking for the one who *usually* spoiled him with these treats, I suspected.

When Karys didn't follow me into the yard, Zell begrudgingly moved back to me, his long tongue peeling one of the treats from my hand. As he ate, his jewel-black eyes fixed toward the room where Karys slept, as if he'd managed to pinpoint her energy, faint as it was.

I soon returned to that room myself. Rieta exited just as I reached for the door's handle, her careworn expression brightening the tiniest bit as she caught sight of me—I hoped it was because she had good news.

"She's awake?"

"Gettin' there. She didn't recognize me when she opened her eyes, though. Called me *Savna*."

My jaw clenched. "Her sister."

"That's what I thought." Rieta clicked her tongue, hands on her hips as she studied the partially-ajar door. She nodded me toward it. "Maybe you'll have better luck. Doubt she'll confuse you with anyone else."

I thanked her and quietly slipped inside.

Karys was far more restless than she'd been the last time I checked on her. Her blankets were twisted up as though she'd spent the last hour tossing and turning. Her ears twitched at the sound of my footsteps. Her nostrils flared. She inhaled deeply, and her forehead wrinkled in frustration, as if she was trying to get her senses to cooperate and zero in on the newest presence in the room.

Her lips moved, but she didn't speak—not out loud—though I heard her voice in my head, a single whispered word: *Dravyn.*

I answered in the same way—a simple thought, directed toward her: *I'm right here.*

Her head tilted toward me, eyes fluttering open and trying to focus.

I kneeled at her bedside, brushing a sweat-soaked strand of hair from her face. "Hello, Wildfire."

Her eyes closed, but her lips curved slightly upwards, recognizing the nickname.

"I made it back to you through the chaos, after all," she said after a moment of concentration. "I told you I would." Her smile faltered as she inhaled what sounded like a shallow, painful breath. "Sorry I'm late."

Something in her voice nearly unraveled me.

I'd come too close to losing her.

Far too close.

"It's all right," I said, taking her hand and lacing my fingers through hers.

She breathed in deeply. Exhaled slowly. Nodded.

The silence stretched between us, full of questions. "But I need to know," I began after a minute, "what exactly *made* you so late? What happened these past days?"

Her hand gave mine a weak squeeze.

I was hungry for details. For answers. I wanted to know what they'd done to her. *Who* had done it to her. Who I needed to hunt down next.

But it was asking too much of her, too soon, maybe.

Reluctantly, I said, "...A conversation for later, perhaps."

She breathed a sigh of relief. Her hand went limp, sliding from mine. Within moments, she was already dozing off again.

I stayed by her side for most of the next hour before deciding to leave her to her sleep. She was conscious again—that was enough for now. She needed to rest.

She stirred once more, however, as soon I stood and started to turn toward the door.

"I felt you," she whispered. "Your magic, reaching for me from the other side of the walls they'd put up. You were looking for me."

"Of course I was."

"For how long? I think I lost track by the end."

"You were missing for nearly five days."

She clenched the blankets and went very still, as if steadying herself under the weight of this knowledge.

"And I would have kept looking for you for an eternity, if that was what it took."

A pause. Then her voice, so quiet I wasn't sure if she was truly whispering or just pressing her thoughts into my head once more: "Even among the chaos."

"Even among the chaos," I agreed.

She settled back into the pillows with an exhausted sigh.

"Rest," I urged. "I'll be here when you wake up. Then we can talk."

CHAPTER 34

Dravyn

Later that evening, Karys surprised me when she appeared in the library, interrupting the tense conversation I'd been having with the rest of our court; I'd been too distracted to sense her coming.

Zachar had only just left my territory.

The Death God had arrived shortly after my last visit to Karys's room. He'd sensed her waking, her magic rising, and had arrived with the intention of speaking to her—another spy sent by the God of the Shade, I assumed; if any of the Shade Court could be trusted to do our upper-god's bidding without question, it would be Zachar.

But whatever this bidding was—whatever he intended to speak to Karys about—he refused to tell me.

I *might* have lost my temper with him over this.

The resulting surge of my fiery energy is likely what had roused Karys from her sleep and drawn her down into the library.

I regretted interrupting her rest, but I would be lying if I claimed I wasn't glad to see her step through the doorway looking far more lively than she had when I left her hours ago. The ends of her hair were damp, and her skin shimmered faintly from the various floral powders and oils Rieta often added into her bathwater.

Seeing her standing there was like coming up for air. Like surfacing from what I thought might kill me, finding myself miraculously alive, yet still dizzy from holding my breath.

I'm alive.

She's alive.

We haven't drowned.

Mairu reached her first, wrapping her in a crushing hug that lasted for at least a full minute, letting go only because the God of Winter stole her away for himself.

Valas said something in a low voice reserved for the two of them—something that made Karys laugh. Despite the irritation I'd felt toward him throughout the past five tension-filled days, I'd never been more grateful for him than I was in that moment; the sound of her laughter was another breath injected into my half-drowned lungs.

Our gazes locked as Valas let her go. She stilled. Her mind was a jumbled mess of thoughts, but I could read her silence; her slightly clenched hands; her eyes, shining with the same emotions I felt; and the soft, relieved sigh that barely passed through her lips...

Dizzy.

Still breathless.

But alive.

She crossed the room to me, studying my face as she came. "You look terrible," she informed me, cheerfully. "Like you haven't closed your eyes in days."

"He hasn't," Valas confirmed.

Moth, who had draped himself like a weighted blanket on the back of my chair, agreed with a chirp.

Karys's teasing smile fell a bit in the corners.

"I'm fine," I said hastily.

Moth rolled from the chair with all the grace of a newborn baby deer, hitting the floor with a loud *thud*. He righted himself and scampered to meet Karys, leaping into her arms, distracting her momentarily. But she continued to study me out of the corner of her vision even as she smoothed his ruffled feathers.

All the things I needed to tell her slammed into me all at once, like taking a sledgehammer to the stomach.

"But I could use some air," I continued, calmly getting to my feet. "Step outside with me?"

She agreed, settling Moth into the empty space I'd left behind and giving him a few more loving pats before following me.

We walked together to the gardens that had become one of our favorite haunts over the past months. She picked fallen flower petals from the stone path while I studied our surroundings, all my senses on edge. I didn't perceive any threatening presence nearby, nor any eavesdroppers, yet the uneasy twisting in my gut didn't subside.

"The God of Death has been here recently, hasn't he?" Karys straightened, a pile of petals cupped in her hands. Her gaze drifted toward a distant spot on the other side of the low garden walls—the very spot I'd last confronted Zachar before he fled. "I can feel his lingering energy."

"Yes. He wanted to speak to you." I unsuccessfully attempted to roll away some of the tension tightening my neck. "I'm sure he'll be back."

"You two fought, didn't you?"

As suspected, she'd felt that energy, too.

"He was being foolish. And I was not in the mood for his games."

She considered this for a long moment, a frown pulling at the corners of her lips, but didn't ask for details.

"I've actually been meaning to speak with the Death Marr again," she said.

I worked to keep the protective snarl from my tone. "Have you?"

"He gave me some advice a few weeks ago. Advice I rejected at the time, but now..." She trailed off, her focus shifting to the petals she held.

She transferred them all to a clenched fist and let them slip through her fingers one by one, using her other hand to direct little bursts of fire at them as they fell. I'd seen her practice her precision and control using similar methods in the past. Even now, as tired as she must have been, she continued her pursuit of perfection.

A slight smile curled my lips at this last thought—though it was short-lived. "Whatever *advice* he gave you, I would be wary of taking it. You know he speaks in riddles."

"Do the Marr speak in riddles?" she deadpanned.

"Oh, you hadn't noticed?"

She snorted. "You really think I haven't realized by now that the gods do not always speak the whole truth?" She angled her face toward me and raised a brow. "For example, the God of Fire is known to keep his true thoughts and feelings and fears to himself, despite how it concerns the ones who love him. Did you know that?"

"I've heard it's a bad habit of his," I said, continuing onward down the winding path through the garden. "But then again, you can't believe everything you hear."

Though my back was to her, I suspected she rolled her eyes at this, which brought another slight smile to my face.

"I thought I would allow you a little more time to rest and recover before I dropped all of those *thoughts and feelings and fears* upon you," I told her as she caught up to me.

She chewed her bottom lip for a few paces before nodding, seeming to understand even if she didn't agree.

We came to the end of the path. An elaborate fountain stood here, its trio of trickling waterfalls the only sound disrupting the heavy air. I watched the water rippling over the basin lined with colorful, decorative chips of glass while Karys continued to turn bits of flowers into piles of ash.

Finally, she spoke again, in a voice still distant and lost in thought: "I wasn't resting particularly well."

The weight in my stomach grew heavier. "More nightmares?"

"I keep going back to the fields outside my old home. The ones you set fire to."

I waited for her to elaborate, but she said nothing else.

"...You're angry about those fires?"

She considered this for another long moment. "Worried, more like. About the mortal world going up in flames. About you choosing between me and that world, and..." She trailed off, regarding me from underneath her lashes, eyes dark and troubled over questions she couldn't seem to force through her lips.

There were no easy answers to these questions—there was only what I felt, foolish as it was. A feeling I would have buried months ago for the sake of simplicity.

There was no chance of burying it now.

"There is no other *choice* for me, anymore," I said. "There is only you. You're the only thing I could think of these past five days, no matter how hard I tried to focus on anything else."

Her reply came slowly. Quietly. Guarded, even now—even in spite of all the walls we'd already torn down to get to one another. "Maybe I'm just not used to people choosing me. So it feels strange."

She lifted one shoulder and let it drop, as though she could really shrug off a lifetime of being pushed aside, lied to, manipulated by her family and allies.

I stared at her, a familiar irritation heating my blood. Not at her, but at every single being who had ever wronged her and put her second to anything. The irritation simmered into anger, and then into a flare of passion that had me reaching for her, pulling her into a kiss.

A hundred other things needed to be said and done in that moment —yet all I could think about was kissing her, finding some way to prove I would choose her above everything, over and over again, for as long as I existed.

Her guarded posture slowly collapsed, her arms lifting, wrapping around my neck. The petals in her hands fell against my back as she unclenched her fists and held more tightly to me, deepening the kiss.

We were both breathless when I finally drew my lips from hers.

"I love you." I dropped my forehead against hers, framing her face between my hands. "And I thought I'd lost you. It was one of the most painful things I have ever experienced, but it made me realize something."

She lifted her gaze to mine, questioning.

"That I would have burned down a thousand worlds to find my way back to you."

She trembled beneath my touch, her breathing uneven as she struggled to keep the tears in her eyes from falling. She eventually gave up on this effort, merely letting them fall as she leaned her head against my chest. I wrapped my arms around her, holding her tightly to me.

We stayed this way for several minutes.

She moved first, pulling away, walking over and settling onto the edge of the fountain. The occasional tear still escaped, winding a shining trail down her cheek, but her brow was furrowed in thought. She braced her arms against the stone beneath her, steadying herself, her demeanor shifting—as it so often did—to that of someone determined to push through the pain and make sense of things.

"How *did* you find me?" she asked.

And so we had arrived at the part I was dreading.

Every muscle in my body clenched with reluctance as I sat down beside her. But I couldn't put it off any longer; she deserved to know what had happened while she was being held prisoner.

So I told her about Cillian.

It was cruel. Unfair. Had she not suffered enough? Lost enough? I hated the world and everything in it a little more with every word I uttered, but somehow, I got the words out.

Her face became a wall as I spoke, hardening further with each detail I fumbled through. The tears continued, but they fell without sound or movement. She didn't even bother wiping them away.

When I'd finished speaking, she stayed silent. A statue at first; an extension of the fountain edge she sat upon.

Then it seemed to hit her all at once.

She crumpled slowly, tucking her head toward her chest, drawing into herself like a withering bloom.

Ten minutes passed. Twenty, thirty, forty…I lost count. She paced. Flung stones into the fountain. Burned away flowers and vines with precise, angry flourishes of her hands.

All the while, I stayed close, giving her space when she needed it, holding her close when she looked as though she might collapse.

It was excruciating to not be able to do anything more than this.

We were sitting atop one of the garden walls, her head resting against my chest and her body wrapped tightly in my arms, when she finally spoke again.

"Cillian must have told my sister I was in Mindoth. That's how she knew to look for me. To target me." Her voice was perfectly even. Emotionless. The practiced tone of one who had far too much experience speaking of betrayals.

"Yes. That's what I suspected as well."

"Savna poisoned me with…something. Something more powerful than anything we've encountered yet."

I fought the urge to reach for my shoulder, where I carried my own scars from what I assumed was the same poison. I hadn't noticed any similar scars on her; maybe her sister had quickly given her an antidote, at least.

"My sister…she believed she was saving me by stealing me away."

"Poison and cages are unusual tools for saviors," I muttered.

"I thought so, too."

"…Thought?" A muscle in my jaw twitched. "In past tense?"

She didn't reply.

Still protecting her sister, even now.

I held my tongue. I knew it wouldn't do any good to argue the matter just then. Not after the day we'd had. I didn't need to voice my concerns, anyway; she could read me easily enough.

"I am not a fool, Dravyn," she said, standing, but not pulling away completely. "I know what she's done. But she ultimately protected me and helped me escape this time. And in the days before that, we actually spoke. On several occasions. And she seemed—at times—like the sister I knew and loved. I know you haven't spoken to your brother in years, but if you had a chance to go back, to talk like you used to…"

My brother's latest words to me slid through my thoughts, stinging just as badly as they had while I stood before him.

You are not welcome here any longer.

Without looking at Karys, I said, "I recently spoke with him, actually. Not as prolonged a conversation or visit as you had to endure with your sister, but it was…enough."

I could feel the weight of her shocked stare. I kept my eyes on the ground, on one of the scorch marks she'd left while setting fires earlier.

"He was their true target that night in Mindoth," I said. "They were trying to kill him—and they very nearly managed it. I dug him out of the rubble myself."

"Is he…okay?"

"He'll live."

She hesitated a moment before settling back on the wall beside me, tucking her hands beneath her, forcing herself to be still in spite of the storm of questions I could sense roaring through her head.

"I went to his palace to ask for help finding you," I said. "That's how I encountered Cillian. He was being held in the dungeon, and I convinced Fallon to let me speak with him. I haven't been back to Altis since, though, and I don't intend to change that."

Her gaze flew toward mine. "What? Why not? You've finally started talking again, isn't that—"

"It's simpler to leave some things in the past."

"He's not a *thing*, he's your brother."

"A brother who still wants nothing to do with me. We're even now; I dragged him from a collapsing building, he helped me find you. And then he ordered me not to return to the royal city."

Her nostrils flared. "Do gods take orders from kings?"

"No, not usually. But this is a special case."

She started to argue before seeming to think better of it—though keeping silent and still remained an obvious effort for her.

I kept talking, partly because it seemed to make her less restless. "He has yet to forgive me for the way things happened on the night of our siblings' murders, and in the aftermath."

She was quiet for a few more beats, considering.

Then she asked, "Have you forgiven *yourself*?"

My stomach dropped.

What a foolish question, I thought, bitterly.

"It's a fair, important question," she countered, as if I'd said it out loud.

"You're getting very good at hearing my thoughts," I muttered.

A corner of her mouth lifted a touch. "Nothing is safe from me, now."

I huffed out a laugh, though I was far from amused. I returned my attention to the burned ground. "Fallon needs somebody to hate. Someone to blame for all the things that have gone wrong in our lives. I can give him that, at least, even though I've abandoned him."

She still didn't argue, but when I glanced her way a minute later, her eyes were glazed over, clearly plagued by troubled thoughts.

Giving her head a little shake, she said, "You're more than that, you know. More than a target for other people's grief and anger and hatred. And you are worthy of forgiveness, whether you believe that or not."

My throat was suddenly too thick to swallow, much less to reply, so I merely gave a noncommittal shrug.

She sighed and leaned her head on my shoulder. "You know I'm right."

"Maybe. But things were easier for you when you hated me yourself, now weren't they?"

"...*Easier* might be a stretch," she said, wrapping her arm around mine and leaning closer. "But simpler, I suppose. I do miss those days, sometimes."

I gave another humorless chuckle. "Yes, you've said that before."

"Several times."

"Should I be concerned?"

"No. Because I don't hate you, you fool." She hesitated. Took a deep breath. "I love you so much it terrifies me. Sometimes it feels like we're one of those glass figures you created...like I'm holding us so tightly we're going to shatter and the shards are going to cut deeper than I can stand. But I can't let go. I don't *want* to let go. Even if it means broken and bloody hands."

She squeezed my arm, burrowing her face more fully into my shoulder.

"Wildfire," I murmured, kissing the top of her head, "we are made of something much stronger than glass."

She breathed out a content, soft little sound, some of the tension slipping from her hold on me.

"If I *do* go back to Fallon," I said after a moment, "it won't be for a family reunion."

She lifted her head, curiosity sparking in her eyes.

"Something he said right before we parted has been eating away at me," I explained.

"What was it?"

"He told me to find you and bring you back to this realm. To leave him to his plans and not look back or interfere in mortal affairs. Tempting, but..."

"But we can't ignore what's happening below. Andrel spoke as though he was preparing to unleash another part of their plans, too...a *grand ending*, he called it."

"You spoke with him over these past days?"

A tremble went through her—an answer in itself.

Of course she spoke with him.

"He was partly responsible for trapping you, wasn't he?"

"Yes."

The way the mere mention of him caused her body to tremble and her pulse to race faster—a reaction of fear, however short-lived it was—made me physically ill.

"What else did he do?" I demanded.

How else did he hurt you because I failed to kill him in Mindoth?

The fingers she had around my arm dug deeper.

Gently, I brushed a hand across her cheek and turned her face toward me.

"I don't want to talk about him." She looked me directly in the eyes, her gaze full of fire and fierceness. "I only want to talk about what we're going to do about all these threats we're facing."

I blinked away the fire blurring my own vision. Forced the rage in my blood to settle.

"I don't know what *plans* Fallon has," I said, once I could manage a calm, rational voice, "but I worry he's underestimating the forces he's up against."

She untangled herself from me and hopped down from the wall. "I'm worried about my sister, too. About the cost of her helping me escape and..." She trailed off with a frustrated sound and returned to her pacing, her forehead creased in thought and her lips moving with silent calculations.

Eventually, she stopped and lifted her gaze to the cream-colored sky. Her lips stilled, but her hands continued to absently draw the occasional path through the air, the way they often did when she was mapping out plans.

"I know that look," I said.

"What look?"

"You're plotting something."

She glanced at me, a slightly rueful curve to her lips, and shrugged.

"Are you going to let me in on those plans, this time?"

"I think we should go to Altis," she said without hesitation. "To your brother. Together, we can find out what he's planning, and maybe while we're in that realm..." Her voice grew quieter toward the end, a telling, pained expression in her eyes.

"You want to see your sister again."

She didn't deny it. "Do you think the king will be able to arrange an audience with her? Somewhere in his city, perhaps—someplace that's neutral ground between my sister and me, unlike Ederis or our old house."

"Possibly," I replied, somewhat reluctantly. "He has no shortage of capable spies and messengers he could use to track her down. But what, then?"

"I want to talk with her as a diplomat and speaker for the gods, this time, rather than as a sister."

"An attempt at ceasefire negotiations?"

She nodded. "She started to listen to me before. And if she holds as much sway over the other rebels as Andrel, then maybe we can stop all their attacks—against us, the humans, and anyone else—before they escalate into something catastrophic. I believe I could bring balance back to the races and realms. I think...I think maybe that's what I'm meant to do. What I've been meant to do all along."

I considered the possibility, as much as I didn't want to—as much as it frightened me. It made some sense. Maybe this *was* the plan the Moraki had in mind when they assisted with her ascension.

Karys was watching me closely, her body tense but her gaze hopeful.

I was still reluctant to agree, unable to shake my concerns about what such a task might require of her, knowing that the upper-gods cared little for feelings or fairness when they made plans and required a sacrifice for them.

But there would be no outrunning the things chasing us, I knew.

So I said, "Wherever you go, I'm going too."

She gave me a grateful little smile.

I did my best to return it.

I'd meant what I said before—that we were made of something

stronger than glass. Something more like iron and steel, forged in flame, twisted and bent into painful shapes, yet still in one piece.

I couldn't say the same about the path stretching before us. It felt uneven. Uncertain. Ready to crumble at the first misstep.

And I couldn't help but wonder how much longer it was all going to hold together.

CHAPTER 35

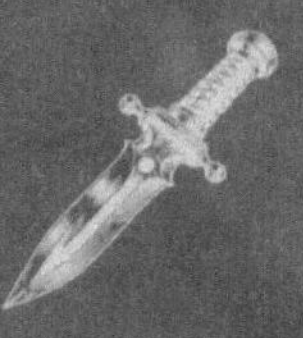

Karys

The interior of the Altis Palace reminded me of tunnels through a vast mountain, with cold walls of marbled stone and few windows to let in natural light.

The tunnel carver clearly had a precise hand and an eye for art, too; every so often we passed incredible works cut into the stone, reliefs that featured scenes from the Kingdom of Galizur's history. Each one was rendered in painstaking detail. I could have studied them for hours, deciphering their stories and taking notes.

But that was not why we had come here.

I stayed close to Dravyn as we climbed higher into the palace, heading for the parlor where we'd been told we could find his brother. Despite the relatively narrow halls, it felt as if I was walking into something much larger, the world expanding around me with every step I took.

The conversation I'd shared with Dravyn yesterday continued to play on repeat in my mind, just as it had been doing since the second we left the garden.

I believe I could bring balance back to the races and realms...

I hadn't realized how badly I wanted to accomplish this before I'd suggested it to him. Now, the thought was all-consuming. It was the answer I had been seeking since I woke up with divine power flowing through my veins. The *why* I'd been trying to grasp, and the *how*—how I could exist in both worlds with purpose in my past, present, and future.

I was meant to be walking this path.

To be the one to bring balance between all these different worlds I was tethered to, in one way or another.

I was certain this was my task, but it felt all the more impossible as we stepped into the sun-splashed room where our target awaited.

Fallon was perched on the edge of a massive white sofa with golden footings. A short sword lay at his side, its jeweled sheath balanced across his knee. He was working on the sheath, securing and reinforcing a few of the sparkling red stones that had loosened from the twisting, ornate pattern on that casing. A pinching, metal tool of some kind flashed in his hand.

He didn't speak right away, giving me an opportunity to study his appearance without distraction. Dravyn had once told me that he favored his father, whereas Fallon favored their mother.

Their mother must have been beautiful, if the King of Galizur was any indication.

His complexion was a few shades darker than Dravyn's golden-beige tone. His hair appeared to be a rich shade of brown until he shifted in such a way that sunlight caught the strands, revealing hints of deep auburn. His demeanor was cool and confident—he shared that in common with his brother, at least. He was so perfectly balanced on the elegant couch that he could have been a posed, impressive sculpture rather than a living, breathing person.

His focus and poise didn't falter even as Dravyn cleared his throat.

"I hope you have a good reason for disrupting my solitude," said the king as he secured a small jewel in the clutches of the shiny tool he held.

"I wouldn't have come here without reason," Dravyn replied. "I've no desire for casual, unplanned visits with you. I would have thought that was abundantly clear by now."

I grimaced at the bitterness infused in his words; we would get nowhere with that tone.

The king's green-eyed gaze swept right over Dravyn and instead moved to me, appraising. "You found her, I see."

"Yes," said Dravyn.

"So our business has concluded successfully, then."

I stepped forward before Dravyn could fire another thinly-veiled insult at him. "I'm afraid nothing is really *concluded*."

The king repositioned the scabbard against his knee and finished securing the gem he was working on before meeting my insistent stare.

"There's something else you want from me? More favors, so soon?"

"The favor would be in your best interest," I said. "Trust me."

His gaze slid over me, lingering on my tapered ears. Like so many before him, he seemed to be trying to figure out what I was and which side I was on. I looked like the ones who had destroyed his training grounds, yet I had walked into this room side-by-side with a god.

So I had his interest, at least—even if *trust* was another matter entirely.

"I'm in a unique position to give you the insight and perspective you need to help protect your kingdom and de-escalate the wars surrounding it." Ironically, it was a position I'd struggled with for months,

But now I was determined to use it to my advantage.

"Another deity here to offer me counsel, hm?" He bared his teeth in a challenging smile.

"Only to those wise enough to listen to it," I replied evenly.

"You're here for some other reason. Admit it, or this conversation is finished." He put the sheath aside and settled back against the sofa, regarding me with a raised brow.

"Very few things are done for a singular reason, wouldn't you agree? Life is not that simple, unfortunately."

He chuckled a bit at this. Then his gaze flashed toward Dravyn, and he spoke in a voice just above a whisper. He used the ancient language of Galizur, leaving me mostly in the dark about whatever was being said; I'd studied and attempted to translate a few of the Galithian books in Dravyn's libraries, but I was far from fluent.

Dravyn replied to his brother in the same language, his tone coiling tightly with irritation along with the rest of his body.

I braced myself for the king's command to leave.

It never came.

Instead, Fallon said, "I want to speak with her alone."

My stomach flipped.

Dravyn shifted his stance, angling his body more protectively in front of me. "Why alone?"

The king picked up the jeweled sheath again, giving it a once-over before leaning down and picking up the sword it was meant to cover.

"Because I'm intrigued by her," he said, carefully sheathing the sword. "Anybody who could make my little brother come crawling to me for help must wield a significant amount of power and persuasion, indeed. And I don't want you or your temper interfering with our conversation."

"This isn't a game, Fallon."

"You've forgotten much about palace life, it seems," said Fallon, rising and stretching with an oddly casual grace. "It *is* a game. But not one I intend to play recklessly. Don't worry."

I placed a hand on Dravyn's arm, squeezing tight, trying to massage some of the tension from his muscles. "I'll be fine," I assured him.

He hesitated, no doubt thinking of the last time we'd split up.

It hadn't exactly turned out *fine.*

But I survived that ordeal, for better or worse, and I would survive this one, too.

Dravyn didn't protest as I stepped away from him, though he did say one last thing to his brother in a low voice...yet more words in their native language that I didn't understand. Clearly a threat, this time; the air grew scorching hot as he spoke. The sunlight itself seemed to flicker.

Fallon looked uncomfortable for an instant but quickly recovered and gestured to the door. "Let's step into my office across the hall," he said to me.

I followed him, trying to ignore the way Dravyn's magic swelled as he watched me go.

Stay calm, I thought—a reminder for both of us.

He didn't reply. But nothing around me caught on fire, so I considered the situation stable for the moment.

Fallon left the door to his office slightly ajar. He walked to his desk against the back wall, but after a silent debate, decided against sitting down. He walked the edges of the room instead, gaze flitting about like a man taking inventory of all the books and other treasures he'd collected. Like he was afraid someone might try to steal them.

Or at the very least, knock them all down.

He eventually threw a glance back toward the room where we'd left Dravyn and asked, "What did you say to get him to come back to this palace?"

"You're his brother. He's wanted to come back here for a long time, I think, even if he would never admit it."

Fallon snorted and moved toward the window, fiddling with the curtain ties, clearly not believing me. "He looked eager to leave the last time he was here—once he'd had his favor granted, anyway."

"He told me you *ordered* him to leave."

The king parted the curtains. Ran his fingers over the window sill and lifted them, inspecting for dust. Several times he did this before wiping his hands on the leg of his trousers and saying, "I suppose I did."

"You regret it?"

"I try not to regret much of anything, as a rule."

Wouldn't that be nice.

"But you *did* tell him to leave and not come back?"

"I thought it would be simpler."

"He thought the same—that staying away would be easier."

"And yet you convinced him otherwise."

"In my experience, Your Majesty, there are very few families who can claim to have a *simple* relationship, anyway. So we might as well try to help one another, for better or worse."

I chose to ignore the dismissive noise he made, and I kept talking.

"That's also part of the reason I've come to see you."

"Is that so?"

He fixed a hard stare in my direction. I briefly froze. All the things I needed to say and do, all the decisions to make and all their consequences and outcomes rattled around in my mind. Loud. Messy. Uncertain..

But somehow, I burned away all the distractions, leaving only the single thing I had to say.

"I need help reaching my sister. She's a leader of the rebellious factions you've been battling with, and if I could draw her away from the other rebels long enough to speak to her on ground that's neutral between us—perhaps somewhere here in Altis—then I believe I could be a mediator of sorts between your army and hers, which would—"

"Invite the enemy into my city?" Fallon leaned against the wall, arms folded across his chest. "After what they did at Mindoth?"

"What alternative do you have planned?"

"Not really any of your business, is it?"

So he was going to be difficult, then.

I stepped closer to him. "Do you realize who you're talking to?"

He opened his mouth to reply, but the sight of me moving even closer made his words catch in his throat.

I came to a stop in a ribbon of sunlight snaking through the parted drapes. My body seemed to absorb the heat from it, drawing smoke and light to the surface of my skin, making it difficult to tell where the sun ended and my magic began. The curtains moved, caught in a warm breeze despite the window remaining tightly shut.

Fallon's gaze jumped between the fluttering fabric and me, calculating.

"Whatever happens in this realm *is* the business of the divine beings charged with looking after it," I reminded him. "I am one of those beings. And if I were you, I would want me to be on your side."

He had to swallow a few times to clear his throat and manage his usual confident tone. "I didn't think the gods took sides. My brother's aloofness and abandonment suggested as much."

I didn't reply right away, my lungs too tight to breathe any words out—because I knew what it was like to feel like your sibling had abandoned you.

It was a particular kind of hurt that I wouldn't be able to heal or even start to untangle within this single conversation.

Yet, I had to keep trying to reach him.

Fallon looked ready to leave. Before he could, I blurted out, "Dravyn wants to protect you, too. That's the other reason we came here."

The king flashed me the same challenging smile he'd given in the parlor. "Then why don't you *gods* simply smite my enemies for me and call it a day?"

"It doesn't work like that."

"And what a pity *that* is."

"I am trying to do this discreetly. Diplomatically. I'd rather not burn anything or anyone to the ground to make a point. And I'd rather not watch *you* continue to make mistakes that will be the equivalent of burning it all down."

He lifted his eyes to the ceiling, studying the tin panels and the elaborate swirls of gold painted upon their ivory faces.

"I am trying to *help* you," I pressed. "I can put an end to the battles around you before they become a full-scale war you can't win."

He kept his eyes on the ceiling. "And all I have to do is send an invitation to the leader of the very beings I have fought to keep *out* of my kingdom at all costs."

I didn't always recognize sarcasm when it was leveled in my direction, but it was impossible to miss it in his voice.

I chose to ignore it.

"Yes. That's all. You can manage that, can't you?"

He slowly lowered his gaze to mine. His expression was stony and proud, reminding me of one of the many stone reliefs we'd passed on our way through the palace.

The seconds ticked by. The curtains whipped more wildly in the throes of my power, casting strange shadows over our faces. Papers on shelves and pages of books joined in the dance of energy, filling the room with sounds of crinkling and rustling.

"For the record," said Fallon, "I don't believe you can change the course this realm is on. And yet..." He stared at me with unabashed curiosity. "You've clearly changed my brother, which I also wouldn't have thought possible."

I exhaled slowly, settling my magic along with all the things it was disturbing.

The king turned his back to me, clasping his hands behind it as he stared at the sliver of Altis now visible through the stilled drapery.

"I'll arrange what I can," he said. "But if you are wrong, you will have put my city and its people in a very dangerous position. I just hope you realize that."

LATER THAT EVENING, I stood on the roof of one of the palace's smaller towers, watching the sun sinking below the vast forest in the distance.

I'd been here for the better part of the last hour. The fields between the palace and the forest were covered with red flowers cast in gold by the sunset, reminding me of the fields of marigold that stretched outside of Andrel's old family home.

I used to find such peace in that place, sitting alone for hours, watching the colors of night and day shift over the swaying flowers. Now all I could think about was the last time I'd sat there.

How everything changed so soon after that moment.

Cillian had joined me that day; I could still remember every word of the conversation we shared. I wanted to shrink at the memory—at the reminder that all I had left of him were memories. But I didn't. Cillian wouldn't have wanted me to. He would have been telling me to focus, to find some way to turn his death into something I could use...

And I had an idea of how to do that.

I hated it. Hated to think of the death of one of my best friends and mentors as a potential stepping stone toward anything *good*.

But it was leverage I could use, and I knew it.

The orders to poison Cillian and the other captives had come from Andrel—I was certain of it. My sister would not have given that order. Cillian had once been her closest friend. There was a chance she didn't even know what had happened, given how expertly Andrel could weave lies.

So when we spoke, I was going to tell her everything Dravyn had witnessed.

I would keep opening her eyes, over and over, until she finally saw what I did.

Assuming she actually showed up, of course.

Fallon had sent a messenger soon after our conversation in his office. I'd been counting the hours that passed since that moment; we were approaching the tenth. The king had offered to let us stay the night while we waited, and Dravyn had begrudgingly agreed once I mentioned that I thought it would be easier to stay in one place—easier and less taxing on my magic that was still recovering after my ordeal at my old house.

Truthfully, I felt fine.

I just wasn't willing to leave for several reasons. At the top of the list was my fear that Fallon would change his mind if I wasn't here and constantly reminding him of my power and presence.

And though I knew it might end in disaster, I also wanted an excuse to keep Dravyn near his brother for at least a little longer. It felt like the only way to start healing the wounds between them.

Despite my scheming, they had managed to avoid each other for most of the day—but at least they were under the same roof again. That was a start.

As the last rays of sun slipped away, I heard footsteps approaching. I turned to see Dravyn walking toward me, cutting an impressive silhouette in the deepening twilight, looking more godly than human just then. I knew he'd made an effort to stifle his divine essence while we were here, but his skin still glowed with a faint glimmer of gold, as if it had drawn in bits of the setting sun.

His lips curved upward—the first relaxed, genuine smile I'd seen from him all day. My heart skipped at the sight, a mixture of happiness and relief tingling through me.

"What are you grinning about?" I asked, smiling back.

"This spot," he replied, taking in the scenery as he strolled closer, "used to be one of my own favorite haunts. I would pass hours up here, sitting on the very edge of the roof. Now here you are. And I don't know...it feels like something's come full circle."

I mirrored his wistful expression, thinking of a younger, less burdened version of him sitting here. "It's a beautiful view."

"Yes," he agreed, his eyes fixing on my face, completely unconcerned about the view behind me.

Blushing slightly, I looked back to the fields and forest, letting my gaze travel the roads that wound to and from the palace, watching for any signs of a returning messenger.

Dravyn came to stand behind me, slipping his arms around my waist and nuzzling his face into the crook between my neck and shoulder. His warm breath fanned over my skin, sending tingles down my spine. His heartbeat pounded against my back.

Even with all the things on my mind, I found myself sinking into that beat, wanting to keep time with it and nothing else. The days we'd spent apart seemed vast, suddenly. Too many minutes, too many hours. My body hummed with want at our reunion, eager to make up for lost time.

I settled more completely against him, sinking my full weight into his warmth, his strength. He supported me with ease, absently trailing his hands along the curves and dips of my waist, my hips, my thighs. I shivered as he dragged his lips and nose along my neck, inhaling my scent.

"Did I ever tell you how much I missed you these past days?" I asked, breath catching on the last word as his mouth found my earlobe and claimed it, covering it in kisses before gently sucking and sliding his teeth across it.

"I missed you, too." His hold on me tightened, one hand dropping to a hip and possessively gripping it. The other traveled up to my throat and splayed across it, the pressure of his fingers increasing until my head tilted to an angle that allowed him to press his lips to mine.

"And I needed you," he mumbled against my lips. "Wanted you. So fucking badly."

I twisted more fully toward him. He moved the hand around my throat up to my hair, tangling his fingers in the loose waves and pulling. Slowly, gently...yet firmly in command. He gathered a fistful of hair and used it to tilt my head to the side, exposing the most sensitive, throbbing pulse-point of my throat.

My mind drifted as his lips and tongue worked against that point until my knees felt weak and ready to collapse into total, blissful unawareness.

Heat snaked out from the fingertips pressed against my hip, winding a wicked path around my thighs before pressing into the space between them.

His control over that fire was very...*precise.*

A second ribbon of heat swept even deeper into my core, and an involuntary noise—something between a gasp, a moan, and a breathless laugh—escaped me. The sound brought my awareness back with it, despite how hard I tried not to let it.

I didn't pull away from Dravyn, but I did crane my neck so I could see all the guards milling about in the yard below. I wondered if they could see us. Hear us.

"Does it make us poor guests if we distract your brother's soldiers with our rooftop antics?" I mused.

He laughed. "You insisted on staying the night here," he reminded me. "And yes...it might be difficult to find a bit of privacy with all of the guards currently locking the palace down. It's not too late to return to our own palace, of course."

I cut him a wry look. "You're still looking for excuses to run away from here, aren't you?"

"That's only part of it." He gave me a roguish grin. "I've thought about stealing you away to someplace more private, several times today —that's true." The hand against my hip flexed, drawing my body more flush against his. "But then again, as I've told you before: I'm willing to fuck you anywhere."

I no longer cared about any of the guards below, all of a sudden.

"Here on this rooftop or back on our own," he continued, tracing my bottom lip with his thumb, "it makes little difference to me. I suspect your moans will sound just as sweet anywhere we go. Your taste will still be divine, whatever the realm."

His mouth returned briefly to my neck—another taste, for emphasis. Then another, and then we fell back into blissful ignorance for a few minutes, lost in one another's kisses and caresses until we were interrupted by the sound of shouting voices and the echoing *clip-clop* of hooves.

I reluctantly peeled away from Dravyn and moved to the edge of the roof for a closer look. My body still hummed with desire, but I was desperate to see if those hoofbeats belonged to the horse of a returning messenger.

My heart sank as I took in the scene below—nothing except carts full of supplies being hauled in and unloaded while palace officials darted to and fro, checking lists.

Dravyn sensed my disappointment. Slowly, he followed me and wrapped his arms around my waist, pulling me against his chest, just as before—but this time I couldn't bring myself to relax against him; I was too caught up in my worried thoughts to return to that enraptured place of moments ago.

"Have you had a chance to talk to your brother much today?" I asked.

"He's locked himself in his private residential hall. Doing his best to avoid me, as expected."

"I think he's glad you're here. He just hasn't figured out how to show it."

"I'll continue waiting on bated breath for my proper welcome home party, then."

"He hasn't thrown us into the streets yet," I pointed out. "That's a good sign, isn't it?"

Dravyn tipped his mouth closer to my ear and mumbled, "I'd keep your bags packed just in case."

I rolled my eyes even though he couldn't see it. "I think I was more convincing than you realize."

He chuckled, the sound low and seductive as it slid across my neck.

"You doubt my negotiating skills?"

He considered for a moment before his lips—now close enough to brush my skin—eased into a smile. "No, I suppose not."

"Such a passionate endorsement."

Another huff of laughter. "How could I doubt such skills," he said, taking my hand and twirling me around to face him, "when I am, after all, a victim of your persuasion myself?"

"*Victim* is an interesting choice of word there."

He lifted my knuckles to his lips, planting kisses across them. "I've suffered greatly beneath your hands," he insisted.

"There's more suffering in store for you if you keep teasing me."

His smile turned mischievous. "Let's hope so."

The curve of his lips nearly had me melting back into his embrace. But a new commotion from below drew my gaze, and this time I spotted a promising-looking rider trotting through the gates. Hope and dread curdled together in my stomach as I looked to Dravyn for confirmation.

"One of the king's messengers," he said with a nod, "judging by the livery he wears."

I raced back inside.

Fallon was already waiting for us by the time we found our way through the maze of hallways and staircases and managed to reach the entrance the messenger had been heading for.

The king had been there long enough to open the letter the messenger carried in, and—I assumed—had already read it several times over. His face was impassive, however. He said nothing to me as he handed that letter over.

He muttered something to Dravyn before he walked away, but I was too absorbed by the sight of Savna's handwriting to pay much attention to whatever he'd said.

The parchment shook in my hands as we made our way toward a small sitting room nearby. I perched on the edge of a creaking chair and scoured the letter like a starved woman hunting cabinets for scraps, for crumbs, for some morsel of any kind—anything that would help fill the aching pit in my stomach.

I couldn't keep still as I read. I got to my feet. Sat down again. Stood again. Sank deeper into the velvety cushions, only to stand back up again almost immediately.

I kept reading the last line over and over again—it was the only one that seemed to stick in my mind long enough for me to understand it:

I'll see you then.

My heart pounded in my throat.

Dravyn was watching me with a mixture of curiosity and concern. "She's agreed to meet you?" he guessed.

"Just after sunrise." I fought to settle my shaking hands, scanning the letter one more time, still doubting its message even as I read it. "And she's coming alone."

"So she says."

I ignored the pessimistic comment, though he was right to be wary. There was a chance she was lying. A chance she'd been forced to write this reply to help Andrel and the other rebels lay a trap for me.

I knew all of these things, of course.

But for some stupid reason, I was determined to cling to the few shreds of optimism I had left. I had to have hope. There would be no future without it.

"She wants to speak with me privately before we go to the king," I told Dravyn.

"...But she's agreed to speak with Fallon, too?"

"It seems that way," I said, holding out the letter to him. "Though maybe I'm biased and looking for positive things that aren't really there."

He took the parchment and read it silently. Then read it a second and third time before he finally gave it back to me. "It sounds...somewhat promising," he admitted.

I folded the letter up and slipped it into the inside pocket of my coat, letting it rest right above the scar left by Andrel's knife.

Somewhat promising was better than nothing.

And for now, it would have to do.

CHAPTER 36

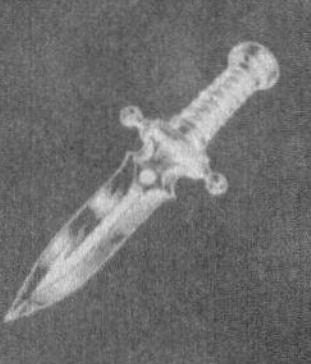

Karys

I couldn't sleep.

Sunrise was only hours away, yet it felt like it would never arrive. Like I was trapped in an endless night that kept repeating itself over and over and over.

Dravyn dozed soundly at my side, one arm draped over my stomach.

I kept still for as long as I could, trying not to disturb him, but restlessness eventually got the better of me. Slowly and silently, I sat up, scooting toward the edge of the bed.

Dravyn's hand closed around my hip, pulling me back. His eyes stayed closed. His breathing remained easy and even. He mumbled my name and something else, but he was clearly still asleep.

Even in his dreams, he was still reaching for me.

Still choosing me.

I warmed at the thought and reached for him as well, intertwining my fingers with his. He squeezed my hand and shifted onto his back, pulling free of the blankets that had bunched between us and putting his bare, impressive chest on full display.

I stopped moving toward the edge of the mattress, caught up in the sight of him.

My gaze swept over the moonlit ridges of his abdomen, up the corded muscles of his arm, along the powerful lines of his shoulder. My stomach clenched at the sight of the new scars he'd gained in Mindoth. Or maybe *bruises* was the more correct term. They were a strange combination of both—dark splotches of discolored skin with a scattering of raised, angry slashes in some places.

Tentatively, I ran my fingers along the longest of the raised marks. As I touched it, I would have sworn I could see the arrow that had caused it, bright and flashing in my mind. I could feel its sharpness. The burning it left behind...

A wave of anguish shot through me.

Dravyn stirred, clearly sensing it. I froze, cursing myself for not having better control of my thoughts and feelings, as he blinked his eyes open. Several emotions played across his face in the span of a few breaths.

Disoriented at first.

Then came a flash of guarded panic as he took in the symbols of his old life that surrounded us.

And then—finally—relief overtook him as his eyes found me.

"I'm sorry I woke you," I said.

"You didn't." His voice was a whisper. One husky with sleep—and maybe something more, given the way his gaze dipped to the plunging neckline of my nightgown as he spoke. "This still feels like a dream to me." He brushed his hand along my arm, hooded eyes still drinking me in. "And I think I'd like to stay asleep."

His voice reignited the desire I'd felt on the rooftop earlier today. I smiled and eased closer, moving my attention from his shoulder to his chest, kissing a trail across it, then down along the hard ridges of his stomach.

My hands slid down along with my mouth, tracing his sides, following the muscular lines that dipped out of sight beneath the low-slung, loose-fitting pants he wore. I paused at the top of those pants, my fingers hooking around the waistband.

I planted a few more teasing kisses on the skin just above that band before arching up and bringing my face back toward his. One of my hands braced against the bed beside him. The other, I kept at his waist, drawing tantalizing circles with my fingertips, caresses that slowly slipped lower and lower.

I brushed that lower hand against the stiffening outline of his cock, pulling a soft groan from him.

Catching his breath, he asked, "Is this the suffering you warned me about on the roof earlier?"

I gave him a sly smile. "At least I gave you a warning."

His hand took mine, guiding it into a firm grip around his arousal. "One I've been thinking about all day."

I smiled as his other hand came to rest against the back of my neck, pulling my lips down to meet his. I sank into the kiss, my body willing and eager to mold itself to his.

My mind, on the other hand, refused to surrender to oblivious desire so easily; seconds into our kiss, I felt the intrusive thoughts prodding—the same relentless, battering worries that had overtaken me during the aforementioned roof conversation.

And though I attempted to continue as though nothing had distracted me, Dravyn clearly sensed something was wrong.

I tried to bury my face against his chest, but he caught my chin and lifted it. His eyes locked with mine; he seemed to be trying to focus on hearing my thoughts. I didn't attempt to block him out.

"Your mind is elsewhere."

I sighed. "Politics, deadly battles, the looming conversation with my sister and all the potential impending, world-altering doom around us... all such horrible mood killers, aren't they?"

He chuckled. Tenderly brushed a strand of hair from my eyes. Didn't disagree. After a moment, he sat up, pushing me upright in the same motion before settling me in his lap and wrapping my legs around him.

I shivered, partly from the amount of skin exposed by my thin nightgown, and partly from the way this position left no space between the most sensitive parts of us.

He circled both the blanket and his arms more tightly around my body. It was more torturous than anything I'd started, the way he pulled me into his firmness and warmth and held me there.

His arousal was still very obvious, hard and occasionally throbbing against my center, yet he didn't seem to be in a hurry to act on it. His touch was gentle rather than eager, taking the time to adjust the blanket so every inch of my chilled arms and shoulders was covered.

His eyes were full of concern rather than lust as he asked, "Have you gotten any rest at all?"

I shrugged.

His gaze slid toward the window, likely trying to gauge what time of night it was.

"I really didn't mean to wake you. If I'm keeping you up, I can sleep somewhere else," I offered.

"I don't need sleep. I've told you before—it's little more than a refreshing habit I enjoy."

"Right, but I just thought..." I trailed off, unsure of *what* I thought. I couldn't focus on any one thing, no matter how hard I tried.

We kept still, wrapped up in one another, for several minutes after that. Time seemed to slow along with us, making the night seem even more endless than before. My thoughts moved so quickly in comparison that it made me feel removed from the stillness, like I was floating somewhere far above this space—somewhere out of my body entirely.

"I won't stop you if you want to go somewhere else," Dravyn finally said. "But I would rather you stay."

Stay.

The word slowed my speeding thoughts to a crawl.

He hesitated, giving me the chance to pull away, to leave.

I didn't move. Didn't protest when he tilted his lips toward mine.

"Stay," he repeated, softly, in between kisses.

I smiled a little when he finally drew back enough to take in my response. "First, I make you suffer under my touch," I said, "and now, I have you pleading for me to stay."

He smirked. "Yes; I'm completely undone and overcome by you. I think we've established that."

"And I've barely even tried tonight. Imagine if I *really* wanted to torture you."

He took my hand, rubbing his thumb thoughtfully along my knuckles. "So ruthless."

I mirrored his smirk.

He raised a brow. "You are the only being in any realm that I'm willing to kneel before. I hope you realize that."

I did. But hearing him say the words out loud sent a pleasant tingle down my spine. "I'll try to wield the power responsibly."

His smirk gave way to a mischievous little grin.

"You're plotting something," I accused.

"Am I?"

"Out with it."

"I had a thought, is all." He gripped my hand more tightly, drawing me farther into his lap, pressing me more firmly against his hard, impressive length.

"A thought?"

"That you should wield nothing tonight." He massaged my hand as he spoke, rubbing and smoothing away the tension that had been trying to curl my fingers into a fist for the past several hours. "You are ruthless and magical and capable of bringing all the gods to their knees," he said. "But tonight...you should relax. *Yield* rather than wield."

"Yield?"

"To me."

He must have seen a flash of panic in my eyes, because his smile turned softer—though a bit teasing—as he said, "You know what it means to *yield*, don't you? To lower your guard? To relax?"

"I'm afraid I don't," I deadpanned.

"Well, let me teach you." The way he said *teach* made my heart skip several beats. It nearly pounded out of my chest altogether when he whispered, "Let me take care of you tonight, the way you deserve to be taken care of."

Heat pooled between my thighs as he leaned closer. Our noses brushed. The hand he'd been using to massage mine moved higher, skimming along my arm, up to my shoulder, rubbing away the tension gathered there, before moving on to the back of my neck.

A shiver of anticipation and desire crept down my spine. And it didn't stop there, this time; it coursed through me until every inch of my skin prickled with awareness. With want.

With *need.*

His other hand moved to the small of my back, rubbing small circles against the satiny fabric of my nightgown. An almost innocent, absent-minded touch, yet it stirred something deep inside me—a flame at my center that burned hotter and hotter with every caress, until my head tipped back into his strong palm and a soft note of pleasure escaped me.

His hand against my back stilled, holding me more securely. His other one shifted from the back of my neck, fingers wrapping lightly around the side of my throat. Tiny little points of pressure, so strong—yet restrained—against me.

And I started to imagine what it would be like to fully trust and relax into that strength.

To let him do whatever he wanted to me.

A thrill went through me at this last thought.

He let out a low laugh. Likely because he'd heard that thought for himself. "Have I successfully distracted you from all the *mood killers* we're facing?"

"For the moment," I admitted.

"Then let's not waste the moment." Without another word, he leaned me back onto the mattress.

The sudden loss of his body heat caused a violent shiver. But the cold lasted only an instant before he was moving over me, fingertips sliding along my body, lingering on pressure points, massaging with precise flexes of power and occasional bursts of heat.

Little by little, he stroked away much of the tension I'd been carrying from the past days.

I closed my eyes. Despite my usual tendency to want to overthink and map out every touch and breath between us, it seemed I *was* capable of letting these things go. Of *relaxing.*

I'd never felt this way with any other lover—comfortable enough to fall asleep one moment, wide awake and eager for more than just his careful, massaging touch in the next.

The longer his hands worked over me, the more pliable I became beneath them. After several minutes, all memory of the tension I'd carried into this bedroom was disappearing. I felt like I was melting into a warm bath, my body unfolding, opening for him in every sense of the word.

His fingers paused at the hem of my nightgown, tracing along the spot where silky trim met the pebbled skin of my thigh.

I sucked in a breath, eager for him to push the cloth aside.

Instead, he left the gown in place. His head dipped to kiss along the trail of heat his fingers had left before roaming higher, lips and tongue pressing and exploring me through my clothing. The combination of the soft, satin fabric and the warm, wet, heavy weight of his tongue felt sinfully good.

But I still wanted *more*.

My hands grew restless, alternating between clawing at my nightgown and tangling in his hair. As I caught a fistful of hair, using it to press his mouth more firmly to my body, he laughed—a hot, delicious puff of air and vibration against me.

I heard his thoughts a moment later: *Relax.*

Keep still.

Let me do the work.

His hands found mine. Pinned them to the mattress. Held them there as he stretched over me, straddling a knee on either side of my body before leaning up to kiss my neck.

Bringing his lips to my ear, he whispered, "Just a reminder...this room isn't fireproof like the ones back home. So you'll have to control your magic."

"Speak for yourself," I purred back. "I'm planning to merely relax and let you take care of me, remember?" I stopped fighting the powerful hold he had on my wrists, keeping perfectly still as he bowed his head toward my chest.

He brushed his face across the swell of my breasts, pausing to admire the stiffened peaks straining against my gown. He took one of those hardened, silk-draped points in his mouth, glancing up at me as he sucked upon it. Our eyes locked. I felt his magic surge, and the room burned hotter for an instant.

He regained his composure quickly. But still, I couldn't resist a small smirk, followed by a teasing brush of my tongue across my lower lip—a gesture that caused his magical pulse to briefly jump once more, even as he obviously worked to keep his cool.

I had more control than it appeared.

We both knew it.

I was still willing to play along, though, when he softly growled out a command: "Keep your hands at your sides."

I clenched my fingers into the sheets and did precisely that, leaving his hands free to let go of me, to move and take hold of the bottom of my nightgown instead.

He rolled it up to my hips, revealing the lace-trimmed undergarment beneath—one fashioned from silken fabric similar to that of my gown, providing no real barrier between my sex and the brush of his fingers, the heat of his breath, the hot lashes of his tongue. That tongue was relentless, licking and skimming until the fabric was thoroughly soaked.

When he slowed and started to pull away, I couldn't stop the sound of protest that slipped through my lips.

His eyes flicked up to mine. Stayed there as he ran his tongue slowly, savoringly, over my most sensitive spot. "As expected," he said, "you taste just as divine here as you do in the middle-heavens."

My breath caught and my stomach fluttered at the words.

Then came his teeth, nipping around my swollen folds but carefully catching only the damp fabric of the garment that separated us. He pulled that garment partially down with his mouth, finished the job with his hands, and tossed it to the floor.

He slipped my nightgown off as well, adding it to the pile of fabric that shimmered in the light streaming through the window. The full, pale moon had dropped lower in the sky since we started, casting the entire space in a bluish, otherworldly light and causing our shapes to throw tall shadows against the walls. Caught between those shadows and the moonlight edging his form, he looked beastly and beautiful all at once.

I didn't have long to admire him before he was leaning over me again, his gaze raking over me as he came.

"You are fucking immaculate." His tone was soft, almost reverent, as he ran his hands and a few quick swipes of his tongue over my newly-bared body.

Then his hands trailed back to my inner thighs.

He eased my legs apart.

I couldn't help but squirm eagerly under his hold, knowing what was to come.

He planted a chaste kiss just above the meeting of my thighs, but stopped there. "Relax," he reminded me with a slightly wicked smile. "And arch your back for me, Goddess."

His low, seductive tone made it nearly impossible to follow his command, but I somehow managed it.

As my back lifted, he piled pillows underneath to support me. Then he moved his attention back to my thighs, his arms hooking around them and steadying me further before he buried his face between my legs once again.

He savored a few more slow tastes, pulling at my thighs as he did, urging them farther and farther apart. The wider they went, the more heightened my reaction was to his mouth. I was practically writhing beneath him, certain nothing could feel better than what he was doing just then, when his tongue penetrated me with a slow, relishing thrust.

I cried out.

He buried his face more fully, pushed his tongue even deeper.

Breath left me, taking the sound of my moan with it. I clenched the sheets so hard I began to lose the feeling in my hands. I could have collapsed into orgasm then and there and been perfectly satisfied.

Dravyn must have sensed that release building in my body and mind, because he pulled away, still regarding me with that slightly wicked smile.

"Not yet," he said, slipping his fingers into the space his tongue had just claimed. "There's more I want to give you."

I tried to catch my breath. Not an easy task as two of his fingers moved against my inner walls with increasingly rapid strokes. A much different sensation than his tongue, but the end result was the same; after a few moments I was breathing hard, doing all I could to settle the fire building in my blood before I lost control and sent this room up in flames.

Dravyn pulled his fingers out and ran them—and the dampness that coated them—over the slickness that had gathered between my legs.

"Already so wet," he commented. "You've been thinking about this all day, too, haven't you?"

I mumbled something that sounded like *yes* in response. I think.

"Stay just like that." He ran his fingers over my center again, then smoothed his hand out across my thigh, applying light pressure and encouraging it to stretch wider once more. "Nice and open for me."

He stepped away from the bed and started to untie the drawstring holding his pants in place. The moonlight seemed to track his movements—a spotlight following and highlighting every tight muscle slicked with sweat and making it impossible to miss the sight of his hard cock springing free as he dropped his clothing to the ground.

He stood there for a moment, stroking himself, eyes leveled on me.

He looked so divinely perfect I couldn't breathe.

Couldn't comprehend that he was *mine*—that he was willing and ready to do whatever I wanted, whatever I needed to *relax*.

Moving back to the bed, he shifted some of the pillows underneath me, adjusting the angle of my body as he knelt before it. My muscles tensed in anticipation while I continued to struggle for breath.

He paused, his gaze searching mine. Watching for any sign of hesitation. But there was nothing there for him to see. The world and all the problems outside of this room, this moment...I'd already let it all go.

I trusted him, whatever came next. Just as I had trusted him to teach me to fly and to wield fire. It was much smaller, this sign of trust I gave him now—a soft exhale, a slight tip of my head. Just enough to say *yes. I want this*. The movement was nothing at all.

Yet it was *everything*.

Everything to not feel vulnerable, even though my position should have made me feel precisely that. To yield to him, yet still feel powerful beyond measure. Desired above all else.

He entered me slowly. My eyes fluttered shut and a soft whimper slipped out as he stretched me, as he throbbed against me in a way that was pleasure and pain twisted into one. His hands found mine and pinned them at my sides once more.

He slid in and out several times with slow, deliberate control, letting me feel each throb, easing me into a rhythm with beats that eventually became more pleasure than pain.

As my body relaxed—*yielded*—more completely, he leaned his mouth closer to mine and whispered, "How would you like to take it, Goddess?"

I kept my eyes closed, still savoring the fullness of him, but a corner of my mouth curved. "Ceding a bit of control, are we?"

"Just for the moment." He punctuated his reply with a more powerful roll of his hips, making me gasp.

A simple command came to my mind as I caught my breath. I whispered it without a second thought: "Harder."

His cock twitched at the word. He pressed one of my hands more firmly into the mattress, bracing himself. His thrusts came faster, slowing only long enough for him to focus on slipping his other hand between my legs. That hand moved against my center while he leaned more completely over my body, driving deeper and deeper with each successive pounding.

A moan rose in my throat. His lips crashed into mine, silencing the sound and every one that followed, only to answer them with feral sounds of his own as he pumped harder. Heat enveloped us, so searingly hot I expected to open my eyes and find the room entirely consumed by flames.

But the only inferno was between us, building in the burning friction of our bodies, in the smoldering fire of our locked gazes. The only scent of smoke came from his skin—that intoxicating smokiness mixed with pine and a spice that was undeniably *him*. It was the only scent I wanted to inhale just then. Maybe the only one I wanted to breathe in for the rest of my existence.

His head started to tip back, but my arms wrapped around his neck, pulling his mouth back down to mine. "*Harder*," I breathed against his lips.

I felt a fresh, powerful wave of desire ripple through him. His eyes found mine again, burning with wild need, all his remaining restraint undone.

"Hold on to me," he ordered.

As I linked my arms more tightly around his neck, he slipped himself out of me and stood, carrying me with ease toward the nearest wall. He pressed my back to it. The plaster was shockingly cold against my hot skin.

Any chill was forgotten an instant later, more heat engulfing us both as he grabbed one of my legs and lifted it. While holding it with one hand, he used his other to guide the tip of his cock back toward my entrance, teasing a few times before finally burying it deep inside of me.

He hooked an arm around my other leg and lifted me completely off the ground as he pounded harder, faster. His eyes were on me the whole time, studying the way I reacted to his every movement, watching for the things that drove me closer and closer to losing control, until finally—

I let go completely.

I forgot everything except the pulse and throb and pressure of him. I came with a cry, pressed between the firmness of the wall and the strength of him. Solid yet floating—I felt like I was back in the middle-heavens, held in his arms as we soared over the ground. All the rush and rapture of falling without any of the fear.

His release chased after mine, catching up to me with one last deep, powerful thrust that triggered another wave of my own climax. We shattered against one another, his arms wrapping more tightly around my body, crushing me against him until we were both fully emptied, fully spent.

We stayed in that position for several moments after, his skin flush against mine, our bodies shaking slightly, our breaths coming in gasps.

His eyes lifted to my face once more. A hint of wildness lingered in their silvery-blue depths, but he settled it and kissed me softly with a gentleness that would never stop surprising me after what I'd witnessed of his power.

He lowered me back to my feet, keeping a light hold on my waist until I'd fully regained my balance. He brushed one last kiss across my cheek and asked, "Are we relaxed, now?"

I couldn't find my voice, so I lifted onto my tiptoes and kissed him instead. He took my hand and gave it a squeeze; we didn't really need words.

He finally let me go, gathering up his clothing and heading into the attached washroom.

I ducked into that room as well, but lingered in it for some time after he left before I finally returned to our bed.

I moved quietly through the space, trying not to think, trying to hold on to nothing except what I'd felt while wrapped up in Dravyn's embrace.

I couldn't help noticing my surroundings, however; a dresser stood against the far wall, an ornate mirror attached to its top, and I caught my reflection in it as I pulled on my clothes and settled down on the edge of the mattress.

I'd made a point of not studying my face any more than I had to, here lately...it only stirred up all the questions I had about my identity. Questions I was tired of asking.

But now I found myself in a trance, unable to look away from the woman staring at me from across the room. Unable to stop thinking of the conversation I'd had with the king. How he had stared at me as well, trying to make sense of who—and what—I was. What I was going to do.

Dravyn had collapsed back into the pillows and blankets. His eyes were already closed. I tried, unsuccessfully, to follow his example, slipping under the covers and curling up tight, as if making myself smaller could help all my doubts and fears overlook me.

After several minutes of lying there, I was still wide awake.

I thought Dravyn had fallen asleep until he moved, hooking an arm around my waist and pulling me toward his chest. His voice rumbled against my shoulder a moment later, "The relaxation didn't last, hm?"

I considered ignoring the question and pretending I was far closer to sleep than I actually was.

I knew I wouldn't be able to fool him, though.

"Why were you studying your reflection?" he asked.

"No reason."

He gave a little snort of disbelief. Then he proceeded to knock his forehead against my shoulder repeatedly—the insistent badgering reminding me so much of something Moth would do that I couldn't help but let out a quiet laugh. Likely what he'd been going for.

I eventually gave into his prodding—*before* he decided to bite my shoulder the way a certain little griffin would have.

"It's just...I feel like I'm somebody different every day as of late," I said. "Every time I look in a mirror, I'm bracing myself, afraid of what I'll see. When does it end? When do I recognize the person staring back? And who will I be after this meeting with my sister tomorrow?"

He was quiet for a long time.

Then, he simply said, "You'll be Karys."

I grabbed one of the spare pillows, clenching it tightly against my chest. "Yes. I suppose. Whatever that means."

He propped himself up behind me, trailing a comforting hand along my tense muscles.

I kept my back to him as I swallowed a frustrated sigh. "I'm sorry."

"For what?"

"I should know who I am by now."

"I don't think figuring that out is a particularly easy task for anyone, whether goddess or human or elf."

"Maybe not. But it's hard to love a person in flux, isn't it?" I was thinking, not only of myself, but of my sister—of all the ones I'd tried to love throughout my life, and all the different versions of them I'd uncovered.

Dravyn gathered me more fully against him and settled back into the mattress with a sigh.

Silence stretched between us—not entirely uncomfortable, but full of questions. Of painful, heavy things that we weren't ignoring, but that neither of us wanted to talk about just then. I was content to leave the conversation here, to let him get back to his rest. These things were keeping me awake, but I didn't need him to suffer alongside me.

I started to tell him this.

Then he said, "Wildfire, do you not understand? I love *who* you are. Not what. Who you are, and who you were, and who you're becoming. Your fire, your ashes, your everything in-between..." The words were a bit slurred, spoken against my skin, growing softer as he drifted toward sleep. But they were certain. Without hesitation.

I kept perfectly still, letting those words sink over me. Trying to convince myself I deserved them. That I could trust them.

Slowly, I rolled over to face him.

His eyes were closed again. Just as well; this way he couldn't see the tears building in mine. I'd cried entirely too often, lately, and I was done with tears for now. I had to be.

His words from earlier resurfaced in my mind—*I won't stop you if you want to go somewhere else.*

A ridiculous statement. I never wanted to leave his side.

Not now, not ever.

And for the moment—as I curled into his chest and closed my eyes—I refused to think of the day ahead, and of all the things that might tear us apart.

CHAPTER 37

Karys

Sunrise finally came.

I rose to greet it alone. Dravyn's side of the bed was cold, his scent faint. But I could still feel his magical energy nearby, so I knew he remained in the palace.

I cleaned myself up and dressed quickly, trying not to dwell too much on what the day held. I would get through it one step at a time, by only *focusing* on one step at a time—starting with leaving this room.

Easy enough.

Except, I froze at the threshold, overcome by a sudden compulsion to get every step between now and my meeting with my sister correct.

In the past, I could usually shake this sort of fear off by being careful about how I stepped into certain places, making sure to lead with the correct foot, to hold my body in the correct posture.

But now a new, even more ridiculous and illogical fear consumed me: *What if I needed to change the way I moved between places?* What if that was the first step to fixing all the things I wanted to fix—through this meeting with my sister and beyond—and I got it wrong?

The questions kept repeating, growing more complicated, spiraling into a paralyzing chorus of what ifs.

What if, what if, what if...

Sweat beaded on my forehead. The floor was rising up, threatening to tip me over. I wanted to crumple to that floor, but I braced an arm against the door frame and I made myself stay on my feet.

I'm not sure how long I stood there, or how long I *would* have stood there if Dravyn hadn't found me.

I heard his voice say my name. Felt him stepping closer. I couldn't seem to shake my paralysis and look up to meet him, though; I was completely frozen. The only thing I could see were blurry, horrible images of all the wrong choices I might make, and what devastation might rain down on me because of them.

"Left," Dravyn said, softly.

My rushing thoughts slowed to a gentle whirring.

"Every time in the past," he said, "it's always been left."

I managed to blink away some of the horrid images flashing through my mind. To lift my eyes and see what was directly in front of me instead. And what I saw was Dravyn staring back at me, clutching a pewter mug full of what smelled like some sort of herbal tea.

I swallowed hard. "And what if I'd gone right?" A mere mention of the possibility sent another thread of fear spiraling through my gut. "In the past, what if I hadn't led with my left foot?"

He considered it—truly considered it, where so many in my past had merely laughed at me when I started asking questions like these. "Then maybe you wouldn't be here. Maybe we never would have met. Maybe everything would be different."

The thought of us never meeting sent a shock straight to my core—a visceral feeling even stronger than the fear currently rooting me in place.

"But you've survived every moment up to this point, even if you set out on the wrong foot," he pointed out.

Yes.

I had.

I stood up a little straighter, prying my hand from the door frame, finger-by-finger. Dravyn offered me the mug he held, and I managed to make myself take it. The solid warmth of it helped ground me more fully in the present, allowing me to finally step into the hallway.

My fear didn't fully subside as we walked. I found myself wanting to count everything we passed—the light fixtures, the floor tiles, the busts of famous Galithian leaders—to make certain the number of them was correct.

I didn't even know what the 'correct' number of these things was. I just needed to double-check things. To control, to hold on to *something* this morning, before I fully stepped into this day where it felt like so many things could slip from my grasp.

I finally found solace by counting the paintings we walked by, then going a step further and organizing them in my mind according to the style they represented. It calmed me enough that I was soon able to manage more coherent, purposeful thoughts, and, eventually, a conversation.

"You're up early," I said, glancing toward Dravyn. "A sunrise breakfast with your brother?"

He smiled wryly at my hopeful tone. "Sorry to disappoint you, but no."

"Where were you, then?"

"I went to check in with Mairu before she started to worry about us too much. And also to remind Valas that we needed him to be paying attention in case we needed his help. And after that..." His voice trailed off. He took a deep, steadying breath.

Curiosity ignited within me, but I didn't want to pry my way into his mind for answers.

Luckily, I didn't have to; his thoughts became clear a moment later —so clear that I suspected he wanted me to see them. That he was showing me what he couldn't bring himself to speak of.

And what I saw was an image of polished stones bearing the crest of the Galithian royal family. They stood on a hilltop dotted with trees with long, flowing branches. A breeze stirred through the memory, swaying the branches and fluttering the navy and silver-colored banners that were planted in an even line behind the stones.

"You went to visit your siblings' graves, didn't you?"

"And those of my parents."

"Alone?"

"You were finally resting well. I didn't want to disturb you."

I frowned, even though the answer was expected. It was who he was at the very core of his being, after all—he would carry the weight of the entire world alone if given the chance.

But the fact that he'd actually gone to visit those graves...it was surprising. A step forward, I wanted to think. Maybe he'd laid some of that weight on his shoulders down while he was there.

I desperately hoped so.

"I did speak briefly to my brother as well," he added after we'd walked in silence for some time. "Not a cheerful breakfast conversation, however. I was curious about what became of the other elvish prisoners being kept alongside Cillian."

"And?"

"None of them survived."

A cold sweat washed over me.

I went back to counting and organizing the various works of art we walked by until my pulse stopped racing and I felt like I could speak clearly again.

"It wasn't your fault, you know. What happened with Cillian."

He said nothing to this.

He had apologized over and over again about it already. Now that we were here, staying directly in the shadow of his family's lives and deaths, it occurred to me that he was probably struggling not to draw parallels between what had happened with Cillian and what had happened with his siblings.

He hadn't been able to save them from death by elvish poison, either.

He was the one who kept apologizing for Cillian, but I was the one who felt guilty now. Powerless to undo the deaths he'd witnessed. To unbreak his heart. All I could do was forgive him and hope it would be enough.

I said none of these things out loud. I only took his hand as we walked, squeezing it as tightly as I could, as I thought of our conversation from the other day. Of what I'd told him, whether he was listening or not—that he was worthy of forgiveness.

You have to forgive yourself for the ones you couldn't heal, I thought. *The ones you couldn't save.*

If today went well, if we could somehow kindle the start of a peace between all the realms and races, then we would end up saving far more than we'd lost.

His hand eventually squeezed mine back; hopefully because he was listening.

We said nothing else until we reached the small office where Fallon had stationed the soldiers who would be helping to facilitate our meeting with Savna. After a brief exchange of information, our helpers filed out of the room, most of them grim-faced and looking less-than-enthusiastic about having been selected for this mission.

I tried not to let their expressions get to me.

I didn't need enthusiasm today; just cooperation.

Dravyn pulled me aside before we left, directing my attention to a small box perched on the edge of a desk, beside the city maps we'd been poring over during our planning.

"The other thing I collected this morning," he said. "It's a gift that Mairu brought me—given to her by the Healing God. Rieta helped fashion it, so it should fit as well as the other things she's made for you."

Inside the box was one of the most beautiful pieces of armor I'd ever seen—a coat of mail that shimmered between shades of white and gold, much like the Healing God's eyes. It flowed as easily as water between my fingers, weighing next to nothing at all, yet I could sense a mighty power radiating softly from it. The same quiet, understated power Armaros carried into every room he entered.

"It will offer protection against any weapon that might try to pierce you, obviously, but more importantly: it's infused with the Healing God's magic—specifically with spells that will help counter the effects of anti-divine venom. The same spells he used to reverse some of the damage I sustained in Mindoth." He rubbed his shoulder. The marred skin there was fully covered by his shirt, but I still winced at the memory of the way his scars had looked in the moonlight last night.

"Hopefully you won't have to make use of this gift," he said. "But I'm not willing to take any chances."

WE REACHED the gatehouse I'd chosen for our meeting point after a quick horseback ride through the waking city.

Even as we left the more crowded areas behind, I could feel all the stares of that city against my back. Could hear the people's whispers, the foundational blocks of rumors being laid. No one had approached us—they didn't dare, given the royal livery of our horses and the small army of guards accompanying us—but the weight of their attention weighed heavily.

Fallon's words echoed in my mind.

If you are wrong, you will have put my city and its people in a very dangerous position. I just hope you realize that.

I gripped my horse's reins with sweaty palms, leading her to the hitching post behind the gatehouse. My lungs could not seem to inhale enough air no matter how hard I tried to focus on my breathing.

The guards were now a quarter mile behind me, forming a barricade to ensure this meeting would not be interrupted. No city folk would leave through this route. No one would enter through it.

The guards remained close enough to intervene quickly, if needed—and Dravyn was even closer—but the gatehouse itself was secluded, neutral ground that only Savna and I would step into.

Exactly what I had requested from the King of Galizur.

The only problem was that my sister was nowhere to be seen.

The messenger who had delivered the particulars about our meeting to Savna *was* here, however. And after interrogating him several times, I finally concluded that he'd done his job adequately. The meeting place and time had been made clear. Savna knew the way, she knew the stakes, she knew my expectations.

She would be here.

I just had to be patient—not a quality I was known for.

How many times had I waited for her to show up, only to be disappointed? Of course that was what my heart wanted to retreat to—that feeling of disappointment and betrayal. I *hated* that feeling. But it was familiar. And so it was comforting.

I forced myself to keep still, to sit in the discomfort for once and simply...*wait*.

And to my surprise, she actually showed up.

She rode into view just as the sun slipped behind a mass of gathering rain clouds. Two riders accompanied her, each one bearing a small white flag.

It took everything I had not to break into a run to immediately go greet her.

That was not the plan.

I held my position, merely watching as the two flag-bearing riders dismounted and held perfectly still next to their horses, their symbols of our temporary truce clutched tightly in their fists.

Savna stepped forward alone.

This was what we had agreed upon—me and her and no one else.

Dravyn was less settled on this plan than I was. He was out of sight, but still close enough that he must have seen Savna arriving, because his voice was suddenly in my head, as loud and clear as if he was standing right beside me.

If any part of this starts to look threatening to you, I am intervening. I won't be separated from you again.

I nodded. *I'm fine. My magic is fully recovered. Ready to carry me away quickly, if need be.*

I held out my hand and summoned a tiny, perfectly controlled flame into my palm, hoping he could see it from wherever he stood. Hoping it would reassure him.

Be careful.

I nodded and started to walk toward my sister.

We met before the barred door of the gatehouse—a door that had been left partially ajar for our use. I didn't go inside right away. I couldn't.

I was too busy staring.

The first thing I noticed were her eyes. The dark circles underneath, the way their usual bright blue had dulled to the color of murky water. She hadn't slept since we'd parted ways. I was certain of it.

The second thing I noticed was the bruise around her neck.

I had a vivid memory of the other night—of Andrel's hand grabbing her throat as she tried to protect me from him.

It took everything I had to keep from igniting more fire in my hands —enough fire to swallow us both up, along with this stupid gatehouse and all my stupid plans for peace talks that suddenly seemed pointless. Impossible.

Are you okay? Dravyn's voice somehow cut through the fury that was slowly encasing me, suffocating out all other sound and sensation.

I had to answer quickly, or I knew he would intervene—which would likely be disastrous.

Yes, I lied. *I'm fine.*

Then I noticed a third thing: A fresh scar ran along Savna's face, slicing across her jaw and dipping down toward the hollow of her throat. The slash stopped just short of the life-giving arteries of her neck. As if he'd been aiming to kill.

"I know what you're thinking." My sister gave me a grim smile. "But it's not as bad as it looks."

The rage that overtook me was so intense, so all-consuming, that I didn't trust myself to speak through it. I closed my eyes and willed another wave of calmness to overtake me.

I'm fine, I assured Dravyn, before he could ask.

"You've been bearing countless scars and bruises on your own for years," Savna said. "Now we're a bit more even, that's all."

"That doesn't make it any better," I said, fiercely. "How could you think I would—"

"Is this *really* what you summoned me here to discuss?"

I snapped my mouth shut.

"It's not, is it?"

"No."

"Focus, then."

It irked me to be ordered around by her—like I was still just her kid sister, nothing more—but I also knew she was right. There was no shortage of things we could spend the next several hours raging about. This wouldn't fix anything, however.

"So here I am," she prompted. "But *why* am I here?"

I jerked my head toward the gatehouse. She moved first. I managed to follow her lead, and once we were inside, I took a deep breath and rattled off the speech I'd rehearsed before I had a chance to freeze up and overthink it.

"The King of Galizur is planning something," I told her. "Retaliation for Mindoth, and for all the transgressions the elves have made against this kingdom before that. A battle to end all others. And Andrel led me to believe he has something similar planned from your side of things."

She neither confirmed nor denied the last part. She was listening intently, though, so I kept talking.

"If we let these sides clash, I fear there will be no coming back from it. This realm will be devastated by such a war. Elves, humans—*both* sides will be ruined."

The room felt small, cramped and dark as it was with all the uncertain, heavy things between us. The only light came from a single square, barred window. Savna moved toward this broken sunlight, but stopped short of it, as if she didn't want to risk being seen by anyone outside.

She lowered her voice when she finally replied—even though we were surrounded by thick stone with no one close enough to hear us. "What do you want from me, Karys?" Exasperation filled her voice, yet there was a genuine plea underneath it.

Tell me what to do.

Tell me how we can fix this.

"I have the king almost willing to listen to my advice," I said. "And he may be willing to reconsider his plans for attack, too, if I can convince him that you might do the same. But I can't do it on my own. I need you to speak to him."

She shook her head, unconvinced.

"I *know* you, Savna," I pressed. "I haven't been there to watch it happen, but I know you have followers who would march with you to whatever ending—you were always the one who could rally others. You have as much control over the rebellion factions as Andrel does."

"I don't think we have enough to stand against the ones who are more loyal to Andrel."

"But you have me, too." I stepped closer, effectively cornering her. "And the divine court I belong to as well—"

She scoffed at the mention of the gods.

"The king is a potential ally, too," I insisted.

"Yes, but Andrel—"

"*He killed Cillian*," I blurted out, frustration taking hold of my tongue and turning it sharp. "He killed every hostage taken that night from Mindoth. Snuck poison into their water so they couldn't spill any secrets. Does that not make you want to at least *try* to stand up to him?"

Her gaze was wild as it fixed on mine, flashing between fear, grief, anger—all the emotions I'd felt since learning the news, all at once.

The one emotion I *didn't* see was shock.

She didn't look as surprised by the news of Cillian's death as I thought she might be.

Realization crawled over my skin. I barely resisted the urge to try and claw the needling sensation from my body.

"...You were already aware of what happened in Fallon's dungeons, weren't you?"

She averted her eyes.

"The sister I knew would have already done something about it."

"It's more complicated than all the things you once knew."

"But you know something has to change. You're destroying each other. Whatever grand plans you all had for reshaping this world are gone."

She shoved past me, making as if for the door, but stopped at the sound of my voice.

"You fought against him once already. You risked everything to help me escape from our house the other night. What's changed in the days since then?"

"Yes, I fought." She threw a glare over her shoulder at me. "But that was for *you*. And it was a moment of desperation. I don't know if the others will fight as I did. Even the ones loyal to me...it's a risk. One that might not pay off for either of us."

"Will *you* keep fighting, at least?"

She seemed startled by the question.

"Savna." Her name cracked as it came out. My throat was so brutally, painfully dry.

Slowly, she turned to face me once more.

"Just answer the question."

She breathed in deep. Exhaled. Over and over. Finally, she whispered, "I *want* to fight with you. For you."

"You want to. But something is holding you back."

"I want to," she repeated, looking me dead in the eyes with a haunting sort of focus. "But I haven't been able to get the taste of smoke from my tongue. I still smell it whenever I breathe in too deeply. I *see* it when I close my eyes—the land outside of our house, our childhood home, all of it...*burning*."

"They were empty fields."

"*This* time. But fire spreads if left unchecked."

"They were fires he sent to help guide me back home."

"...Home?" The word rolled like a boulder from her lips, heavy and clumsy, hitting the ground between us and cracking it open. The start of yet another chasm between us.

I'd realized it months ago: That Dravyn was home for me now. This was the first time I'd ever said it out loud to her, though—or to anyone, maybe.

It was painful to watch the way my sister shrunk away from my words. But I didn't take them back. I wouldn't apologize for moving on. For changing. Not anymore.

She collected herself and calmly asked, "Is that how you were able to vanish into the flames? You really are a divine being, now, aren't you?" Her eyes glazed over, as if she was reliving the memory as we spoke. "There one moment, gone up in smoke the next...it was...frightening to watch."

"Burning yourself away can be surprisingly therapeutic," I muttered.

"Fire spreads," she said, again. "And it destroys things." She blinked back into awareness, and her gaze jumped to the burn scars covering my face. She looked away just as quickly, as if she hadn't meant to let her eyes wander so carelessly over this ugly reminder of our childhood games and mistakes.

Months ago it would have been *me* looking away first, trying to keep her from staring.

Now I kept still.

I called attention to those ugly marks, even, effortlessly flexing my magic enough that it brought divine symbols to my skin and set the old scars alight.

I was no longer ashamed to let these things burn brightly.

Proof of my power, not my mistakes.

"It does destroy," I agreed. "But it can also forge and reshape things. Weld them back together. And there is more to me than the fire he gave me. More to my power, my plans, my story—all of it. And I can prove it; I just need you to trust me."

Her eyes slowly returned to mine. She stared at me and my glowing scars for a long moment. Inhaled deeply, and said, "You've changed." Her lips quivered with emotion before splitting into a crooked smile. "When did you become the brave one, while I became the coward?"

"You aren't a coward. You've only been doing what you thought you needed to do to survive." I fought the urge to reach for the scar near my heart—the one scar, the one mistake I was still struggling to make peace with. "I know the feeling. It takes courage to survive that. And it will take *more* courage to change things."

The clouds outside moved, more of them sliding over the sun, taking away what little light we had. The birds chattered louder in the sudden shadow, and a breeze stirred—everything felt like it was shifting.

Whether for better or worse, I wasn't sure.

"I'm trying, Karys," she whispered. "I am. I just don't know how to start. How to see beyond surviving the next battle, or trust your gods the way you do."

The chasm between us was cracking wider—dangerously wider—while the edges of it threatened to cave in.

I leapt across it anyway, taking her hand as I said, "You could just... meet them. Meet the God of Fire, at least. Maybe that would help."

She was quiet for a painfully long moment before she replied. "He's close by?"

A corner of my mouth lifted. "He's hardly let me out of his sight since everything that happened at our old house."

"Well," she said after another pause, forcing an obvious lightness into her tone, "I suppose it's a good thing you have *someone* looking after you, if I can't be around to keep you out of trouble." Despite her light tone, her expression remained wary, her eyes darting to the window over and over as if anticipating a fiery entrance from the god in question.

"He isn't going to smite you," I said dryly. "I won't let him."

"As if *I'd* let him," she said with a smirk, tossing her hair behind her shoulder and striding toward the doorway without hesitation. Back to her usual confident self, just like that.

Once outside, she surveyed the companions who had ridden in with her—both of whom remained on the distant hilltop—and she gave them a signal of some kind.

Then she whistled low, calling her horse.

I watched her adjusting the saddle and headgear with an anxious ball growing in the pit of my stomach; she hadn't really given me an answer, had she?

Was this it?

Were we done, just like that?

She swung into the saddle. I trailed to her side, staring up at her just like I had so many times when I was young. Only, I wasn't begging her to me with her, now.

She looked ready to bolt. To set off on whatever mission awaited her.

I tried to make peace with the possibility, to steel myself against the oncoming hurt.

But she didn't leave.

"This God of Fire...he was the younger brother of the king in his mortal life, wasn't he?" She spoke without really looking at me, and continued without giving me a chance to answer. "So I likely would have met him eventually, anyway, as long as I have business with Fallon. We might as well get it over with."

The knot in my stomach loosened a bit.

I focused my thoughts in Dravyn's direction once more, summoning him as calmly as I could.

Almost instantly, he emerged onto the road in the distance, on foot, leading both of our horses. A burst of warmth flared through the air as our gazes met, causing my sister to gasp.

"You'll get used to that," I said.

Dravyn cooled the air as quickly as he'd heated it. He'd once again attempted to look more human than usual, too, but the rising sun at his back—even as diluted as it was by the gathering clouds—ruined any chance of that. He was power and perfection in this realm and every other, and everyone present knew it.

My sister drew in a long, shaky breath as she watched him approach. Her horse nervously stamped its feet and attempted to turn them once more toward the other elves, but she refused to let it. She sat tall, her shoulders drawn back, her chin lifted.

I stood perfectly still, watching the meeting with a mixture of hope and horror.

I had faced the wrath of gods. Solved their sadistic trials and tests. I had traveled between worlds and battled against armies of all shapes and sizes. Had flown with wings made of fire, wielded weapons of the same flame, endured betrayal and poison and countless other things...

But this.

This was the most anxious I remembered feeling in a very long time. Maybe because my hopes for this meeting were so high that—should this experiment fail—I felt like the fall back to earth might kill me.

Savna spoke first, kicking her horse into a trot and riding closer to appraise the deity approaching us. "*Dra' Zerachiel*, God of Fire and Forging, Destroyer of Worlds and—" she threw a glance in my direction "—Captor of Innocent Elven Maidens."

A muscle ticked in his jaw.

I held my breath.

He rolled the tension from his shoulders and said, "Just Dravyn will suffice."

The breath left me in a soft, slow sigh.

My sister glared at him in much the same way I imagined *I* had done during our first meeting. A glare full of complicated, conflicting things —a generational hatred and fear tempered by a need to cooperate for the sake of bigger, more important things.

Finally, a corner of her lips edged up in that confident, familiar way of hers. "Dravyn it is, then."

Dravyn gave her a cordial nod before letting his gaze shift to me, searching my face for signs of anything amiss, still questioning whether I was truly okay after the tense meeting I'd just endured in the gatehouse.

I hurried forward and took the reins from his hand. "Our royal guard awaits us," I reminded him as I swung onto my horse's back. "As does the king."

Both he and my sister still looked wary of one another, but neither one objected.

And somehow, despite all the forces battling against it, the three of us set off together toward the palace.

CHAPTER 38

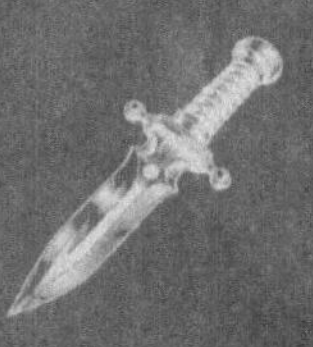

Karys

It was taking too long to get back to the palace.

Maybe it was the silence between us making it feel longer. Or the tension weighing down our movements, making every step seem to drag. Or maybe this whole situation was some fever dream that existed outside of time and reality—maybe I'd never actually woken up this morning.

I almost started to believe this last thought until Dravyn slowed his horse, his gaze darting suspiciously at our surroundings, and he said, "This is a different route than the one we took earlier."

The statement startled me; it wasn't like me to not notice a change like this.

One of our escorts slowed as well. "A disturbance of some kind took place on that earlier route, soon after we passed through," he informed us. "It's been dealt with, I'm told. Nothing to worry about—we're just being extra cautious."

But the soldier clearly seemed to be worrying as he picked up his pace, leaving the three of us to exchange an uneasy glance.

As the soldier trotted just out of earshot, Dravyn's glare swung in my sister's direction. "You came into this city alone, as agreed?"

"I swore I would," she replied, stiffly. "And I kept my promise."

I pushed my horse between them before Dravyn could comment on her record of promise-keeping. "We're almost back to the palace," I said pointedly. "Let's just keep going."

They led their horses away from one another, each hugging as closely as they could to opposite sides of the road while I remained in the middle.

Finally, we turned onto the street that led directly up to the palace gates. Dravyn's former home stood like a beacon among the increasingly dismal day, the brick facade bright in the somber lighting.

A bolt of lightning flashed, its brilliance reflecting in the silver-domed tower that reached high from the palace's center. It was such an arresting sight that at first, I didn't notice anything else on the road we were trotting along.

When I finally did pry my eyes from the palace, I still took note of little that directly surrounded us...because there was nothing *worth* noticing.

No sound. No movement. No signs of any life, at all. The street and its houses were clearly inhabited—clothes hung to dry on lines, chickens pecked in yards, dogs barked.

Yet not a single person walked among any of it.

My skin crawled with warning.

Then, a flash of movement: Someone darted across an upstairs window. Someone who didn't want to be seen, I thought. Someone who had the high ground. A vantage point.

A shiver rippled through my horse. I absently rubbed its neck, whispering calming words while my gaze darted to all the places where threats could be lurking. A few more flashes of movement caught my eye—all too quick for me to make out much more than vague shapes as they snuck past doors and windows. They all appeared to be dressed from head to toe in black, and they were clearly following our movements. Flashing signals to other figures in other houses.

We passed a wide balcony draped with Galithian flags. Aside from wind chimes clinking lightly in the breeze, there was no movement here.

There was only a horrifyingly still shape stretched across the boards, halfway in the house and halfway outside—a lifeless body. Its bare feet pushed between the balcony railings. Small feet.

A child, maybe.

Bile rose up, acrid and stinging in the back of my throat.

Something told me there were more bodies tucked away out of sight.

Dravyn pulled his horse up beside mine, inhaling deeply, scenting the air. I didn't have to ask what he smelled. I smelled it too.

Elves.

And blood.

"The houses..." I began.

"They've been infiltrated."

Arrows flew from several different balconies in the next breath, striking the ground all around us.

A massive *bang!* sounded in the same instant, spooking our horses and making it impossible to steer them away from the second deluge of arrows that quickly followed the first.

I spotted the nearest masked assailant and started to summon fire into my palm. My horse panicked even further at the surge of magical energy. I leapt from the saddle before the beast's panicked bucking got us both impaled, wings flaring from my back and lifting me higher, slowing my descent so I could twist in mid-air and take aim at the masked attacker I'd spotted.

This all happened in the span of a few heartbeats—yet Dravyn was still faster; before I touched the ground, he was in front of me and my horse, summoning magic of his own. A wall of fire sprang up, dazzling and bright, thick enough that no arrow could have passed through—

An unnecessary wall, I quickly realized.

Because most of our attackers weren't even aiming for us.

They were aiming for my sister.

Savna had gotten separated from us. She was some twenty feet back, crouched beside her horse, which was kneeling in an awkward, crumpled heap on the dusty road. Arrows protruded from the creature's neck. Savna was distracted, frantically trying to assess the damage, so busy trying to soothe the horse that she was oblivious to the full extent of the danger taking shape around her.

I screamed her name.

She looked up just in time to see the arrowheads glinting before they were released. She hit the ground and rolled, narrowly avoiding three different shots. Springing back to her feet with a lethal grace, she quickly assessed the area, searching for cover.

I raced toward her, wings tucking behind me, the fiery concentration of their power propelling me forward with a reckless, inhuman speed.

Savna took cover in a narrow gap between two houses as I crashed to a stop in front of her.

I looked up again, finding more attackers drawing their arrows and pointing them in our direction.

My own arrows shot from my hand with little conscious thought—arrows made of fire that embedded deep in the bottom of several balconies and rapidly ignited the wood, consuming it and sending the archers crashing to the ground.

There were countless more attackers already spilling out of houses, thundering down the street, leaping from the balconies before Dravyn or I could set those balconies on fire. They all wore the same dark attire and masks, and they carried more than just bows—weapons of all shapes and sizes flashed, clinked, clattered.

A group of sword-wielding assailants was swiftly approaching us. My sister drew her sword as well, the metallic shriek of it echoing off the high walls of the houses rising on either side of us.

I backed deeper into the corridor, positioning myself more squarely in front of my sister and starting to summon a shield of flame for us both.

Dravyn cut a path through the group of approaching swords to reach us—a raging storm of wind and fire that killed several and sent countless others scattering in all directions. As he reached me, he guided my attention toward the bridge in the distance; another heavily armed group was crossing it, heading our way—Galithian soldiers.

"We should let them take it from here," he said.

I nodded. We could have killed all of these elven assailants easily enough. But we'd likely send half this city—and its innocent population —up in flames in the process.

"You can carry your sister away?"

I nodded without hesitation, even though I'd never actually managed to transport someone else alongside myself. But Savna wouldn't relax enough to let Dravyn carry her, I was certain—so I was her best option for escape.

I would manage, somehow.

I turned to relay this plan to Savna just as an attacker appeared on the other end of the narrow passage we'd taken shelter in. He'd been trying to sneak up on us. Failing this, he broke into a crazed sprint, his curved blade drawn and ready at his side.

My sister turned to face him, ducking at precisely the right angle to avoid the strike and then countering with one of her own. In a single, fluid motion she swooped down and then rose back up, plunging her sword into his gut.

As she twisted her weapon free and kicked the attacker to the ground with a grunt, I was briefly transported—as I'd so often been over these past weeks—back to our younger years, to all the times I'd admired the way she fought. The way she protected me.

She was still the sister I had always admired and looked up to, in so many ways.

But now we were facing a bigger battle than ever before.

And it was my turn to protect her.

While Dravyn held off the rest of our attackers, I grabbed Savna's arm and pulled her out of the fray. I needed more open space, away from the houses and everything else, where I could focus and fully unleash my magic and let it wrap itself properly around us and carry us away.

As I hurried her along, I began to focus my power. The surge of it must have felt overwhelming to someone not used to it; Savna stumbled and dug in her heels, yanking her arm from my grasp.

"Karys, what are you—"

I spun wildly toward her, sending bits of flame peeling off my body —which did nothing to settle the panic in her eyes. A few of the embers caught on the trees surrounding us. The sound of crackling leaves and the scent of wood smoke filled the air.

"I can get us both away from here, but you have to *trust me*," I said, as calmly as I could. "You have to relax into my power, to want to go with me, or it could end very poorly for you."

Her eyes widened further as I reined in the embers drifting around us and extinguished the smoking trees with a clench of my fist.

The symbols on my skin burned brighter. I redirected the flames I'd collected, fusing them together and turning them into ribbons that I started to wrap around us.

In the same moment, I spotted a trio of our attackers weaving through the trees, trying to hunt us down.

"We have to go!" I shoved my hand out.

My sister hesitated only a moment before she reached back.

An arrow struck her outstretched arm.

A shallow scrape, nothing more, but the scent of her blood undid something in me.

A furious cry rising in my throat, I turned my power on the ones approaching us. While I focused on the one who had fired the arrow —ending him with a spear of flame shot straight through his neck— the other two swung wide and closed in on us from opposite directions.

Savna fell into step beside me, sword in hand.

I forged those ribbons of flame around us into a sword of my own.

And for a moment, we were again our younger selves, reborn into our old life—a life filled with the two of us fighting back-to-back. Watching over one another. Where I stumbled, she stepped in to lift me back up. Where she missed her mark, I followed up and struck with more precision.

We were invincible.

Until we weren't.

Until I went one way, impaling my target with my blade of flame, searing my way through his heart.

Savna went the other way, dealing with her own attacker with the same sort of finesse—knocking him off his feet and stabbing smoothly into his chest when he struggled to sit up.

But there was another taking aim; I twisted around just in time to see him darting out from behind a nearby tree, silent as a falling leaf.

Lightning flashed, illuminating the whites of his eyes, wild and wide.

Thunder followed at the exact moment he stabbed the blade into Savna's back—a sound that seemed to fit the sensation of my heart collapsing into nothing, nothing, *nothing*.

My sister was looking at me as it happened. Starting to reach for me again. Ready to trust me. To let me carry her away from all of this. As her attacker withdrew his weapon, she dropped slowly to her knees before tumbling face first onto the grass.

I stumbled toward her, reciting my next steps to myself, trying to force myself to stay focused.

Slow the bleeding.

Get her away from here.

Save her, save her, save her—

My earlier suspicion was proven true; my sister had been the target of these assassins. And now that she was motionless on the ground, the one who had stabbed her seemed completely uninterested in me.

He took several steps back, sword still held at the ready, but only appraised me with a cold, distant look as I fell at my sister's side and gathered her into my lap. Remembering the divine mail I wore—and the magic it was infused with—I pulled her closer to it, hoping that the Healing God's power might seep into her somehow.

I held her the way she used to hold me when I was sick—enveloping her entirely in my arms, folding my body over hers until we were one singular being, our heartbeats echoing one another's, my breaths in sync with hers, even as they became shallow and slow.

I pressed a fist against the wound on her back, trying to stop the flow of blood. That blood quickly soaked through my sleeve and trickled down my arm, but I only pressed tighter.

Whatever magic lies within this armor, whatever healing power still sleeps within my elvish blood, let it pass to her

The chaos in the distance raged on.

I could sense Dravyn still battling within it. He wouldn't leave until I was gone, I knew; so of course he was still fighting, still drawing as many as he could away from us. He'd killed plenty—the stench of blood and death, of scorched skin and bones, was overwhelming—yet more had managed to peel away from that main battle; they were making their way toward me, surveying the scene. Sizing up the goddess before them. The blood soaking me. The smoke spiraling around my arms—all that remained of the fires I'd started to wield moments ago.

I barely glanced their way. There were too many to count at just a glance, but I didn't care. Didn't care that I was outnumbered. That I felt cold and empty of all fire, divine or otherwise. That I could barely breathe.

I didn't care about *anything* else except the weight of my sister's body in my arms. I saw nothing else. Felt nothing. Heard nothing...

Until the one holding the sword—the sword stained with Savna's blood—spoke.

"You were warned," he said.

I swallowed away the bitter dryness coating my throat. "...What did you just say?"

"The message we were instructed to give you," said the elf, cooly. "You were warned."

Andrel's words from days ago snaked into my mind.

You've already lost enough. I would so hate for you to lose anything else...

Slowly, carefully, I untangled myself from my sister. Laid her shivering body on the ground. Rose to my feet. My blood-soaked clothing stuck to my skin. Heat flared around me, drying it, turning the cloth stiff. Symbols ignited across my body, blazing so brightly they could be seen even through my armor.

Quietly, I said, "I have a warning for him, too."

I struck my right hand outward. Flames ignited in my hand, stretching all the way up to my shoulder. Another flick of my arm, a bit of concentration, and the fire gathered into the familiar-by-now shape and weight of a makeshift blade.

The elf who had stabbed my sister cocked his head and narrowed his gaze, lips parted as if to answer me.

I silenced his reply by flinging that flaming sword forward with such swift, incredible force that he had no hope of avoiding it. It struck his chest and exploded, swallowing him in a ball of heat and light.

The group of approaching elves slowed, their expressions wary.

My eyes darted over them, counting.

One. Two. Three. Four. Five. Six. Seven.

My sister's attacker lay dead on the ground, little more than a melted and singed, gruesome impression of a body.

I pulled the fire around him back into my control, reshaped it into a weapon. As soon as my hold on it was secured, I struck my left hand out and repeated the same motions as before, forging a second blade.

With all the divine power I possessed, I swung both of the blades forward, crossing them before me and sending forth a wave of fire from the combined points—a wave that built and spread until it became an inferno that leveled trees and bodies alike.

It was over within seconds.

Nothing survived. Everything had been reduced to ash and cinders —or so I thought.

Then I heard footsteps scrambling off to my right.

I turned my furious gaze toward the only thing still moving—a female elf who had managed to take cover in a ditch that my fiery wave had merely skimmed over.

She tried to run faster.

I flew after her, knocking her to the ground. She attempted to roll away, but I shoved a boot onto her chest, holding her down.

Jerking my head toward the closest pile of charred, ruined bodies littering the ground, I said, "Pass that *warning* to Andrel for me, won't you? And let him know he's next." I let the fire of my wings fall away, guiding some of the embers into the shape of a long sword that I pressed near her throat. "Swear to me you won't leave out any details of what I've just told you."

Her wide eyes shifted toward those burned bodies, then back to me, over and over.

"*Swear it,*" I growled.

She nodded frantically. "I-I swear it."

Slowly, I lifted my foot from her chest.

And without another word, I went back to gather up my sister's lifeless body, wrapped it in a cloak of divine fire, and carried her away.

CHAPTER 39

THE FIELDS OUTSIDE OF MY OLD HOME WERE BURNING AGAIN.

And this time, I had set the fires.

I'd needed to release. To get rid of some of the magic eating away at my insides—or else I would have done far worse than the small massacre I'd committed back in the tree-lined grove in Altis.

We'd ended up back at my old house because it was the easiest place to go. Because it was in the mortal realm and still blanketed in the magical residue from the fires Dravyn had set days ago. Despite how passionately I'd sworn to myself that I would never return here, there had been no better choice; I wasn't sure how Savna would fare if I tried to carry her into Nerithyl, especially now that she was injured.

Injured.

Not dead.

Over and over, I kept reminding myself of that. Telling myself that it was not over. They had not killed her. They had not killed Dravyn. They had not killed me. They *wouldn't* kill me. I was a goddess. I was fire and fury, perfection and power, and this was not my ending.

But my sister...

Of course they had gone after her.

I should have known I was putting her at risk, asking her to meet me. I should have been better prepared to protect her.

But no.

I was a fool who couldn't even protect my own flesh and blood, much less save the realms from the wars threatening them, as I'd hoped to do. I'd only ended up killing more. Causing a bigger mess.

I took a deep breath.

Tried to focus on the things that *weren't* a disaster.

Dravyn was safe. I was safe. My sister was barely conscious, but still alive. *Injured*. Not dead.

This is not an ending.

But I had never felt so ready for everything to be over.

I wanted to collapse to the ground, yet I kept moving. Weaving through the flaming fields on my own, letting the tendrils of heat scour my skin. Mentally sinking into the magic within that heat. Bolstering the magic where it felt weak, sending some of the flames so high they could likely be seen for miles around.

I *wanted* them to be seen.

I wanted them to serve as a warning to all our enemies. To one enemy in particular.

Come close to this house again.

I fucking dare you.

A reckless challenge, I knew, when we were better off lying low while my sister recovered. Which was why I wasn't surprised when I looked over my shoulder and saw a section of the distant field barely smoldering, the roaring blaze I'd set reduced to nothing more than charred and smoking ground.

Someone was putting my fires out.

I felt a cool breeze caress my skin moments later, pulling my attention away from my broken and battered thoughts. I didn't have to look in the direction of that breeze to know it was Valas approaching from the east. His power preceded him, countering and starting to calm my own just by its mere arrival.

"Sorry to undo your impressive work," he said, flashing me a crooked smile, "but it was getting a bit warm for my taste."

I folded my arms across my chest and simply nodded. I didn't want to argue. Or even talk. But I was not entirely ungrateful for his company, either, so I kept silent when he fell into step beside me.

Together, we walked the perimeter of my family's land. I continued to occasionally set fires whenever I grew restless. He never asked me to stop. He only put out the worst of them with simple flourishes of his hands, gestures that filled the air with sparkling crystals that hissed into steam as they clashed with my power.

"I've just come from Altis, if you're curious," he said after a few minutes of walking. "The city is secured. The fires in and around it have all been put out."

"And the king?"

"Not thrilled with how things unfolded, as you probably guessed. Rumors are he's mobilizing troops at Mindoth and elsewhere, preparing to march northward."

"Toward the Hollowlands? Toward Ederis?"

"One assumes." He sighed. "He already had these forces lined up and ready, but now..."

Now he has no reason to believe peace is an option.

Because I'd failed to hold up my end of the deal.

He was surely furious at me, at my sister, at anything and everything associated with us. Angry that he'd taken a chance on me. How many of his people had the elves killed to get at my sister?

I thought of Dravyn, of the complicated tension between him and the king, and my heart sank even further.

I'd made things between them worse instead of better.

He had to be worried about his brother. Yet he wasn't in Altis. He wasn't here, either—he'd traveled back to Nerithyl, to the territories of the Stone Court, in search of Armaros. He was on better terms with the Healing God than any other member of our own court, so he'd gone to him on my behalf—or my sister's, rather—seeking something that might help claw Savna back from the deathly edge she balanced on.

Mairu had arrived in his place; she was currently watching over my old house, and over my sister, while I walked through my fires and tried to decide what the hell I was supposed to do next.

Everything I came up with felt wrong.

My very existence felt wrong—like I shouldn't have been here at all. Like I'd taken a thousand wrong turns; my obsession with maps and charts and patterns had not protected me from getting lost the way I'd so desperately wanted it to.

I'd stopped walking without realizing it. Tears tickled the edges of my eyes. I blinked them away and jogged to catch up with Valas, who gave me a long, searching look.

"I told the King of Galizur I could fix things," I said, eyes straight ahead, focused on putting one foot after the other. "A ceasefire. I wanted that more than I've ever wanted anything."

The Winter God continued watching me closely, his magic rising, settling over me and my simmering rage and grief like a comforting, weighted blanket.

Quietly, I said, "I thought I could fix it all."

"Bit of a lofty expectation for yourself, wasn't it?" I glanced over to see him smiling, as usual, but his eyes were sad.

I scrubbed the heel of my hand across my own eyes, swiping away the tears before they could fall.

"It wouldn't have been such an impossible task if I hadn't gotten it so wrong from the very beginning," I said, voice tight with the fury I felt toward myself. "I've had so many chances where I could have undone mistakes I made, but instead, I only made more. With my magic, with the gods, with my sister. And with Andrel." I couldn't help the shudder that rippled through me at the mention of him. "With my sister out of his way, there will be no opposing voice within the rebellious ranks he leads. I was so desperate to pull my sister away from him that I didn't think everything through the way I should have. I should have been smarter. Instead, I've given him more power. I've given him entirely too much power for years, now, and all he's done, and all he will do—"

My throat swelled with emotion, choking me into silence. The rage building, filling up my heart and lungs and everything else, ensured I didn't find my voice again any time soon.

Valas was quiet for a long moment before he said, "I don't know if anyone's ever told you this, but you are not responsible for anything he's done. Not to you or otherwise."

My heart thudded painfully hard against my chest.

I didn't know what to say to this.

It didn't undo any of the things that had happened, but something in the words soothed some of the rage building in me—or maybe it was his magic at work again, breathing cold, fresh life into that rage, turning it into something new.

Still anger, but a more purposeful kind.

He was primarily the god associated with Winter, but I was reminded now of the other things that fell under his domain. Like a certain kind of death—that which led to rebirth, just as the dark days of winter made tired hearts reach more eagerly for spring.

It was interesting, all the different powers of this divine family I'd found myself a part of, and how they conflicted and complimented one another—particularly when it came to different echoes of death and rebirth. Mairu, the Goddess of Change. Dravyn, whose fire could destroy, but also scour things clean. Zachar, who could suspend death and shepherd souls through it. And, of course, the god who walked beside me now...

It made me wonder once more at the depths and shades of my own power, and think again of the conversation I'd had with Zachar about letting things go.

I'd crash landed in the middle of them all, and in some ways, I'd been stumbling around ever since, trying to discover where my true strength actually was.

The words Dravyn said to me soon after I'd emerged from the Tower of Ascension played in my head again, as they so often had over the past weeks.

Fire will be the magic that comes most easily...but there's more to you than what I gave you. The Moraki granted you power in addition to mine, and it's impossible to say how much, or what you might shape that into.

I walked on with all these thoughts tangling up tight in my head. My feet were numb, my chest tight, my skin burning.

Valas stayed close, the cool weight of his power continuing to soothe my aches, both physical and otherwise.

"I may not be responsible for the things Andrel has done," I said, eventually, breaking the silence, "but I still want to fix things. Heal things."

Deep down, it was all I'd ever wanted to do.

I just kept getting it all wrong.

I choked back a sob at this last thought. The tears still trailed silently down my cheeks, but I managed to keep my breaths and words relatively steady.

"I don't think I've ever told you this," I said as my old house came into view once more, "but I used to have actual healing magic, when I was a mortal. Or, at least, I could sense the places where healing power had pooled, and I could draw it from those places. From the very earth, sometimes. I created recipes for all sorts of ailments, too, and everyone swore that when I made them, my touch infused them with extra healing power."

Valas tilted his head toward me, his attention clearly focused for once.

"And I always thought the Marr became exaggerated versions of the beings they'd been before they became divine—but then I ascended, and I think I lost whatever talent for healing I possessed."

"Did you?"

I gritted my teeth. "My sister is dying. The world is splintering. Everything feels broken beyond repair, and I don't even know what piece to reach for first. And even if I did, things will never go back to the way they were—so I can't fix anything I set out to fix."

"What if they aren't meant to go back to the way they were?"

I opened my mouth to argue.

Then I realized I once again didn't know what to say.

Valas didn't elaborate. He was uncharacteristically quiet as we reached the house. While I went inside to check on my sister, he stayed in the yard, pacing and occasionally kneeling in the overgrown grass, swiping through it as if searching for something.

Mairu met me at the door of my sister's room—or ran into me, more like, as she was so lost in thought that she didn't notice me until it was too late.

She quickly transformed her distracted expression into something more optimistic. "She's resting easier, I think. The pain medicine you gave her earlier helped."

I could tell she was forcing the words, the smile.

"Tell me the truth." I braced myself against the doorframe. "You can sense energies of living creatures, so you know better than most how Savna is *truly* faring."

She hesitated.

"Just...tell me."

"Her life force is very faint, Karys. It's getting fainter."

I swallowed hard. "Thank you."

She tried once more to press her lips into an optimistic smile, but didn't quite manage it. "Dravyn will be back soon, I'm sure."

My magic swelled at the thought, giving me courage to move.

As I stepped into the dimly-lit room, it was impossible not to draw comparisons to that fateful day over five years ago, when Savna had disappeared. When I'd stumbled into her room and found her bed coated in blood.

I'd changed her blood-soaked clothing earlier. Made sure her sheets were clean. Wiped away all the drops that had gotten on the floor.

Yet the stench of blood lingered.

Whether from the most recent wound in her back, or a trick of my memory, I wasn't sure.

I pulled up a chair next to her bed and numbly lowered myself into it. My hand fumbled for her wrist, feeling for her pulse.

So, so *weak*.

I slipped from the chair, dropped instead to my knees. Buried my face against the mattress, my fingers clenching the sheets next to my sister's still body.

"Please don't leave me again," I begged, softly. "Not now."

Not when you finally started to come back to me.

I couldn't stop thinking about her hand reaching for mine just before the arrow struck it.

Every time the scene played in my mind, I felt a little more sick.

I kept vigil by her bedside for as long as I could bear it. Then I stood, moving around the room, tidying and organizing, humming softly to myself. Trying not to think of the past. Not five hours ago. Not five years ago. Just...now.

I only needed to survive this moment.

One breath in, one breath out.

One foot after the other.

I went outside once more, and I found Valas close to where I'd last seen him—in a wild, overgrown section of the yard.

The area was filled with trash and debris. The remnants of the old storehouse that had once stood in the corner made up most of the junk; there were splintered, weathered boards, rusted nails, bits of broken jars that had lined the building's shelves.

Valas held two pieces of those broken jars, studying them.

I gave him a curious look, and he gestured for me to follow him as he walked over to a clearer section of the yard.

He leaned against a stretch of rundown fencing, dropping the shards onto the ground next to him, and said, "Did you know, in the mortal kingdom I was born in—Olithia—they have a tradition of never throwing away broken things if they can help it? It's considered bad luck to do so." He pointed at the jagged pieces beside his boots. "So they keep shattered bits of jewelry, pottery, decor—anything and everything. They collect it in ornate boxes and put them on display. Like shrines to mistakes, almost. And they often forge these pieces into something new, binding the brokenness in all sorts of creative ways. There are regular festivals to celebrate the remaking of these objects, even, that most of the royal city participates in."

He took the golden bangles from his wrist and placed them on a nearby stone paver.

"Melt them," he instructed.

Still curious about the point he was making—and happy to have another target for the still-smoldering fire inside of me—I did so without questioning him.

As the bracelets turned to liquified metal, he nudged the broken pieces of the jars closer to me. Understanding, I took one shard and pressed it into the sticky glob of molten material, then grabbed the other and affixed it to the same stickiness.

"The masters of this art form have other tools and materials they use, of course, but this is essentially the same thing." He cooled the melted gold with a gentle, icy wind as he spoke, fastening the shards of ceramic more permanently together.

I leaned against the fence beside him, holding up the still-fragile, but now singular, piece. It wasn't a perfect match. Even with his aid in cooling the adhesive, the shards continued to slip and slide and settle against one another. It looked messy. Crooked. I kept waiting for one to break off, fall to the ground, shatter.

Yet they never did.

"A disastrous first attempt at the art of it," Valas said, grinning his usual teasing grin, "but my general point still stands. And you'll get better with practice, hopefully. I mean, you can hardly get *worse*."

I aimed a punch at his arm, which he avoided with a graceful little spin. He danced out of my reach and moved back to the long grass, gathering up more broken things.

Fighting the urge to both smile and roll my eyes, I went back to studying the joined shards.

The two pieces were not from the same jar, I noticed—they could not have been more different in terms of their designs. I didn't know if Valas had chosen them on purpose or not, but I couldn't stop staring, comparing the two patterns.

They complimented one another, I decided.

And something about the shining gold in between them brought me a sense of peace as I stared at it.

I was still studying it when I sensed movement in the bushes behind me.

Strange energy accompanied what sounded like a small, rustling creature, but by the time I turned and pinpointed where that sound and energy was coming from, the creature causing it was disappearing into thin air, leaving nothing but swirls of sparkling, purplish-black residue in its place.

"We've had an audience," Valas muttered, sauntering back to me.

I took a few cautious steps toward the bushes, running my fingers through the magical residue, which clung like ink to my skin for an instant before evaporating. "I've seen one of them before."

Valas didn't seem particularly surprised by this. "A *tellesk*," he informed me. "They serve the Moraki. Usually the God of the Shade, to be exact—the creatures share his power to read minds, emotions, and the like."

"He's been watching me through them over this past month, hasn't he?"

"Through them and who knows what other methods."

I stared at my fingers, now completely clear of the ink-like substance. Nothing to see, yet my skin still shivered.

My *entire body* shivered—not with fear, but with possibility.

These creatures showing themselves now, of all times...it seemed almost too obvious. Too coincidental. Impossible to ignore.

As I lowered my hand, I looked to the sky, thinking of the heavens I'd become familiar with over the past months. And then beyond Nerithyl—higher than that place I'd started to think of as *home*.

A plan started to form in my mind.

But could I manage it?

There were no maps to where I needed to go.

No clear guideposts.

And I would go alone—I *needed* to go alone. Too long had I spent looking to other people, to other powers to hide behind. My sister's rebellious dreams. Dravyn's fire. I loved them both, but I couldn't exist merely as a shadow or an extension of either one of them anymore.

If I was going to bring balance to all these different worlds I had tethers to, then I was going to have to forge a new path through them.

My own path.

"I know the look of someone considering a chaotic decision," Valas said, "and you have it."

I gripped the fused shards of ceramic tightly, bringing the shivering in my hand to a stop.

"Come on. Out with it."

"...The tellesk share his power," I recited, lowering my gaze back to the bushes the creature had been hiding in. "So does that mean focusing on the energy this creature leaves behind might help my own magic carry me to wherever the largest concentration of that energy is?"

Valas considered the question. "...Yes," he answered, carefully. "I would think so."

"And that place is the dwelling of the upper-gods themselves."

The Winter God's brows rose, but he didn't reply.

"I'm not wrong, am I?"

"It's...*possible* for us to visit those upper-heavens, at least for a short amount of time. Usually only when we're invited, though."

"I'm not waiting for an invitation," I said, fiercely. "I think a certain upper-god owes me a conversation."

Valas fixed me with a familiar look—one that was part exasperation, part admiration, part amusement.

"If the God of Fire asks, I tried to talk you out of it," he said, dryly. "And I thoroughly warned you about the consequences of not treading carefully where the Moraki are concerned."

"He'll understand why I needed to go," I said, more to myself than Valas.

Dravyn would be worried, but in the end, he wouldn't stop me. He would empower me. It was what he'd been doing all along, after all—he had given me fire, showed me the way to unfold my wings...but then he'd let go and let me fly on my own, stepping in only when it looked like I might crash to the ground.

If I wanted to soar to the highest heavens, he would be there to catch me whenever I came back down, I knew. However I came back down.

But this was a dangerous new game I was thinking of playing.

And even if I won it, deep in my heart, I knew there was a chance I wouldn't come back to him at all.

CHAPTER 40

Karys

IN THE SHADOW OF GATHERING STORM CLOUDS, PRESSED against the weather-worn outer walls of my old house, I was waiting.

After giving the tellesk—and all their previous visits—some more thought, a pattern had occurred to me: I realized these creatures almost always appeared during the moments when I was at my weakest, emotionally or otherwise. They could read emotions and thoughts, Valas said; it seemed to me that they were *feeding* off these things, as well.

So I'd been making sure to give them plenty to eat.

After every trip to check on my sister, I walked back outside and made certain *not* to try and calm myself down for once. Like throwing bait into the water, I let my confusing thoughts and emotions cast off me without any attempt to reel them in.

On my third trip outside, it had finally happened: I spotted another shadowy creature slinking through the bushes, its shining eyes fixed in my direction.

Mairu had been by my side, too, her controlling magic ready to seize the beast and hold it still.

It remained in her hold, now, while I braced myself against the wall and soaked up all the knowledge she could give me about the place I was attempting to reach—and the upper-god who would hopefully be there to meet me.

"Are you certain about this plan?" she asked, for what might have been the twelfth time.

I nodded confidently, showing none of the trepidation I felt. "I'm going. And I'm ready to do this."

She studied my face, searching it for lies, before eventually relenting with a sigh. "I'll pull my magic away quickly so it doesn't interfere with yours. You'll have to be swift to catch the creature."

I thanked her and started creeping my way toward the rustling bushes. I couldn't see the creature itself, only its movements and the few scraps of energy that managed to escape Mairu's hold.

"Be careful," the Serpent Goddess called softly—and then released.

The spidery tellesk let out a terrible noise as it finally skittered entirely free of her spell. It tumbled and spilled from the shelter of the bushes, all long legs and swirling, chaotic energy.

That shadowy energy cocooned around the creature the way my threads of fire often surrounded my body before whisking it to somewhere else, leaving nothing behind as they unraveled.

I dove before it could completely disappear, catching it around the middle, trying to ignore the brutal chill of its shadows and the way its spindly legs flailed and scurried against my arms. Its body gave in an unsettling way—I thought maybe it was made purely of shadows until a tighter squeeze had my arms finally closing in on something solid.

Its legs continued to creep and crawl against my body, scrambling for grip. The chaotic energy around it exploded outward, enveloping me in a cloud, as if I was squeezing a powderpuff.

I held in a cough, eyes watering, but managed to call forth my own magic and surround myself in ropes of flame.

While I surrendered to the weight and pull of these ropes, I simultaneously focused on the tellesk's energy, thinking of nothing else except finding *more* of it—the greatest concentration that existed in this realm or any other.

I pictured that energy sinking into my own. Willed my fire to use it as a guide until, finally, I felt myself being lifted away from the mortal realm.

The chill of the tellesk's power overtook my warm magic more completely. It was so overwhelming that I could no longer think of anything else, even if I'd wanted to. I felt nothing, touched nothing, breathed in nothing except the dark bits of energy. The more I inhaled, the more my awareness slipped. The more weightless my body seemed to become.

I reached a state of complete surrender that lasted for perhaps a heartbeat, or maybe for a lifetime—however long it took, I eventually tumbled from the embrace of the transporting magic and into some-place new.

I landed on my hands and knees upon sandy black ground.

Straightening, I gasped, eyes widening at the beauty before me.

I was standing in a garden awash in a pale, silvery glow, surrounded by blooms of every shade of white and blue imaginable. Trees with gnarled trunks and tangled branches towered above. A stream ran through it all, its waters milky and shimmering. The scent of spice and jasmine filled the air.

The darkness was lit only by a smattering of star-like dots in the dusky purple sky. After my eyes fully adjusted to the low lighting, I noticed a narrow path edged by smooth, perfectly circular stones that glowed with a soft white light.

I followed this path out of the trees and into a bright field covered in long, swaying blue grass.

As I inhaled the crisp air above this field, I knew I'd made it to Valla; the feel of magic was the same as in the middle-heavens, only magnified a hundred times over. It was enough to crush me if I stood still too long and focused on it too much—I understood now why the Winter God said most visits to this realm were short ones.

But I wasn't afraid.

The power here was overwhelming, yet I'd been prepared for far worse, based on what I'd seen of the God of the Shade and the creatures he created.

Instead of terrifying shadows and scores of creeping, threatening beasts, the field I pushed my way through was bright and full of docile life, teeming with curious, firefly-like insects and swirls of sparkling, beautiful magic that made me feel perfectly aware yet entirely calm whenever I passed through them.

I kept walking.

A house soon materialized at the end of my path. Its design was relatively simple, featuring stacked stone and wood beams reminiscent of the small cottages that dotted the human villages around my old home in the mortal realm. Except there was nothing *small* about it; it sprawled as far as I could see in both directions, and the closer I came to it, the taller it seemed to loom.

By the time I reached the front door—which was partially ajar—I was certain it was magic making the dwelling grow.

A twinge of doubt struck me as I stared at the warm light slipping through the cracked door. But I'd already come this far, so there seemed no point in hesitating now.

I let myself inside.

Only to immediately freeze at the sight before me.

The interior looked *exactly* like my old home, down to the scent of cooking spices, woodsmoke, and freshly-tilled earth. I could hear familiar laughter, too. My father's. My sister's.

I tucked my chin toward my chest and shut my eyes.

Opening them again, I lifted my head, and the scenery had changed —now it was the tent where I'd last seen Cillian. Except it was empty. Sounds of a battle rose at my back. It smelled of blood and dust, metal and fire.

Another blink, and it was all gone.

Over and over, my surroundings flashed before me, changing with every blink, becoming all the places I'd been, all the memories that haunted me.

"*Enough,*" I said into the churning scenery.

I was *here,* now, and I would not be defined by those past places, those memories, any longer.

As soon as this thought crossed my mind, I tightly closed my eyes again. The house grew quiet. I peeked and saw it had changed yet again. But it was an unfamiliar sight, now; still quiet, and with a settled feeling about it—blinking no longer shifted any of its pieces.

The permanent design it had taken on was made up of wooden walls, narrow corridors, and shelves lined with both books and trinkets of all kinds, from crowns and goblets featuring shining gemstones, to small, intricately detailed figurines made of all different varieties of wood and stone, to some objects I couldn't readily name.

I itched to organize the decor according to their colors and shapes, but I kept my hands to myself and continued walking.

I moved deeper inside, choosing hallways mainly based on how brightly they were lit. My Fire magic didn't seem to have any effect on the torches that lined the halls, even when I tried to brighten them. My feet made no noise against the plush, silver-white carpet. The smell of leather and books slowly overtook the spaces around me, and I heard soft music playing from some distant room that I never managed to find.

After several minutes of exploring, I reached the end of a hallway and found myself stepping into a vast space. Not a proper room with a door or windows, but simply an expansion of the hall itself—one with curved walls and yet more shelves filled to the brim with a wondrous amount of different objects.

A man sat in a large, straight-backed armchair next to a fireplace filled with white flames, clutching a silver cup. Black, raven-like birds hopped around his feet, leaving shadowy trails in their wake. Feathers drifted about the room, along with bits of shining ash that seemed to be originating from the white flames dancing in the hearth.

The man spoke without taking his eyes from this strange fire: "Karys of Mistwilde. Elf. Rebel. Mortal..." He lifted the cup in his hands toward his lips, inhaled from it, but didn't sip. "Or...Karys, Goddess of Fire and Forging. Immortal being of the Shade Court." The cup stayed poised just out of reach of his mouth as he slowly cut his gaze toward me and asked, "Are you here to ask me which one of these sides you belong to?"

"No."

"No?"

"I'm here to tell you that I don't belong to either of them."

He lowered the cup, staring into the shining eyes of the bird closest to his boot as if he was consulting the creature.

Then he gestured to a chair across from him—one that I was almost certain hadn't been there before—and said, "Sit down, won't you?"

Phrased as an invitation, yet it sounded more like a command in his quiet, powerful voice.

I gathered every scrap of courage I could and made my way to the chair.

The fireplace brightened as I sat down, fully illuminating the man— *the god*—across from me. Malaphar. The Dark God. The Moraki responsible for enlightening the world with all shades of knowledge, blessing its creatures with souls.

I'd seen him before, but never quite like this. He looked slightly more approachable than in the past—or maybe it was me who had changed, who was no longer content to cower at the sight of him.

He was—predictably—beyond beautiful in a terrible, otherworldly kind of way. His face looked as if it had been hewn from a slab of white marble; strong, smooth, its pale color oddly multifaceted in the light of the fire. The shade of his eyes reminded me of the stream I'd seen when I first arrived in this realm—a milky sort of blue with iridescent qualities. His usual black wings were missing, but the feathers drifting around the room seemed eager to be made into those wings; they kept gathering at his back only to be dismissed by a subtle shake of his head or a twitch of his hand.

He appraised me for a long moment. Sipped from the silver cup he held. Dropped it. Snapped his fingers, and it disappeared in mid-air, leaving behind nothing but purplish-grey smoke. Weaving his fingers in and out of this smoke, he said, "Explain yourself."

I stared into his unsettling eyes, gripping the leather armrests for support.

Slowly, my tongue loosened, and I began to unleash it all—all the steps that had led me to this moment. All the things that could have stopped me, had I allowed them to.

I told him the words his servant, the Death God, had spoken to me weeks ago—words I finally understood.

But death must come first. I wonder; could you wield that, too?

Death. Destruction. Rebirth. Change.

I was all of the gods of the Shade Court. But more than that—I was all the things I had survived, all the things I'd learned to rise above and to let go of. I still carried these things, but I commanded them, now, and not the other way around.

And I still believed I could use them to build a bridge.

I'd failed my first attempt at this in Altis, but it was not the end of me. That failure had only strengthened my resolve.

I could be the golden bond that brought the jagged pieces together, messy and slippery as they might be. I could connect it all, make it into something new. Guide it with whatever divine ability I possessed.

And this—all of this—was what I told the dark, terrifying being who sat across from me.

He listened without interrupting, rarely blinking his unsettling eyes.

When I finally finished, he leaned back in his chair. Swirled the silver cup back into existence with a precise flourish of his hand. Took a few sips, and then finally asked, "And what is it you want from *me*?"

I didn't hesitate. "You've been watching me closely since the moment I emerged from the Tower of Ascension. Sending spies and servants to trace and manipulate my steps—the tellesk. The Death God. And who else? You had some scheme in mind when you allowed me to ascend; I know you did."

His pale lips pulled into a clever smile, revealing a flash of sharp teeth.

"I can only assume you intended for me to fall into this role of the mediator between realms," I pressed. "I understand now that this is what I'm meant to do—so I only ask for the power to do it. I know you're capable of granting it, whatever it might look like. You and your fellow Moraki can build and level realms at will. I will protect the things you built, if only I—"

He held up a hand.

I sucked in a breath and held it, forcing myself to stop talking as I braced myself for his answer.

It was a long time before it came.

He continued to study me as he held out his hand, encouraging the black bird at his boot to hop into his palm.

The bird swiveled its head between the two of us, beady black eyes alert. Judging, it felt like.

"Yes—you have always been a link between the realms," Malaphar finally said, while scratching under the bird's chin. "I was only waiting for you to realize it."

The space around us seemed to shrink to a much less intimidating size.

Malaphar, however, remained intimidating, becoming even more so as he stood and rolled his shoulders—an action that drew the swirling feathers of the room toward him, gathering them across his back.

He crossed the room, heading to one of the many shelves, eyes narrowed on an object in the very center of it. When he walked, some of the feathers at his back rearranged themselves, tumbling downward and forming a cape that fluttered out behind him.

"We made a mistake, trying to crush the Velkyn so quickly and completely," he said.

I had to work hard to keep my jaw from dropping.

I couldn't believe he'd just admitted to making a mistake.

"My brethren will not admit to it, but myself...I am the god who imparted knowledge upon the world—all shades of it, good and bad— so how could I not speak up about such problems? How could I not— to use your word—*scheme* up some solution to fix things?"

It seemed like a rhetorical question, so I didn't reply.

We stood silently for a long moment. The shining ash and dark feathers continued to swirl around the room, continuously reminding me of where I stood, and who I stood with.

I wondered over and over again at the absurdity of it all—how I had gone from setting rebellious fires in mortal temples to here in the highest of heavens, standing before one of the most powerful beings in our known world, asking for his help and guidance.

Malaphar tilted his face toward me and said, "I do, indeed, have something to give you."

I should have been wary, a small voice in the back of my head reminded me—yet I felt nothing except a buzzing, purposeful exhilaration.

"It is a kind of magic that the majority of elves could never comprehend on their own. Nor humans, for that matter." He returned his attention to the shelf before him, reaching for the small, unassuming object he'd been staring at earlier.

It was a dagger.

A wave of his hand brought more feathers toward him, swirled them around the sheath, making the patterns on it glow with a silvery light for several seconds before the weapon moved of its own accord, slipping free of its casing and floating for a moment before gently rocking back down to the shelf.

It was a beautiful dagger, shining and black, with subtle etchings in the blade that matched the ones upon its sheath.

"This dagger is called *Antaeum*," Malaphar said, picking it up and offering it to me.

I took it with trembling hands.

It was nearly weightless and bitingly cold to the touch.

"It is a gift. A carrier of restorative, protective power created by all three of the Moraki. We perfected it some time ago; we only needed somebody willing to wield it. To plant it in the heart of the elves' rebellion. I've had my eye on you as a potential vessel for some time. The other two were less convinced. But you've proven them wrong. They didn't expect you to survive the trials set forth by the Marr, to begin with. And when you managed ascension, they expected you to become a slave to the divine magic you'd been granted, to turn your back entirely on the elven race you rose above."

It would have been easier to do that. Countless times, I'd wished I could turn a blind eye to everything I'd once known. But I never could manage it.

A weakness, I'd always thought—my need to remember every side.

Yet the upper-god before me clearly thought otherwise.

He replied as though I'd spoken out loud. "To see all sides of things is a rare gift."

I clutched the dagger more tightly. My Fire magic rumbled in response to the questions piling up in my mind, but it didn't rise to the surface; the dagger's power seemed to be placating it.

"If I wield this...if I plant it, as you said...what happens next?" I couldn't help but ask. "Will I remain as I am now?"

"Not as a middle-goddess, no. But a divine being, nonetheless. *The*

Arbiter of Realms, I will call you. Born of earth, forged in divine fire, tempered by your own knowledge and experiences, by the blood you've spilled, and by the things you've carried—the anger, the hope, the trials, the failures, the triumphs. All of it."

All of it.

All the mistakes I thought I'd made....even those had helped bring me to this moment, shaping me into the unique being capable of this task before me.

Now I simply had to see things through to the end.

Easier said than done, I was sure.

"You would not have been able to pick up Antaeum without being ready to do so," said the God of the Shade, his quiet, authoritative voice rumbling through my mind, drowning out some of my lingering doubts. "I would not have been willing to give you its power until I was certain you were the balance point our world needed."

I turned the dagger over and around in my hands, trying to get used to the feel of it.

Determined to get used to it.

"Now: There is a specific task you must complete in order to fully awaken the power of Antaeum. Consider it your final trial before your *true* ascension can take place."

I'd expected no less.

I stared at my reflection in the shining black blade as I calmly said, "Whatever trial awaits, I am not afraid of it."

"Good."

I took a deep breath and lifted my gaze to his.

"Wherever you plant this dagger will be a point of new life," he explained. "It is potential power. It is potential peace. It is up to you what ultimately is allowed to flow from it, and over it, and who is allowed to take from its energy. It has the power to save the Velkyn, both from themselves and others, but it will need to be planted in the heart of their rebellion, as I told you—allowed to finish killing off that which must die to allow for new growth."

"But the anti-divine runes, and all the poisons they've created..."

"The dagger's power, once awakened through the proper ritual—and wielded properly by you—will render all they've created useless."

"Useless?" I repeated, breathlessly, awestruck again by this tiny dagger and the apparently limitless power it contained.

The quiet voice in the back of my mind was back, telling me to be wary once more.

I no longer hated or feared the gods as I once did, but could I trust everything Malaphar was telling me—and the things he almost certainly wasn't?

"It will also return to them some of the divine blessings they seek," he said, again answering me as though I'd voiced my concerns aloud. "Not all they had before—which is why they will need a divine leader to look to. To guide them as they rebuild their lands into something different, something better. With you as their goddess and guide, the lands around the Antaeum's Point will flourish. You have my word on that. And, if all goes well, we may see fit to establish other points like it."

I could see it, almost—a world where my sister and the other elves had a true place to belong again, rather than merely a cursed hiding place. A world where they had power equal to the other mortal beings of Avalinth.

Would it be enough to calm the rebels and the rising tides of war?

"Can you do this?" Malaphar asked.

Goddess. Guide. Balance point.

The expectations were high.

But I had not come here expecting low ones.

So I managed to swallow down my doubt and give him a firm answer. "I can."

He bowed his head in acknowledgment—an almost reverent gesture that seemed strange from one so much more powerful than myself.

I secured the dagger in its sheath and clutched it to my chest. Bracing myself, already, for the days ahead.

"One last thing: You may not speak of this gift to any other divine being. Not even to him."

I didn't have to ask who he meant.

But the thought of keeping such a secret from Dravyn made my stomach curl.

"This weapon will change the course of history in all realms. The

Marr are better off not knowing about it, or the plans we have for it. Do you understand?"

I didn't want to agree, but felt I had little choice. "Yes."

"Good," he said, gesturing toward a narrow wooden door on the opposite side of the room—one I knew for *certain* hadn't been there a moment ago.

I couldn't help hesitating and looking back one last time before I went through it.

"You have more questions, Arbiter?"

I was almost afraid to ask them. But I couldn't get myself to move while they were still in my heart, weighing me down. "If my power shifts into this different form, this different kind of goddess, what becomes of the God of Fire?"

What becomes of us if I step into this role? Of the magic he gave me? Of the home I found with him? Will we ever see each other again?

I didn't ask these last questions out loud. I didn't have to. This god before me was the keeper of all knowledge, which included every secret I might have tried to bury—reading minds and emotions was as effortless as breathing to him.

He turned away, his attention again on one of his raven's, which was pecking out one of the loose feathers on the floor.

"Focus on the final trial I've given you," he said, more to the bird than me, "and I trust you'll know the path you must walk when you come to it."

CHAPTER 41

Dravyn

I RETURNED TO AVALINTH AFTER SEVERAL HOURS SPENT talking and negotiating with the God of Healing, and then helping him create the tonic I now carried—one that I'd been instructed to give to Savna.

The first thing I noticed upon touching down in the mortal realm was that Karys was missing.

"Don't panic," came Valas's voice, almost immediately. I turned to see him reclining against the side of Karys's old house. He looked as if he'd been waiting for me.

"Where is she?" I demanded. Her magic felt faint—not in this realm. Yet I hadn't felt her when I was in Nerithyl, either.

Valas pushed away from the wall, a troubled expression darkening his gaze. "I was only instructed to tell you she was safe," he said, "and that she'd be back soon. She didn't want you to worry."

As though that would stop me.

"You know more than that," I insisted. "I can see it in your face."

"Maybe." He summoned a crystal of ice to his palm and walked it back and forth between his fingers—a habit he sometimes fell into during the rare instances when he was nervous. "But I'm going to let her explain things when she gets back," he said. "I'm curious about what her actual plans and reasoning are, too."

I scowled; I was not in the mood to be patient or to play guessing games.

"That bottle you have there," said Valas, "it's from Armaros, I hope?"

I shifted the tonic to my other hand and gave it a shake, holding it up for his inspection even though I was annoyed by his change of subject.

"Karys's sister is not doing well. You may already be too late."

Too late.

Just like I'd been with Cillian.

I couldn't—*wouldn't*—fail her again.

Loathe as I was to do it, I shifted my priorities and forgot about tracking down Karys for the moment.

As I started toward the house, Moth appeared in a flurry of feathers and fire, startling me—though I should have expected him; I'd ordered him to stay behind, but following commands was not his strength.

It had been too long since he'd seen Karys, too. So there would be no keeping him away, no sending him back home.

Knowing this, I didn't protest when he perched himself on my shoulder and accompanied me to Savna's room.

Once there, he hopped down and started to rummage through her belongings; sniffing under furniture, rooting through drawers, snatching blankets and pillows in his claws and dragging them in every direction.

Savna slept on, oblivious, even when he leapt onto her bed and inspected her more closely. He appeared confused, for a moment, by this elf who looked so much like Karys but clearly wasn't her. He trotted back to me and clamped his beak around my ankle, tugging, as if he wanted me to follow him in his search for the real Karys.

"You and Zell are both lost without her, aren't you?" I mused, prying his bite off and shoving him toward the hallway. "Go on, wait for her outside, why don't you?"

While he plodded sulkily from the room, I stood perfectly still, silently reciting the instructions the Healing God had given me while watching Savna for signs of life.

She was, as Valas had warned, barely hanging on.

I'd planned to hand this tonic from Armaros over to Karys and let her handle its administration. But now she was nowhere to be found, and time was of the essence.

Knowing her, she'd be glad I had this chance to *bond* with her sister. Another chance to mend the brokenness between us all, just as she wanted my brother and me to do.

I smiled wryly at the thought and, sighing, made my way over to the bedside, shaking the glass bottle as I went. Uncorking it sent spirals of whitish-gold, magical residue fluttering into the air, along with the scent of citrus.

It wasn't a remedy she needed to ingest, thankfully; her skin could absorb it easily enough. There was a basket of medical supplies on the shelf next to her bed, so I took some of the cloths from it and soaked them in the citrusy substance.

The magic within this concoction would seep into her body and reverse the damage and blood loss she'd suffered, while simultaneously restoring her energy. I only needed to distribute it evenly over the wounded areas, and then there was nothing to do except...*wait.*

Once the job was finished, I drew a chair up beside the window on the far side of the room and sank down into it. It creaked under my weight as I leaned back and raked a hand through my hair.

It wasn't like me to not be able to keep still, but I found myself fidgeting as the minutes passed. Shuffling my weight from one side to the other. Picking at invisible loose threads on the chair cushion. Tapping my fingers against the windowsill.

I finally stuffed my hands into the pockets of my coat instead, hoping that would keep them still.

As I did, my fingers brushed against the heavy silver ring in my right pocket—a family heirloom that I'd been carrying since our trip to Altis. Fallon had given it to me. Had flung it at me, practically, and I'd accepted it against my better judgment, in spite of all the unwanted memories it stirred when I looked at it.

It traditionally went to the youngest in our family, so it wasn't meant to be mine—it *wouldn't* have been mine, if not for that fateful night of blood and poison all those years ago.

I squeezed it tight, rolling it around between my fingers.

Such a small trinket, but it weighed so much.

I was drifting dangerously close to clear memories of the night my siblings had died when Savna gave a sudden cough and rolled in my direction.

"You look like you're contemplating murder," she mumbled.

I softened my expression but otherwise didn't reply.

"Not mine, I hope." She breathed in deep, an effort that made her wince. "Though if you are considering it, there are knives under my bed. Very sharp. Should get the job done quickly if you've any sort of skill."

"I don't need knives to provide you with a quick death," I reminded her.

She laughed a humorless, bewildered sort of laugh. "Right. Of course."

We were quiet for a long time before she spoke again.

"Where is Karys?"

"Away on divine business, I'm afraid."

"That figures." With a great deal of effort, she fought her way upright, propping pillows behind herself so she could stay there.

Her face was alarmingly pale, her skin slicked with sweat. But her heartbeat sounded stronger, and she smelled considerably less like death than she had earlier. Or maybe it was just the pungent odor of the Healing God's medicine covering up everything else.

"She's...divine." Another weak, bewildered laugh. "I keep forgetting that, somehow."

"Maybe because you don't want to accept it," I suggested.

"Maybe." She turned her tired gaze my direction, though she seemed to have a hard time focusing it on my face. "It's hard to change the way we see people, isn't it?"

Lucky for you, I thought, *or else she would have abandoned you a long time ago.*

I sank deeper into the chair, my hand once more in my pocket, turning the ring over and over as I considered what Savna had said.

It *was* difficult to change the way we saw people; maybe that was why I couldn't bring myself to fully let my guard down around this elven woman—because I'd only ever known her as a source of pain to the one being I cared about more than anyone else.

Savna was quiet for a time, her gaze fixed on something outside the window. "I feel miraculously better. You gave me something, I assume? These cloths against my skin...they carry the god-awful scent of magic, among other things."

"Yes."

Her face scrunched up, I assumed from a combination of the scent and the confusing, tense situation we'd found ourselves in. "So, you saved me."

"For her sake, not yours," I said, bluntly.

"Understandable." She dropped her gaze to her hands, absently tracing the lines along her palm for a minute before she said, "I've made a lot of mistakes, haven't I?"

It took several moments before a reply came to me, and several more before I could bring myself to say it out loud. "You have. But she would want you to forgive yourself."

"Forgiveness." She scoffed. More to herself than me she added, "You don't know the half of what I've done."

"No. I don't." I pulled my hand from my pocket. Clenched it into a fist in order to keep myself from immediately reaching for the ring again. "But I do know your sister."

The words Karys had spoken days ago rang through my mind for what might have been the dozenth time: *You are worthy of forgiveness.*

Savna stared at me, clearly at a loss for words, as I got to my feet.

"The remedy I gave you is from the God of Healing himself," I told her. "It should continue to help you mend. Keep those cloths pressed over your skin, let your body continue to absorb the magic."

"...Thank you."

I inclined my head, then turned toward the door.

"Hey. Mister, um, Lord God of Fire...Sir?"

My hand stilled against the tarnished handle. "Just Dravyn will do," I reminded her.

"Right. Dravyn." She hesitated. "I just...I wanted to thank you for taking care of her when I couldn't."

I stiffened, unsure of how to reply.

"For giving her power, and for saving her. For...everything."

"She was powerful enough before I came along," I replied, glancing back one last time before pushing the door open, "And she did most of the saving."

"Still. Thank you."

I acknowledged the words with another dip of my head before leaving.

I encountered Mairu on my way out of the house. Moth had burrowed himself snugly into her arms; it never took him long to find someone to take pity on him and offer him attention.

"I've been patrolling the area," she informed me. "It's oddly quiet."

"Let's hope it stays that way for a while."

Between the terrifying display Karys had put on in Altis, and the fact that we had one of their leaders in our control...something told me the elven forces were likely scrambling to find order amongst themselves, if nothing else. It wouldn't last, but it was allowing us to catch our breath in the meantime.

"How is Savna?" Mairu asked.

"Better."

"Are you all right?" She cocked her head, a concerned little smile on her face. "You look as if you went to war in that room with her."

"She's awake. We were just...talking."

"About...?"

"I don't know. Feelings."

"Oh, the horror," she said, eyes dancing with amusement.

"Spare me the teasing and just go watch over her for me," I said. "I'll take over patrolling duties."

She agreed, transferring Moth to my arms before heading inside.

The griffin watched the sky while I scanned the fields and forests.

Thankfully, we didn't have to wait long before Karys returned.

I sensed her approaching, and my own magic rose in reply, brightening and helping to guide her in.

A fiery wind swirled as she entered the realm, gathering bits of dry grass and other debris toward it as it built. The embers in the center of the whirlwind began to shift into the shape of her body, and seconds later she stepped from the fire, shaking sparks and ashes from her hair as she came.

Moth leapt from my arms and bounded toward her, snapping and swatting at the stray bits of fire, tumbling through the grass and making a predictable spectacle of himself.

"You've gotten good at that," I told Karys as she finished materializing and the last of the smoke and fire that had carried her faded away.

She lifted her attention away from Moth, smiling a bit as our eyes met. "It's easier when you're more certain about where you want to go, isn't it?"

"It is," I agreed as she drew nearer.

Her expression turned strange as we came together—though I had little chance to study it before she was closing all of the remaining space between us and lifting onto her tiptoes, pressing her lips to mine.

Her arms circled around my neck. My hands gripped her waist, steadying and lifting her higher, deeper into the kiss.

We remained locked in this embrace for a full minute, at least, until I finally pulled away—only because of the uneasy weight growing in my chest.

"Wildfire..." I said softly, "why does it feel like you're kissing me goodbye rather than hello?"

Her eyes were distant, unwilling to meet mine.

Moth curled at our feet, sniffing her boots, the fur along his back standing on end.

Now that I wasn't distracted by the feel of Karys's hands and the taste of her kiss, I realized what was making Moth so uneasy.

That powerful energy surrounding her, the scent of a far wilder, more powerful magic that didn't belong to either of us...

"Where have you been?"

She finally met my concerned gaze. "We...we need to talk."

The words made my balance sway.

"You should check on your sister first," I said—because, apparently, I was a coward who wasn't truly prepared to talk about where she'd been. "She's awake, now. She was asking for you."

She hesitated only a moment before agreeing.

I followed her into the house but lingered outside of her sister's room, granting them privacy. Their conversation continued until well past sunset, while I steeled myself for whatever would follow it.

I already knew the answer to my question from earlier—she'd been to Valla. The upper-heavens. I'd only visited that realm a handful of times myself, but it was impossible to forget the feel and smell of the magical energy that filled it.

I could guess at her reason for going, too—she had likely demanded an audience with one of the gods who dwelled there. Admiration swelled in my chest at the thought, but beneath it lay fear.

What had she talked to the Moraki about?

What was she planning to do?

I grew restless waiting inside, so I went back to patrolling the yard and beyond. I checked in with Valas and Mairu countless times. I spent much of the time soaring above it all, twisting and turning through the sky, the embers shearing from my wings sizzling as they passed through the low-lying clouds that were heavy with the promise of rain.

I was sitting on a stone bench in the center of the yard, head bowed in thought, when Karys finally emerged from the house.

Moth flew from his perch on the roof to greet her. His tail and ears drooped when she didn't immediately gather him up in her arms as she usually did; she was too distracted to see him—she nearly walked right past me as well, until I cleared my throat, making her jump.

"Is everything all right?" I asked.

She shook her head. Moth made a pitiful mewling sound, and she finally crouched down and opened her arms to him. She hugged him tightly as she straightened, her eyes darting around the yard. "Valas and Mairu, are they..."

"They're close by."

"Good. I need to speak with Mairu. I'm going to require her magic for something."

I tilted my head, curious.

"I need to borrow my sister's shadow, one last time."

"You've been practicing the divine's ability to speak in riddles, I see."

She gave me a grim smile. "Gather the others," she insisted, "and I'll explain as much as I can."

HOURS LATER, deep in the middle of the mortal realm's night, I walked alone along the edge of the fields surrounding Karys's old house.

To my left, a forest loomed. The twisted, shadowy branches seemed a fitting reflection of my dark and tangled thoughts. I was still going over the meeting we'd had, still trying to make sense of all the things Karys had told us.

And the things she *hadn't*.

She'd gone to Valla, as I'd suspected.

To Malaphar, as I'd feared.

And next, she planned to go deep into the territory of the elven rebels once more. To strike at the heart of their operation, she'd informed us, and undo the corrupted magic they'd created along with everything else.

Beyond this vague plan, she'd shared frustratingly little. We'd gone in circles for the better part of an hour while she explained what she needed to do, and why, but the *how*…

There was more she wasn't telling us.

Too much more.

It was not her fault, I didn't think; I suspected the God of the Shade had bound her to secrecy regarding some details of their plans. Whether by way of an actual spell or merely a spoken oath, there were secrets he'd insisted she keep from me. And if she failed to do so…

I clenched my hand into a fist, stifling the fire that had started to build in my palm.

Breaking her oath to such a powerful god would only make things worse.

So I was left with no choice but to guess at how I could possibly help her. How I could keep her safe.

I continued to study the woods as I walked, considering disappearing into them for a minute until I felt a stirring in my chest that made me turn back toward the house.

Karys was crossing the field, making her way toward me.

Her hair whipped about in the damp breeze. Her skin glowed

faintly, the magic inside of her shining a light that was particularly noticeable in the pale cast of the cloud-covered moon.

Stunning, as always.

I would never tire of seeing her walking in my direction.

She studied my face as she reached me, the familiar, grim smile curving her lips once more. "You're angry with me, aren't you? Is that why you haven't come back to the house?"

Despite the very real rage simmering in my gut, I shook my head.

"No. I'm not angry—not with you." I took her hand. Pulled her closer. Kissed her forehead before gathering her against my chest and burying my face against her hair. "Never with you."

She angled her face so she could gaze up at me. "I should have told you I was going to Valla. But I was afraid I would lose my nerve if I waited too long."

I brushed a hand across her cheek. She shook slightly against me, as if all of the plans and fears she carried were rattling against her insides, trying to overtake her.

"Walk with me," I said, taking a step back and grabbing hold of her hand. "Show me more of this forest; you know all the paths through it, I'm guessing?"

She nodded slowly.

Of course she did—she likely had entire books filled with hand-drawn maps of the area.

We spent the next several hours exploring it. She showed me the places where everything notable grew—berries for foraging, flowers for picking. She took me to the places where magic pooled, and explained the way she had always been able to sense that earthbound power, to find magic-infused herbs and roots that she used in healing recipes of her own creation.

Thunder soon rolled overhead, but she ignored it, focused as she was on bringing me to the places where she had wandered alone when she needed to think, then to all the nooks and crannies where she and her sister had built forts and castles and all other manner of make-believe things.

Finally, we stopped to rest beside a small stream.

She settled atop a large, flat boulder, her eyes on the stream as the first raindrops began to disrupt its clear water.

"Did you mean it," she said, after a minute, "when you said you loved *who* I was, and not what? You were half-asleep when you spoke those words the other night so I...I didn't know if maybe..."

I turned to find her staring at me, holding her breath.

I couldn't think of the right words to say.

Not at first.

So I focused on action instead, reaching into the inner pocket of my coat, pulling out that ring I'd been carrying with me since our visit to Altis.

"My brother gave me this when we were in the royal city," I told her. "Traditionally, it goes to the youngest heir in my family. With my younger siblings gone, it's now mine to give to whomever I wish." I stepped closer, holding it out to her.

She plucked it gingerly from my grasp.

"An heirloom of my mortal life—but I've also been infusing it with my own divine power during these hours I've carried it, while we were apart and I was thinking of you."

She summoned a bit of her own power, a small flame that floated beside the ring and allowed her to study its details more clearly. The silver band was molded in the shape of two wings that held the oval centerpiece. Three diamonds ran in a diagonal line across the center, signifying the three regions that my ancestors united to form the Kingdom of Galizur.

"It's beautiful," she said, slowly offering it back.

"Keep it."

Her lips parted in surprise. "It's beautiful, but I can't take something so important, I..."

I knelt before her, taking it and slipping it onto her finger as I said, "You're more important."

Her eyes flashed to mine. Holding her breath again.

I twisted the ring around her finger, marveling at how perfectly it fit. Like it was meant to be there.

And I finally thought of an answer to her question.

"There is no limit to what I would give you," I said, still kneeling before her. "What I would burn down to get to you. What I would build with you, forge for you. Wherever you go, whatever you become, I love you. And I will find my way back to you, no matter the chaos between us, and whatever the battles we face in the coming days." I traced my thumb across the ring, igniting the magic I'd been pouring into it until the diamonds in its center flickered with firelight. "Please tell me you believe that."

She traced the diamonds, her own fire stirring, warming the air as she said, "I do."

I rose to meet her lips, pressing her back against the rock. We sank into a kiss just as the clouds opened up and unleashed the full deluge they'd been threatening.

We were soaked within moments.

Rainwater mingled with the taste of her fire. As our kiss deepened and our surroundings heated, the drops began to hiss as they hit, slowly enveloping us in a cloud of steam.

We stayed tangled together, soaking wet and steaming, until the sun came up and started to chase away some of the damp dreariness.

She was curled against me, her breathing slow and even, when she stirred, huddled more closely to me and said, "The battles we'll face in the coming days..."

I steadied her as she sat up, rearranging herself in my lap so we were face-to-face.

She visibly steeled herself further before she said, "Whatever happens in the end, I need you to trust me."

I stared, searching her face for clues about the things she hadn't been able to tell me. About whatever trial Malaphar had appointed to her. Clues about where she was planning to go, what she was planning to do.

Finding none, I planted one last lingering kiss on her lips, swallowing the last of the raindrops still clinging to them.

"I trust you," I whispered against her mouth.

But as she kissed me back—harder than she ever had—I had the strange sensation that she was returning the fire I'd given her, only now it burned more brightly and fiercely than ever before.

CHAPTER 42

Two days after my meeting with the God of the Shade, I stood at the edge of the Hollowlands, my sights once again set on Ederis.

The heart of the elven rebellion.

In a matter of minutes, I would be driving my way toward that heart.

And my sister—fully healed thanks to the magic of Armaros—was coming with me this time.

I would be taking on her appearance with the help of Mairu's magic, and we would both be traveling into the hornet's nest that was Ederis with the same goal in mind.

We had mapped out our exact routes, our precise targets, and made certain we wouldn't overlap one another. It would still be dangerous. Incredibly dangerous.

But it was the only plan we could all agree on.

Savna still had followers within Ederis. As many as Andrel, at least. And could maybe gain more, once she returned and revealed that she had survived an assassination attempt—an act of violence that hadn't

435

surprised *me*, but which might surprise others and turn them away from Andrel's leadership.

My original plan had been to go alone, but Savna refused to be left behind.

She would be better at winning over any extra supporters and getting them to do as she commanded, she had argued—and I couldn't disagree. So I would focus on alerting the ones who already followed her, letting them know of our plan to refuse to continue to fight under Andrel's banner.

Together, we would turn enough against him that he would have no choice but to rethink his goal of launching a full-scale war against the human kingdoms.

That was the first part of the plan.

Once it was in motion—and most of our enemies were moving out of the city, away from me—I would focus on making my way to the place I believed to be the 'heart' of the rebellion.

And there I would unleash Antaeum, which was currently quietly tucked away against my back, hidden beneath my coat.

I kept expecting Dravyn or the others to pick up on the dagger's energy. To spot it, at least. To ask where I'd gotten it. But it went entirely unnoticed; whatever Malaphar had done to cloak its power from them, it was working.

I only hoped it proved as powerful as he claimed whenever the time to wield it arrived—a time that would have to come sooner rather than later.

Because while we stood there, plotting and preparing to sneak our way inside Ederis, the forces at Mindoth and the surrounding posts of the Galithian Army continued to mobilize and march toward us. Help was coming from neighboring kingdoms, as well—a rare alliance of human-kind all converging toward a single goal: To eliminate the elves before they could declare their full war.

As my sister and I finished finalizing our routes and reciting our goals, Valas returned from his mission of scouting out the moving human troops.

He soared down in the form of a serpentine dragon that looked remarkably similar to the shape Mairu often shifted into.

"How many?" Dravyn asked in place of a greeting.

"Two-thousand strong, at least," Valas said, shaking away the last of the scales from his arms. "They're marching through the Naudren Pass."

"Approaching from the west," Dravyn muttered. "They'll likely set up in a blockade formation along the Hollowlands' edge."

"There's a nearly permanent encampment along the west-facing edge of those lands, stretching for miles up from the human's territory," my sister informed us. "So they'll be well prepared to defend themselves and outlast any siege."

"It could end up an indefinite stalemate," Mairu said, almost hopefully.

But Savna shook her head. "It will be too tempting—all of those humans sitting so close to our protected lands? Andrel will order an attack before long."

"The numbers are greater than we hoped," Dravyn said solemnly, "but that doesn't change our plans. The three of us still have our work to do, and Karys and her sister have theirs."

While my sister and I infiltrated and disbanded the elves' forces from inside Ederis, the three of them would do what they could to slow the oncoming storm of human soldiers.

There was little time to second guess this plan, and even less to say goodbye.

Valas moved first, sprouting ice-glazed wings with a roll of his shoulders before striding toward me, cupping my cheek, and leaning his forehead against mine in a conspiratorial kind of way.

"I would tell you to be careful," he said, "but I don't think it would do any good."

"I'll be exactly as careful as the situation allows for," I told him.

"Exactly the sort of less-than-reassuring doublespeak I'd expect from a divine being," he said, grinning. "I'm so proud of how much you've learned, and how horribly I've managed to influence you."

"I have a long way to go to reach your level of horribleness."

"That's very true," he said, stepping back and giving me a wink. "You still have plenty to learn." With that, he leapt into the air, summoning an icy blast of wind and unfurling his wings fully to catch that gust, letting it carry him into the bright morning sky and nearly out of sight.

I felt Dravyn's eyes settling on me. The ring on my finger warmed as I looked over and met his gaze.

"You need to go," I said, even as I walked toward him, fighting the urge to grab his arm and hold him close. "Stay with Valas so he can't do anything foolish."

"He'll still manage to do that, either way," Dravyn pointed out.

I laughed as I brought my lips to his, partly to hide the true, more painful surge of emotion that overcame me as I kissed him goodbye.

"I love you," I whispered, hoping with everything in me that this would not be the last time I got to say that to him.

"I'll see you soon," he replied, pointedly.

This is not our ending.

I wasn't sure who thought the words—me or him—but there they were in my head, and I held to them as tightly as I could as I watched him take to the skies alongside Valas. His wings were even more impressive than the God of Winter's had been, the fiery span of them stretching no less than ten feet, with each beat summoning more embers that built upon their solidness.

My sister was still staring at the display, eyes wide and lips parted in awe, when Mairu stepped in front of her.

"Hold still," the goddess commanded, golden threads of magic sprouting from her fingertips as she pressed them to my sister's face.

Savna flinched, but ultimately managed not to flee, even as the Serpent Goddess's power swelled.

The ribbons of gold lengthened and completely wrapped around my sister's body, where they held for a breath until Mairu snapped her fingers and unraveled them all in a blink.

They flew toward her outstretched palm, twisting into a neat ball of shining gold as if wrapping around an invisible spool.

She beckoned me toward her, guiding that ball of energy into me as I approached. It sank, warm and heavy, into my chest. As the magic settled and spread through my body, I felt myself changing. It seemed different than other transformation spells she'd used—deeper. More powerful.

"Well, *this* is incredibly unsettling," Savna said, peering around the goddess and watching just as I felt the magic tickling around my eyes—shifting them from green to blue.

"It's not the most unsettling thing I've witnessed during my time among the gods," I assured her.

We shared a nervous laugh over that, and then I closed my eyes as the last parts of Mairu's spell finished washing over me.

Within moments, I had finally become the person I'd always wanted to be—but only so I could finish the task of becoming who I was *truly* meant to be.

The irony was not lost on me.

"I've left a temporary mark on your sister as well," Mairu told me. "You'll be able to track her by its divine energy if you find yourself in a desperate situation." She grimaced as she shook the last threads of gold from her palm. "Well, *more* desperate than our present situation."

I tried to give her a reassuring smile. "Thank you."

She wrapped me in a quick hug in response. Then she looked to the sky and, after an encouraging nod from me, she followed Valas and Dravyn's examples, unleashing dragon-like wings that carried her swiftly away.

Once she had disappeared from view, my sister drew closer to me, gaze darting back and forth between my transformed appearance and the sky.

"The details of what we're going to do to settle things after we scatter and disarm Andrel's loyalists...couldn't help but notice those plans were scarcely discussed," she said, staring at the spot where Mairu's winged body had faded from view. "Is this lack of details common with these gods and their plans?"

"Yes," I said with a snort, thinking of all the poor communication I'd witnessed among the divine. "But this time, it's not their fault."

She fixed me with an expectant look.

"They don't know the extent of what I'm planning, because I...I couldn't tell them."

"Do *you* even know what you're planning?"

"I know...enough."

"That's terribly reassuring."

I sighed, my hand slipping under my coat and finding the hilt of the dagger Malaphar had given me.

I couldn't keep this secret solely to myself any longer—and the Dark God had said nothing against sharing it with a *mortal* being.

My sister had always been my secret keeper...so maybe she could be that again, at least one last time.

"My plan revolves around this," I said, slipping the dagger from its sheath and holding it out to her. "It's a gift from one of the Creator Gods."

She slowly took it, studying the blade's etchings with the same cautious wonder I had.

"The magic it yields will replace the wards around Ederis," I told her, "and render all of the anti-divine magic in the area useless. It's meant to become a point that will establish a new age of elves."

She stared at me. "It will undo our protections, you mean."

"And replace them with something better."

"So they claim." She shoved the dagger back at me as though it had suddenly grown hot to the touch. "How can you be sure the gods aren't playing games with you? Or just using you to finish wiping out our race?"

I snatched the weapon from her hold. As my hand closed around the grip, the etchings on the black blade pulsed with silvery light for a fraction of a moment. An incredible sense of power overtook me in the same instant.

I settled myself within that power and answered my sister in a calm, decisive voice: "Because I am too powerful to be played with, now," I said. "And they wouldn't need *me* if they truly wanted to finish killing off the elves. What they need is a divine being who can help restore order. Someone who can navigate the various realms and races. Don't you understand? If I don't succeed in doing this, then they likely *will* simply swoop in and finish the job of killing you all off. It's simpler, after all. This is my—*our*—last chance at restoring balance."

She considered me and Antaeum for a long moment before carefully reaching for it again, giving it a closer look.

No matter how she twisted and turned it, the blade never reacted to her touch—only to mine.

"It's tied to me," I said quietly. "I'm meant to wield it. To fix things with it." I took the dagger and sheathed it, averting my eyes, avoiding the concerned look she watched me with. "And I'm stronger than I used to be."

"I know you are."

"Then trust me."

Trust me.

The same plea I'd made to Dravyn the other night. It was asking a lot of both of them, I knew.

But I would not let them down.

"Fine," my sister said, after a long pause. "The Hollows await—lead the way."

I moved much more quickly through said Hollows—more confidently—than last time. Because I was stronger than I used to be, yes—but I also had all the insider information my sister had provided me with, in addition to the disguise of her appearance.

As we passed through the wards meant to keep divine magic out, Antaeum provided help, too.

A shimmer went through the air so quickly I would have missed it if I'd blinked. I didn't understand what was happening at first, not until I took a moment to stop and catch my breath...and I realized how easily I could do so.

The unbearable pressure I'd fought against during my last trip through this place was no longer a problem.

The dagger had negated it.

A positive sign of greater things to come, I hoped.

As we approached Ederis, my sister and I went in opposite directions. She would stick to the outskirts of the city—areas I was less familiar with, anyway. We wouldn't cross paths again until Mairu's magic wore off, and we both had plenty to do between now and then.

I had a map in my mind—one Savna had helped me construct; that was all I needed from this point. It guided me to the places where she thought I was most likely to run into the targets we'd chosen. Many of the ones I sought were rebels I'd known, at least in passing, from my younger years. And I rarely forgot faces.

My disturbingly exact memory, along with my sister's instructions, provided enough guidance; within the first two hours spent darting from one point to another along my mental map, I managed to speak to seven of our targets.

From these chosen leaders, ripples began to spread.

Soon I was beginning to sense it—the stirrings of movement, the whispers of possible change. A nervous yet determined sort of energy was soon rising all around me.

I hoped my sister was having similar luck.

And I hoped she was safe.

But I couldn't help but wonder...

What if we'd miscalculated?

What if there were far more rebels who wanted her dead than we realized? We'd assumed Andrel was the one responsible for ordering the attack in Altis. That no one else would act so brazenly, so brutally against Savna.

But what if we were wrong?

What if they tried again while she was here, and I wasn't there to save her this time?

"You're alive," came a sudden voice, just as I started to duck into the shadows of a building to collect myself and calm my racing thoughts.

I turned toward Andrel with the same cool, unhurried confidence my sister would have used. "Surprised, are you?"

His face split into the wide, charismatic grin he usually reserved for winning over the more reluctant rebels. "*Thrilled*, more like. I heard what happened in Altis. I thought you were finished, for sure."

Of course you heard, I wanted to snap. *You're the one who ordered it to happen.*

But he would only deny it, and I would risk revealing too much before I was ready to reveal it.

So instead, I calmly recited the words my sister had suggested I use if and when I encountered him.

"We have traitors in our midst, as we feared," I said. "I spotted a member of Lensa's inner circle leading my assassination party—the one who shot the first arrow, as a matter of fact."

"An arrow she'll sorely regret before the end."

"I plan to make her regret it," I agreed.

Andrel started to walk, indicating for me to follow him.

The divine dagger at my waist shivered with power.

I wanted so badly to plant it in Andrel's back.

But I knew how divine trials worked. And the Moraki who had handed me this trial had been clear that the dagger I held was meant for greater things than the filthy blood of this traitor before me.

I would have my revenge before the end.

But not yet.

Not yet, not yet, not yet...

Every inch of my body rebelled against the idea of following him anywhere, but I made myself keep up appearances, trailing a short distance behind him.

He summited a hill and gazed into the distance, toward the Hollowlands, which were covered with a light veil of mist.

"Any and all potential traitors and cowards..." he said as I caught up to him, "they'll all be crawling back to us soon enough."

The confidence in his voice chilled me to the bone, but I didn't let my fear show. I only agreed with him, mirroring that confidence as best I could.

His gaze slid toward me, appraising me a little too closely, so I quickly changed the subject.

"There's an army marching toward us, coming from the Naudren Pass—I encountered them on my way back to you." I offered up this information freely—information he likely already knew—just to further convince him we were still on the same side.

He dismissed it with a chuckle. "We're more than prepared for them."

"They number at least two-thousand strong," I said, still calmly. "An alliance from multiple kingdoms."

"And we number more than double that."

I tried to twist my tone into one of curiosity rather than horror. "...How?"

He chuckled to himself, as if enjoying some private joke.

I continued to stare at him, until he finally answered me. "I took the liberty of making a few changes to our strategies while you were away. Switching from a defensive to offensive posture, to begin with. As soon as we learned of that marching army of allied humans, we mobilized our own.

"I knew we'd eventually lure them toward our lands—and they have no idea how many we are actually hiding within the darkness of the Hollows, or what sort of alliances we've formed for ourselves. They are vain, indeed, to think we couldn't match whatever forces they conjured up."

It took everything in me to swallow the bile in the back of my throat and say, "I always said vanity would be their downfall, didn't I?"

The space between where we stood and where Dravyn and the others were was vast, impossible to see across even if it *hadn't* been covered in fog.

I stared into the distance anyway, as if I might see some flash of fire or glint of ice—some powerful display that would give me hope that things were not as dismal or impossible as they were starting to seem.

"It should be an easy enough victory," Andrel said, sounding almost bored.

"...It should be a massacre."

"Exactly. One that is likely beginning right about now." He turned to me with a smile. "Shall we go enjoy it together?"

CHAPTER 43

Dravyn

The king was here.

My arrogant, fucking fool of a brother.

Here.

I'd caught his scent almost immediately after we'd settled onto our vantage point along the top of a cliff—one that overlooked the main encampment being established by a rapidly increasing number of human soldiers.

And now—after a minute of furious searching—I actually *saw* the idiot.

"Focus," Mairu urged. "Just because he's here doesn't mean he's going to be leading the charge into battle."

"I doubt he's here to surrender, either," Valas put in, earning himself a scowl from the Serpent Goddess.

I turned my back to both of them—and the bustling war camp—for a moment, doing my best to *focus* as Mairu insisted.

I had to.

There was too much at stake to think only of my brother, even though all I wanted to do in that moment was fly down and confront him.

Fucking *idiot.*

"There's movement in the trees at the Hollowlands' edge," Mairu said suddenly. "Lots of it."

I slowly turned back around, and the three of us watched those trees for several minutes, trying to gauge what kind of numbers we were up against.

We would use our magic to keep the humans and elves separated, biding time for Karys to accomplish whatever task Malaphar had appointed to her—that was our plan, in its simplest form. And it would be easier than keeping the two sides separated at Mindoth, I thought; there were fewer natural barriers to contend with, here—no raging sea, no underground caves.

Even so, something about the amount of movement in those trees was...unsettling.

"How many are there, Mai?"

She closed her eyes and breathed slowly in, slowly out, several times, feeling for the energies of the hidden bodies. She could usually pinpoint the auras of individual beings even in the largest of crowds, but...

Judging by her confused silence, there were too many here to easily estimate.

"That can't be right," she finally whispered, blinking her eyes open and narrowing them on the rustling trees once more.

A few human soldiers had ventured closer to inspect the movement, but nothing emerged to meet them.

Not yet.

"Worse numbers than we feared?" Valas guessed.

She didn't answer, but the horrified expression on her face said enough.

"You'd think we would have learned to assume the worst by now," Valas moaned. "Why am I such an eternal optimist? It honestly makes no sense."

While the Winter God continued to have a conversation with himself, I moved stealthily over the clifftop, getting a better view of that camp taking shape below us, sizing up their numbers as well as any potential strong or weak points.

There was another cliff like the one I stood on almost directly across from me. Together, they pinched in the land below and created a narrow passage that would be easier to defend. The majority of the camp was already behind this narrow point, save for a few smaller companies patrolling the areas closer to the Hollowlands.

Among those smaller companies, of course, was my fool of a brother.

Fallon was on horseback, trotting dangerously close to the Hollows and its hidden dangers. He sat tall and proud in the saddle, shouting commands, his voice occasionally rising into a booming rallying cry.

"We should funnel all of them back behind that narrow spot," Mai said, walking over to me even as she kept her eyes on the trees. "So they'll have to go around these cliffs to get to one another—which will slow both sides down, at least."

"My thoughts, exactly."

We wasted no time.

She went first, wings soundlessly unfolding and carrying her down the cliffside. She landed gently in the crook of a dead tree, just close enough to better see which soldiers were giving the orders.

Her magic could control every tiny twitch of a body—every breath, every heartbeat—but with so many to deal with, commanding each individual body would be difficult. So she merely took hold of the leaders among them and twisted their will into her own, guiding them into a hasty retreat toward safer ground. The rest of the crowd, I assumed, caught a subtle piece of her power as well—enough to help persuade them to follow those leaders without question.

Within minutes, they were all funneling toward the larger group, past the narrow passage, gathering a safer distance from the Hollows.

Mairu landed beside me once more, still guiding her targets with subtle movements of her hands.

Valas was perched on the opposite cliff, now, scanning the edge of the forest, plotting his next move. He waited until we signaled, then he leapt, taking on a form that was little more than a cold swirl of pale energy—one that blended almost seamlessly with the cliff face. As he shot away from that cliff, twisting and turning along the edge of the forest, a thick layer of ice overtook the ground he passed over.

I kept my human-like form for the moment, dropping with the brief aid of wings and landing close to the pinch-point between the two cliffs.

I pushed an invisible, searing wind toward the human's encampment, driving the last of the lingering soldiers more quickly toward it.

Once the area was clear, I sent ropes of flame out in a line across the narrowest part of the path. Then I built upon that line, creating a wall that neither elf nor human would be able to pass.

As the barrier began properly roaring with power and heat, I flew back to our higher vantage point, settling down on the very edge of the cliff to survey our work.

Ice covered the ground all along the Hollows' edge, which would make it nearly impossible for the elves to charge out with any sort of speed or control.

At that narrow point Mairu and I had agreed upon, my wall of fire continued to burn higher. I finished the job from where I now stood, filling in the weaker spots that this view allowed me to see.

But before the wall closed off completely, I caught sight of a small company of humans on the wrong side of my wall—the one group who had somehow escaped Mairu's hold.

My brother was leading them.

I leapt from the clifftop, wings flaring out behind me, curses flying from my mouth.

The ground shook as I landed before him, spooking his horse. He cut the reins sharply, preventing it from bolting, then jumped from the saddle to finish calming the beast.

He turned his glare on me once the horse was still. "Dravyn? What is the meaning of—"

"*Fall back*," I growled at him, "get behind the wall I've built for you before you get yourself and everyone else in your company killed." As I spoke, I lifted a hand toward that wall of fire, parting a small section of it to allow him and the other remaining riders to pass through.

The shift in power and light made his horse skittish again. Fallon stumbled a few steps before managing a more commanding hold on it.

"I'm not retreating," he snapped.

"You won't win this battle. There are more enemies than you realize within those trees."

His expression—cold and angry, hard as steel—didn't change.

"I warned you of their numbers before. Why didn't you *listen*?"

"It was this, or allow them to keep driving deeper and deeper into my kingdom, into my cities—"

"They don't want to lay siege to your cities. They were trying to lure you toward their own territory so they could draw you in and devour you here, where they're at their strongest—and you've fallen for it."

He blinked. Shifted his gaze to the ice-edged forest then back to me. Appraising. Considering my words, maybe.

But he said nothing.

I knew my brother well enough, even after all the things that had come between us. Knew he would never admit that he'd gotten this wrong.

How could he, when he had thousands of soldiers looking to him for leadership?

The wall of fire grew as my concern grew, the flames tumbling more violently, reflecting my increasingly fast heartbeats.

Fallon jerked his gaze toward the brightening, burgeoning wall. It stayed there for a long moment.

And as my brother stared at those flames almost longingly—as though he was thinking of sacrificing himself to their growing heat—I thought I finally understood something after all these years: The weight he carried as a king.

A king whose rule was, according to many, the only thing standing between the human territories and the rise of these elves who were building the foundations of a rebellious empire so close to his kingdom's border.

"Tell your soldiers the gods have chosen your side because you made the decision to bravely march forward and confront your enemies," I said, quieter. "That should help you save face."

He looked momentarily furious at the idea of needing to *save face*.

But it passed quickly, and the expression left behind was a confusing mixture of regret, stubbornness, and resolve.

Finally, he placed a hand on the saddle and prepared to leave.

I started to just let him go, but my mouth was moving again, words spilling out before I could stop them.

"You may have felt like you've been alone these years," I said as he hoisted himself up, "but I've had your palace wrapped in protective magic for years. Even if you couldn't see it. Or feel it. You are more than just a *king*. And I need you to fall back because I need you to survive this. Just so you know."

He adjusted the reins of his horse and turned it away from me—toward safety—without another word.

But he paused after only half a step.

Glancing over his shoulder, he said, "If their numbers are as great as you claim, then this isn't a battle you can likely win, either. Even as a god. They have weapons that can strike successfully against divine power—we saw them in Altis."

"Yes."

"So what can you possibly do against these monsters?"

"There are powers greater than any the middle-gods can wield. And things are in motion, now—they only need time to come to fruition. We only have to keep the situation from escalating beyond repair in the meantime."

His stone-faced glare returned.

"You just have to trust me," I told him.

Trust me.

The same words Karys had said. The words I'd been holding on to like a lifeline these past two days.

I *did* trust her.

But it was not a feeling I could easily explain to the skeptical king before me. And again, I knew what my stubborn brother was thinking.

Trust you? As I trusted you to negotiate a ceasefire?

But he said nothing.

Which was a kind of progress between us, maybe.

My brother and I were still caught in our quiet stalemate when a small explosion went off behind me.

I looked back to see powder raining down over a large swath of ground, landing upon the divine trap of ice Valas had laid.

Melting it.

The powder hissed as it hit the ice and ignited. Secondary, smaller explosions of violet-colored fog popped up all along the forest's edge.

The first line of elven warriors emerged through this fog, wearing masks of white, their clothing patterned like the pale grey trees they'd been hiding among. It created an eerie effect—their bodies being hidden by a combination of these patterns and the swirling fog, their movements only noticeable when one of their masks caught a bit of the overcast sunlight.

"These monsters won't be stopped," Fallon said through clenched teeth.

"*Fall back*!" I said again, giving his horse a swat on the hindquarters to get it moving. It lunged into a gallop—beyond ready to run by this point—and he didn't try to stop it. To my relief, he managed to direct it through the opening I'd created in my barrier.

I doubted he would retreat entirely. It would not be that easy. But at least he was out of my way for the moment.

Now I could focus on the growing disaster behind me.

After sealing off the wall of fire, I turned just in time to see another bomb landing against the glittering, ice-coated ground. Another explosion. Another blanket of dust landing upon Valas's ice, another series of explosions *pop pop popping* and filling the air with an even thicker layer of noxious fog.

The ghostly elven army advanced in earnest, now, their relatively silent movements adding to the overall haunting effect they created.

Some drove straight for the wall of fire I'd made, pulling more of their small bombs from the bags slung across their chests.

Other groups began splintering off, charging in opposite directions. They *could* go around the cliffs and converge from both directions—arguably a worse situation than all of them simply pouring straight forward. It would take them longer to accomplish it, but the end result...

Valas caught my attention, and we wordlessly coordinated our next moves, taking to the sky and heading off every group we could get in front of. Closing off paths with magic. Forcing them to waste their finite supply of magic-negating bombs. Slowing them down even further.

While we worked from above, Mairu's magic worked from hidden places alongside the moving army, sowing confusion and chaos into their ranks.

She focused on controlling the ones who carried the bomb-filled slings across their chests, forcing them to launch several of those bombs in wrong directions. Not only did this waste the weapons, but it also created several scuffles among the soldiers as they argued over orders not being followed.

Little by little, the composed, quiet, ghost-like lines began to break down.

Yet even as they did so, the situation continued to go from bad to worse.

Because their numbers simply kept increasing.

How could we possibly stop them all?

This emerging army, and the rest of it still hiding in the woods... most of this first wave had answered Andrel's command to assemble, to attack. Yet there was no telling who was loyal at their core, and who could be swayed back to a more reasonable position if given the chance.

And soon, the ones loyal to Savna would be secretly weaving their way into the fray as well, hopefully impossible to tell apart from the others until the moment came to reveal themselves. Maybe this was already happening.

So we couldn't unleash our true power—couldn't slaughter them indiscriminately.

But we had no time to be *delicate*, either.

I decided to focus on the ones directly attacking the barriers Valas and I were planting. I went back to the largest of those barriers—the first one I'd established—and took aim at the group currently trying to destroy it.

As they closed in on my wall of fire, so did I, sending a new line of flames lashing toward them. They scattered in all directions—but they didn't go far before gathering their courage and turning back to the fight.

Back and forth we went.

I kept driving them away until they were no longer close enough to throw their bombs at the wall—but this didn't entirely stop them;

arrows flew next, with balls of exploding powder affixed to their heads. They cleared a smaller area, and with less force, but they struck faster and in more places at once.

Several flew uncomfortably close to me as well. I wasn't sure the effect that powder would have on my current form, but I wouldn't risk a repeat of what had happened in Mindoth.

I soared higher, out of range of the archers. From just above the top of the cliff, I continued to rain fire down upon them.

They grew bolder, several of them sacrificing themselves in order to get closer to the wall and destroy it, continuing to press on even as their fellow warriors caught fire and fell beside them.

And all the while, the numbers pouring from the Hollows kept increasing.

I tried to be strategic with my aim. Tried not to add any more than necessary to the already overpowering stench of blood and fire that filled the air.

When this strategy began to fail, I flew even higher—high enough to see the human encampment on the other side. I was considering landing on that other side, preparing them for the onslaught to come, when a strange sensation slammed through my chest and distracted me.

For several seconds, my vision blacked out.

I couldn't breathe.

Yet nothing had struck me.

It wasn't my own pain, but one I felt through the divine bond of my court. And the desperate cold that followed, it felt like—

"VALAS!"

With the sound of Mairu's sudden cry came a wild burst of her magic. That magic caught the trees in a merciless grip and bent them as if she had them between her fingers, snapping them as easily as twigs.

I veered sharply in mid-air, turning in the direction I'd last seen Valas, searching for the reason behind Mairu's scream—

There.

He was on the ground, barely visible behind a group of converging elven soldiers.

I raced toward him.

Mairu reached him first, touching down on the ground directly beside him and lifting her feral, furious gaze to the circling soldiers.

She struck out a hand. Her fingers bent at odd angles, curving like the talons of her dragon form, and then she closed them into a fist.

Even from where I stood, I could feel the rippling expanse of her power. Could hear the gasps of the soldiers as their hands flew to their throats, and the sound of their heartbeats stuttering to a stop.

They dropped as if their legs had been cut out from under them.

I landed seconds later, fire preceding my approach, encircling the three of us in a protective ring.

Valas did not move, even as the ring burned hotter. His chest had been slashed open, and what bits of skin I could see were already taking on a look similar to the wounds I'd sustained in Mindoth—except his looked much darker. Deeper.

I carefully started to gather him in my arms, preparing to carry him somewhere safer, somewhere less crowded.

"Leave me be," he moaned, struggling against my hold. "I'm fine."

"Be quiet," I snapped.

He actually listened.

Which was how I knew he was severely injured.

As I finally settled his disoriented self against me, he opened his eyes. They were disturbingly blank for a moment before they caught on something behind me and immediately widened in horror.

I couldn't help following his gaze.

The trees at my back were rustling again, shaking and swaying as if in the throes of a building earthquake.

The largest wave of elven warriors yet exploded from those trees seconds later, heading directly toward us.

CHAPTER 44

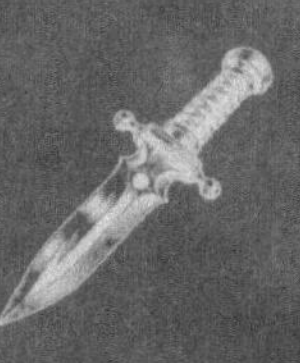

Karys

After several tense minutes, I managed to slip away from Andrel by claiming I needed to go to my private quarters, to retrieve my weapons and armor before I could join him on his march through the Hollowlands.

It was a believable lie—my sister's sword, *Godcleaver*, had once belonged to our father, and she rarely went into any important battle without it.

Of course, I had no idea where her quarters even were.

Nor did I have any intention of actually retrieving her sword.

The only weapon I needed was the dagger at my back.

At first, I'd worried Andrel wouldn't go without me. But soon enough, he got caught up in the swelling, rebellious energy all around us, swept away by the countless others heading off to join the battle at the edge of the elven territory.

The city was emptying of most of its soldiers, as we'd planned—the ones secretly most loyal to my sister leading the charge as we'd been quietly instructing them to do.

They would move quickly, catching up to the forces already mobilized. Then, when the moment was right, they would turn on them. Disarm them. Throw Andrel's strategies askew and help the gods stall the battle long enough to allow me to do what I needed to do.

Mairu's magic was beginning to fade. I was becoming myself once more, and my sister would take over as the sole version of her, joining the army marching outward. Triumphantly leading it after surviving the attack against her in Altis...

Everything was going according to plan.

I only had to focus on my next part of this plot: Finding the heart that Malaphar had mentioned.

In the back of my mind, horrible scenes of a battle were starting to form—images I feared were being inadvertently passed to me through our court's divine connection. But I pushed them down and worked on recalling the directions my sister had given me.

When I'd mentioned the *heart of the elven rebellion* to her, her reply had been almost immediate: In the very center of the city, there was a grass field filled with flowers, stretching away from a stone monument.

The same monument I'd encountered the last time I snuck into this city.

So at least I had no trouble finding it.

It was more than a memorial to the dead, apparently; it had existed long before Dravyn killed the poor souls whose names were etched into the stone's surface. Originally, that stone was placed as a shrine to the ones who had discovered the first anti-divine runes; a copy of those runes was inscribed on the back of it. I'd been too distracted by the names on the front to notice it last time, but perhaps that inscription was part of the reason the energy in this area felt so strange to me.

If there is a heart beating in Ederis, my sister had told me, *it is likely buried near that white stone.*

Behind the towering rock, I found a patch of ground that looked strange. Nothing grew upon it, and the dirt was an odd shade of blackish grey. As I drew closer, I noticed the same runes here as on the back of the monument.

I withdrew Antaeum.

With all the strength I could gather, I lifted the dagger high and slammed it into the cold earth.

It pierced easily and sank in deeply—up to my forearms. I kept a tight hold on the dagger as it hummed and warmed, briefly filling the air with the scent of scorched dirt.

But nothing else happened.

Hands shaking, I drew it out. Wiped the dirt from the blade. My touch caused the etchings to glow momentarily, which encouraged me to try again.

I willed more of my divine magic to accompany the strike this time.

Still nothing.

There was movement to my right.

A narrow road separated me from the rest of the city—but some passerby had seen me and hesitated at the sight.

Much of the city might have been moving out, but there were still a fair number staying behind. And Andrel likely was not far away yet.

I couldn't risk drawing too much attention to myself.

I clutched the divine dagger to my chest and crept farther from that narrow road, into the shadows of a small, locked outbuilding.

A feeling of impossibility threatened as I pressed against that building and out of sight, studying the weapon in my hands.

What now?

The longer I hid, the faster my mind raced—and the more vibrant the violent sights and sounds in my head became.

I was almost certain of it, now: These mental glimpses I kept receiving...they were not in my imagination. I was inadvertently getting updates on the battle my divine family was fighting far in the distance.

As soon as I admitted this to myself, a stronger surge of chaotic thoughts and feelings hit me, crescendoing in a terrible sensation of pain that shot through my back—like I'd just slammed into the ground, knocking the breath from my lungs.

Something was definitely wrong.

What was happening at the Hollows' edge?

I pushed away from the building, frantically pacing the small yard in front of it, trying to think.

Where else could I try to plant this stupid dagger?

Should I just abandon it and go aid the others?

Was this part of the trial? A trick of some kind? Maybe I wasn't supposed to be in this city at all. Maybe I'd made a mistake, keeping the dagger a secret. Maybe it had been a test to see if I would blindly follow orders, and I was *meant* to challenge said orders.

I didn't know, but I was sure of one thing: Whatever happened next, I had to get to the rest of my court.

I just hoped I wasn't already too late.

Sheathing Antaeum, I broke into a run.

I raced through the city at a wild, otherworldly pace. Each slap of my feet against the dirt was like the pound of a war drum beating faster, more frantic, with every second.

I could still feel Mairu's magic tingling in my skin—I was likely a mixture of my sister's appearance and my own at this point, but it didn't matter; I didn't slow down long enough for anyone to even try to identify me.

Once I was out of the city, I flew. My wings sprouted more effortlessly than ever before, carrying me up, up, up above the trees.

It wasn't hard to find the battle—the scent of blood and magic was impossible to miss.

I followed that scent trail for several minutes, until I heard shouting, thundering boots, clanging weapons growing louder and louder. Smoke filled the air, along with strange drifts of purple mist.

An acrid, nauseating scent soon stood out, even above the blood and smoke. From those purple clouds, I suspected. More poisonous weapons the elves had developed.

Another sharp sensation struck through my core, accompanied by a horrible sense that something was falling. Something was fading.

Another vision flickered through my mind. It was accompanied by the familiar feel of Dravyn's warmth, this time, and so it was easier to focus on it, to hold on to until I could make sense of it.

Until I could see what was happening through his eyes.

The image that formed was almost perfectly clear. An actual setting appeared: flat stone, surrounded by boulders and sparse trees—a dip in the top of a cliff, it looked like. A hiding place.

A still body lay in the middle of it.

Valas.

I froze in shock at the sight, forgetting for a moment that I was in the air. I plummeted several dozen feet before finally regaining my senses. I pulled up sharply. The world spun around me. My thoughts tumbled and roared until I made my lips move with a command for myself.

Find them.

I could track Dravyn through this chaos.

I'd made my way back to him through worse.

Within minutes, I managed to find the familiar threads of his power and weave mine through them, tying an invisible knot between us so I could pull myself toward him.

I made certain to swing wide and fly high—above clouds of concealing smoke and powder—so I wouldn't draw attention to where I was going.

Once I was confident of my destination, I descended as quickly and silently as I could.

Dravyn rose to catch me, breaking my recklessly fast landing and bringing me safely to a stop.

I ran my hands across his chest, his arms, up to the sides of his face, making sure he was truly solid and safe.

Then I immediately dropped to my knees beside the God of Winter.

"Don't touch his wounds," Dravyn warned, placing a hand on my shoulder and gently holding me back. "The poison might be contagious."

That poison had turned most of his body an unnatural shade of pale blue, yet his godly features still looked beautiful even in this sickening sheen. Like he'd been preserved by the cold glamour of his own magic.

His breaths were so shallow they hardly moved his chest at all.

Open your eyes, I silently begged, *open your eyes and say something stupid. Make me smile, make me believe something foolish.*

The silent pleas made no difference.

I shrugged out of my coat and draped it over his lifeless body. A useless gesture, maybe, but I didn't know what else to do.

He looked oddly small underneath the pile of canvas cloth. Oddly fragile for a god. It made everything else feel unbearably breakable and painfully impossible.

The sound of distant footsteps scrambling over the rocks grabbed our attention.

Dravyn darted toward the sound, bracing a hand against the nearest boulder tall enough to hide his massive frame. As he peered around it, I moved to his side as well, and we both searched the sloping cliffs for signs of an ambush, but...

Nothing there.

Tensely, we held our position and continued our watch.

After a minute, I couldn't help glancing back at Valas and whispering, "What happened to him?"

"The Velkyn's numbers were much higher than we anticipated."

"I know—I mean, I spoke with Andrel, and he said something along those lines." My breath stuttered in my chest. "I should have tried to warn you all. I'm sorry, I..."

"It would have made little difference," he replied, quietly, eyes still trained in the direction we'd heard footsteps echoing from. "We're here, and we were going to have to face things regardless of the numbers. Did you accomplish what you needed to in the meantime?"

Another crushing feeling of failure squeezed my heart.

He glanced at me out of the corner of his eye. His gaze caught on Antaeum; without my coat covering it, the sheath at my back was perfectly visible.

Before either of us could mention the weapon, a surge of new energy struck me—the divine marker Mairu had placed on my sister's skin was still intact, and it was drawing nearer.

Creeping closer to the cliff's edge, I scanned the battle far below.

I felt Savna well before I saw her. She was leading a small group of warriors into the fray, making as if to help another group that was trying to extinguish a wall of divine fire.

I looked at Valas, hesitating.

"I'll stay with him," Dravyn said. "Whatever you're planning to do, do it *quickly*."

I met his gaze one last time. Nodded. Straightened to my full height despite the heaviness in my limbs, my heart, my lungs.

Then I was off again before I could dwell any longer on my failures, launching myself from the cliff and careening downward.

I landed silently and moved as stealthily as I could, keeping away from the largest crowds, making my way from smoke cloud to smoke cloud—and using magic to create more of that concealing smoke when necessary.

As soon as I was within easy sprinting distance of my sister, I forgot about all else. I leapt over a few dead bodies—two that were burned husks, three that were ice-glazed statues—and nearly collided with my sister as she spun toward the sound of my approach.

She heaved a sigh of relief at the sight of me.

I gave her a quick embrace. "You managed to gather as many as I did, I hope?"

She nodded, her confident smirk the exact remedy my doubts needed just then. "Did you think I'd let you outdo me?" Her bright eyes swept over the battlefield. "They're moving into position now, drawing near to the ones Andrel considers his leaders. We should have enough to disarm those leaders."

"Good."

"I'll just need a way to communicate the signal when we're ready for it." She lost herself in thought for an instant, still surveying the chaotic field around us, until her eyes widened and darted back to me. "But you're here. Why are you here? The heart you were searching for—"

"Wasn't where we thought it would be."

She frowned.

"I'm not out of ideas, yet, don't worry. Just keep things as controlled as you can in the meantime. Keep moving your loyalists into position."

She looked worried, but ultimately didn't try to stop me when I moved, racing away as if heading to the next part of my plan.

It had been a lie.

I *was* out of ideas.

But that had never stopped me before.

And as I always had in the past, I began to break down my surroundings in hopes of figuring out some sort of solution. To search for signs, for symbols...all these elves surrounding me...did one of them hold the key to the heart's location?

If not in Ederis, then where?

Somewhere in the Hollowlands?

Who could lead me where I needed to go?

I started to summon wings, intending to consider the problem from above. But before I could get airborne, a violent shudder went through me.

A quick search revealed a possible reason: A large barrier of fire Dravyn had put in place was breaking down; an entire section of it had just been dissolved—a target of the elvish weapons that were responsible for that acrid, foul-smelling purple smoke.

As I watched, another section suffered the same fate. This second bit of destruction rumbled through me hard enough to drop me to one knee.

The ground shook as dozens of elves raced toward the dissolving barrier. I braced my hand against the dirt as best I could, trying to keep my balance, as I looked over my shoulder and took in the sight of the fire wall falling completely away.

The elves roared through the new opening.

A flood of humans was there to greet them.

The two sides collided like a river striking rocks, bodies hitting and spilling to the ground, tumbling and stumbling over one another.

The waiting humans outnumbered the elves in this particular spot of the battle. They swung their swords without pause or mercy, the sounds of blades hitting armor and skin making me wince.

There were bits of scattered flame still lingering around from the destroyed barrier; bodies were tripping into them—or being thrown into them—and the scent of scorched flesh became the most powerful, horrible smell in a sea full of powerful, horrible smells.

The sudden cry of a dragon mercifully pulled my attention toward it.

Mairu.

She twisted into sight high above the battle a short distance away, talons and fangs flashing, golden scales shining in the dim, smoky daylight.

Savna balanced on her back—this was her way of catching the attention she needed, it seemed; hundreds had already stopped to stare, marveling at the sight of the beast with a mixture of horror and awe.

My sister was watching the same breaking point I'd been watching.

More and more humans gathered to this point, weapons drawn, determined to stop the elves from advancing.

All over the battlefield, more and more of these clashes were beginning to happen.

We had no divine connection, but I could tell by Savna's stoic, resolved posture that we still shared the same thoughts—it was time to intervene. The tide needed shifting.

I heard her cry rising moments later, crystal clear and carrying all the way to where I knelt: "Lay down your weapons!"

It was the cue. The agreed-upon phrase to activate the next part of our scheme.

Savna's loyalists didn't lay down their weapons.

They turned them on Andrel's leaders, as planned.

All at once they struck, disarming in most cases, striking with more violence in some. Confusion reigned. Forward marches ceased.

Many of the humans slowed their charge as well, watching the strange scene unfolding before them.

And still—like I had so many times in the past—I kneeled in the middle of it, a witness to both sides, uncertain of where to go next.

Antaeum trembled against my back.

I gripped its hilt, trying to think.

If I could simply find out a way to wake its power, then all the soldiers here would be witnesses to whatever magic it contained—magic that would supposedly fix all of the madness surrounding us.

And maybe this was the answer I'd been looking for.

As I held the dagger more tightly, a thought occurred to me. Quiet at first, but growing rapidly in size as the seconds passed: The idea that just as the Moraki had left my scars for the world to see, maybe the heart was not as hidden as I'd believed it to be.

Maybe it was beating close.

Very close.

The idea was both terrifying and freeing.

Slowly, I rose to my feet, staring again at the madness rushing all around me. I felt oddly still and silent compared to it all. Smoke filled my lungs, like it had on the day I broke through the barriers surrounding my old home and found myself standing in a burning field.

The same mixture of horror and possibility overtook me now as it had then. The same sense of pain and realization. Of strength in spite of weakness.

Move, I told myself now, same as I'd told myself then. *You have things to finish.*

I spotted a small plateau a short distance away and walked toward it, climbing the rocky outcropping that led to its highest point.

Mairu and my sister swooped overhead, close enough that I could see the concerned, questioning look in Savna's eyes.

I waved her away.

"Meddling again. Because of course you are."

I wasn't surprised to hear Andrel's voice.

After all the battles we'd endured against one another, it seemed fated that we should meet one last time.

"You never fucking *learn*, do you?" I turned to see him scrambling up the rocks, huffing for breath as he reached the same large, flat stretch of stone I stood on.

He didn't move with his usual grace.

Instead, he advanced on me with a wild, merciless gleam in his eyes, the sword in his hand already dripping with someone else's blood. He skipped his usual arrogant speech, too, and moved immediately to attack, aiming the sword toward my chest.

I ducked, sweeping around behind him.

He twisted and darted for me again.

The only weapon I carried was Antaeum, so instinctively I whipped it from its sheath, gripped it with both hands, and threw it up just in time to parry his blow.

He slammed into my smaller blade with enough force that it rattled my teeth and bones and made the muscles in my arms feel as if they were in danger of ripping apart.

I dug in my heels and pushed back.

Divine strength surged through me. Heat enveloped me. And the dagger in my hands began to hum, the symbols on the black blade gleaming more brightly than ever before.

Andrel's sword was suddenly, briefly overtaken by a crackling, silver-colored energy—Antaeum's power, undoing whatever runes he'd fortified the weapon with.

He stumbled back, nearly dropping that blade in shock.

I started to lower my dagger.

But he wasn't done.

The feral glimmer in his eyes returned, and he threw himself at me so quickly, I didn't have time to consider a counterattack.

I flung myself backward, trying to get out of his reach only to realize I had nowhere to go; the edge of the plateau was somehow right behind me, and this side was much steeper than the one I'd climbed up.

He took aim at my legs, preparing to cut my balance further away from me—

An arrow of pure flame struck his face first, knocking him backward and setting the collar of his shirt and part of his hair alight. He hit the ground and rolled to put the fire out.

I hadn't summoned that fire.

Dravyn landed a moment later, positioning himself between me and Andrel.

I reached for the ring he'd given me. My world again seemed to slow, the battles all around me growing silent, distant.

The idea that had struck me earlier grew bolder.

But all I saw for a moment was Dravyn.

The god who had carried me from my old life months ago, into one I never could have imagined. The god who had protected me. Challenged me. Chose me.

Fought for me until the very end.

I wished I had more time to tell him how much I loved him. How much I hoped what I was about to do would somehow heal him, too. How he was so convinced he couldn't be redeemed after the mistakes he'd made, yet he had saved me in more ways than I could possibly explain. He'd given me fire, and wings, and reminded me that I had strength enough to save myself—and to save others.

I had strength enough to do what I needed to do now.

But there was no time to tell him all of these things.

No time to do anything except put more space between myself and Andrel, racing to the other end of the high platform I'd chosen, putting myself in position, all while thinking words I hoped would reach Dravyn—

Trust me.

I felt his eyes on me.

He'd paused his pursuit of Andrel long enough to fix a stare in my direction. His expression was torn, his response frantic in my mind, *What are you doing?*

I turned away from him.

What came next would be easier if I didn't have to see his face while I did it.

As I balanced Antaeum in my hands, the God of the Shade's instructions overtook my thoughts once more. One sentence in particular kept playing over and over in my mind.

...I became certain you were the balance point our world needed.

Me.

Of course it was me—I was the key to waking up the power sleeping within this dagger, just as he said. But some parts of me had to finish dying off to allow for new growth. And this blade held the key to that death.

I exhaled slowly.

My final trial was over.

I knew the answer.

So I lifted the dagger high, gripping it with both hands—

And I plunged it into my heart.

CHAPTER 45

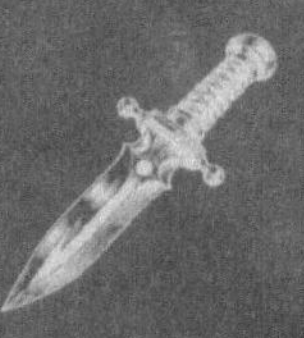

Dravyn

The world was shifting.

Breaking apart beneath me.

And I wanted it to swallow me whole and never spit me back out.

If she is going, take me too.

But when my vision cleared and my surroundings stopped reeling, I had not moved. Nothing had taken me.

So I was forced to watch what was unfolding.

Silver and black energy wove a tangled web around Karys's body, bleeding out from the spot where she'd stabbed herself. Little fires slipped between the ribbons of that energy, as if fleeing from it. They extinguished almost as quickly as they flew away from her.

Even from a distance, I could see how pale she was becoming.

Could see that she wasn't moving.

I ran, throwing myself down beside her, gathering her against me. Her body was already stiff. Devoid entirely of color. As if that knife she'd plunged into her chest had not only killed her, but sucked her dry of all her spirit, all her magic. Where had she gotten that knife? What had it done? And *why*?

Dead.

She was dead.

This could not be.

Because I would not let it happen. I would *never* let it happen. I'd sworn it. I would have protected her from every single hurt, every threat, every beast in every heaven and hell and everywhere in between. From *anything,* no matter the cost.

But this...

She'd done it to herself.

Why?

I couldn't move.

Andrel shook free of his stupor before I did. I heard him sheathing his sword, shuffling his stance.

Then he *laughed.*

My eyes flashed toward him.

He started to back away, still smiling.

As soon as he took a step, Karys's body caught fire, igniting into a violent pyre, its flames so thick they blinded me from all else.

Not knowing what else to do, I held even more tightly to her. Her flames had never bothered or burned me before, and I didn't care if they did now. I held to her fire like it was the very air I needed to exist.

My wildfire, my goddess, my breath...

But her body was growing lighter, slipping away from me no matter how fiercely I clung to it. Turning to threads of flame like it did whenever she transported herself...except the threads did not immediately whisk away into nothingness.

They pulled her body away from me only to gather again and weave into a different form—into the same mythical creature I'd seen on the day we'd first practiced flying together.

A phoenix.

Just as before, the creature didn't stay long.

But this time, as it faded into the air, some of its fire fell into a new shape that *did* stay behind: A sword.

The last of her fire, forged into a fitting weapon to finish things with.

It hung in the air, solid and waiting. I stood and reached for it, and it dropped directly into my outstretched hand.

Andrel had paused his retreat, caught up for a moment in the sight of all the magic unfolding around us. As his gaze fell to the sword I now held, he slowly backed away.

Then broke into a run.

I was faster.

There were no words exchanged. No hesitation. No other thought—there was nothing except the feel of the blade of fire in my hand and the pounding of my feet driving me closer, closer…

Close enough to grab him and yank him to a stop.

I didn't stab him in the back.

I whipped him around to face me before throwing him to the ground.

Then I pressed the tip of the sword into the exact same place where he'd left that scar on Karys, right near the heart.

"I am not the God of Death," I growled, "but I have connections. And so when your sorry, fucking pathetic excuse for a soul makes its way into the Afterlands, I am going to personally escort it straight into the deepest hell."

I didn't give him a chance to reply.

I stabbed, shoving the blade cleanly through his chest, twisting it viciously as it went.

The sword ignited and engulfed his writhing body.

As the flames rose, I released the blade and took a step back. Within seconds, he was burned beyond recognition—just another body in a battlefield full of them.

Nobody and nothing, just as he deserved to be.

But it was not as satisfying as I'd dreamed about.

A victory, but a meaningless one in the wake of what I'd lost. It felt hollow.

I felt hollow.

Unbalanced.

I surveyed that battlefield still rumbling around me. The fighting was subdued, now, with most of the participants either confused or distracted. But there were still swords in hands, poison in the air, blood pouring from wounds. There were still plenty of questions left to answer. Plenty of things that needed to be fixed.

Before I could decide on what my next move might be, a silvery light exploded at my back.

I spun around to see the phoenix-like creature alighting on the same stone plateau it had first emerged above—only it was no longer made purely of fire. Instead, this creature she had shifted into was solid, her feathers a mixture of faintly glowing shades of blue, violet, and scarlet. The same silvery light that had caught my attention surrounded her.

As I stared, that silvery energy flowed out from her, carried on a cool, mist-filled breeze that rattled the trees, stirred up dust, swept over the battlefield and cleansed it of the scent of blood and poison.

It washed over every being in sight, turning them all toward her. Swords dropped. Whispers filled the air. Soldiers kneeled, and the ones who didn't bow of their own accord were soon slipping into a daze that had them wandering, looking to the sky, shaking their heads.

It was more than awe taking over them—it was something supernatural, something beyond any power I had ever witnessed in any realm.

What was this magic?

Whatever it was, it continued to pour from her for several minutes. The cool breeze soon made several laps around me, lifting my hair, pulling at my clothing. Drawing me toward her.

I followed that pull.

The world no longer felt as if it was tilting sideways.

She watched me approach through green eyes that were familiar, yet altogether something new. Something brighter.

But as I made my way up onto the rocky plateau, the last of the silvery light left her, and all the color seemed to drain from her body in the next instant.

I froze.

She blinked. Bowed her head.

Then she rose with a mighty flap of her wings, disappearing into the bright sky, leaving behind nothing except a pile of ash and feathers.

CHAPTER 46

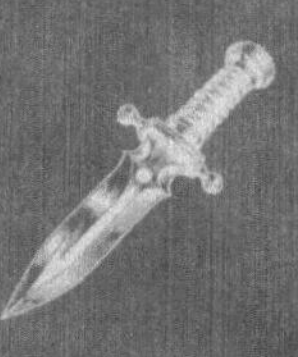

Karys

A BIRD WAS SINGING SOMEWHERE NEARBY.

I was dreaming of a morning long ago. Back when I was a child. Long before I knew much of wars or blood or betrayal and surviving, or of rising above these things. I'd been very sick. My fever made me delirious, and for five days I didn't wake.

I didn't remember much about those days, aside from the sound of a sparrow singing outside my window—and a voice.

Wake up, Karys. Please wake up.

My sister's voice, on the verge of tears.

She told me later that it was the most frightened she'd ever been. She stayed by my bedside for all five days, and she ended up needing a doctor herself because she refused to eat or drink if I couldn't do either of those things.

She would have followed me to the grave if I hadn't woken up, I think.

But I'd heard her voice, and somehow, I'd decided I was going to answer it. That I was going to keep fighting. Rise into something new. Something better.

Wake up, Karys.

It was not only my sister speaking to me this time. It was Dravyn. Mairu. Valas.

So many were calling out to me.

Waiting on me.

So I again made the decision to rise.

To wake.

I was not in my room when I did. There were no birds singing. No doctors, no family, no allies. There was only me, a lush shoreline of grass, and a shallow stream.

I strode toward that stream and peered into the water.

I was still myself, only brighter. Cleaner. My dirty, battle-worn clothes were gone, replaced by robes of silver and white. My dark hair fell in loose, wild waves, tamed only by a silver circlet resting on my head —one with diamonds that matched the ring Dravyn had given me, which was still securely fixed on my finger.

The scars on my face and neck were very faint, impressions that only revealed themselves when I turned in precisely the right way, looking for them.

I finally lifted my gaze away from my reflection.

Across from the stream, something was resting in the grass.

Antaeum.

But it wasn't alone. A second dagger accompanied it, this one with a blade that was stunningly white, etched with golden symbols that shone brighter as I approached and knelt beside it.

One light, one dark.

Balanced.

As I picked up the daggers, the scenery whirled around me. Faster and faster. The spinning would have made me panic, once upon a time. But I knew where I needed to go. Who I needed to see. I knew I could find my way.

So I merely reached out with both hands, a dagger in each—balancing me—and I brought myself to a stop.

Everything stilled. I blinked, and as my eyes opened, I found myself once more on the top of the cliff overlooking the battlefield.

Except it was no longer a battlefield. It was changed—and still changing. The landscape was blooming into something wild, something with a beauty almost beyond description.

I sheathed my daggers and walked to the edge for a closer look.

Grass took root where there had been only dry stone. Little rivers had started to appear, forming crystal clear waterfalls that pooled in places where blood had once stained. Both the smoke and the poisonous clouds filling the air were disappearing, and in the clearer air, a scent of jasmine and honey was rising.

Elves and humans alike stood among the shifting land, their expressions a mixture of confusion and awe. But there was no animosity to be seen; at least for the moment, a feeling of strange, otherworldly calmness permeated all.

"Karys?"

I turned to meet Mairu's shocked gaze. She raced toward me but drew up just short of embracing me, curiosity overtaking her features. "Your energy, it's...changed."

I breathed in deep, a smile warming my face. "Yes. It's a bit of a long story."

She contemplated asking about that story for only a moment before deciding it was more important to finish embracing me.

"How is Valas?" I asked as she pulled away.

She fixed me with another close look, considering my strange new energy for another moment. "The light that washed over this battle-field...it seemed to cleanse the poison from his body as well, and he's..." Her voice grew thick with emotion. "He's okay, I think."

She led me to the same spot where I'd last seen him, where he was now propped up against a tall, skinny tree.

I crouched before him, giving him my best impersonation of his chaotic grin. "You look absolutely terrible."

He grinned back. "Haven't had much time for all the beauty sleep I require, here lately."

I laughed, tears springing to my eyes, and threw my arms around him.

"Easy," he groaned, "the gaping hole in my chest is still a bit tender, if you couldn't tell."

I eased up but didn't let go completely. After a moment, *he* was the one squeezing tighter, all while laughing softly despite whatever pain I might have been causing him.

I drew away when I heard footsteps, followed by a soft little gasp— my sister.

We stared at one another for several beats, both at a loss for words.

It seemed impossible that we were both standing here in one piece. That we had somehow ended in the same way we began—together. Despite all the mess and uncertainty between us.

The right words to capture these feelings never did occur to either of us. So we merely drew together and took each other's hands, pressing our foreheads against one another's and breathing in the same air, sighing in the same relieved way.

The only thing that could have pulled me from my sister just then was a warmth that suddenly radiated from the ring around my finger—a reminder that I still hadn't seen Dravyn since my return.

I clutched that ring to my chest and went to peer over the edge of the cliff once more, searching for him.

It was easy enough to know where to look. Though the magic coursing through me had changed—shifted into something that was more my own before anyone else's—the impression he'd left on it was still there.

We were still connected, and I would recognize his magic anywhere, I was certain.

I leapt from the cliff, soaring down and landing close to where I felt the strongest pulse of that magic. My wings were no longer made of fire; they were sleek and tapered, made up of bird-like feathers.

Like a sparrow's, I thought, only with bolder, more fiery coloring.

Dravyn stood with his brother at the edge of the encampment that was slowly disbanding. The two were deep in conversation—a serious talk, from the looks of it, but not an angry one. If anything, they seemed to be consoling one another.

It healed a part of my heart to see it.

As I walked toward him, all the lingering soldiers turned to watch me pass. Walking through the mist-like energy still floating over the area made me feel bolder, brighter. That silvery energy gathered toward my body without any effort from me, settling on my skin and making it glow softly.

Heads turned my direction. Eyes lowered. Voices called out to me.

I didn't answer.

I just kept walking.

It was Fallon who saw me first. Shock registered slowly in his eyes. Then his face softened in a way I'd never witnessed from him. He placed a hand on Dravyn's shoulder. Nodded in my direction. Took several steps back, out of my sight, and I forgot he existed at all.

I forgot everything else as the God of Fire turned toward me.

Our eyes met, and my breath caught exactly as it had the very first time I'd seen him in his divine form.

I recalled the first words I'd said to him that day: *This is a dream.*

It felt like a dream again. Except better. Because now I knew I was actually awake—and now he was walking toward me, swooping me into his arms, crushing his lips against mine.

It was a brief kiss; he quickly drew back so he could study me closer.

I smiled. "Do you remember when you asked me if I would ever stop surprising you?"

He laughed, shaking his head in disbelief, his fingers trembling slightly as they brushed across my cheek.

"And I told you I didn't plan to?"

His hand stilled against my face. "I hope you never stop," he said, lips tilting closer to mine.

I don't know who moved first. Who started the kiss. Who wrapped their arms more tightly around the other. Who fell more fully, more completely into the other.

I only knew I never wanted it to end.

When that ending inevitably came, I breathed in deep, fully at peace for the first time in as long as I could remember.

Yet I knew there was more to do.

The world around us teemed with unsettled energy. Beautiful, but messy. Still in need of more of my magic. My guidance.

I knew what came next. A bittersweet part that I wasn't looking forward to, but one that couldn't be put off for much longer. There was too much work to be done.

We rejoined the others, and once we were all together, I did my best to explain the things I hadn't been able to before—the meeting with Malaphar, and why I'd made the sacrifice I had, and what that meant for the future of all of us.

"Where will you go now?" Savna asked.

"I am the being now responsible for maintaining balance and peace between the realms," I said, "so I'll go wherever I'm needed. In this realm or otherwise."

Her brow furrowed in thought, a tiny frown starting to form on her lips.

I cupped her chin, lifting it up the way she used to do to me whenever I was sad about something. "I'll need you to help me put things back together where the elves are concerned. So you should be expecting me soon, once I've mastered my new magic a little better."

She nodded, the corners of her mouth turning slightly upward.

We hugged goodbye, and for once it didn't feel like an ending—merely an *I'll see you later.*

Valas caught my eye as I turned away from her, wearing his usual sly grin. "It's going to be boring without you in the middle-heavens constantly setting fire to things."

"You'll have plenty of time to nap, at least."

"Which is good," he said, yawning, "because it's going to take a lot of beauty sleep to recover from today."

Mairu scoffed. "Something tells me it won't be *that* boring with your chaotic ass still around, causing trouble." She turned her golden eyes toward me. They were shining with tears that she hastily blinked away. "But all the same, you'll stop by soon, I hope? Keep things interesting for us."

I agreed with a hug. My shoulder was damp with her tears by the time I stopped squeezing her and stepped back.

And at last, I turned once more to Dravyn.

The others drifted away, granting us a moment of privacy.

A moment that stretched into several more, until he eventually took my hand, and we walked to the edge of the cliff together. The air was fully cleared now, no trace of smoke or anything else shading it, and the world seemed to stretch endlessly out below us.

"I will never be far from you," he promised, "no matter the realm you find yourself in. And you can always come home to me."

"I know," I said—and it was that knowledge that encouraged my heart to beat more courageously, making me less afraid of the waiting world and its vastness.

Because he was right: No matter where my new magic took me, whatever endings or beginnings or in between places it led to, I loved him, and he loved me, and there was no amount of change or distance that could undo that.

There was work to be done, now. Lots of it. But I could see the roads I needed to take. Like bright, shining trails unfolding across a map of the peaceful future I would help guide into existence.

I kissed Dravyn one last time—for now—letting his warmth wash over me.

Then I leapt from the edge, wings unfurling, and I soared boldly into whatever trials awaited me next.

EPILOGUE

300 Years Later

In the realm of Mistwilde, a young elvish woman by the name of Soraya stood on a hilltop overlooking the capital city of Irithyl, admiring the sweeping view.

Water flowed everywhere she looked, falling over countless surfaces, gathering in turquoise pools, winding between buildings. The air glittered with mist that caught the setting sunlight and turned to gold. A soft, sweet scent wafted up from the pale blue flowers covering most of the city's yards. The houses those yards belonged to were arranged in neat rows stacked precisely on top of one another, each one boasting countless windows of colorful glass. It somehow looked both perfectly planned and yet entirely natural—a wild city carved from the earth by precise and thoughtful hands.

Sora clutched a silver ring as she studied it all, her thumb absently tracing over the band, which was molded in the shape of two wings that held an oval centerpiece.

The hilltop was called Elleras. It was a sanctuary filled with gardens and shrines—a place the inhabitants of Irithyl often retreated to when they found themselves in need of peace. Of balance. And in the sanctuary's center stood a towering statue of the immortal being responsible for such things: the Arbiter of Realms, they called her.

Her story was one that all the children of Mistwilde learned at a young age—because it was this being who had brought a divine essence back to the elves over three hundred years ago, giving them a point to build their future upon.

A peaceful kind of magic often flowed even from mere statues of the Arbiter. The one Sora leaned against now, however, carried more than a feeling of peace; there was a wildness about this sculpture, she'd always thought—and she was not alone in that thinking.

When the sun hit it just right, some swore they saw fire rippling across the Arbiter's body. Blazing in her eyes. Burning through the scars upon her face. Flaring like wings out from her back.

This was why Sora had chosen this spot for her work.

And this was why a captive audience of villagers sat before her and the Arbiter's statue, their eyes wide, their hands clutching glass daggers with feathers tied around the hilts, modeled after the ones the Arbiter herself held. Even the youngest of the village children had ceased their bickering and tumbling, and they now sat perfectly still, eagerly awaiting what came next.

For today was Forging Day, which meant a reprieve from the chores and routine of their everyday lives. It meant food, dancing, celebration —and most importantly, it meant *stories*.

And Sora—though still young by elvish standards—was already regarded by many as the greatest storyteller they'd encountered in a generation.

Among her most popular tales were those she told of the love story between the Arbiter of Realms and the God of Fire. And, as Forging Day celebrated the union of these two divine beings, Sora had predictably found herself in high demand by villagers eager to get swept up in such a story.

She surveyed the eager crowd before her, still smoothing the silver ring between her fingers.

Sundown was nearly upon them, which meant it was almost time for the festivities to begin in earnest. It had been a particularly spectacular sunset thus far. A good omen—one that meant the God of Fire had been to the mortal realm recently.

He and the Arbiter shared two palaces, most of the legends claimed: one in the mortal realm, and another in the middle-heavens. A sky painted in swaths of red and gold meant the Fire God had descended into the mortal realm to stay with his divine soulmate. When the skies turned dreary and grey, however, it meant the Arbiter was gone from this mortal realm, off to the middle-heavens to stay amongst her divine family.

She always came back, of course. Any storms that rose in her absence always subsided, and they were often followed by the most spectacular displays of bright and burning skies—further proof of the Fire God's devotion to her. They followed one another across the realms, across centuries, through the rise and fall of kings and queens and all manner of other things. There was chaos in the skies between them, at times, but balance and beauty always returned.

And it was their devotion to one another—and the balance that came about because of it—that was the cause for celebration on Forging Day.

Sora had told their story for years, in this city and its surrounding villages, and nobody questioned her authority on the matter; perhaps because she spoke as though weaving together precise memories of the divine, rather than mere myths of them.

Plenty of the Mistwilde elves had claimed they were direct descendants of divine beings, or otherwise divinely-touched...

With Sora, some of the elders wondered if it might have actually been true.

No one knew where she'd truly come from, after all. Or where she went when she left Mistwilde—which was often. A handful of witnesses claimed they'd seen her disappearing into thin air, even. These disappearances were occasionally preceded by flashes of fire, or—just as often—by an icy wind so intense it could not have come from anywhere but the divine realm, from the Winter God himself.

The Marr of the Shade Court seem to have their eyes on this one, the elves whispered.

Though *why* she was so closely watched was a matter of friendly debate.

All anyone knew for certain was how Sora had simply emerged from the mists surrounding their capital city one day, decades ago—a young woman with bright green eyes and hair that was oddly pale compared to most elves from this region.

She'd carried little else aside from the ring she held in her hand now, but had been sitting astride a strange golden horse, and accompanied by a small griffin—creatures that were occasionally seen following her throughout Mistwilde even to this day. The horse was a rarer sight, but the griffin was fond of children, especially, and those children had quickly learned that they could summon the creature by scattering offerings of sweet cakes and shiny things—much to their parents' dismay.

Sora and her company were a curious addition to their realm, to say the least...but her appearance had ushered in a renewed sense of peace and protection for the capital city—one that perhaps surpassed their mortal understanding. And so she had been welcomed by Irithyl's leaders, and soon became a leader of the realm in her own right; a historian, a storyteller, a shining reminder of the link between the elves and the divine.

She closed her fingers over the band of that ring she'd carried for so long—a gift from her parents. One given to her, their youngest daughter, when she'd first mastered her ability to transcend realms. A promise had accompanied it: *You can always come home to us.*

She glanced toward the sky. After a short search, her eyes caught movement—a flash of golden scales she doubted anyone else noticed.

The Marr of the Shade Court did indeed have their eyes on her; they were eager for her to return to them, for her to finish her task and join them for their own celebration of this day.

Familiar warmth blossomed in her chest. Confidence followed, and she looked back to her captive audience and finally started to speak, the words flowing from her like a song she'd sung many times before: "Once upon a time, an elf set off to wage war against the divine..."

It always began this way.

The parts in the middle were what changed with each telling, because they were twisted, messy, occasionally wrong before they were ultimately made right—the sort of winding path all the best love stories traveled along.

The legend of these two divine beings grew bigger each time Sora told it—but it always began the same way, and it always ended the same way, too.

On and on she went with her tale, until she felt she had done justice to all the pieces, until she'd put them together in a way that resonated. Until the celebration was properly underway in the city below, and fires were burning all throughout it, throwing light onto the countless stained windows and other sculptures of colored glass, washing the side-walks and waterways in a kaleidoscope of hues.

As music drifted up from the city center, Sora stepped away from the statue of the Arbiter, drawing the crowd's attention toward her one last time.

"Once upon a time, an elf set off to wage war against the divine," she repeated, eyes alight with a blaze that most would have sworn came from within. "But the God of Fire met her flames with his own. Together, they burned away the lies and the hatred, until all that remained was a promise. A choice. A love."

She held the ring out, letting its diamonds catch the last rays of fading sunlight, and spoke the last words of her story in a whisper, like a promise she meant to keep—

"And out of that love, reforged a world."

The End

THANK YOU FOR READING!

I'm so grateful to readers like you for picking up my books! If you enjoyed Karys and Dravyn's story, please consider taking a moment to leave a quick rating or review.

And be sure to check out more of my work at www. smgaitherbooks.com!